52 V

Barry Lillie

Flatfield F

Barry Lillie

You can follow Barry on the following platforms:

www.facebook.com/barrylillieauthor
www.instagram.com/barrylillie2
www.twitter.com/barrylillie1

For news about new releases and free content
sign up for Barry's Book Club here:
www.barrylillie.com

Copyright © Barry Lillie 2024
Cover design © Flatfield
Published by Flatfield 2024

The moral right of Barry Lillie to be identified as the author of this work has been asserted in accordance with the Copyright, Designs and Patents Act of 1988.

All rights reserved. No part of this publication may be reproduced, stored in a retrieval system, or transmitted in any form or by any means, electronic, mechanical, photocopying, recording, or otherwise, without the prior permission of the copyright owner of this book.

This novel is entirely a work of fiction. The names, characters and incidents portrayed within are the product of the author's imagination. Any resemblance to actual people living or dead is entirely coincidental.

Barry Lillie

This book is dedicated to:

My mother, for the inspiration

and

My sister-in-law, Patsy Jones.

And all the brave women who have fought breast cancer.

"You are never too old to set another goal or to dream a new dream." — C.S. Lewis

~ Dr Chopra ~

Friday, 5 March 2010
I shall die earlier than I previously expected. My best prognosis is twelve months, that's fifty-two weeks, three hundred and sixty-five days and can you credit it, we're not even in a leap year.

***

"It is with regret that I have to inform you that the cancer has returned," Dr Chopra had said from behind the safety of his desk. "But it's not as straightforward as before." He looked uncomfortable and glanced down at the keyboard in front of him.

I guess delivering bad news never gets easier.

The outcome of my consultation was that my breast cancer, which was in remission up until a recent check-up had returned. When I say returned there's a small lump in my armpit that minor surgery can deal with but the worrying thing is there's now a tumour in my brain.

Dr Chopra's dark brown eyes seem to soften and become a milky colour. (Caffe-latte I imagine Lisa would call it.) "I'd like to be honest with you Mrs Bickerstaff." Len put his hand on my knee and I nodded my head, an indication that I was happy for him to be frank. "Metastatic breast cancer in the brain is extremely rare and so it currently has no cure, some treatments can help to control it, meaning people can live longer."

"How much longer?" I whisper.

"It's not an exact science. On average, the median survival rate from diagnosis is three to six months but with treatment it is possible to extend this to twelve months."

The room fell silent. Three pairs of eyes darted from one face to another until Dr Chopra spoke again. "I'm very sorry."

I said nothing.

"Mrs Bickerstaff, do you understand everything that I've said?"

"Yes, Doctor, but ask me again in a few weeks when the new tumour's taken hold."

***

This morning, I've been awake for what seems like hours, but in reality, is just minutes. Yesterday's conversation is hula-hooping in my consciousness, every word fastened to my memory like discarded chewing gum to a pavement. I slide a foot out of the duvet and wriggle my toes around like five, fat, fleshy thermometers assessing the temperature of the room. Deciding it's too chilly to get out of bed, my foot is returned to the warmth inside. Just then, as if in an attempt to warm me further, a rush of hot air brushes against my leg. Len has silently broken wind. Two seconds later, out of the top of the duvet, the aroma of physiologically recycled lamb tikka emerges. I know I should get out of bed and escape this assault on my olfactory system, but I'm unable to. I'm not physically incapable, just emotionally.

My mind skitters back to the hospital visit yesterday.

***

As we'd walked along the harshly lit hospital corridor, every earlier visit played in my head, fuzzy at the edges like an ancient videotape. That first uneasy appointment and examination by a junior doctor. The second for a discussion with a consultant, (things must be bad I had thought). Then the letter arrived, booking me in to start treatment.

"Do you know how many times we've been here in the past eighteen months?" Len said, pulling me back into the present. I shrug and shake my head. "Forty-two… Forty-two trips. If we didn't have our free bus passes that would have amounted to £403.20. We spent less than half that on our honeymoon."

"I'm surprised you can remember that far back," I replied. "Five days on Anglesey in a caravan."

Back in the day, that was considered upmarket."

"Upmarket," I said. "Five days of drizzle and an unstable caravan."

"There was nowt wrong with that caravan."

"It was positively dangerous, every time you got amorous, I'm sure it moved a few feet closer to the gas bottle store."

Len laughed, "That could've been explosive."

"Good job when it came to sex, you were more of a sparkler than a rocket then."

Smiling, he hugged me publicly, something he rarely did, then said, "We'll be okay, you and me."

"We always have been," I told him, "Now stop mauling me you daft tray-cloth, and let's get the bus home."

Len, bless him, had tried his best to change the mood. Drinks in the Wedgwood Arms, a pint of brown ale for him and a Dubonnet and lemonade for me. "Queen's favourite tipple," he said, putting his pint glass down and wiping his mouth with the back of his hand.

"What, brown ale?"

"No, you daft beggar. Dubonnet."

"Oh."

Our drinks were followed by a visit to the Rose of Kashmir and we ate our dinner in silence. I liked the companionable calm, it meant we didn't have to talk about what had happened, or what was going to happen.

***

So now I'm in bed with a flatulent husband, and staring at the clock, willing the second hand to go backwards in a futile attempt to delay the foreseeable when there's another rumble beneath the duvet. I take that as my cue to get up.

The kitchen is cold, always has been. The extension tagged onto the back of the terrace not having enough room for both fitted units and a radiator. However, as with most houses in our street, there's always room for a dog basket. Cupping my morning brew, I watch as the dog squats in the backyard, not a pleasant sight, but one that oddly makes me feel alive. It doesn't matter what's going on in my life, the dog will still need feeding, emptying and cleaning up after.

Up until eighteen months ago when I had my surgery, my life – in my opinion – was quietly normal. I had no great plan, no agenda, in fact, it could be said that I've always been one of life's plodders. Human ballast, giving stability to the world around me. School led to a job in a potbank, where I met Len. This in turn led to marriage, kids and furniture on a repayment plan.

My husband, Len. God love him, is not, and has never been by any stretch of the imagination a sex symbol. He's more of your paint-splashed slippers and roll-ups sort of a man. We'll have been married forty-four years, in June. Most of those years have been happy, a few sad. Several monotonous, and thankfully, less than a handful have been downright miserable. We've created two wonderful children. I use the term, 'we' loosely, as Len's contribution was over faster than an Olympic sprinter with Crohn's disease. One minute I was sipping a cherry brandy at the local club and the next I was in the doctor's surgery clutching a jam jar filled with pee.

Although my life has been what I'd call, average, it could never be said to have been mundane. I may never have won tickets to the *Britain's Got Talent* final or set up my own tinned mackerel business, But my life has been rich in many other ways, and I did once stand behind the Potteries TV personality Anthea Turner in a post office.

I think most people would welcome an opportunity to reflect upon their life, I, however, don't. I don't want to wallow in the past, because life is about moving forward, not reflecting. I can still thread a needle without the need for spectacles, mash potatoes by hand and bend down far enough to cut my toenails.

It's just my left breast that's no longer there.

~ 52 ~

Thursday, 11 March
We need a Battenberg," says Lisa.

"Whatever for?" I ask pushing past a young mother with a child whose face is smeared with something that looks unmentionable.

"We can't have a family get-together without a Battenberg."

"Chocolate," the woman with the child says.

Sorry?" I reply, puzzled by the stranger's interruption.

"Chocolate. Betty-Anne can't eat it without getting it everywhere." Betty-Anne, I think, now there's a name that literally advertises the requirement to be bullied in secondary school. "That's nice," I reply and smile as the brown-faced imp is ushered away in the direction of the cheese counter, thus giving Lisa the opportunity to slip the pink and yellow confection into my shopping trolley.

"Do you think we should get some olives?" Lisa drops a couple of packs of frozen sausage rolls in among the shopping.

"Olives, who for?"

"Our Victor. His sort are partial to things like olives."

"His sort? He's bloody gay, not Mediterranean. Come on you barmpot let's get this lot home before the prawn ring starts to defrost."

The blame for my having to endure the trip to the supermarket with my daughter lies firmly at my husband's door. In the aftermath of Dr Chopra's prognosis, Len hasn't said much, not because he doesn't know what to say, but because after all the years of our being together, he's learned to read the signs. I know men find it hard to understand the inner workings of the female psyche, and heaven forbid they're pushed into having an opinion on wicker table mats. But when faced with a watery-eyed wife, the good ones like my Len have no difficulty interpreting the signals.

After a particularly ponderous episode of *Midsomer Murders*, I told him of my intention to keep a diary. Len said he thought it was a good idea, he even dug out a new hardbacked notebook from a drawer in the sideboard for me. Then out of nowhere, last night, he said, he thought we ought to tell people sooner rather than later. I told him I needed a few more days to let the consultation with Dr Chopra sink in before I subjected myself to concerned looks from family and friends. He continued, saying that we should at least tell the family. Eventually, I conceded and so I planned two gatherings, hence this shopping trip with Lisa. An informal get-together where the surprise guest is cancer.

***

Over the past few days, I've drunk enough tea to fill the swimming pool at Festival Park's Waterworld. I've perfected the art of sitting in silence and I've discovered tissues placed strategically around the house. Len's allowed me space to sob, even volunteering to go to the pub when my misery turned to anger. But the best support he's given is allowing me the time to reflect on my situation alone.

He has had his moments. A couple of nights ago I woke at 2:00 a.m.. The space next to me was vacant, so I pulled on my dressing gown and went downstairs to see where he was. I was about to turn the light on when through the window I saw him standing outside in the backyard, his head bent forward with his shoulders rising and falling.

I'd never seen him cry before.

Years ago, when we lost our first child, I did the crying and he made the tea. I guess back then spouses had more defined roles than they do today.

I crept back upstairs, took off my dressing gown, got into bed and waited. He eventually came back, he slid beneath the duvet saying, "The dog needed to go out for a pee."

Letting him know I saw him wouldn't achieve anything.

***

The day of the family gathering arrives and I'm elbow-deep in water, rinsing lettuce whilst keeping one eye on our temperamental oven, when the phone rings. "It's your sister," Len calls from the middle room. "She wants to know if it's formal wear or casual."

"Tell her it's come as you like."

"She says will you be okay with her wearing trousers?"

"Tell her she can wear a bloody straitjacket for all I care."

I'm placing sausage rolls onto a cooling rack when Len walks into the kitchen. "She said it might be a problem at a finger buffet."

"What might?"

"Wearing a straitjacket might make it difficult to juggle a plate and a glass."

"At least it'll stop her interfering with the cold platters."

My sister and I have what can only be described as an edgy relationship. It's not that we don't love each other, we just don't have a single thing in common. She has ideas above her station and enjoys trips to the theatre, while I'm more grounded and watch the soaps. And she has a habit of taking over, especially when it comes to food presentation. I could spend hours making sure everything looked faultless, that the sandwiches were cut into perfect obtuse triangles and that the coleslaw had a balanced ratio of cabbage to carrot and she'd still interfere. She can't help herself. She calls it obsessive-compulsive disorder. I call it rude.

Later with the table groaning under the weight of enough food to feed the Port Vale Supporters' Club I'm upstairs groaning at the weighty decision of what to wear.

Ever since the surgery it's been high necklines and buttons. My old cleavage revealing outfits have been consigned to the back of the wardrobe or dropped into one of the many charity bags that fall through my letterbox with alarming regularity. I'm standing looking at myself in the mirror and even though it's been months since I had the surgery, I still haven't become accustomed to being lopsided. I chose not to have reconstructive surgery, I thought it best not to eat into the hospital budget. Besides, I'm past bikini wearing age and it's highly unlikely I'll be approached by Marks and Spencer to front their next UK bra advertising campaign.

Time's ticking away and I've narrowed it down to two outfits when there's a knock on the bedroom door. "Is everything okay Mum?" Victor calls from the landing.

"Yes love, just making my mind up what to wear."

"Can I come in?" The door opens and my son steps into the room, in his hands he holds a carrier bag and out of the top I can see red and gold wrapping paper.

"What do you have there, love?"

"Just a little something I thought you'd like; I saw it in a charity shop window. I used some leftover Christmas paper to wrap it up."

I tear open the paper to reveal a picture; a bridge in watercolour with the sun reflected off the water below. "Oh, Victor, thank you."

"Do you like it?"

"Yes, it's lovely. I've wanted a picture of the Rialto Bridge for years."

"So come on, let's see what you've picked to wear."

Victor looks at the choices I hold up for him and his nose wrinkles, "So it's between something floaty with layers that hide your shape, or an ethnic-looking skirt with embroidery panels to pull focus from the upper body."

I nod and he takes the clothes from me, "This," he says holding up the layered one, "will make you look like a walking trifle, and the other," he scowls as he tosses it onto the bed, "wouldn't look out of place as a wall decoration in an Indian restaurant."

He rifles through my wardrobe, I'm anxious as hangers slide across rails accompanied by his vocalisations of disapproval, until he stops and withdraws a dress with a sweetheart neckline. "You've always looked lovely in this."

I shake my head, "It's not suitable anymore, the neck's too low."

"Nonsense, all it needs is a bit of a zhuzh and some bling."

"No love, what it needs is a second breast."

It's Victor's turn to shake his head – since my original diagnosis, he's been the strongest of my children. His attitude has always been positive and he was the first person to point out that the world around me will continue whether I choose to fight or give up. It's a bonus too that he has an excellent eye for detail and a real flair for fashion. Now, I'm not one prone to reinforcing stereotypes, but I used to think it was because he was gay. That was until I met his friend Gareth, who is the only gay man who can make a pig's ear out of matching a pair of jeans with a t-shirt.

Victor hands me the dress and I step into it. He zips it up the back before slipping a sheer scarf over my left shoulder, pinning it at the centre of the neckline with a faceted brooch. I turn to look at my reflection and a tear threatens, but a kiss from my son beats it into a hasty retreat.

"You look smashing love, I—" Len says as I walk into the middle room, there's a knock at the front door and the dog barks over the rest of his sentence. "Go and get that Vic," Len shouts and puts his arm around my waist. "Are you ready for this, duck?"

"I am," I reply, wishing I felt as certain as I sounded.

"Shall I show everyone into the front room?" Victor yells from the hall.

"Yes love," I shout back. Like everyone else around here, we tend to live in the middle room. The parlour is for special occasions like today.

I'm removing cling film from plates when I notice that something is missing from the table. "Where's the Battenberg gone?" I say to myself, as Lisa walks in with her husband, Mac. I take everyone's coats, putting the Battenberg disappearance out of my head and Len makes a drinking gesture with his hand to Mac and the two of them retire to the kitchen where the cans of beer are stacked.

"Do those kids have to play football in the street?" Lisa says as she places a foil-covered dish on the table, "Devils on horseback." She walks over to the window and the glass wobbles as her knuckles bang against it. "Oi, get away from that car if you know what's good for you."

"Hello Beryl love, Len let me in the back door," says Vera as she enters the room. Seeing Lisa at the window she nods in her direction, "What's going on?"

"Something about devils riding horses near Lisa's car."

"No Mother, there are no devils outside, just kids."

"Kids, devils, they're all the same no matter what you call them."

"No Vera, the devils on horseback are in that dish over there."

"They must be riding small horses."

"They're not really riding horses. They're Nigella's."

"Who's Nigella?"

"Off the television. The devils on horseback are hers."

"And does she know you've got them?"

"They're hors d'oeuvres."

"I thought you said they were Nigella's?"

"They are." Lisa's face is starting to colour. "They're prunes wrapped in streaky bacon."

"Really, so who was riding a horse near your car?"

I see Lisa take a deep breath, about to continue when Len comes into the room to tell me my sister has arrived. "Harold sends his apologies," she tells everyone, the scent of violets saturating the air around her.

"Trouble with his bowels again?" asks Vera, her query provoking raised eyebrows.

"Vera, there are some things we don't discuss in polite company."

"That's as may be," replies Vera. "Tell me are you and Harold married yet or still living over the brush."

"We're not living over the brush, as you so eloquently put it, Vera, everybody knows that our relationship is purely platonic. Harold is just a lodger of mine."

I can see Vera is ready to respond, and so to diffuse any potential unpleasantness, I nudge Len, who tells everyone to help themselves to food.

The get-together is pretty soon in full swing, glasses are filled and emptied and filled again and the buffet is going down a treat; that is apart from Lisa's contribution, the occasional hand hovers over the dish followed by a furrowed brow but the devils' and their horses remain untouched.

I'm sitting on the sofa with Saffron, whose party dress is showered in the flaky pastry raining down from the sausage roll that she's devouring when she looks up at me and says, "Have we got cake Nan?"

"No love, I did buy one but it seems to have vanished."

"But you can't have a party without cake."

"Talking about parties," says Mac, "You still haven't told us why we've been invited here today." I look across at Len and he picks Saffron up from my knee and takes her into the kitchen, mumbling something about needing help to find the dog. I stand up, smooth down my dress and adjust the scarf over my shoulder and suddenly feel nervous. Come on you silly woman, I think to myself, it's only family, they're not going to bite your head off. So, I clear my throat. "As you know, we went to the hospital last week… Len and I."

"Everything's okay though, isn't it?" Victor asks, I can hear the concern in his voice.

"Well, you see things are sort of—"

Suddenly lost for words, my hands shake and everyone looks at me, faces expectant for news.

"Things aren't as good as we'd hoped," Len says, standing in the doorway, all eyes on him now. "The cancer's come back," eyes flick back in my direction. "We've been told that something called metastasis can happen. It's when a cancer spreads to another part of the body." All eyes are back on Len in this tennis tournament of dire news delivery. He looks across at me, nods and winks, it's my turn and the eyes are back on me.

"They've found another tumour."

"Oh love," says Vera, her face falling faster than a bridegroom's underpants. "You will be okay, won't you?" I shake my head and look down at the floor, I feel ashamed; guilty of upsetting everyone. A diseased party pooper.

By now Len has joined me and with his arm across my shoulder, he tells everyone about the prognosis and I watch as the sorry collection of bewildered people in my front room shuffle uncomfortably from one foot to the other. I'm about to say something when Saffron runs in.

"Nan, the dog's been sick in the kitchen and it's pink and yellow."

I snigger, then I begin to shake until I can contain it no longer and laugh out loud, "Oh well, at least we know where the Battenberg went."

~ 51 ~

Thursday, 18 March
I'm standing on the front step waiting for Vera, looking along the street I can see that spring has almost arrived. In the pavement cracks a few weeds are starting to burst forth. The tiny blue flowers of a spindly-looking speedwell move in the frigid air and an early yellow-headed dandelion stands proud in defiance. It's a nice morning; the sun is shining and the wind has been packed away for the day.

This street where I've lived all of my married life has changed over the years. When the pottery industry declined, people moved on and empty houses were sold to landlords. There developed a swift turnover of tenants that came and went; some doing a moonlight flit. This constant change of neighbours means it is difficult to get to know anyone properly, greetings are exchanged but names go mostly unknown.

When we first moved into our house a potbank stood opposite. Every morning and evening the pavements would be filled with workers, dust-covered men and women in blue smocks, their arms white from working with clay. The factory was demolished in the 1980s and what remains is an open space populated with buddleia bushes and littered with pieces of discarded furniture, no longer useful or loved.

Vera comes around the corner and beckons to me. I wave back then leaving the door on the latch I nip back inside and switch on the kettle. "Morning Beryl," she calls from the hall as she closes the front door. "How are you feeling today?"

"I'm as I was yesterday," I tell her as she joins me in the kitchen.

"I got these." Vera rummages inside her shopping bag and removes a cardboard box. "Choux buns, from the new cake shop that used to be the building society."

I pour boiling water over tea bags and she reaches up and removes two tea plates from the cupboard.

We're in the middle room when I tell her I've heard from the hospital, "They want to remove the lump in my armpit next week."

"Will you be in long?"

"No, it's minor surgery the doctor said, should just be an outpatient visit, but I'm to pack an overnight bag just in case."

"And what about the…" Vera taps the side of her head with one hand and with the other places the choux buns onto the plates.

"The tumour is more convoluted. I need another assessment."

Vera bites into her cake and cream is forced out of the sides in two white waves. The drizzled chocolate on the top cracks and sloughs down her blouse. I watch as she scoffs the bun before sucking the icing sugar and cream from her fingers. I pour the tea and she begins telling me about a man living in her street who she suspects is fiddling his invalidity benefit, "Bold as brass he was," she says. "Up a stepladder washing his windows, giving them a good buffing with a chammy too. This is him who can't get out of the house without his mobility scooter." As she's chatting away, she's eyeing my choux bun, I pick up a knife, cut it into two and slide one half over onto Vera's plate. "You sure?"

"Yes, but cake before lunch? We're being a bit backwards today."

"Sod it." Vera chuckles fresh cream around her mouth. "Let's live dangerously."

Cakes eaten and tea drank we settle into the armchairs and picking up Victor's iPad Vera says, "What's this?"

"It's an iPad. Victor got it, they've only been around a week or so, he pre-ordered it from Dixons." I take the iPad from her and using a tea towel wipe away the smear of cream on the screen.

"I'm not sure I could have one of these. I don't think I'd be able to figure out how to use it."

"They're quite easy once you know how."

"I'm not good with new-fangled things, I'm only just getting used to opening tins of spaghetti with a ring pull."

"Look I'll show you." I press the button that wakes up the screen; there's no password and quickly the Google search engine is awaiting its instruction. "You just type in what you want to know."

"Anything?"

"Yes, and it searches for the answer."

"Like for instance Mary Berry's date of birth?"

"Yes, if that's what you want to know." I tap the keys on the screen and turn the iPad to face Vera. "There you go. Mary Berry, born 24 March 1935."

"Oooh," exclaimed Vera, "it's her birthday next week."

"Looks like it."

"So, this goggle can find anything for you?"

"Google. Yes, I think within reason."

"Can it find last week's lottery numbers?"

"Yes."

"What about next week's?"

"Now you're just being silly. Here." I hand her the iPad and stand up. "I'll make us some sandwiches for lunch, I've some nice ham in. Is that okay with you?" Vera nods her head as she's looking back at the screen with eyes as wide as beachballs.

I'm buttering slices of wholemeal when she calls out to me from the middle room, "Did you know that pigeons can tell the difference between Picasso and Monet?"

"That can't be right."

"It says here that a 1995 study showed that the birds can differentiate between the two artists."

"Well, I never. Do you want chutney or onion?"

"What kind of chutney, Branston or that plum stuff from the Lidl?"

"Either."

"I'll go with onion." I'm shaking my head as I reach into the veg rack for an onion. "Here's another one for you Beryl. Did you know that you can hear a blue whale's heartbeat from over two miles away?" I switch on the kettle to refresh the pot of tea and as I walk into the middle room Vera is silent, staring at the screen. Sensing me she says, "How do you turn it off?" She's tapping at the screen unsuccessfully so I reach over and take the device from her. As I turn it over, I notice the website she's been looking at, the page has, secondary brain cancer, in a bold font.

"I tried to look for the bus times from Burslem to Leek," Vera mumbles in a feeble attempt to cover her tracks.

"It's okay." I pick up the teapot and take it into the kitchen, and I'm pouring boiling water into it when I realise Vera is standing in the doorway. "I'm really sorry," she says. "I didn't mean to upset you."

"You haven't, Vera love. I've already looked up what to expect, but not a word to Len or Lisa."

"Very well," Vera says with a conspiratorial wink, "What are your plans for next week?"

"Apart from staying alive? I'm thinking of inviting Doreen and Mavis over for a coffee morning to tell them my news, maybe Elkie too if she's free."

"That'll be nice," Vera replies and the conversation moves on to Mrs Khan's new curtains, "They don't match her three-piece, I told her as much, just after I'd phoned the butcher to order some collar bacon."

The house feels empty when I'm alone again. Vera's chatter fills the space when she's here and her snippets of incidental news help to distract me from my thoughts. Thoughts that race around like toddlers in a playgroup, crashing into each other, picking themselves up and then running across the space again. I think about what will become of Len when I've gone. How will he cope without me, will Lisa and Victor rally round and support him through his grief? I'm sure they will, but what about them? I think about Vera, without me, will she be lost, her days will change, and gone will be the cups of tea served with a slice of gossip. Her routine will be broken and simple things cross my mind, like, will she walk down this street again like she did this morning?

Life changes all the time, change is unavoidable. Some things in life are predictable, almost expected. You know when you buy a punnet of strawberries, there'll be a rotten one hidden in the corner, and no matter how much you scrub them, your husband's underpants will still turn grey.

Living is the car horn that sounds as you're out walking, making you jump, and it can be the dog mess you step in when you've forgotten to pop a packet of tissues inside your handbag.

However, some things are not predictable. Like falling in love, winning a raffle or finding a lump where one shouldn't be.

~ 50 ~

Wednesday, 24 March
I've a few friends coming over for sandwiches and coffee and so I'm in the kitchen trying to decide which china to use. I plump for the harebell design that I got from a factory shop sale in early 1979, as Mavis can be a bit ham-fisted and so I dare not let her near my Royal Albert.

While I'm laying out the cups and saucers in the middle room, Len is having a quick whip round with the vacuum cleaner and I can hear him muttering to himself as he tries his best not to cause the dog a serious injury. For the past nine years, the daft hound cowered beneath the dining table as soon as the vacuum was wheeled into the room, however a few months ago we invested in one of those new ones with a ball rather than fixed wheels, and now whenever we get it out, the dog thinks it's playtime and chases after it like a puppy.

"I swear one of these days it'll get its ears sucked up," Len says as he winds the flex around the handle.

"It'll only happen once," I tell him as I spot a few crumbs next to the skirting board.

When Len takes the cleaner into the kitchen, I bend down and tap the floor where the crumbs are to attract the dog's attention and with its tail swaying from side to side it hoovers them up.

"What time are they arriving?" Len calls.

"Around ten-thirty, Vera said she'd pop in earlier to give me a hand with some sandwiches but I told her not to bother."

"Is there anything else you'd like me to do?"

"Yes, could you put up the picture that Victor gave me last week?"

Len sets to with a tack and a hammer and I busy myself opening a tin of pink salmon. It would have been red, but it's not a special occasion, only revelation coffee with friends.

"What do you think?" Len calls as there's a knock at the back door. I'm about to go to it when it opens and Vera steps inside.

"It's a bit chilly out there," she says, unravelling the scarf from around her neck and noticing the hammer in Len's hand, "Are you doing a bit of DIY?"

"He's just put up a picture," I tell her before we all walk into the middle room.

With our arms folded across our chests, we stand in silence looking at the gilt-framed print, Vera and I tilt our heads to the left and then hold them upright again. "It's not level," she says. "The right side needs to come down a bit." I don't agree, I think the left side needs to drop a little and Len shrugs and says, "Looks okay to me."

There's another knock, the front door this time and we can hear familiar voices on the step. "I'm off," Len says as he grabs his coat and makes a break for the kitchen. I open the front to Mavis and Doreen just as Len leaves through the back and the sudden draught sucks the middle door shut with a bang."

"It's a bit parky out there," Mavis says as she takes off her coat and drops it over the back of the sofa before plopping down in the chair nearest the fireplace. Doreen folds her coat neatly before placing it on a dining chair. I'd offer to hang it up for her but knowing she has a thing about coat hooks stretching fabric I say nothing.

It's a constant wonder how these two women, who are so different from each other, have managed to remain friends for so long. Mavis is short and squat. A ruddy-faced woman who is apt to speak without considering the consequences. Doreen on the other hand, is tall and willowy with pale skin and pencilled-in eyebrows as severe as her honesty.

"Who's for coffee?" chirps Vera taking control, and the three of us purse our lips whilst making grateful noises.

"Is this all of us?" Doreen asks standing with her back to the fire; the heat beginning to create a blotchy effect on the back of her legs. "Just one more to come," Vera calls from the kitchen, "Elkie's popping in too."

"Elkie," Mavis says. "I wouldn't have thought this was her kind of thing."

"Why ever not?" I ask.

"Well, you know, she's…"

"Pretentious," chips in Doreen.

"No, she's not. She's quite nice when you get to know her."

"Oh, come on Beryl, of course she's pretentious. Anyone who changes their name has to be pretentious." Vera pours the coffee and Mavis reaches out and takes a cup followed by a handful of biscuits, burbling something about only having had a couple of mouthfuls of Shreddies for breakfast and her blood sugar dipping. Doreen tosses her a sidelong glance and takes the cup offered to her by Vera.

"I don't think she changed her name," Vera says tucking a biscuit under the cup balanced on her saucer.

"Come on, of course, she changed her name," continued Doreen.

"No, apparently her father was a big *Vinegar Joe* fan."

"Don't you mean vinegar tits?"

"No Mavis, you're thinking of *Prisoner Cell Block H*," I point out.

"And I suppose," says Doreen, "her marrying Steven Brookes was just a coincidence?"

A knock at the door brings the room to silence. "That'll be Elkie," I say, before making my way into the hallway. I'm halfway along the parquet when I hear Mavis say, "I wonder if she'll bring a bottle of lilac wine."

The laughter stops as Elkie enters the room. Vera's already poured a cup of coffee for her and holds it out to her. "Here you go love, that'll chase the cold out of your bones."

"Thanks, Vera," Elkie says accepting the drink, "Hope you don't mind, I've brought my own sweeteners." Mavis nudges Doreen who's silently mouthing the word, 'pretentious' as the small white tablet drops into Elkie's cup. "That's a nice picture, Beryl. Is it new?"

"Yes, Victor gave it to me last week, when we had a little family get-together."

"It looks like—" Mavis begins, but her words are cut off as the bottom half of the digestive she's dunked into her cup breaks off and plops into her drink. "Bugger, pass me a spoon please Vera."

"Venice," says Doreen finishing off Mavis's earlier observation.

"Yes," I reply. "It's the Rialto Bridge. I've always wanted to see it."

"Oh you must," Elkie says. "I went a few years back. Venice is lovely."

"Smells, they say," moans Mavis, scooping the dissolved digestive out of her tea. "Anyway, how was it?"

"It was very crowded and so you have to keep your wits about you. It's very easy for people to get separated from their family."

"I don't think Mavis was enquiring as to your holiday habits," says Doreen.

"How was what?" Vera asks, looking confused.

"The family do-dah last week," chips in Mavis, "how did it go?"

"Ooh! Well, there was a bit of a palaver when Beryl told them the cancer had returned. It's in her head now."

"Returned?" Doreen exclaimed.

"Yes, thanks, Vera. The whole point of today was to reveal it delicately, not to blurt it out like a costermonger. Anyway, everyone, I've been thinking about what to do next and I've decided that I'll try the thing that zaps my brain but I'm not going back on the chemo."

"She's not said anything to Len yet, so keep it under your hats," chips in Vera which solicits supportive smiles from Mavis and Elkie. "She said she's had enough. I think she's being very brave."

"I think she's being a bloody idiot," says Doreen, her eyebrows raised high like barriers at a level crossing.

Before the conversation has the chance to turn into an argument, I add my two-penneth. "I understand what you're saying Doreen, but after all the treatment and the surgery I've already had over the past eighteen months, I just can't be bothered to go through it all again."

"But there must be something they can do," asks Mavis.

"Not really. I can't face feeling washed out and sick from the chemo, and what for, the chance that I might have a few extra months."

"Good for you," Elkie says in an attempt to raise the mood. "Do you know what you want?"

"I know what she wants," Doreen butts in, "someone to talk some bloody sense into her."

"What you need, is a bucket list," Elkie says ignoring Doreen's comment.

"A bucket list?"

"Yes, it's a sort of list of all the things you want to achieve before you kick the bucket."

"I don't know." I shrug. "I can't think of anything I'd like to do."

"What about going to Venice?" Vera proposes.

"Well, yes, I suppose there's that. But I can't think of anything else I've always wanted to do."

"What about a parachute jump?" volunteers Mavis.

"What about you shutting your cakehole," says Vera.

"Is there anything else you'd like to do?"

"Well, actually there is. I've always wanted to see a certain film."

"Beryl Bickerstaff, I'm shocked," says Doreen: level-crossing eyebrows once again.

"No, you daft tray-cloth," I tell her. "I'm not talking about a mucky movie."

"Well, then what film is it?"

"It's an old George Formby one called *Boots! Boots!*"

"And what's so special about this film?" Mavis says as she picks at the foil covering the salmon sandwiches.

"Well, the film had its premiere here instead of London and my father took my mother to see it when they first started stepping out together."

"They had the premiere here in Stoke?" asks Mavis, the sandwiches now exposed by the rip she's caused in the foil.

"Yes, well Burslem actually," I tell her as I remove the remainder of the foil from the plate. "You see my parents named me after Beryl Ingham, a famous clog dancer who was married to Formby. She was in the film too and I remember my mother telling me that my father had said that Beryl had kind eyes."

"And what about you Elkie?" Doreen says. "What birth name did your parents give you?"

"Elkie, of course," she says rising from her chair and picking up the plate of sandwiches. "Mind you it's been a source of embarrassment since I got wed, I can't tell you how many people in call centres have asked me to sing them a few bars of 'Pearl's a Singer' once I've told them my married name. But as my husband says, anyone who thinks I might have changed my name can't be too clever, because everyone knows Elkie the singer doesn't have an 'E' in her surname. Sandwich, Doreen?"

~ 49 ~

Thursday, 1 April
"It's certainly the right day for making stupid decisions," Lisa says. "The problem is I don't know who the April fool is, me or you."

I knew that telling my daughter I'd opted to forgo any more chemotherapy would elicit a negative response. But I'm not prepared for her decline into teenage mode. "Stop sulking and let's talk about this like adults."

"Like adults. Like adults!" the repeated words rising an octave. "You tell me that you're not having the treatment needed to cure you and then expect me not to be upset by your decision."

"There is no cure. Chemo will slow down the disease, but in my case, it will not delay the inevitable."

Lisa's bottom lip juts out and the room becomes heavy with silence as we sit looking away from each other in an atmosphere as cold as the tea untouched in our cups. In an attempt to break the impasse, I open a packet of biscuits and I'm tipping them out onto a plate when Lisa rises from her seat and looks out of the window onto the backyard. "What does dad think about it?" she says, breaking the silence.

"Your father agrees with me."

"That's not the impression he gave me."

She turns to face me with her back to the window blocking out the feeble April sunshine and making the room dark and oppressive.

"Come away from the window and sit down, you're making the place look untidy," I tell her. "Have you eaten? What did you have for breakfast?"

"Mother," she sighs loudly, "I didn't come here to discuss my morning meal requirements. Look, I think you should talk to Dad."

"Me and your father are all right, we've already discussed this."

"I can't believe you're being so selfish."

"Selfish?" I reply, coughing as a stray custard cream crumb lodges itself at the back of my throat. "You think I'm being selfish?"

"Yes, you are. What about the rest of the family?"

"What about them?"

"Don't we have any say in what happens?"

I pause for a while, collecting my thoughts and working out what to say. Lisa looks irritated by my silence and sniffs again loudly. "For goodness sake, use a handkerchief," I tell her. "If the treatment decision was left up to the family, what do you think would happen?"

"We'd insist that you have it."

"Exactly." I shake away a twinge in my temple that threatens to develop into a headache and as the custard cream crumb hasn't quite dislodged itself, I take a sip of my cold tea. "You'd insist. Now who's being selfish?"

"So, we're expected to just sit back and watch you fade away."

"No. You're expected to respect my decision and support me."

Lisa still hasn't touched her drink so I nod my head towards it. She does as instructed and picks up her tea. She sits stony-faced taking noisy sips from the cup, and I get up and walk towards her.

"I understand what you're saying." I stroke the top of her head, smoothing her hair as it makes its way down to her shoulder. "But, love, you really must see things from my perspective."

Her shoulders begin to shake and I can see tears beginning to form in the corners of her eyes. She puts down her cup and standing slowly she comes into me, and with her face buried into my neck she hugs me and for a second or two she's like the child she once was, finding solace in the arms of her mother.

"I don't think I can go through with the treatment; I want to enjoy the time I have left, not spend it feeling sick or lying upstairs in bed like some guilty secret."

In an attempt to lift the mood, I tell her about Elkie's suggestion of making a bucket list. I'm recounting last week's coffee morning when she pulls away from me. The tears are still there but the well in her eyes has changed into a pit of anger. "A bucket list," she spits, more of a statement than a question. "You're unbelievable. So, rather than accept any help from the hospital, you're going to spend what time you have left engaging in ridiculous stunts?

"No. It's not like that, it was just a fun suggestion."

"Save it," Lisa says picking up her coat. "It's obvious that you'll do whatever you like regardless of the family's wishes." I have no chance to reply as she stomps out of the room and down the hall, slamming the front door in her wake.

Now I'm angry.

I spend the remainder of the morning simmering: I'm like a red wine jus in a Michelin-star kitchen. The only difference is that instead of reducing, my annoyance grows.

The back door opens and the dog bounds inside, "Look who I found outside," Len calls as he walks inside closely followed by Vera. "Shall I put the kettle on?" he asks.

"I can do it." I answer rather snappily, "I'm not completely useless yet."

"Are you all right Beryl?" Vera asks as she removes her headscarf.

"Yes, Vera," I say as I take the kettle over to the sink and begin filling it with water. "I can do that, love," Len says and I give him a look that lets him know I have a problem with his suggestion.

Call it instinct, possibly fear, or more likely years of marriage, but Len knows when to make himself scarce. He withdraws to the kitchen with the dog almost inside his footsteps.

"I noticed that they're having a nearly new baby sale down at the church hall today," Vera says. "Do you fancy popping in?"

"Nearly new baby sale? What's on offer, slightly soiled, second-hand toddlers?"

"I can see that you're out of sorts," my friend says. Knowing that it would be pointless to hide the reason for my bad mood, I tell her all about my conversation with Lisa earlier as the kettle spews steam.

"So are you going to write a bucket list?" she asks, vigorously stirring the teabags in the pot sending the spoon clacking against the inside of my teapot like a clapper in a dull sounding bell.

"Am I buggery." I restrain her and take the spoon before she does my teapot any damage. "I've got no desire to do something daft just because I've been given a reduced life expectancy. Besides could you really see me on the end of a bungee rope?"

"Not with your bosoms," laughs Vera.

"Bosoms? You've forgotten Vera, they're singular now not plural." Blushing Vera splutters as she apologises, I smile before starting to laugh. "Just imagine it. I'd look like I was strapped to a zeppelin in free fall."

Vera has started to laugh too, "Not to mention when the elastic snaps back," she says. "Your nipple would end up in a different postcode to your feet."

"I tell you what I am going to do though," I say. "I'm going to enjoy the time I have left. Maybe I don't have a list of unusual things I want to achieve before I climb aboard that bus to oblivion, but I'm going to embrace each day that I am given and live whatever life I have left to the fullest. I've started a diary, something to leave for the family to look at when I've departed."

"Good idea," says Vera, "now grab your coat then and let's get down the church hall and have a look at those bargain babies."

**

Len looks glum when I return home. The result of an hour or so stewing, or has he spoken with Lisa? "Hello love," he says, "Do you fancy a cuppa?" I tell him no thanks and hang my coat on the hooks at the foot of our stairs before slipping out of my shoes and into my slippers.

"Lisa phoned while you were out." So now I know the reason for his hangdog look.

"Did she?" I reply. "I suppose she told you what happened this morning?"

"Yes, she says she's sorry."

"I should think she bloody well is."

"She's just worried."

"She's worried," I tell him as I get settled into my chair: The one nearest the fire. "I'm hardly jumping for joy myself. I've spent the past three weeks thinking about my situation, trying to decide if I'm doing the right thing. I've had so many thoughts bouncing around my head lately that I've felt like a human maraca."

Len does something completely out of character, he eases himself out of his chair, comes over and kisses me on the cheek. Stunned, I ask him why he's done it. "Because I love you," he says with a wink.

"Give over you soft wallop," I say, thinking that after forty-three years of marriage, it's a bit late to start blushing. "How do you feel about my decision not to have any more chemotherapy?"

"It doesn't much matter," he says.

"Of course it matters. Lisa has made her feelings clear and I'd like to know yours."

Len settles back into his armchair, the years of wear showing both on the man and chair. The dog rises from the floor and sits up as its man strokes its head. "I remember how the treatments made you feel before and, well I can understand that you don't want to go through that again." I nod in agreement, not wanting to revisit the memories of sickness and loose bowels following chemotherapy and the cocktail of drugs that made me feel lethargic and wasted.

"I'm not going to lie," he says. "I'm pleased that you're going to give the laser ablation therapy a try. But the decision about treatment is yours to make. End of discussion." Was it the light or did his blue eyes look diluted? "But I'm not happy with this bucket list nonsense."

"I'm not interested in bucket lists," I say reaching over and squeezing his hand. "I'm just going to embrace the time I have left and maybe try a few new things along the way."

"What sort of things?"

"I don't know yet. But I can assure you that I won't be abseiling down Stoke Town Hall."

"Just think of all the pigeons you'd disturb if you did." He says chuckling. We both turn our heads as the front door closes and into the middle room walks Victor.

"Hi Mum, Dad. What are you two doing?"

"Discussing pigeons and abseiling," says Len.

"You're bloody nuts, you two. What's for tea?"

"Pie," I tell him, "I got a couple while I was out with Vera looking for a second-hand baby.

"Lovely," Victor says his face a mask of confusion. "I hope it's not a pigeon pie though."

~ 48 ~

Tuesday, 6 April
With his birthday due next week, I'd asked Len what he'd like to do to celebrate. I know he'll be happy with a few pints at the workingmen's club. He gave me his usual, 'I want no fuss speech' that continues with, "We're lucky to still have a traditional ale and entertainment venue in the next street, as most have gone to the wall." I'm still undecided if the demise of these clubs nationwide is solely down to the lack of working men or could it be the wane in popularity for lacklustre cabaret.

I spoke with the family and we all decided that it might be nice to celebrate his birthday at a restaurant for a change. Victor showed me a review in the local paper for a new Italian place that has opened, and despite Len being a little huffy about the idea at first, when he saw how much it would mean to me, he agreed, "Just as long as we can end the evening at the club," he'd said.

After the dinner dishes have been put away, I check the dog is in its basket and pull on my coat and step outside. It's only a short walk to the bus stop and within a few minutes, I'm on the 3a to the city centre.

How the town centre has changed, it's only 8:00 in the evening and there's very few people around. I remember years ago when I was in my twenties, the streets would have been filled with people, eager for the hospitable embrace of warm public houses with their welcoming beery aroma. Smoke rooms would be full of men having a swift half before a night shift, and the lounges with intimate alcoves and ashtrays advertising pale ale would host courting couples. Now most pubs have a man dressed in a black coat watching the door and there are no longer ashtrays on each table. Len's always said that cheap supermarket alcohol would encourage people to stay at home, he may have been right.

Outside the restaurant, I peer through the window at the interior bathed in an orange glow. There's a handful of diners at tables and I can hear a mandolin playing *'Funiculi, Funiculà.'* I read the menu that's pinned inside a wooden display box beside the door and note that there's quite a good selection of pizza and pasta meals and for the Italian-phobic there are a few English options. Deciding I've made the right choice of venue I push open the door as the music changes and Pavarotti begins to sing *'Di Quella Pira.'* His robust timbre is a perfect accompaniment to the chequered napkins and dishes of parmesan on the tables.

"Can I help?" says a young man in a shirt that needs to be introduced to a steam iron.

"I'd like to make a booking please."

"If you'd like to take a seat," he says, "I'll fetch Carmel, she handles the bookings." As I wait, he unscrews the cap off a bottle of mineral water and places the bottle and a glass down in front of me.

I'm sipping the fizzy water when Carmel arrives with a page-a-day diary. She has skin the colour of butterscotch and I think to myself, she'd be more aptly named caramel. After licking her finger, she begins leafing through the diary. "I'm all over the place tonight. I've just got back from my holiday."

"That'll explain the tan," I reply.

"Oh no, I'm always this colour." I'm beginning to blush, embarrassed in case I've offended her. I open my mouth to apologise when she says, "It's sprayed on, I go to Bronzed Bods in Burslem every fortnight to top it up. Mind you it doesn't half make a mess of my bedsheets. Here we are, 11th of April. How many will be in the party?" I give her the details and after leaving my telephone number I'm once again outside as Pavarotti trades places again with more plucking mandolins.

I'm walking towards the bus station, built in the 1970s with a gallery of faintly Moorish concrete arches that house a shuttered parade of shops, now looking hopeless and unloved. I pause as I pass Hanley Town Hall, which is illuminated by coloured lights that constantly change, bathing the exterior in hues of pink to blue to green. Last month in the local paper the council were saying they're struggling to fund the household recycling costs but it seems they can waste our council tax payments on coloured light bulbs. I shake the negativity from my thoughts and walk over to wait at the bus stop. The interior looks unwelcoming, even the lone pigeon, head bobbing as it strolls along the pavement has one eye out for muggers and teenage tearaways. "Are you waiting for the Tunstall bus love?" a woman calls out to me.

"Yes," I reply.

"It's already gone, it was seven minutes early. There's not another for an hour and then that's the last one." I thank her and am just deciding whether to wait or take a taxi when the combination of an April breeze and the fizzy water makes its presence felt.

The public facilities at the bus station were closed months ago in an effort to curb drug taking and rough sleepers. Rough sleepers, who coined that phrase? Years ago, people living on the streets, were called, the homeless, rough sleepers implies they're choosing to sleep in doorways out of choice. With my bladder feeling like an over-inflated balloon, I have no option but to pop into a pub and use their facilities.

I push open the door and immediately see the sign for the ladies and so ducking down the corridor I nip inside and become ensconced in a cubicle. "Come along, Beryl," I tell myself, "just pee and go."

Cocooned inside the safety of a cubicle I hear someone else enter the room. "He's a bit fit that Kirk, isn't he?" the stranger's voice says as she enters the cubicle next to mine and closes the door noisily. "Have you seen his bum in those tight jeans?"

"Ooh yeah, it's so peachy, I could bite it," a friend responds. "I wouldn't kick him out of bed for farting."

"Me neither."

"Come on, can't you pee any quicker, we'll miss our go if you don't hurry up."

"I'm coming now. Oh shit!"

"What's wrong?"

"There's no loo roll in here."

"Just use your knickers and go commando, it won't be the first time."

"I can't with this skirt, everyone will see my lady bits when I sit down." I remove the roll attached to the wall and pass it under the cubicle. "Thanks," the voice next door says as she takes it from me before calling to her friend, "I'm coming now." The roll is passed back under the cubicle to me and as the toilet next to mine flushes the occupant says, "I don't care what Natalie says I'm being Cheryl whether she likes it or not."

"But Natalie is always Cheryl. She says she has the same style."

"Bollocks has she. Natalie's more Cheryl Baker than Cole." Laughter explodes, bouncing off the tiled walls and with a squeak the door opens and the two girls leave the room singing, 'Making Your Mind Up.' I wait a few more minutes before opening the cubicle door. Intrigued by the conversation I wonder what the girls could have been talking about. After a quick glance at my reflection in the mirror, I walk along the corridor that leads to the bar and push the door open. I step inside and am enveloped in the atmosphere; the buzz of conversation and the chink of glassware surrounds me. From the corner, a shrill laugh erupts and I turn to see a group of girls with smiles as wide as their waists. They bang shot glasses down onto the table before making their way to the makeshift stage in the corner of the bar. Music kicks in and the five girls start to sing, 'Sound of the Underground,' whilst having an unsuccessful stab at what looks like a complicated dance routine. Laughter reverberates around the room as the rotund girl in the middle of the group attempts a high kick, which results in her splitting her trousers. With her knickers on show, she wiggles her backside at the audience, and a group of men nearby give her a rousing cheer.

As I watch this spectacle my apprehension disappears. None of the people have glanced across and muttered remarks about me being here alone, no one has sucked their teeth in disapproval and, apart from an old man who gave me a rather salacious wink, no one has taken a blind bit of notice.

The five girls leave the stage and a young man announces that there'll be a short break and that the karaoke will resume in twenty minutes. Feeling bolstered, I order a drink and find a seat in the corner. On the table in front of me is a folder with pages inside individual plastic pockets. I pick it up and glance at the worn sticker with a mix of upper and lowercase letters.

It reads: After choosin a sonG Please fill In Slip & hand to Ruth.

"Thinking of having a go?" a voice beside me says, I look up and see the young man who had made the announcement smiling at me.

"No, I don't think so," I say shaking my head.

"Go on, you might enjoy it." He winks, his dark fringed eyelid closing and opening slowly. "If you do fancy a bash, fill this in and hand it to Ruth over there." He points out a plump girl with pink hair who is missing a front tooth.

I watch as he walks over to her and whispers something into her ear, which results in a laugh you could grate cheese on. Ruth leaves his side and walks over to the music system set up at the end of the room and taking the microphone she taps it with her knuckles creating an ear-splitting squeal of feedback. "Okay, everyone, you have just five more minutes to fill in your song choices before Kirk takes over." She waves to the young man who had spoken to me earlier and now I know who Kirk is.

I open the folder and I'm running my finger down the list of songs when it falls upon one that makes me smile. "Thinking of doing one?"

I look up to see Ruth looming over me. "I'm not sure."

"Go on love you only live once."

"You're telling me," I say, before taking the pen she's offered me. How odd that phrase is, but remarkably true.

Here I am, I have one life that's now in jeopardy, (I'm being rather dramatic there) so let's take this opportunity to do something that pushes me, (as they say on the telly) out of my comfort zone. I want to enjoy the moment, who knows a similar one might not come along again.

As the entertainment gets underway again and the first person takes to the stage, I decide I'm in need of some Dutch courage and so order a second drink. I'm walking back to my table and begin to wonder what the people of the Netherlands call the need for alcoholic bravado when Simon, a six-foot blond with freckles and a tattoo of a naked woman on his forearm breaks into a gravelly rendition of 'Hey Jude', and when I say gravelly, I mean hardcore. Next to take the stage is Karl and Sarah and they offer up a duet from *Grease*. Sadly, Karl lacks the sex appeal of John Travolta, and Sarah with her unfortunate nose and wide forehead is more Isaac Newton than Newton-John.

I'm beginning to lose my confidence and I'm thinking of slipping off into the night when my name is called. Suddenly I'm riddled with fear as Ruth comes over to escort me to the stage. "Oh well, here we go," I mumble under my breath as I position myself in front of the television screen. I take my reading glasses out of my handbag, and pop them onto my nose as the song title appears on the screen: The strumming guitar and tick-tick-tick of the hi-hats of the first few bars begin the play. There's no going back now, this will be a surprise entry in the diary I think and I take a deep breath and begin to sing, "We have all the time in the world…"

Three minutes and fourteen seconds later, I'm beaming as the room swells with applause. "That was brilliant," Kirk says. I know he's just being kind because I've no experience of singing, except while waiting for the tumble dryer to finish its load.

"I was off key I think."

"No, you were great. Is it a favourite?"

"Not really, more tongue in cheek actually." I look at my watch. "Bugger I'll miss my bus if I don't get a wriggle on." I swap my spectacles over again and I'm already buttoning up my coat as Ruth takes the microphone, telling everyone its last orders at the bar before she begins to belt out the Kelly Marie classic, 'Feels Like I'm in Love'. Her vibrato is so pronounced that I'm sure the fillings in her back teeth must be working themselves loose.

Just my luck, I'm stepping outside as the bus is leaving the bus station. There are no more buses until morning so I return to the pub and I'm just inside the doorway about to call a taxi when Kirk spots me. He's lugging a speaker up the corridor as I lift the payphone receiver. "Everything okay?" he asks.

"I've missed the last bus," I reply.

He pauses, using his foot to keep the door open and stares at me for a moment. "Do you have far to go?"

"Tunstall, just off the high street."

""Really?" He heaves a speaker into the back of a Berlingo van and slams it shut. "I'm passing there. I could give you a lift if you don't mind waiting a few minutes?"

"No," I say declining his kind offer. "I couldn't possibly put you to any trouble."

"It's no trouble, honest. Just as soon as the gears loaded up I'll be on my way." He opens the passenger side door and tells me to wait inside, "It'll be much warmer than standing outside."

"I'm not the sort of woman usually taken to accepting lifts from strangers," I say as the van pulls out of the pub car park. "In fact, this is the first time."

"That's okay, it can be our secret." I don't need to look at him, I already know he'll be smiling.

"You're a very kind man," I say.

"And you're a cracking singer."

"That was the first time I've ever sung in public. This whole evening has been a catalogue of first-time experiences."

"Really?" he asks but doesn't push it.

"Mind you, I don't think I'll be making a habit of visiting pubs alone. Besides, truth be told after a couple of vodkas my memory tends to resemble a crotched blanket."

We're just pulling up outside my front door as I tell him about the conversation I overheard in the ladies. He laughs and I ask what's so funny. "They'll have a long wait if they think they stand a chance with me."

"Are you already courting?" I ask.

"No. Single sadly, no one wants me."

"I can't believe that. A good-looking lad like you, there must be scores of girls falling over themselves to get a date with you."

"That's the problem," he says with another wink, "they're girls."

The penny drops as my front door opens spilling yellow light onto the pavement. "Is that you mum?" asks Victor.

"Yes love," I reply, "This is Kirk, he's kindly given me a lift home." I'm just about to step inside my hallway when I turn to see Victor leaning into the van's open window to say thank you. I give Kirk a wink, nod to my son and then enter the house to be greeted by the dog with its tail going ten to the dozen.

~ 47 ~

Sunday, 11 April
I'm pouring a cup of tea when I hear the letterbox rattle. I walk into the hall and lying upon the mat is a small mountain of mail. A couple of coloured envelopes, a handful of white ones and sticking out at an odd angle a brown one. Call it instinct. Call it whatever you like. I already know what the brown envelope contains. I scoop up the post from the mat and walk back into the middle room, where I drop it onto the dining table and go back to my morning cuppa.

In the corner, the television is broadcasting the early morning news. The female presenter is doing her utmost to remain calm while trying to get a word in edgeways, as her male counterpart is ranting about whatever he's got his teeth into. Meanwhile, the politician invited onto the show sits there as passive as a cadaver.

My eyes kept flitting from the screen to the pile of mail and back again. Finally, unable to concentrate, I switch the television off and pick up the envelopes. There are six of them. Two are junk: A special offer for digital television services and a holiday brochure for the Outer Hebrides and three are addressed to Len, which look like birthday cards. Leaving the final brown envelope addressed to me.

I pick up the butter knife and using my handkerchief wipe the toast and jam residue from it. I slide it between the envelope flap and with one quick slice it's cleanly opened. I remove the white sheet inside and beneath the National Health Service logo, my initial appointment for the laser treatment is printed.

I'm returning the letter to the envelope when in walks Victor. "Morning mum. Any tea in the pot?"

"It'll be stewed now," I tell him, "I'll make a fresh one."

"Looks like Dad's got a good few birthday cards," he calls after me as I leave the room. "Mine's upstairs, I'll bring it down after I've had some breakfast. Is there any bacon in?"

"Yes love," I say lighting the grill. "Sit down and I'll make you a sandwich."

Minutes later I'm walking back into the room, with the sandwich on a muffin plate, to find Victor examining the brown envelope. "Is this from the hospital?" he asks.

I nod and put the bacon sandwich in front of him. "It's an appointment, just a consultation, next week."

"Bloody hell, that came through quick." Victor peels back the white bread and looks up, "No brown sauce?"

***

It's mid-morning, Vera pops over to say she'll be meeting us at the restaurant later but can't go out for a drink afterwards as she's halfway through a TV whodunnit two-parter. I tell her about the appointment and ask if she would be available to come with me. She asks why I don't want Len to come and I explain that he's already had enough time off work with my illness. "I'm sure they'd understand," she says.

"Probably," I reply, "but with cutbacks and imminent layoffs I don't want to give them any reason for thinking about getting rid of him."

"They wouldn't do that would they, he only works three days a week?"

"Len told me last week, that head office has said, they've got to get rid of a couple of part-time staff."

"What's the country coming to when they need to make old men redundant?" Vera shakes her head. "Anyway, I've got to nip into town and return a shower cap to the pound shop."

"Why, is it faulty?"

"No, it's perfectly fine, but they've got them for forty-nine pence in Wilko." I bid her goodbye and watch her walk up the road before closing the front door.

***

We arrive at *Trattoria di Roberto* early, "Gives us a chance to have a pre-dinner drink," says Victor, who's dressed in an immaculately pressed shirt balanced with a pair of black jeans. Len's in his suit, the machine washable one that does for all occasions, everything from entrance to exit and the bits in the middle that constitute a lifespan.

The waiter is taking our drinks order as the door opens and in walks Vera. She stamps her feet on the mat, exclaiming loudly that her toes are as numb as a dentist's patient. "Bloody freezing out there, I hope I'm not late?"

"Len's ordered you a drink. Lisa and Mac are still to come."

"You look nice Victor."

"Thanks, Vera."

"He's got a date after," I tell her, as Victor blushes.

"Anyone we know?" I'm about to tell her about my evening with Kirk and the karaoke when Victor coughs and says, "No one you'd know." The waiter delivers our drinks when Lisa walks in. "Mac's just parking the car," she says, avoiding eye contact with me.

It's been ten days since Lisa and I had our argument and during this time relations have remained frosty. She has called at the house a handful of times to drop off and collect Saffron, but we've only exchanged the bare minimum of words.

She walks over to the table, bends down and kisses her father on the cheek after wishing him a happy birthday. She gives me a weak smile before parking herself between Victor and Vera. "What's everyone having?" she says, picking up a menu and hiding her head behind the burgundy and gilt, wipe-clean cover. "We've not decided yet," Victor says.

"I have," pipes up Vera. "I'm having a prawn cocktail to start."

Mac arrives and after ordering himself a half of lager and a vodka for Lisa, we all sit in silence reading a menu each. "What's *funghi ripieni*?" asks Len.

"Stuffed mushrooms," says Victor. "I've had them before they're nice."

"What are they stuffed with?"

"Why don't you read the menu, Dad, it'll tell you what's in them." Lisa says without looking up.

"Don't speak to your father like that," I'm still annoyed.

"I was only saying…"

I'm about to respond when Len looks across and discreetly shakes his head, silencing me.

"I can't find anything I like," moans Mac. "I'm not really into foreign food. Why didn't we just go for a curry?"

All menus are lowered and eight pairs of bewildered eyes look across the table at him. All, that is, except for Lisa, after so many years of marriage she's used to her husband's peculiarities.

"I think I'll skip the prawns," says Vera, "and save some room for a portion of tiramisu later."

With our orders scribbled down, the waiter walks off to the kitchen as Carmel strolls over to ask if everything is okay. We all mumble in agreement. "And is this the birthday boy?" she says. Not being a man at ease with public attention Len looks uncomfortable as Carmel stands behind him, both hands upon his shoulders, his eyes widen as she continues, "And what a good-looking man he is. How old are you today, Mr Handsome?"

Now ten pairs of eyes look across the table as Len sheepishly tells her he's sixty-six.

"You don't look a day over fifty-five," Carmel says with a wink, and my husband's eyes now dip as a pink flush colours his cheeks. "I'll have the waiter bring you a birthday drink over, what would you like, wine, grappa?"

"Do you have a brown ale?"

"I … err not … erm … sure," a flustered Carmel says, "I'll look to see if we have the Italian equivalent."

Victor and Lisa snigger and Len turns to them and just says, "What?"

With the starters over and the plates cleared away, Mac orders another round of drinks as Victor turns to Lisa and tells her about my forthcoming hospital appointment. "So, you've finally seen sense?" she says.

"Your mother's agreed to make enquiries into laser ablation treatment," Len says.

"About time too."

"They're just enquiries, nothing more." Lisa opens her mouth to reply, but a stern glance from her father puts a stop to her intention. "Whatever your mother decides is final, so let's put an end to this pettiness."

The waiter arrives and puts a lasagne down in front of Vera and what can only be described as a bolster cushion in front of Victor. "Bloody hell," Mac says, "What's that?"

"It's a *calzone*, a house special."

"A cal-what-ay?"

"A pizza folded over and filled with Bolognese sauce."

"Looks like a bloody giant pasty."

Lisa looks across at me, smiles and rolls her eyes before leading the table into laughter as Mac sits wondering what he's said that's so funny.

With our meal over, the waiter is clearing our table, the tablecloth being scooped up collecting the crumbs and our memories and despite it being a Sunday, another group of people look over in readiness to take our places. Victor's paying the bill as Len helps me on with my coat. "Thank you," he says, as he tosses my scarf around my neck as if I were a prize on a hoop-la stall before whispering, "I love you, you daft old bird."

Mac retrieves his car from a nearby car park and he and Lisa promise to drop Vera at home on their way. Victor opens the taxi door and I climb in beside Len. "You have a good night," he says as he closes the door. "I'll try not to be too late." I catch Len winking at his son, and the taxi pulls away.

***

The club is crowded when we arrive. The committee had decided a few months ago that they needed to inject some much-needed life into the place, and so had voted to stage an evening of entertainment and bingo every second Sunday. Most evenings there's just a handful of old stalwarts clinging to the bar keeping the till open, but tonight the main room is packed to capacity.

Len manages to find us a seat and I'm taking off my coat when I hear my name called out. Julia Watkins is waving at me from across the room. She's a nice enough girl but a little brash in my opinion. Julia is one of those girls who can often be seen sporting a love bite on her neck as if it was a badge of honour and come rain or shine you can guarantee she'll be wearing a skirt no bigger than a wet wipe. She comes from the estate that backs onto our street. Like all estates, it has its problems. These range from youths hanging around at night drinking and riding bicycles that are too small for them, to kids thinking it's hilarious to swap people's hanging baskets around. There was an argument not long ago when Harry Mountford woke up one Sunday morning to find his hanging baskets had been swapped over with his neighbour Reggie Boyle's. Well, the upshot was Harry preferred Reggie's baskets and refused to give them back. It took two police officers and several cups of tea to get it sorted out, but that said, by and large, the estate is pretty trouble-free.

"Hey, Beryl?" she calls again.

"What?" I call back, trying to be heard over, Candy Dreams, a duo from Birkenhead, who are murdering a Nat King Cole classic.

Len looks up from his pint and gestures with his eyes that it might be best if I went to see what she wants. "Okay," I say, getting up, "but don't let anyone nick my seat, I won't be long." Len smiles and goes back to hearing how Bernard Copland had fastened himself to Norris Mackenzie's dado rail with a hot-glue gun.

"What's up, Julia?" I ask reaching the table she's sharing with three other girls.

"Do you wanna come out with us in a couple of weeks, it's Sonia's hen night, it'll be a laugh?"

"Yeah, it's gonna be a blast," chips in a girl dressed all in black with hair the colour of limes.

"Oh, I don't think so." I say, "You don't want someone of my age slowing you down."

"Oh come on, you should let your hair down," says Rachel Eckersley, who was sitting next to the lime-haired girl. "Me mum's gonna be there so you'll have another oldie to talk to, you could even bring Vera along if you like."

"Yeah and hold the coats," snorts a girl I hadn't seen before, who had so many facial piercings she'd short circuit a metal detector.

"I'll think about it," I say and I make my way back to Len as Candy Dreams begins an all-out assault on the senses with a Spice Girls medley.

"What did she want?" Len asks with one eye on the two girls singing.

"Oh, something and nothing," I tell him in a non-committal manner.

After Candy Dreams have finished telling us what they want, what they really, really want, followed by a final zigazig-ah, they leave the stage for a short break and Julia Watkins passes our table juggling two pints of lager and what looks like two gins; I guess it's gin, as wedged down her cleavage I can see a bottle of slimline tonic water.

A thought fleetingly dances across my mind, reminding me that as I was now sans cleavage, I'd never be able to do that with a bottle. I shake away the preposterous thought and smile at Julia and pointing to the bottle I say, "I bet that's cold."

"Not half," she replies. "It's made my bra damp." Hearing the word bra, Len looks up from his pint and I'm pretty sure Julia turns back to add, more for his benefit than mine, "Hey Beryl, I'll have to be careful I don't take anyone's eye out. My nipples are standing to attention like little soldiers."

52 Weeks

~ 46 ~

Tuesday, 20 April
"Who's getting married again?" Vera asks as we sit on the hard plastic chairs in the oncology department.

"Sonia Murphy I've told you already, she's having the hen party Thursday."

"Sonia Murphy?"

"You know, stout girl with bleached hair."

"With a harelip?" My eyes roll upwards as I recall an image, then shaking my head I say, "No that's Rosie Clarkson, but they do look similar. She was in the newspaper two years ago, can you remember, she won a pie-eating competition."

"Did she?"

"Yes, she beat a bevy of blokes from the pub and that big girl out of the butchers. She won a year's supply of meat pies."

"Meat and potato or steak and kidney?"

"Sorry?" I ask a little confused.

"What flavour pies?"

"Does it really matter?"

"Well you know me; I've never been keen on kidney."

I decide it's best to end the thread of the conversation there before it becomes life-threatening. Vera's life.

I try my best to steer the chat back on track and tell her that Sonia's mother works in the chip shop on Summerbank Road.

"Is she the little woman, with the tattoo of Ronnie Corbett on her arm?"

"Yes, that's right," I say after breathing an inward sigh of relief, the penny having finally fallen.

"So, what about her?" Vera asks.

"She's getting married."

"Who? Her with the tattoo, I thought she was already married?"

"No, not her, Sonia."

"Sonia, who?"

"Her daughter, Sonia."

"Is she the rather dumpy one with hair like straw?"

"Yes," I groan.

"Is she the one that they call Range Rover?"

"No that's her sister Beverley, and it's four-by-four, not Range Rover."

"Really, why?"

"Because she has four children by four different men." Vera sits thinking for a while, a look of confusion on her face until she says, "That explains it. I thought it was because she had a lot of boot space."

I'm enjoying a vision of myself, beating Vera about the body with a rolled-up copy of Staffordshire Monthly, when a nurse pops her head around the door and tells me, that they are ready for me. I stand up and smooth down my coat and Vera rises to join me, telling me that I look a little stressed and should learn to relax more.

I scan the table for a spare magazine.

We're ushered into a square room which gives the impression of being inside a cube. The plastic chairs have been replaced with padded faux leather ones but the harsh fluorescent lighting remains the same here as it is in the waiting room.

We sit in silence and wait for the man sitting at the desk, who is tapping on a keyboard to acknowledge our arrival. Several minutes later, between clicks of a fingernail on plastic, he looks up. Brown eyes register our presence and a perfunctory smile invades the corners of his mouth.

"Good morning Mrs…" He double checks the notes on the desk in front of him, "Bickerstaff. I'm Rajrishi Banerjee. Raj for short. I'll be overseeing your treatment. Before we start do you have any questions?"

"Will she go bald again?" asks Vera. Raj looks across at me, his eyes questioning. "I'm just wondering, because, you see, they've had some nice bandannas at the Rowfers shop in Hanley and I could get one for Beryl's birthday."

"There will be some hair loss, but it won't be as extensive as the loss that results from chemotherapy." Picking up a booklet from the desk he hands it to me. "This will answer any questions you may have."

"Thank you," I whisper. "Will it hurt?"

"You will feel a little discomfort, but nothing to worry yourself about. Most patients suffer no adverse effects from the treatment." He stands up and walks towards me. "We just need to take a couple of measurements."

"We?" queries Vera, "will I need my reading glasses?"

"Sorry?"

"For the measurements we need to take, I won't be able to see the ruler without them." The realisation flows over Raj's face like a veil being lifted over a bride's head. "Sorry, when I said, we, I meant me or rather I. But also, we, meaning the oncology department."

"Ignore Vera," I say hoping to move things along, "Just imagine that she's on day release from a home for the bewildered."

I pass Vera the booklet to read, while Dr Banerjee proceeds to make a note of the circumference, diameter and radius of my head. "We'll use these measurements to construct a protective mask," he tells me.

"Protective mask?"

"It's so that we only target the tumour during treatment and protect the healthy tissue and your eyes. It's perfectly normal."

"Yes, if you're a bloody welder," pipes up Vera. Her input once again prompts a puzzled look from Raj as he moves back to his desk and begins to click at the keyboard once more. "Now Mrs Bickerstaff, I'm eager to start the treatment as soon as possible. I'll make an appointment for you at the same time in two weeks. We'll confirm this in writing. Is that all right with you?" I nod and his eyes flick from me to the screen and back to me. My acceptance taking less than a second to be documented.

"Very well." Raj is standing and proffering his hand. "We'll see you in two weeks. That's, we the hospital and not…"

"I understand. Thanks."

"Well, that wasn't too bad, was it?" Vera says as we stand waiting for a bus to take us back into town. I smile back, I don't have the energy to reply, but inside my head, I'm screaming. In fact, I'm yelling at the top of my lungs, I wasn't being measured for a sodding hat.

"Beryl?" Vera whispers, as we sit side by side on the bus, "I've been thinking."

"What about?"

"This hen night, next week. I think I'll give it a miss."

"Oh, right," I reply. Then I think to myself, probably best.

I decide I need to buy something to wear if I'm going to go to Sonia's hen party but preferably without Vera's help. I love the woman to death but there is a limit. So once we've said goodbye I pop into the Cats Need Care charity shop to see if they have something that's both inexpensive and suitable. I'm preoccupied, deliberating if three pounds is a little too much to invest in a lemon-coloured high-necked blouse that I'm only going to wear the once, when I feel a tap on my shoulder.

Startled, I drop the blouse back on the rail and turn around to see Margaret Watkins. Her large, hooped earrings, heavily outlined eyes and gravity-defying black beehive making her look like a demonic Minnie Mouse. "I'm glad I've bumped into you," she tells me, "Our Julia says you're coming out on the hen night with us."

I nod, transfixed as the slash of crimson in the middle of her face, opens to reveal tombstone-sized teeth. "I can't tell you how pleased I am that there'll be some of us older girls there."

"Older. More like ancient," I say, then seeing her brow furrow, I quickly correct myself and shift the emphasis onto myself, "Unlike me, you're still young enough, to fit in with the younger girls."

"It's going to be such fun; we've booked a stripper called Ebony Knight. He comes recommended by the girl from Bargain Booze, she says his willy is massive."

"That'll be nice," I mumble, as I spot Mavis and Doreen looking at me, their faces paintings of disapproval. "Hello Beryl," Doreen says, her pencilled eyebrows raised like two ticks in a schoolboy's jotter.

I'm searching for something to say as Mavis picks up the lemon blouse I was thinking about and holds it up to the light. "There's a slight stain on the front," she says.

Doreen steps in to inspect the garment, "Looks like gravy."

"I think someone's already attempted, unsuccessfully, to shift it," Mavis says placing it back on the rail. "Oh well, never mind."

"I've got some biological powder that'll get rid of that," Doreen says.

"I suppose for just three pounds I could give it a try," Mavis replies picking the blouse up again.

"You could cover the stain with a nice brooch," I tell her.

"You can always bring it back if it won't shift," Doreen remarks and saying their goodbyes they take the blouse over to the cash register.

"I hope," I say turning back to Margaret, "it's not going to be too raucous."

"It'll be great fun. We're all meeting at Fusion, that new wine bar on the high street, at eight." She leans in and gives either side of my head two noisy air kisses and then breezes out of the shop knocking against a display of dog-eared paperbacks sending a PD James tumbling to the floor.

~ 45 ~

Thursday, 29 April
After tea, with the dog asleep in front of the fire, Len looks up from the television and says, "How would that work if you don't know anyone in Jamaica?"

"How would what work?" I say, confused.

"This competition on the telly, they've just said, you can win a luxury stay with a friend in Jamaica. I don't think I have any friends in Jamaica." The dog opens one eye and looks up at its master and I just shake my head in disbelief.

"You've not forgotten, I'm going out tonight?"

"No love." The television takes his attention again; using the remote to flick through the available channels, he asks, "Is it that hen thing?"

"Yes. But I could give it a miss. I mean if you've anything else planned."

"I have got something planned." He opts for a hospital program, where Fern Britton is making her way through accident and emergency to see a child that has managed to get a silverskin onion lodged in its ear. "Me and Norris are joining a couple of blokes in town for a game of crib."

Briefly, he looks away from the screen and rummages in his trouser pocket before retrieving a crumpled twenty-pound note. "Here, have a couple of drinks on me."

"Thanks, love." I'm tempted to kiss him but decide against it. The television once again grabs his attention and Fern is now sitting on a hospital bed laughing loudly as a pensioner tells her about the fun he had the day they removed his catheter.

***

Later on, I'm standing outside Fusion, a wine bar where music spills out onto the street like open-air tinnitus. I got over my fear of entering a drinking establishment alone at the karaoke bar and squeeze between the two heavy-set gentlemen dressed in black suits with barely a blink. Once inside I spot Sonia straight away. She's hard to miss being dressed as a nurse, which I think is odd when she's actually a bricklayer. She has a bridal veil clipped into her bottled-platinum hair and a learner driver plate on her back. I make a mental note to enquire if the L-plate was meant to infer she was inexperienced with men, and if it was, maybe it was too late as she'd already got a five-year-old daughter named Tiffany.

"Beryl's here," she slurs through nicotine-stained teeth and she points towards the table where her party are sitting. "Thanks for coming, help yourself to bubbly."

"Thanks," I say, taking a glass of fizz that turns out to be Lambrusco rather than champagne: I wasn't surprised.

"Let me introduce you to everyone," Margaret says clapping her hands which is futile as it can't be heard above Florence and the Machine playing at a phenomenal volume. "Ladies, this is Beryl."

I'm introduced to the other women at the table. Marjorie tells me she has an iguana at home named Keith. Cynthia, a taxi driver with a florid complexion, whoops with delight every time someone mentions it's time to get a fresh round of drinks in. I already know Elkie of course and sitting beside her is Ruth, a plain-looking woman who's so slim that sideways on she looks like a five-foot two-inch pencil. "Pleased to meet you," she says taking my plump hand in her bony fist. "I've never seen a black man's thingy, have you?" I tell her I haven't but I'm sure it'll be much like any man's thingy, unsightly and not much to get worked up over.

The lime-haired girl I'd seen previously introduces herself as Natalie, telling me she's doing a drama degree in the hope of landing a substantial part in Emmerdale. I'm about to respond when Julia walks over and looking at the glass in my hand says, "Get that down your neck, we're moving on."

"Moving on to where?" I ask, hoping it would be somewhere with reduced volume.

"The Potter's Wheel, we've booked a room."

Leaving Fusion, we walk behind Sonia in pairs, like a trail of inebriated bridesmaids, as she lurches her way through the streets attracting attention from young lads along the way. Many of these prize specimens offer her a 'good seeing to' if she wanted one last fling. Her response to them all is a two-fingered salute.

We enter the Potter's Wheel, a tired public house with an equally tired clientele, most of whom probably work the land on the nearby council allotments. It's the kind of place where old men clutch pints of pale ale and talk about fertiliser, while their wives sip a sweet sherry, swapping stories about grandchildren and trying to remember when they last had a hot flush. Our entrance disrupts the tepid atmosphere and the pump room hushes as every head turns to look at us. "Hey lanky, are you here for my hen night?" burbles Sonia, striking up a conversation with a coat stand.

"Upstairs!" The publican behind the bar barks at us, "Function room's up there." I'm about to follow the others up the stairs when I'm surprised to catch sight of Len and Norris at the far end of the room. Luckily they appear too engrossed in their game of cribbage to notice me.

We're met by more girls, some of whom had been in earlier to get the room ready. Banners hang from the walls, garish proclamations of best wishes and good luck. Balloons and streamers swing from light fittings, and a long table runs the length of one wall, its surface supporting various sandwiches, sausage rolls and other pastry-based snacks.

At the far end of the room is a stage and flanked on either side by a wooden box with coloured bulbs behind a Perspex panel, stands a mobile disco, the words, Party Central emblazoned across the front.

"I'm gagging for a butty," Marjorie says as she falls upon the buffet and stuffing a mini Scotch egg into her mouth she tells us, she's had nothing to eat since breakfast that morning. A whoop in the corner courtesy of Cynthia indicates that the upstairs bar has opened and picking up a mini quiche and a cheese sandwich Marjorie retreats to get a drink.

"I hope these aren't meat flavoured," says the pierced girl as she helps herself to a handful of crisps, "Being a vegan means social eating can be difficult." I've discovered that her name is Verity and she comes from what is often regarded as an upmarket part of the city. An area where families live in detached houses with four bedrooms, but only have a need for three of them.

Julia announces that Carlton, the owner of Party Central is running a little late due to being stuck behind an articulated lorry on the ring road and that we should all dive into the buffet before Marjorie scoffs the lot.

I'm about to tackle a ham bap when Natalie screeches, "Sonia's in the toilets, snogging Kenny Jackson."

"Really?" I say, shocked, my ham bap midway from plate to mouth.

"It's nowt to worry about," Julia says. "It's just a snog. Sort of last-minute fling before she gets tied down." The door to the ladies flies open and an overexcited Ruth, shouts, "O.M.G. Sonia's on her knees doing … you know what to Kenny."

"This I've got to see." Margaret puts her plate down and rushes across the room.

"Me too," laughs Verity, as the main toilet door opens and a red-faced youth appears zipping up his flies with Julia and Elkie in tow.

"Come on Kenny lad give us all a go," laughs Julia.

"He can't," Elkie says. "There isn't enough to go around."

"Is Sonia all right?"

"Yes Beryl, she fell asleep."

"What! As she was—"

"Yes halfway through, doesn't say much for Kenny does it."

The racket created by a roomful of inebriated women would have been terrifying for most men, but not, Carlton. "Don't worry, here I am," he calls out as he strides into the room. Late thirties but attempting to pull off his mid-twenties, his confidence travels two steps ahead of him. "Let's inject some life into this party," Carlton says, thrusting his hips forward as the lightboxes burst into life. "What does everyone fancy?" he shouts into the microphone. "A good seeing to," is Cynthia's answer, but it's lost as Kylie Minogue starts to tell us that she can't get someone out of her head.

Quickly the dance floor is filled with gyrating bodies and a couple of lads who've gate crashed are told to sling their hooks. The buffet has been demolished and the solitary member of staff behind the bar is working flat out to keep everyone topped up with drinks.

I'm sitting nursing a gin and tonic, while Ruth tells me about her recent Mediterranean cruise. Apparently, apart from spending the first two days suffering from sea sickness and experiencing a far from riveting trip to a tortoise reserve on Corsica, she'd had a wonderful time. The music fades as Carlton announces that the special guest has arrived and anyone wanting a drink should get to the bar before the show starts. Cynthia whoops again and Julia shouts that someone should fetch Sonia.

"She's in the bog, chucking up," Verity calls back and a few minutes later, supported by a girl on either side, Sonia emerges, minus her L-plate with her veil splashed with vomit.

Carlton is given his cue and the current song fades out and a tribal rhythm fades up. The roomful of females gives a cheer as Ebony Knight enters from the kitchen, which has become his makeshift dressing room. I think the term dressing room is an odd one, as he's clearly wearing fewer clothes now than when he'd arrived.

The tall, muscular man moves around the room pausing briefly at tables to let the women gaze at his torso that's toned and the colour of premium quality chocolate.

Reaching our table, Marjorie blushes as he leans in flexing his muscles for us, Julia gasps and Margaret squirms with delight, and I do my best to avert my eyes. He must have guessed that being shy, I must be fair game for some fun, because he then turns his back on me and starts to wiggle his little loin-clothed backside at me.

"Hey, Beryl's got it going on," Julia shouts.

"Lucky sod," a voice in the crowd calls back.

Ebony Knight offers me his hand and shyly I accept and rise from my seat. He walks me into the centre of the room, whispering into my ear as we walk that I'm safe and all he wants me to do is rub some baby oil into his chest, and if I feel uncomfortable I can sit back down. "No, I'm fine," I whisper back, not sure where my confidence has come from. I'm manoeuvered to a seat placed in the centre of the dancefloor and with the audience shrieking and whistling he reaches beneath the chair and produces the oil, drizzling it over his pectorals. Guided by him I begin smoothing the oil onto his skin in large circular motions. My hands travel down his washboard stomach as he gyrates, giving the impression he is deriving pleasure from my touch. With his back to his audience, he mouths the words, 'Are you all right?' I nod and he winks then breaks away. He roams the room like a panther, sleek and alluring, allowing ladies to rub in the oil that glistens on his skin. Julia makes an unsuccessful attempt to grab beneath his loincloth and I'm sensing he's used to this from the way he deftly escapes her lunge. He approaches Sonia who is now fast asleep with her head in a puddle of alcohol, he wriggles his hips above her head, while mobile phones and pocket cameras are removed from handbags and the scene is captured for posterity. The music changes, the tribal rhythm is replaced with a sultry salsa and he turns, moving towards me swinging his hips from left to right as he comes closer. With every dip of his hips Cynthia whoops, her vocal habit now beginning to get on my nerves. Within just a few feet of me, he hooks his fingers into the waistband of his loincloth and slowly reveals himself and I think Margaret has been reliably informed by the girl in Bargain Booze. He turns to face the others and screams of delight ring around the room. The tribal music fades up again and he dances from table to table, staying just long enough for them to see but not touch. Then in an instant, he's out of the room and back in the kitchen as cheers and applause threaten the aging plaster of the Potters Wheel function room.

"Beryl, you lucky sod," Margaret shouts. "If I'd have been that close I don't think I'd have been able to hold myself back." I suddenly realise I'm still sitting there in the middle of the dancefloor, as Party Central, booms back into life, with the Black Eyed Peas proclaiming they've gotta feeling.

As the dance floor begins to fill again, I walk over to the kitchen door, knock and open it just wide enough to enquire if our guest is decent, which, considering that just minutes before, I'd had his naked body, inches from my face seems like an odd question.

"Come in, I'm dressed," he says, packing his loincloth into a sports bag. "I've come to return this," I say, handing him the bottle of baby oil.

"Thanks, I'm Leroy by the way. Mum was a big *Kids From Fame* fan, whoever they were." His face opened up into a wide, beaming grin and taking my hands he wiped the oil from them, telling me that he was studying to be a doctor and the stripping helped to top up his student loan.

***

That night as I climb into bed next to Len he asks me if I've had a good time, I tell him that despite my initial reservations I have. "So, will you be making a habit of this hen night malarkey?"

"No," I reply, honestly. "It's all a bit overrated if you ask me."

"I suppose so." Then with a nudge of his elbow, he asks, "Would you like to rub some baby oil on my chest?"

"Would I buggery," I reply and turn off the bedside lamp and roll over.

~ 44 ~

Tuesday, 4 May
I can tell Len is less than enthusiastic about going to work today. He's taking his time over breakfast, spending longer than usual dipping his crispy bacon into the yellow yolk of his fried egg. "Is everything all right?" I ask, seeing he's almost finished.

"Yes," he lies, sliding a piece of bread around the plate, mopping up the last of the yolk and brown sauce.

"Are you going to eat that, or just wipe the pattern off the plate?"

"I'm not in the mood for it today."

"Why ever not?" I ask, lifting his empty plate from the table and walking into the kitchen, dropping it into the bowl of soapy bubbles, before pulling on my rubber gloves. I pop my head back through the doorway and watch as he puts his now empty mug down. "I'm off the shop floor again today."

"I thought you liked working in the warehouse?"

"I do." He lifts himself out of his seat with the enthusiasm of a condemned man and makes his way into the hall where his coat is waiting for him.

Since being made redundant, following the decline of the local pottery industry, like many of the men his age, Len's found it difficult to adjust. His life after has been a succession of temporary jobs. Another stint at a china maker, to once again be let go and a period of unemployment that he felt ashamed of. A year ago, he secured his current position, three days a week at a large national DIY store and once more he began to feel useful again.

"So what's different today?"

"I'm working with Arthur."

Of all the members of staff at the store, Arthur is the one that Len has least enjoyed working with. He's told me the man is nice enough, but they just didn't have a single thing in common. What with him being an ex-potter and Arthur coming from a teaching background.

Len walks back into the room, picks up the plastic box that contains his lunch, before coming into the kitchen and giving me a peck on the cheek. "Oh well love, best make tracks," he says, as I pull the rubber gloves from my hands. "We all have to do things that we don't want to do at some time."

"We do," I say, as I watch him shuffle out of the back door and into the yard, where he gives the dog a pat on the head before disappearing through the back gate.

***

I'm once again sitting on the hard plastic chairs in oncology, this time however I'm alone. I made the decision not to mention my appointment to Len, and after the last visit, I didn't think my nerves could stand another appointment with Vera. I pick up one of the out-of-date magazines and try to read an article about a podiatrist who is walking from Doncaster to Northallerton to raise awareness of fungal infections and athlete's foot, but it fails to keep my attention. I look at the clock, three minutes have passed since I last looked. Flicking through the pages I'm about to settle on a news article about the decline of canoeing in Swansea when a nurse arrives at my side.

"Mrs Bickerstaff?"

"Yes," I say putting the magazine down.

"I'm Victoria and I'm here to take you through for your treatment." She's a cheery girl, with pink cheeks and moss-green eyes. She has an ideal face for the nursing profession, open and welcoming, in fact, you could say it was expertly designed for the job. "There's nothing to worry about," she says, leading the way.

I'm led into a room where a woman is monitoring a computer screen and Raj is tinkering with another keyboard. Raj looks up and saying nothing acknowledges me with a discrete rise of an eyebrow. I allow Victoria to lead me behind a screen, where after asking me to change into a gown she leaves me alone.

I hear Raj and the other woman talking, but it's all technical jargon and suddenly fear takes hold of me and I'm unable to undress.

"How are we doing?" Victoria asks from the other side of the fabric divide. "Do you need any help?"

"Yes please," I muster just enough energy to make myself heard.

"What's wrong?" Victoria says her eyes as comforting as a warm blanket.

"I'm scared."

"Everything will be all right." She picks up the gown from the bed. "Here, let me help you?" Victoria helps me out of my clothes and into the gown, before taking me back around the screen and into the room. "Everything's fairly straightforward. Have you ever seen that film, *Alien*," she says, "Where Sigourney Weaver sleeps in a sort of space-age capsule?" I nod wondering where the conversation is going. "You see that pod-shaped thing over there?" She points to the bed with what looks like an upside-down barrel suspended above it. "Well, you just lie there and we zap the troublesome tumour. Mind you, there is a downside."

"What's that?" I ask with trepidation.

"You have to wear this." She holds out a clear plastic helmet and smiling, says, "It makes you look like an extra from a *Star Wars* movie."

"Better that, than having a creature exploding out of my chest." I'm feeling more relaxed as the conversation takes my attention away from the procedure. I think I can see a sparkle in Victoria's eyes, but it's probably just the reflection from the strip lights above. I return her smile and within seconds we are both laughing. I watch as her enormous bosoms lift and fall and think to myself, it's a good job she works here and not maternity, those beauties would cause quite a stir at breastfeeding time.

I'm made comfortable on the special bed and Raj explains the procedure before fitting the helmet. "Are you ready?"

I mouth, 'Yes,' close my eyes and before I know it Raj is telling me it's all over. I'm told to remain on the bed and to try not to move as I'm wheeled to the far side of the room.

"Everything okay?" Victoria asks.

"Yes, it felt a bit strange, but it wasn't unpleasant, a bit like an imaginary bullet really."

"The NHS frowns upon laser Russian roulette so it's a good job Dr Banerjee's got a steady hand." The mask is removed and a porter arrives to wheel me into a curtained bay for my recovery. "After twenty minutes you should be fit enough to go home." Victoria's friendly wink fills me with warmth and in a few minutes, I'm sleeping.

***

I'm feeling surprisingly well when I get home, there's no headache or nausea and apart from feeling a little dehydrated, everything feels normal. I open the back door and the dog bolts out into the yard to greet Len who's just come in through the gate.

"Good day?" I ask as he drops his empty sandwich box into the sink.

"Bloody bloke's a pillock. Any chance of a brew?"

"Take your coat off and sit down, I'll put the kettle on."

With a mug of steaming tea and a couple of ginger nuts in front of him, Len starts to tell me about his day. In readiness for the forecasted influx of garden related summer sales, the company anticipates, he and Arthur have been put in charge of erecting a shed outside. Arthur, being a retired mathematics teacher put himself in charge of calculations and measurements, while Len's job was to lug the wooden panels around with a trainee by the name of Shane. "He's not a bad lad, young Shane," says Len, "Once you get used to the lisping caused by his pierced tongue." Apparently, Arthur had not been content with his assumed position of team leader and felt that as he was the person with the mathematical experience it fell to him to drill the holes required for the fixing screws. "I told him," Len says, "It's all right knowing a tangent from a hypotenuse, but when it comes to drilling, you need to have a steady hand and know what you're doing."

My mind returns to Victoria's words earlier about Dr Banerjee. "So what happened?" I ask.

"Well, I was holding the door frame up, while young Shane steadied the side panel and Arthur started to drill into the wood, but the daft bugger went through at an angle."

"Is that bad?"

"Is it bad," he laughs, mouth open and molars coated in biscuit. "He only went and drilled straight through the frame and into Shane's wrist."

"Oh my, is Shane all right?"

"Yes, fortunately, the drill bit went through his watch face before it could do any damage."

"He was lucky."

"Yes, and do you know what happened next?" I shake my head as my husband sniggers, obviously relishing his tale. "Arthur looks up and sees the drill bit sticking up out of the wood with shards of watch glass sticking out and says, 'What's that?' and young Shane looks at him, right serious like, and says, 'looks like forty-five degrees to me Stan.'"

"Oh well, "I say, as Len starts laughing, followed by coughing and a red face. I collect the empty tea mugs and in the kitchen, as I empty a tin of peas into a pan I remember my time at the hospital and call out to Len. "I guess not everyone can be blessed with a steady hand and a good aim."

~ 43 ~

Tuesday 12 May
It's almost midday and so far I've dusted, polished and tripped over the dog twice and now with the beds stripped and the sheets bouncing around inside the washing machine I think it's time for a break.

I'm sitting in front of the television with a cup of coffee as *Bargain Hunt* starts. Today two brothers from Cleckheaton scour a car boot sale for antiques in the hope of selling them on for a profit. In my experience, the format of this show is somewhat flawed, as all the previous contestants have ended up making a loss. The elder brother, who appears to harbour a capricious streak is smitten with a silver-plated denture holder when my telephone rings. I mute the sound as the practical brother takes the denture holder and sets it back down firmly upon the pasting table that's doubling as a stall.

"Is that you Beryl?" it's my sister.

"If it isn't," I reply, "then someone else has just tidied the house and answered the phone."

"There's no need to be flippant."

"I'm sorry. What can I do for you?"

"I don't have time to chat, so I'll get straight to the point," she says. "I had to take Harold up to the hospital this morning for some keyhole surgery on his knee. It was a last-minute appointment and to say it's made a mess of my plans is an understatement." As usual, getting straight to the point is something my sister has trouble with. She is the only person I know, who would find giving a lost motorist succinct directions an uphill struggle. "So," she says, continuing her diatribe, "I did have plans for next week, a theatre trip with a friend. But I couldn't possibly leave Harold alone to fend for himself. The doctor says he'll need to use a wheelchair for a week or so, and I can't have him scuffing my skirting boards, can I?"

"No, of course not, but—"

"Beryl, please don't interrupt, I don't have time to gossip. The reason I'm calling is because I now have two theatre tickets going begging. Now I know it's probably not your thing, but if you'd like them, you're welcome to them and you never know, you might actually enjoy the experience. I'm about to say thank you when she bids farewell and the line goes dead.

***

I've almost finished putting the freshly ironed sheets back on the beds when Lisa arrives. She lets herself in and calls up the stairs that she's put the kettle on. "I'll be down in a min," I call back, "Just got to put a clean sheet on our Victor's bed."

"I don't see why he can't do his own bed," Lisa says, as I enter the middle room, "he's old enough."

"I don't mind; it gives me something to do."

"You do too much and with your condition, you need to slow down."

I don't bother responding when Len walks into the kitchen. "Hello love, bring a cup in with you, there's a fresh pot in here."

"What's for tea?" Len drops his coat onto a chair.

"I've defrosted some haddock." I pour him a cuppa, before taking his coat into the hall and hanging it up.

"I was just telling Mum she shouldn't do so much," Lisa says.

"And I've already said, I don't mind. I'd go mad if I didn't keep busy."

"Dad, I think you and Victor need to pick up some of the slack."

"Do you love?" says Len, slurping his tea. "Any chance of a biscuit?"

"I'll get you one," I say, making my way into the kitchen.

"No, you won't. If Dad wants a bloody biscuit he can get it himself. This is exactly what I'm saying."

"But, it's only a biscuit."

"It's only a biscuit now, but then you'll cook the tea and I don't doubt it'll be you washing the dishes while Dad and Victor watch the telly."

"It's too late," Len says.

"Why?"

"Because I've drunk me tea now," he says putting his cup down.

"For goodness sake dad!"

"You'll never guess who called me earlier," I say in an attempt to change the subject. "My sister," I tell them about Harold's surgery and the offer of spare theatre tickets. Lisa grins and seizes the opportunity. "Get your coat," she says to me.

"Why?"

"I'll run you over and you can pick up the tickets and while we're gone Dad can cook your tea."

"What!" Len says.

"Come on Dad, how difficult can it be to cook some fish and chips?"

"But..." I begin to protest.

"Come along mum, I'm sure dad can cope."

"In forty-three years of marriage, I've never left your father to cook the tea."

"Well then, this'll be a first. Another thing to tick off your bloody list, a new entry for your diary."

I allow myself to be shepherded into my coat and down the hall. Just as we're about to leave Len calls after me. "Yes love?" I reply.

"Where do you keep the tin opener?"

***

"Wipe your feet." This is my sister's standard greeting as she opens her front door. "We've not been in long and Harold says the analgesic's starting to wear off."

"Lisa's brought me over for the tickets, save you posting them."

"That's good of her, now can you hurry up in, the draught's not good for Harold's summer bedding."

"Marigolds?" I ask, looking at the trays of young plants on the windowsill.

"African," my sister replies and closes the door. "You'll no doubt want a cup of tea." We nod as she extends her arm and for the second time, I'm herded along a hallway. "I don't have any of that supermarket tea, you like, mine's a popular branded blend so I do hope it'll suffice."

"Yes, that'll be fine," Lisa says, "and you do have yak's milk, don't you?"

"Flippancy! You get it from your mother." She raises an eyebrow in disapproval before walking into her kitchen.

"So," I say to Harold who's sitting in a wheelchair looking miserable, "You've had surgery then?"

"Yes."

"Was it painful?"

"No."

"Did the hospital loan you the chair?"

"Yes."

"Will you need more treatment in the future?"

"Maybe."

"Don't get Harold started," my sister says as she places a tray of tea things on her occasional table. "You'll never shut him up and when you've gone I'll be left to deal with his incessant prattling." I glance across at Lisa and notice she's trying her best to stifle a laugh. We're passed a slice of Victoria sponge on a side plate decorated with cornflowers before the tea is poured and for the next half hour, we sit sipping as my sister tells us about a recent outing to a candle factory she enjoyed with the women's institute.

"Well, it's been fascinating," Lisa says, "but we have to leave, dad's cooking tea."

My sister's eyes half-close and flicker before she says, "Dinner, Lisa." Then turning her attention to me, "Did I hear correctly, your husband is left at home cooking?" I nod my head; speaking would be futile as she's taken another breath. "All I can say is I hope he doesn't set fire to the kitchen. Mind you, I doubt he'll know a spoon from a spatula."

"We'd better get going," Lisa says, "We might need to help the fire brigade rescue the dog." She's tossed a reproachful glance from my sister and we catch sight of Harold camouflaging a smile with a yawn. We say goodbye and slip away as the front door closes quickly, banishing any breeze from the hallway and Harold's African marigolds.

***

"You're back just in time," Len says. "Get your coat off and park yourself at the table." The tempting aroma of fish, chips and non-brewed condiment floats into the middle room as he opens the kitchen door. I remove my coat and Lisa hangs it in the hall for me as I sit at the already laid dinner table. Len slides around the door jamb and then reappears with two plates brimming with chips, peas and a golden piece of battered fish. "There you go, love," he says, putting the plate in front of me.

"I'll leave you to have your tea in peace," Lisa says and kissing her father on his cheek adds, "Well done Dad."

"I'll see you out," I say rising from the table.

"No, you eat up while it's still hot. I'll see myself out."

I wait until the front door closes before I say to Len, "They've always done nice chips, haven't they?"

"Who?" says Len, trying his best to look as though he doesn't understand what I've just said, but failing miserably.

"The chip shop on Summerbank Road."

"How did you know?"

"Because the haddock I defrosted earlier wasn't battered."

~ 42 ~

Saturday, 22 May

Two evenings ago, Lisa and I made use of the tickets donated to us by my sister and went to the theatre to see, *As You Like It*. You know the one. Persecution, wrestling and cross-dressing, but that's Shakespeare for you. And just let me say, that had the Bard been born a Maureen and not a William, there'd have been fewer plays written and more bedsheets ironed. Anyway, we got to the point where Jacques recited the famous, 'Seven Ages of Man' speech, and I was sitting in the gloom listening to the actor waffle on about mewling, puking and pantaloons, when I thought, what about the three ages of motherhood. First, we're life-givers and nurturers, then best friends and confidants until finally we become unpaid help.

Now nothing illustrates this more than when your progeny have offspring of their own. When my daughter gave birth, I was on hand to administer words of comfort and advice. Months passed, and during this time I was required to listen to the minutiae of daily drudgery and keep her intimate secrets – piles aren't anyone's idea of fun. Until finally, when teething's replaced with tantrums, the occasional spot of babysitting becomes a career move.

Despite telling me to do less housework, Lisa's got herself a part-time job and so with selective memory, the task of childcare falls upon my shoulders.

Yesterday she dropped off my charge and I'm left with specific instructions. The child must be fed at twelve-thirty to maintain a routine, I must limit television viewing to just one hour and under no circumstances administer sweets, as the e numbers facilitate bad behaviour.

I'm watching as my middle room begins to bear a resemblance to a primary school obstacle course when the telephone rings. I'm a firm believer that telephone manufacturers should invest in a pre-programmed range of ringtones that indicate the mood of the incoming call. And let me say, if this service was available then this call would have been heralded by something akin to Stravinsky's, *The Rite of Spring*. I pick up the receiver and on the other end of the line is my sister: Two calls in as many weeks, I feel honoured. She's frantic; bleating on about Harold's fall down the stairs that morning and the price of blown vinyl wall coverings in B&M. I say stairs quite casually as she lives in a bungalow and the sum total of risers in her home numbers three. Apparently, Harold had tried to descend the aforementioned stairs without assistance, had toppled over and broken his walnut pipe. Now I understand most people would think a damaged smoking implement hardly constitutes a disaster, but apparently, it does when at the time it's clenched firmly between your dentures as you tumble headfirst onto the shag pile. Anyhow, the upshot is Harold has broken his top plate, grazed his cheek and singed the carpet in a place that's virtually impossible to hide. Why my sister allows him to smoke in the bungalow beggars belief but add to this the fact that she has plans to meet friends in Milford Haven and the whole fiasco becomes a disaster of epic proportions, second only to the destruction of Pompeii.

So it's left up to me to gather up all the child-related paraphernalia, button Saffron into her duffle coat and navigate my way up the high street. I'm just passing that well-known shop that sells items for a pound when I'm stopped by a lad in a kagool. He flashes his photo I.D. card at me and says, "Would you like to join the fight to save whales?"

"No," I say, "I spent a weekend in Dolgellau last year and it seemed positively thriving to me." I try to push past but he's obviously well versed in the art of paramilitary chugging, he side steps and the bag of my granddaughter's paraphernalia over my shoulder wedges me between him and a lamppost.

"I'm sorry," he says, "I don't think you understood, have you ever heard of CAJWO?"

"Didn't they have a hit single in 1983 called 'Too Shy?'" I ask.

"No madam, you're thinking of Kajagoogoo. I represent CAJWO, the campaign against Japanese whaling organisations. Can we count on your support?"

"Look, love," I tell him, "You're joking if you think I've got time to chat about endangered cetaceans whilst lugging around half my body weight in plastic unicorns, wet wipes and Peppa Pig DVDs." He opens his mouth to reply but thinks better of it and just smiles and moves on to bother some poor woman in a poplin raincoat.

***

Three buses and a short walk later, I'm spotted by my sister's neighbour, Sidney, and he offers me a lift in his Austin Allegro, complete with a faulty heater that spews forth like Etna. Apparently, despite attention from a local mechanic, it won't switch off, which must be a nightmare during an Indian summer. Are we still allowed to say that, or in this climate of political correctness is it now a summer of ethnic origin?

We arrive at my sister's and opening the front door she says, "You look moist."

I toss her a cursory glance and say, "Yes, and you have the social skills of Benito Mussolini." I push past, trying not to scuff the wallpaper and ask if there's any chance of a brew.

I decide it's best I let Lisa know where I am, so I rummage through my handbag for my mobile phone, I eventually find it with a half-chomped dog chew stuck to it. I remove the chew and pop it onto a side table then send her a text as she's not allowed personal calls during work hours. With Saffron happily watching the TV, I pop into Harold's room to see how he is. He tells me he's fine apart from the fact that it's taken him three hours to eat his breakfast. Ever likely, what sane person would give a gummy old man granola? I'm about to have words with my sister when he tells me, he insisted on having it, thinking it'd soften. "And what do you want for a mid-morning snack," I say, "pork scratchings?"

Now changed into a cerise-coloured mohair two-piece, my sister pops her head around the door to say goodbye. She blows us both a kiss, saying she has a train to catch and should the child be gnawing on a piece of dried pig's ear? I tear into the living room and begin to wrestle the dog chew from Saffron who howls like a demented parakeet causing Harold to question my maternal skills. "It's all right," I call, deciding to let go of the chew, no doubt like the dog, she'll get bored when her jaws ache. Who knows, it may even help with her bad breath, well, they've done wonders for the dog's tartar. I know it sounds cruel, but if you can't be honest about your own, then it's time to stop buying ready-made pastry and lock yourself away in the coal shed.

Now I will never understand my sister's relationship with Harold. He's quite laid back, while she's one of those compulsive types. You know the sort, a place for everything and everything in its place. You only have to move one of her knick-knacks and she becomes so anxious that you need a neighbour on stand-by with an EpiPen. The last time someone accidentally moved one of her Capodimonte figurines, she was on the phone to the insurance company telling them she was concerned that the house had been subjected to subsidence.

But I will say that she's made Harold's room very nice for him. Although I don't think the nautical theme's a good idea, not for a man whose wife left him forty years ago to take up a job as a kitchen assistant on a North Sea ferry. That would explain his persistent state of irritability, I guess the last thing you'd want to see on waking is an anchor and a balsa wood lighthouse. Mind you, he's no trouble, in fact, you could say Harold was easier to take care of than the granddaughter. Well, let's face it when you're missing your top teeth the most you can do is mumble incoherently and suck tinned spaghetti.

With lunch over, I'm putting away the dishes, when the front door opens and in walks my sister. "I thought you were meeting friends?"

"Train problems," was all she said as she closed the door, and in my opinion a little harder than the situation required. "So there's no need for you to stay now." I knew it would be futile to argue with her, she was obviously annoyed and experience has taught me that she's best given a wide berth in moments of vexation. "I'll just give Len a quick call. He can pick me up, he's only working a half day today."

"Don't waste your money; I'll get Stan to drop you off."

"I'd rather not," I say, "I don't think I could bear another journey in that menopausal motor, it's like stepping back ten years."

"It's a classic," she says.

"It's a death trap."

Len arrives and beeps his horn to let me know he is outside. I watch my sister raise an eyebrow; she hates people who beep car horns outside the house to attract attention. I know she's hoping that he'll stay in the car, as she has never properly forgiven him for telling an inappropriate joke about Margaret Thatcher at one of her local conservative party functions. I retrieve the dog chew that's now discarded on the sofa, say goodbye to Harold and air kiss my sister in the hall, before lugging Saffron out to the waiting car. "How's the Tory tigress?" Len says as I buckle the child into her booster seat.

"Seething, "I say climbing in beside him. "She missed the train."

"Oh well, at least Milford Haven was spared a visit." I gave him one of my, be careful what you say in front of the child looks and he changes the subject. "Have you had a nice day Saffron? Would you like Granddad to take you to the shop for a treat?" I was about to protest when the child burbles an affirmative response, so not wanting a repeat of her parakeet impression, I concede and say, "Just drop me off at the traffic lights near the shops and I'll walk back."

Len pulls over and I get out of the car and wave to Saffron and set off for home. Imagine my shock and surprise as I came around the corner to see the street filled with people. Two police cars are parked diagonally across the road and parked close by is an ambulance, its flashing blue lights bouncing off the blackened windows of unlit houses. A substantial crowd has gathered on the other side of the blue and white police tape tied between two lampposts. "What's going on here?" I say, "Has someone had an accident?"

The bystanders turn to look in my direction, and then in biblical unison, they part as my daughter comes pushing through towards me. I can see that she's angry. "Mother," she screams, "how could you be so irresponsible?"

"What do you mean?"

"She's lost ... Saffron... She's not in your house."

"Of course she isn't," I say. "Don't be stupid."

"Stupid," she says. "Stu…pid." This second over-enunciated, stupid, raising an octave and a half. "You're the one that's been stupid. Mother, I'll never trust you again."

"What are you blithering on about?"

"The police have been here all afternoon looking for Saffron. I've been out of my mind with worry."

"Why?"

"Because of the text you sent me." She holds her over-priced multi-functional handset up in front of me, and I read: At sister's, Saffron is home. "How could you go out and leave her at home?"

"Did you honestly think I'd leave Saffron alone? And even if I had didn't it occur to you to call me at my sister's? The message should read, Saffron is good. It's that stupid predictive text on my mobile, it must have changed the word."

"If that's so madam," says a police officer who's been eavesdropping. "Where is the child now?" Just then two headlights come around the corner and a car with a familiar rattle drives towards us.

"She's over there." The officer looks confused. "She's in that car with her granddad, he took her to the shop for some sweets."

The crowd collectively exhale, sharing their relief and I smile inwardly knowing that Saffron will now be going home full of e numbers.

~ 41 ~

Tuesday, 25 May
I found some stray hairs on my pillow this morning. Not a substantial amount, just one or two, but that doesn't stop the paranoia kicking in. Len, ever the pragmatist tells me it isn't worth obsessing about. "Did I complain when I was getting thinner on top?" he says as he hands me a morning cuppa. "Look at it from my point of view, less hair means more money saved."

"How do you work that out?" I ask.

"Less hair means fewer trips to the hairdresser." His reasoning may be flawed, but I can't help but laugh.

Over the past couple of weeks, I've had further short sessions of treatment and apart from the hairs on my pillow, I haven't suffered any side effects, something that Len says bodes well.

It's surprising how a brain tumour can affect your daily existence. This little blob of cancerous tissue dictates so much. It takes up my time in visits to the hospital, it alters the way other people interact with me and also, without it, I wouldn't have decided to record my final year in my notebook.

***

Len's gone to work and I'm enjoying a second cup of tea when I take out my notebook and look at what I've written already. Things that cancer has delivered to my door. I've visited a public house alone, something Lisa takes for granted and my mother would never have done. I've been to my first hen party, enjoyed my first karaoke experience and to top it off, I saw Ebony Knight's todger, up close and personal.

With my teacup draining beside the sink, I catch sight of myself in the small mirror on the windowsill. I pick it up and tilt it so I can have a closer look at where I think my hair is thinning. I can't see any change and I'm about to have words with myself when there's a firm knock at the front door. As usual the dog barks and goes tearing up the hall, its claws clacking on the fake oak parquet. "Get out of the way, you daft bugger," I tell it as I open the door just wide enough for the dog's nose to investigate.

"Morning Mrs Bickerstaff," Kirk says. "Victor must have dropped his phone in my van last night. I thought it best I bring it 'round, in case he needs it."

"Thank you, Kirk, that's very kind. Do you fancy a cup of tea?"

"I wouldn't say no to a coffee," he says.

"Come in," I say, and with the dog's head clamped between my knees Kirk steps inside and I re-heat the water in the kettle.

"How have you been?" he asks as he dunks a biscuit into his coffee.

"Not too bad, I've had a few sessions of laser therapy now."

"What's it like?"

"Boring actually. I have to lie perfectly still and as soon as they're ready to start you can guarantee my nose begins to itch, and because you're not allowed to move I can't reach up and scratch it."

"Sounds a right pain in the arse... Sorry."

"No need to apologise. It's not that bad really. It's the disruption to your life that's the real nuisance." I hand the booklet given to me by Dr Banerjee across to him. "I spotted another way in which the cancer interferes with everyday life this morning." I point to the article about how people with brain tumours are prohibited from driving. His eyes scan the page before he looks up at me and says, "But you don't drive."

"I know that, but, what if I wanted to?"

"Do you?"

"Well no. But what if I wanted to?"

"Have you never wanted to drive?" he asks, placing the booklet back down.

"Len said, years ago, that I'd be a danger to other road users if I was let loose. But thinking back I would've liked to have had a go at it."

"If you fancy a lesson in the van one day, let me know. We've got a big private car park at work. I could let you have a spin around." Kirk looks at his watch and tells me he needs to get back to work. "Tell Victor I'll call him later." He gets up to leave. The dog sees this activity as an indication of the front door opening again and resumes its barking. I endure another bout of dog wrestling in the hall as Kirk says goodbye.

***

"Are you mad?" Vera says as she squeezes the loaves of bread on the supermarket shelf. "If you ask me that laser has fried your brain."

"It's just a driving lesson," I tell her, watching as she drops a loaf into her basket, leaving several others suffering from a Vulcan nerve pinch that Mr Spock would have been proud of. "What's Len got to say about this?" she says.

"Nothing, I haven't mentioned it to him."

"And what does that tell you?" Vera's now manhandling a lemon, her lips pursed as if she's been sucking the yellow fruit. "That this is a stupid idea."

"I just thought I'd be fun, another thing to write about to share with my family when the inevitable…"

"So…" dropping the lemon into her basket and giving me eye contact "…when is this lesson going to happen?"

"Tomorrow, Kirk's picking me up at three."

"Well, if you ask me, I think you should take up a new hobby, it might take your mind off this lunacy."

"A new hobby. Such as?"

"Doreen was telling me that Mavis is a wizard with a crochet hook."

"Just what the world needs, more bloody antimacassars."
***

"You and Victor have been seeing quite a bit of each other," I say to Kirk as we sit inside his van.

"Yes, he's good company."

"It's about time he found himself a nice young man."

"If you don't mind me saying, you and Len seem pretty relaxed with Victor's sexuality."

"When he told us he was gay, I expected Len to be upset, but all he said was, there's nowt we can do about it, so there's no point making a fuss."

"How I wish my parents had been as reasonable. They still haven't fully come to terms with it. They still tell people it's just a phase that'll pass one day."

"I'm sorry to hear that. Would you like me to have a word with them?"

"It's okay, it's not like we're a very close family anyway." For the first time since meeting Kirk, I notice he's not smiling. "Right, Mrs B, let's get started."

"Call me Beryl."

"Okay, Beryl, let's start with the basics."

I'm finally sitting in the driver's seat. I've depressed the clutch and accelerator a few times and allowed my foot to hover over the brake as Kirk explains the mechanics of driving. The car park is empty apart from a bottle bank at the far end and the small white van that I'm sitting inside. My heart beats quickly, threatening to exit my chest as I grip the key in the ignition and turn it. The engine roars and Kirk asks me to ease off the accelerator. "We'll just sit here for a while," he says, "let you get used to how much pressure you need to apply."

I have a couple of goes at changing gear, getting accustomed to the combination of foot and hand action before Kirk says he thinks it's time to release the handbrake. We lurch forward and come to a stop. "You've stalled," he says, "You need a little more gas." I turn the key again and within seconds the van is hopping across the tarmac with short jerky movements like a robotic kangaroo. "I'm sorry," I say, as we bounce around inside. Kirk smiles, telling me I'm doing fine and before long the kangarooing is replaced with a smooth movement, albeit a very slow one.

"You're driving," he says, his smile so wide that he's in danger of swallowing his head.

"I can't wait to see Len's face when I tell him." I do a complete circuit of the car park and although Kirk did grab the steering wheel at one point, saying I was too close to the bottle bank, I'm pleased with myself. I apply pressure to the brake, come to a stop and after securing the handbrake I turn off the engine, satisfied with my one lap.

"That's another first for Beryl Bickerstaff," I say aloud and turning to my grinning passenger, I beam back before saying, "Who'd have thought smiling could be contagious."

~ 40 ~

Wednesday, 2 June
Len is less than impressed when I tell him about my driving lesson. "I'll be having words with Kirk, the damn fool idiot, what was he thinking." I try to placate him, almost begging my husband not to say anything and I promise never to do it again. "Just look at you, you're washed out."

"I'm okay."

"You need a day's bed rest," Len says, as he uncharacteristically plumps my pillow, "I'll fetch your tablets and you can stay here." I try to tell him that I'll be all right but find myself on the receiving end of raised eyebrows that put me in my place.

"Morning, Mum," Victor says, popping his head around the door. "What you up to today?"

"Your dad says I'm to stay in bed and rest."

"Take advantage of it, I know I would given half the chance."

"Are you seeing Kirk today?"

"Not today, I'm going into town with Lisa to get something for Saffron's birthday next week."

"Oh yes, of course, I need to get organised. I can't lie in bed when there's a birthday party to sort out."

"You'll do as you're told." Victor wags his finger at me and I think to myself, as much as I love you, Son, you'll never be able to disguise your sexuality. Len comes back with a steaming mug of tea. I prefer proper china but he's never been able to carry a cup and saucer without slopping it. "Here, get this down you," he says removing two digestive biscuits from inside his trouser pocket, "It'll set you up for the day."

"I was just telling Victor that I need to get up and start organising Saffron's party."

"You'll do no such thing. Now take your pills and get some rest." I swallow my tablets, resisting the urge to retch as the foul-tasting medication hits my taste buds. "But, I'll be bored lying in bed with nothing to do."

"You need to stay put and recuperate." I smile and he smiles back, "Right, I'm off to work and I don't want to hear that you've got out of this bed before midday." He closes the door behind himself, then re-opens it and adds, "Unless it's to pee."

***

I do as I'm told and stay in bed until later when I'm feeling much better. I'm allowed to collect Saffron from school and sitting side by side on the bus she says, "Nan, will you be going to heaven soon?" The bus is crowded and the woman sitting across the aisle looks over. So I give her one of my, don't kids say the funniest things look, before lowering my voice and saying, "Why would you ask that?"

"I heard mummy and daddy talking last night."

"And what did mummy and daddy say?"

"That you're going to the hospital for laser terribly." I look into her innocent eyes and pull her into me for a hug.

"It's laser therapy and I'm not going anywhere, not for a long time."

"Promise?"

"I promise. Now we need to think about what we're going to do for your birthday on Saturday."

"Uncle Victor said he wants me to be a princess."

"Well, if Victor wants that, we shan't let him down." The bus stops and we head up the road that's flanked on both sides by red-bricked terraced houses, their front rooms hidden behind the net curtains that hang at the large square windows.

"Is mummy coming for me, or is grandad taking me home?" Saffron says as we come to a stop outside the front door.

"Your mummy's coming for you, why?"

"Grandad always takes me to the shop for some sweets when he takes me home."

"I think you have quite enough sweets young lady." She looks disappointed as I open the door and we step inside and she runs to Victor who's standing at the foot of the stairs.

"Lisa and Mac are waiting," he says then picking Saffron up and holding her aloft, swinging her from left to right, says, "Who's my favourite girl?"

"I am," she screams.

"Did she behave herself, mum?" Lisa asks as I enter the middle room.

"Good as gold, but I need to speak with you both."

"Shall I put the kettle on?" Lisa asks, her question followed by, "Mac, go put the kettle on." Mac drags himself out of his seat and plods into the kitchen. I hear the kettle being filled and pop my head into the hall asking Victor if he can keep his niece entertained. "Would you like to see what I've got for you?" Victor says and Saffron coos, her shoulders rising with her smile. Mac pops his head around the door to ask Lisa if she wants a drink too and I ask him to come in and sit down.

"We're so sorry, Mum," Lisa says after I tell them about the conversation on the bus earlier. "I had no idea she was listening." I can see she's upset so I don't labour the point, I just ask them both to be a little careful what they say in future.

"Don't worry," says Mac, "we will be." The door bursts open, the sudden commotion causes the dog to wake up and let out a frightened yelp.

"Look what I've got," Saffron says, as she twirls around the room with a silver-coloured tiara balanced on her head. "Uncle Victor buyed it for me, so I can be a proper princess."

"Bought it for me," corrects Lisa.

"No, he buyed it for me."

"You look lovely," I say, before turning to Mac to ask if that tea was going to arrive anytime soon.

"Nan, have you ever been a princess?" Saffron asks.

"Don't bother your nan," Lisa says, making a grab for her daughter, who deftly sidesteps her mother.

"It's all right," I say, offering my hand to Saffron. She takes it allowing herself to be drawn into me. "No, love, I've never been a princess."

"That's a shame because you can't be a princess now."

"Why not?"

"Because you is too old." Her honesty makes me chuckle even if her grammar is lacking. "You could be a queen. Because a queen is always old and can walk into rooms without knocking." Victor opens the door and the room erupts with laughter, leaving him and Saffron looking very confused. Saffron is on the verge of tears and sensing this I tell her she's a princess our royal family would be proud of.

"Don't be silly Nan," she says, tilting her head as she looks me square in the face. "I can't be a real princess, not until I've married a prince anyway."

"In which case," Victor says, "you'll have to be our princess." Saffron thinks about what her uncle has said for a few moments, then she takes a deep breath and says, "I will, but only if Nan is the queen."

"That's it," Lisa says taking control, "it's sorted. The theme shall be a royal party. Mum, you'll be the queen and Saffron the princess."

"Will Uncle Victor be a prince, sweetheart?" asks Mac.

"Don't be silly, Daddy," Saffron says, "he can't be a prince, because princes always marry pretty ladies and I heard you tell mummy last week that it was good that Uncle Victor has found himself a nice boyfriend." Laughter fills the room at Victor's expense once more.

***

The day of Saffron's party arrives and Len and I are ushered out of the house so that Victor can prepare for the festivities. It's a warm June morning and as we stroll through the park, it could be said that just like the song, June was, actually, 'bustin' out all over.' The borders are filled with summer bedding, the purple of early lobelia contrasting with the red of greenhouse-forced salvias. A few late flowering anemones sway in the light breeze, their pastel petals beginning to fade and pass over in readiness for the brash, hot colours of summer. We stop at the little café by the redundant bandstand and we're enjoying a cup of tea when Len says that he hopes the kids will keep an eye on the dog, and we both agree that we don't want a repeat of the Battenberg incident.

After our brief refreshment break, we're walking home when we meet Vera, who tells us she's on a mercy mission, as her neighbour Mrs Khan has experienced a backyard laundry related catastrophe, and despite living in England for the last fifty years still hasn't learned the English for washing line. "I'll do my best to get there on time," she says, before turning on her heels and heading off down the high street. Len and I take a slow walk home.

After several hours decorating the front room, Victor allows us to take a look inside. The walls are adorned with red, white and blue bunting and the table is resplendent with patriotic paper plates and napkins. At the head of the table is one of our dining chairs, draped with a damask fabric and at a jaunty angle is pinned a cardboard crown. "That's your throne," Victor says.

I look at my son and feel a pricking behind my eyes. "It's lovely," I say, my words masking the tear that threatens to make its way down my cheek.

"We want to give the impression of a street party."

"You did well, Son," Len says, and my heart stirs as I watch a father pat his son on the back. "Right, let's get the room locked up before that bloody dog comes in."

"You two put your feet up in the middle room," says Victor. "I've just got to bring Saffron's presents down from upstairs and then we'll be ready to go at four o'clock."

***

Mac pulls up outside the house at exactly four. Car doors open and Lisa, Saffron and two of her friends spill out onto the pavement. With the dog banished to the backyard, the front door opens and three small girls in frothy party dresses rush through. "Look at my dress, Nan," Saffron squeals.

"Are we having jelly?" A skinny girl in a peach creation asks while a plump girl in lilac pushes past asking if she can see the dog.

"Hiya Mum," Lisa says, looking tired. "They've worn me ragged. Any chance of a cuppa?" I tell her that Len is in the middle room and Victor has left strict instructions that no one is to go into the front room until he says so.

No sooner have I closed the front door when there's a knocking and I open it. Vera has arrived with a small girl and a timid-looking boy, "Their mother's dropped them off with me to bring." Mac is close behind and he tells Lisa he's had to park the car a few doors down as there's some dog mess in the road and he can't take a chance on one of the children treading it into his new car mats.

I'm closing the front door again after letting in another two children, one being another boy, whose nose would benefit from the application of a handkerchief. "How many more," I ask, and Lisa does a head count before saying she thinks that's all of them. Vera's serving hot beverages to the grown-ups while Len struggles to hand out paper cups of juice to the children when Victor appears in the doorway. "What do you look like," says Mac laughing. Victor is dressed in a pair of red tights and a short black bolero jacket with gold epaulettes. On his head is perched, what can only be described as a hat previously rejected by the mother of a bride, complete with a plume of magenta feathers. And in his hands is a copper reproduction hunting horn.

"My god," Lisa laughs, "Looks like the charity shop did well this week."

"Ladies, gentlemen, distinguished guests and brats," he says. "We welcome Her Royal Highness, Queen Beryl of Stoke on Trent and the *very* beautiful Princess Saffron to this party." He lifts the hunting horn, purses his lips and blows; it gives forth a sound resembling a muffled fart and the children cheer. Eager to get at the cakes and jelly they follow Victor the few steps up the hall towards the front room.

He pushes open the door and music floats out, "It's Viennese," Vera says. "I let Victor borrow one of my André Rieu CDs. It's called Im Krapfenwald'l."

"Sounds it," mutters Len, who's never been impressed with classical music, saying it's for posh folks who can't be bothered listening to words.

We all sit around the table, with an adult inserted into the mix after every second child, Saffron sits at the foot of the table and I make my way to the head. On the wall nearby is a large portrait of our Queen, and Mac, who's quick to take credit for replacing her majesty's face with mine says, "I did that on my computer."

"It's very nice," Vera says, "although I'm not sure it's legal."

"It's hardly an act of treason," Lisa says, obviously a little put-out. "It's just a bit of fun."

"Why does she have a beard," asks Len.

"I had to blur the edges," Mac says, "Beryl and Queen Elizabeth have different shaped chins."

I look around at the happy faces of the children as they tuck into their party food. Saffron has egg mayonnaise down the front of her party frock, and the timid boy is now trying his best to force a cocktail sausage up the other boy's nose, possibly in an attempt to stem the flow of mucus – you can't blame him. "Are you okay?" Victor says, placing his hand on my arm.

"Yes Son, it's perfect. A day I'll remember for as long as I can."

"Come on, let's leave talk like that for another day. I'm just going to nip into the kitchen to fetch some more cake for the brats." I give him my well-rehearsed smile, the one that tries to convince the recipient that I've forgotten my plight for a few minutes.

"Victor?"

"Yes, Mum?"

"Promise me you'll take some photographs of today, for when people want to remember." He smiles and nods; behind his eyes I see a shadow, something dark that stalks his emotions, momentarily dulling the brightness in his eyes then Len calls for everyone to raise a toast to the birthday girl and the table calls for a speech as Victor returns with a plate of sliced Battenberg. Saffron watches as he places it onto the table and overacting she clears her throat and says, "Look everybody, dog sick cake."

~ 39 ~

Thursday, 10 June
No matter how many times I visit Dr Banerjee's office, I still feel nervous as I step through the door. I've now had almost seven weeks of treatment, totalling twelve sessions and I'm here for my evaluation, so it's an important meeting.

"Have you come on your own, today?" Dr Banerjee asks, looking up from the file on his desk. I nod and swallow hard, "I chose to come alone," I say, "but I'm beginning to wish I hadn't."

"Well," he says, shifting in his seat; he looks as uncomfortable as I feel. "I've looked through your notes, and I'm…"

"Is Victoria around?" I ask and Dr Banerjee is visibly taken aback by my interruption and mumbles that he's not sure. "Is it possible you could find out?"

"I suppose I can," he splutters. "Is it important?"

"I need a friendly face."

He closes the folder on his desk rises from his seat and leaves the room, leaving the door ajar. In the waiting room, I can hear the sound of someone sobbing. Gingerly I get out of my seat and peer through the crack in the door. Sitting on one of the orange plastic seats is a woman and she's dabbing at her eyes with a tissue that looks in danger of disintegrating. I cough, making my presence known and ask if she'd like a fresh tissue. She can be no more than thirty years old but her eyes carry a sadness that ages the soul. "Thank you," she says, as I step into the room and hold out a pocket-sized pack of tissues. She goes to take one but I insist she keeps the whole packet, "I've another one in my coat pocket," I say. "I've been coming here for some time now and I learned a while back it pays to bring extra supplies."

"Thank you."

The door at the far end of the room opens and in walks, Dr Banerjee followed by Victoria. "Hello Beryl," she says, her smile brightening up the otherwise dowdy room. "What can I do for you?"

"Can you sit with me while I get my evaluation?"

She looks at Dr Banerjee and then says, "Of course I can."

"That's if you're not too busy."

"I was just going on a break, so it'll be okay." I apologise for dragging her away from her tea break and tell her I'm maybe just being silly. "Nonsense," she says, taking my hand and leading me back into Dr Banerjee's office. "I'll be happy to sit with you."

I can see that Dr Banerjee isn't completely happy with my request. He strikes me as a sensitive soul, not adept at doling out bad news, and I'm sure he'd have preferred to have continued where he'd started a few minutes ago and have it all over with by now. He flips open the folder and picks up where he left off, "I'm sorry Mrs Bickerstaff, but despite our best endeavours there's only been a minimal response to the therapy."

I reach into my coat pocket and squeeze the spare pack of tissues. "So, are you saying nothing's changed?" I'm beginning to think that he looks uncomfortable with my question. On every visit he's been the figure of authority; knowledgeable and in control and now he just looks lost.

"There's been some reduction in the tumour size but not as much as we'd have hoped." I begin to shake visibly and it's now Victoria's turn to swallow hard, she looks across at Dr Banerjee, her eyes urging him to say something. He looks at her and then back to me. "I think it's best if we have a break from the treatment and work out where we're going to go from here. Like I said, there's been a small reduction in size and density, so, maybe, a new regime later will give us better results?"

"Maybe?" I shrug.

"I'll finish recording your evaluation and we'll write to you in due course." No sooner has he finished speaking as he rises and opens the door for me.

"I don't know who that was harder for," I say, once I'm back inside the waiting room, "him or me."

"He isn't the best here at giving out bad news."

"Is that what it was? Bad news."

"Well, let's say it wasn't as positive as you'd have liked it to be." Victoria smiles and takes a purse from her pocket. It's pink and round, with a pair of googly eyes and a blob where I assume a nose was once fixed. "Let's get a drink, it's only a vending machine I'm afraid and apart from the tea, everything else seems to taste like oxtail soup."

We stand outside and sip our tea from plastic cups and I thank her for her honesty. I tell her that I never wanted the laser therapy. "I just want to get on with what time I have left and enjoy it." I expect her to look shocked, but she doesn't.

"You'd be surprised how many people feel the same."

"Really?"

"Yes, not everybody wants to put themselves through it." She throws the dregs of her drink onto the poorly maintained flower bed in front of us. "What will you do now?"

"Now. I'll just get on with living. Well for as long as I can. I only tried the therapy because my daughter kicked up a fuss." I mention this as I drop my empty cup into a litter bin.

Victoria turns to look directly at me, her green eyes were less moss coloured in the sunlight and more jade. "You need to stay positive Beryl. I can remember my grandmother once saying to me, that positivity is better than any medicine. She had a terminal illness too, back when there were very few treatments out there. The family were all resigned to her passing away within months, but because she was an irrepressible old bird she outlasted everybody's expectations. Even her doctors were amazed. A few days before she died, she told me it was all down to remaining positive. That and being obstinate." Victoria looks at her watch, "Cripes, I'd better dash, I've an old man to shave," she says. "It's a good job I don't drink coffee, the last thing you need with an aged scrotum is a shaky hand and a caffeine rush."

She hugs me and then bounces away with an arm across her ample chest, limiting bosom movement. I smile, thinking, there's so much rise and fall inside her bra she could call her breasts Anton du Beke.

***

I'm standing at the bus stop when a small blue car pulls up, the passenger door opens and I bend to look inside. It's the woman I saw earlier in the waiting room. "I'm going towards the town centre; would you like a lift?" At first, I'm a little taken aback, but she has a kind face and I'm sure that even if she does turn out to be a serial killer in disguise, the CCTV camera mounted on the lamppost will have recorded an image of her number plate.

"Thank you for the tissues," she says as the car pulls away from the kerb, "it was very kind of you. I'm Kate, by the way." We're exchanging pleasantries when she asks if I'd like to join her for a drink. I'm about to point out that it's a bit early in the day when she says, "There's a lovely little coffee shop just a few minutes from here."

Kate turns right and almost immediately she pulls into a small car park. There are several terracotta planters dotted around, that contain summer bedding; fiery red geraniums and pink-striped petunias and as I climb out of her car I spot a familiar face planting up hanging baskets. "Hello Reggie," I say. "Doing a spot of moonlighting?"

"Hello, Mrs Bickerstaff. I'm planting these baskets up for my niece. She recently opened this place; a new venture, so I'm sprucing it up for her. Mind you, I do have to put a bloody padlock through the chains though, to stop any of the thieving buggers 'round here from nicking them."

"I'm sure they'll be lovely," I tell him smiling. Obviously the Harry Mountford episode is still raw in his memory.

At a table, I'm spooning sugar into my cup when it becomes obvious that Kate needs to talk. "It's nice in here," I say.

"Yes, I only found it a week or so ago."

"The prices aren't too bad either."

"Yes, they're very reasonable."

There's a long pause in the midst of our inconsequential chatter and then out of nowhere Kate blurts out, "I have cancer by the way." I look up from my coffee and resist the urge to shout, 'snap' as it wouldn't be appropriate.

"I thought as much, what with the both of us being in the oncology department. They tend not to send you there if you've got a problem with a recurring bunion." Kate smiles across at me and her shoulders go from looking like there's a coat hanger inside her blouse to relatively loose. "I wish I could be so light-hearted about it."

"I've had a lot of time to come to terms with mine," I say. I tell her my story and she listens attentively without interruption, occasionally nodding at parts I feel she can relate to. She tells me that she was diagnosed with an aggressive form a few months ago and hasn't yet mentioned it to anyone. "I haven't even told my husband."

"I know men can at times be worse than useless," I tell her, "but I don't know what I'd have done without the support of my Len."

"I don't know how to tell my Gareth. Where do I start? He'll be devastated."

"Imagine how he'll feel if you don't tell him?" I reach across and put my hand on top of hers, "Just start at the beginning, you can't carry this around by yourself."

She nods as the tear that's been threatening her eye socket makes an appearance. I reach into my coat and hold out the packet of tissues and she starts to laugh. "Ever had that feeling of dèjá vu?" Kate dabs at her eyes again. "I'm so glad you were at the hospital today; I think meeting you will help me to start the process of making sense of my illness.

"Can I give you a piece of advice I've recently been given?"

"Please."

I look out of the window at Reggie as he fastens a padlock to a newly planted hanging basket and say, "Positivity is better than any medicine."

~ 38 ~

Monday, 14 June
It seems I can't open a magazine or put on the television without some minor celebrity telling the world that she's changed her hair colour; because she's worth it.

I've never considered changing the colour of my hair before. I've always been happy with mousey-brown, and to be honest, it wasn't the current advertising bombardment that made me think about doing so, it was Elkie. Who over the past year has gone from blonde to brunette and back to blonde, including a few weeks of dabbling with red tones. On Monday she happened to be passing and dropped in with a carrier bag full of periodicals. "My nephew's just started working in a newsagent," she said. "He gets to take home all the magazines that don't sell. I wondered if you'd like some." I thanked her for her kindness, and ever since, I've been sifting through an abundance of titles, everything from 'Amateur Pigeon Fancier' to 'Your Pregnancy'. I've been equally as kind and donated a bundle to Vera and dropped off a small selection at the doctor's surgery. I just hope there's someone out there who'll find the copies of 'Narrowboat Life' interesting, whilst waiting for a repeat prescription.

***

"Have you ever dyed your hair?" I ask Vera as we sit in the Belly Buster café in town.

"Once," she replies, studying the menu. "They should laminate it."

"What, plastic coat it?"

"Sorry?"

"Laminate hair?"

"No, you daft doughnut, these menus. They should laminate them, then they'll be able to wipe them clean."

"What's that got to do with dyeing hair?" I ask.

"Nothing, but I've had to pick off a blob of dried-on brown sauce just to see what tomorrow's special of the day is."

"And was it all right?"

"I don't know I've never had the special on a Tuesday."

"Not the special, the hair dyeing, how did it turn out?"

"I didn't much care for it."

The waitress brings us our frothy coffees and I stare out of the window, wondering if Vera and I have ever had anything in common. I watch a young woman with blonde highlights stroll past, the added colour, shining in the sunlight. Then, a young man with a slash of blue added to his black hair stops to light a cigarette, as his companion, a girl with satsuma-coloured curls picks at a spot on her chin.

"Are you thinking of changing your hair colour?" says Vera, as she spoons sugar into her coffee. "I'm not sure it'd be a good idea."

"Why ever not?"

"After your treatment, it might not be safe."

"To be honest Vera," I say, "I don't think I'm radioactive and besides, I couldn't give a tuppence about safety."

"You've changed, you have, Beryl Bickerstaff," she says. "You've become…" She pauses, looking for the right words. "Rebellious. Yes, that's what you've become, rebellious."

"Don't talk soft. I'm only thinking about changing my hair colour. I'm not planning on having my remaining nipple pierced and applying enough mascara to frighten small children."

"So what colour are you thinking of having?"

"I'm not sure. I've always wondered what it would like to be blonde."

"Diana Dors or Helen Mirren?" she says blowing across the surface of her coffee to cool it. I must look confused because she lowers her voice and leans in and says, "Well there's the trashy blonde and the classic sophisticated one."

"And into which of these categories does Ms Mirren fit?" I ask, but Vera just stares past me, remaining tight-lipped. She takes a sip of her coffee and then says, "Blonde doesn't always look glamorous, take Hillary Clinton, she's had her hair lightened but no matter what style she wears it in she always manages to look like a bag lady." I agree and we finish our coffees in silence before parting company outside the café. Vera heads off in the direction of the market; apparently, her nephew has asked her to keep a lookout for a kitchen timer in the shape of a red tomato and I make my way to the chemist.

I'm standing in the queue at the dispensary waiting for Len's prescription to be processed when I spot an offer for hair colour. I pick up the box and I'm reading the claim that the product will change my life by adding a touch of sophistication, when the woman behind the counter calls, "Bickerstaff." I confirm my address and hand her the box, "I'd like to buy this too," I tell her and as she bags it she gives me a quizzical look.

***

I've just finished cutting the excess fat off some braising steak and peeled the potatoes in readiness for our tea, and with a few minutes to spare, I decide to attempt the hair colouring. As the dog wolfs down the trimmed fat, I read the instructions carefully but decline to bother with a skin allergy test. After years of working in the pottery industry, I'm sure I've built up enough immunity to minor skin irritations. In the bathroom, perched on the side of the bath I mix the contents of the bottle and tube and look at the instructions once more, they make the application of the product look easy.

It isn't.

52 Weeks

I try parting my hair into four sections. It's not easy when the product tells you to apply it to dry hair. I start at the back of my head, as instructed but find this difficult. It's impossible to apply the evil-smelling foam accurately while trying to look over your shoulder and watch what you're doing in the bathroom mirror. Even an Indonesian contortionist would have difficulty applying it, without it sliding down her back and bleaching the waistband of her knickers.

Eventually, I give up and plop it all on the top of my head like an under-whipped meringue and rub it through my hair. I encase the foam that is now warming my scalp inside the plastic bag provided and top it off with a towel cum turban. I check the time and pad downstairs to make myself a cuppa. Stirring my tea, I feel the day catching up with me; fatigue now being a regular guest in my daily routine, so I drop down into my chair with my drink on the table beside me and wait the thirty minutes the dye needs to turn my mousey-coloured hair to honey blonde.

***

"Are you all right love?" Len says, gently shaking me awake, "And what is that awful smell?"

"Beggar," I say realising I'd dozed off. "What time is it?" I don't wait for a response. I shoot to my feet and with the urgency of a pensioner with a prostate problem, I dash out of the middle room and up the stairs. I lock the bathroom door behind me and whip off the towel. I gingerly remove the plastic bag, half expecting my now severely lightened hair to come away with it. Luckily it seems to have survived an extra forty minutes of chemical saturation. Once rinsed and with the conditioner applied and washed out I gently rub my hair with a towel before looking in the mirror. Confronted with my image, I gasp – I know it sounds dramatic, but I did actually gasp. "Bloody hell, Beryl," I say aloud. "You look like one of those trolls the kids win on travelling fairs."

"Are you all right up there?" Len calls from the foot of the stairs.

"Yes, love," I reply as I run a comb through the wild white mop on my head. "I'll be down in a minute. Can you put a light under the potatoes on the stove for me?"

I leave the bathroom and with the aid of a hairdryer, I attempt to fashion the whitened thatch into a style that a young Hollywood starlet would be proud of. Sadly, I fail miserably, and reluctantly I make my way downstairs, looking more Steve Davis than Bette.

"Vera's just popped in," Len calls coming in from the kitchen closely followed by my friend. "Bugger me," he says, his eyelids stretched to their limit. "What have you gone and done to yourself?"

"I fell asleep."

"Oh dear," says Vera, "shall I pour the tea?" I nod and she pours three cups of strong tea and Len, without taking his eyes off me lowers himself into his chair. "Why have you done that?"

"It wasn't supposed to turn out like this." I pick up the empty hair dye packet and show them the picture of the smiling blonde on the front with her hair, honey-coloured and healthy-looking.

"So how come…" it was Len's turn to pause before finishing his sentence "…it looks like that?"

"I left it on too long."

"Do you know what?" says Vera, as she hands me a cup of tea, "for the life of me, I can't think who you remind me of."

"I'll book myself into Gloria's hair salon and get it fixed."

"I'd hope so," Len says. "We can't have you celebrating our wedding anniversary next week with what looks like shredded cotton wool on your head."

"Myra Hindley," Vera suddenly blurts out.

"What?" Len and I say in unison.

"That's who you remind me of… Myra Hindley, she…"

"Yes, we know who she…"

"Shall I fetch you the Yellow Pages?" Len says rising. "You can look up Gloria's number."

"Yes," says Vera, "and open it at D for disasters."

~ 37 ~

Friday, 25 June
"I'm sorry I couldn't fit you in any earlier," Gloria says as I lower myself into the chair. "We've been so busy these past few weeks. It always goes a bit bonkers in here at the start of the holiday season."

I look at myself in the mirror opposite. I'm wearing Len's Port Vale bobble hat that obviously looks out of place on a warm June morning. Apart from the young mother who is reassuring her young daughter who's protesting as a stylist gives her a trim, I'm Gloria's only customer.

"Okay," Gloria says, "Let's take a look at this disaster you told me about last week on the phone." I grab the bobble on the top of the hat and pull it up, allowing the white mop of abused hair to become exposed. I hear Marie who was standing beside the worktop coffee machine snigger and Gloria screws up her eyes as my handiwork is revealed in all its glory. "The good news is," she says, "it's salvageable."

"And the bad news?"

"Until it's grown out, you'll have to use twice as much conditioner to stop your hair feeling like a pan scourer."

Marie comes over and places a mug on the shelf below the mirror, "Latte, Mrs Bickerstaff," she says and reading the embarrassment on my face, she smiles, winks and then says, "The dandelion clock look is very on trend at the moment."

I appreciate her trying to lift the moment, and return the smile before saying, "Who'd have thought it, me a trendsetter."

"Give me a shout if you need anything else.

Gloria sets about combing, teasing and twisting my hair. "If you wanted to go lighter you should have come to me."

"It was a spur-of-the-moment decision or rather an act of madness," I tell her, then I explain that I fell asleep in my chair.

"I think we can rescue it, love. It'll probably be a shade lighter than your natural colour; do you think your Len will mind?"

"As long as I'm presentable for tonight, I don't think he'll mind what colour it is, I think he'll just be happy to see the end of this exploded mouse nest."

"Why what's happening tonight?"

"We're having a party, it's our forty-fourth wedding anniversary today, so he's hired the upstairs room at the club for a bit of a do."

"Forty-four years, that's an achievement. Marie," Gloria says, turning away. "It's Beryl's wedding anniversary today, be a love and nip to the baker's and get us all a cake, take the money out of the till," and turning back she adds, "I'll be happy if me and Mick last half as long."

With my hair washed and conditioned and with the ends trimmed I sit and wolf down a chocolate éclair as the colour beneath the tin foil wrapped around it begins its repair job. Marie makes us all a fresh cup of coffee and Gloria's telling me about her recent pregnancy scare – she had told me previously that children were not a part of her career plan for a few years yet. The bell tinkles as the salon door opens and in walks Doris Platt.

"Hello Beryl," she says seeing me and slipping out of the eggnog-coloured cardigan that frankly does nothing for her wan complexion. "How long has it been?" I was tempted to say, not long enough. But when you're sitting with chocolate fondant staining the corners of your mouth and wearing a foil helmet that Lady Gaga would be proud of, flippancy feels wrong. "Must be a good few years now, not since the factory shut down."

"Too many years. Mind you, I have to admit, I don't think I could go back to eight hours with clay under my fingernails as I sponge cup handles."

"This way Miss Platt," Marie says, leading Doris to a vacant chair. Beverley will be with you shortly."

"Do you ever miss it, Beryl?"

"Sometimes I do, but my Len says, life is for living in the now, not moping around wishing for what you once had."

"Very wise. How is Len?" she asks.

"He's well, thanks."

"It's Mrs Bickerstaff's wedding anniversary today," Marie says as she hands Doris a mug of coffee, "forty-four years.".

"Really," Doris says, her lip quivering, "who'd have thought it." I watch as she takes a petulant sip of her drink, and winces as the hot liquid enters her mouth. Fixing on a smile she returns her gaze towards me and says, "I hear you've not been well."

"That's right."

"I can't recall who told me… Margaret Watkins, I think. Cancer, wasn't it?"

"Still is."

"Oh, I see, is that the reason you're here?" she tilts her head to the side then whispers loudly, "Hair loss is it?"

"Bitch." I hear Gloria say through clenched teeth, as she opens a foil envelope to check on the progress of the hair dye. "No Miss Platt, Beryl's here having a spruce up ready for her party tonight." Gloria indicates to her assistant who had earlier been dealing with the mother and child that she'd like a word. "Beverley's almost free. Shampoo and set isn't it?" As Beverley joins us Gloria leans in and whispers, loud enough for me to hear. "Feel free to splash her."

"You're terrible," I say.

"Well, she gets right up my nose. Right, looks like your colour is ready." Gloria removes the last of the foil strips and I'm reclining, my neck in the recess of the backwash basin having the dye rinsed away when I hear Doris complaining that Beverley has been cack-handed and that the collar of her blouse is now sodden. Beverley can be heard apologising, as Gloria and I suppress our laughter. "I know it's not professional," Gloria laughs, but sometimes, needs must."

"We've never got on," I tell her as I'm lifted back into an upright position and my hair is gently buffed. "She's always carried a torch for my Len you see, and it all came to a head forty years ago after bull week." Beverley has now applied the setting lotion and curlers and leads Doris to the far end of the salon, where a dryer hood is lowered over her head. Flicking a magazine open she sits and waits for her style to set.

"What's bull week?" asks Gloria.

"It was two weeks before the pottery factories closed for the holidays. Workers would go into work before their shift was due to begin and they'd complete a couple of hours of extra work giving them a head start on their daily counts."

"Whatever for?"

"Back then we got paid piecework, the more pieces we completed the more money we made. And as we got paid a week in arrears, the work we did two weeks before the holidays topped up our holiday pay and that week was called bull week." Gloria was now blow-drying me, the brush felt good as it swept through my hair which was now officially light ash blonde. "So, how come you and Doris fell out?"

"We were never friendly; in fact, she was what they'd call nowadays a bit of a bully. It was common knowledge that she'd had her eye on Len for a long time, but he wasn't interested. Well, it was bull week and me and Len were getting wed in the potters' holiday and of course, the both of us put in extra hours each day so that we'd have some extra cash to spend on our honeymoon. But sadly, when pay day came the extra money that I expected didn't appear in my wages."

"How come?" Gloria asks as she fiddles with the hair at the side of my head, manoeuvring it into position so that it covers the small thinning patch left over from the laser.

"Back then my maiden name was Pike and like Doris, I was a cup handler. Doris was my supervisor and one of her duties was to put out and collect the clocking on cards at the beginning and end of each week. Well, what happened was, alphabetically our two cards were side by side on the wall by the machine, so it made it easy for her to do what she, allegedly did." Across the room, Beverley lifts the dryer hood from above Doris and hands her back her cardigan. I watch as Doris looks in a mirror and pats her now stiff style. "Thank you, Beverley," she says, slipping an arm into her cardigan, "That'll do nicely." She pays at the desk and before leaving bides me a goodbye, saying she hopes to see me again soon. As the door closes behind her I say, "Not if I see you first."

"Come on," Gloria says, "Tell us what did the dreadful Doris do?"

"Well, she never bothered doing extra hours during bull week, but what she did do was hide another clocking-on card behind hers with my name on it, and every time she clocked on and off, she did the same with this other card. At the end of the week, she presented the duplicate card to the wage office and not my actual one."

"So you just got paid for normal working hours?"

"Yes. I didn't get any of the unsocial hours allowance or the extra piecework."

"What happened?"

"I went to the wage office to complain but as my manager wasn't around at the time, they said there was nothing they could do until after the holidays."

"That's a bummer," Beverley says, now joining us.

"After the holiday, I went back to the wage office to ask about the underpayment and they showed me the card they had received three weeks previously that showed just normal daily hours. Luckily, my manager confirmed that he'd seen me do the extra hours, and also the piecework counts that he'd logged in his ledger. Eventually, they paid me what I was owed, but they couldn't prove that Doris had interfered with the cards. A week later two of the girls from the belt I worked on told me they'd seen Doris in the toilets stuffing a clock card inside her handbag, and that they had seen the name Pike on the top of it."

"Sneaky old cow, I'd have had it out with her."

"There was no point, I'd already won."

"How do you work that out?"

"I had Len, and in the finish, Doris Platt has remained unmarried."

"Karma that is Beryl," says Marie. "Fate always gets you in the end."

Gloria finishes styling my hair and I'm more than happy to see the restored version of myself in the mirror.

"No I couldn't," Gloria says refusing payment. "Call it an anniversary gift from the salon."

"Thanks. I'll make a donation to a cancer charity in your name, and you must … all of you … come to the party." And minus the Port Vale bobble hat, I leave with my head held high and a feeling of sophistication, something my previous encounter with a hair colourant had failed to accomplish.

***

That evening, we arrive at the club and as we enter the room we're greeted by friends and family who have turned up to share the evening with us. I wave to Gloria who is standing with Marie and Beverley near the doors which lead to the toilets. "Len, there's a pint in over here for you," shouts Bernard Copland, his arm still bandaged after the nail gun incident. The staff at the club have done a sterling job with the usually dingy upstairs room. The curtains look like they'd been laundered, the small parquet dancefloor is polished and it looks like the cleaners have had a flick round with a duster and polish, even the tables and chairs have seen some activity with a cloth.

Victor and Lisa have laid out a sumptuous buffet along one wall, and Kirk's karaoke machine is ready beside the dancefloor with Ruth behind it putting the laser discs into order and testing the various knobs and buttons in front of her on the sound desk. Vera has been in charge of decorations. Streamers stream across the ceiling interspersed with balloons and what look like metallic jellyfish.

On the wall above the buffet table is a huge blown-up poster, of one of our wedding photos. I guess that's down to Mac and his computer. Len, dressed in his father's suit complete with carnation buttonhole is squinting in the sun while I stand beside him in my bridal gown beaming like an imbecile – we look so young.

"You look lovely, Mum," Lisa says admiring the dress I was wearing.

"Victor helped me choose it," I say, "but I'm not sure about this belt?"

"Nonsense," Victor says, leaning in and kissing me on the cheek. "The belt brings in your waist and makes your bangers the star of the show."

"Banger," I reply.

"Best pair of bangers in the room," laughs Len, "even if one of them is a falsie."

Ruth taps a microphone and welcomes everyone before asking Len and me to join her at the karaoke machine. As we walk across the parquet floor I become anxious about the prosthetic I'm wearing. what if it slips? Are people noticing it? Kirk greets us, asking the gathered people to give us a round of applause and as the clapping subsides he says, "Welcome everyone. Before the evening gets underway, Len would like to say a few words." He hands the microphone to Len and being a man of few words, I wonder what it could be that my husband has opted to share with our guests.

"Is this on?" Len says loudly into the microphone.

"Yes," a handful of people shout back over a ripple of laughter.

"All right, I'm not one for yakking in public, so I'll keep this short," he says, then turning to me he takes a small box out of his inside jacket pocket. "Beryl, when you agreed to be my wife forty-four years ago, you made me a happier man than I ever thought I could be. But there's always been one thing I have regretted never being able to give you…"

"There's nothing…"

"Bloody 'ell, dunna interrupt me woman, I'll lose me flow." Another ripple of laughter dances around the room. "There's summat that I wish I'd been able to give you years ago. He presses the small box into my hand and passes the microphone back. "I hope you like it love," he whispers.

The room falls silent as I undo the small bow on top of the blue velveteen box, slowly I lift the lid and nestled inside is a ring. I take it out and look at the gold band that has been channel set with red and white stones. "Sorry, I can't afford diamonds," Len says. "The stones are white topaz and beryl."

"There's a gemstone called beryl?" I say, looking up with watery eyes at the man beside me – my man.

"Yes. Lisa helped me choose it. The jeweller told me that if you wear beryl, they say, you'll enjoy a life full of love and affection."

"And that's what you've given me."

"My darling, for the time we have left together that's all I can promise you." And for the second time in my life, Len slips a ring onto my finger and takes me in his arms before publicly kissing me.

~ 36 ~

Wednesday, 30 June
Here I am standing on the school playing fields wearing a high-visibility vest with a whistle hanging around my neck and a blue lanyard with my photographic I.D.

It's sports day and parents are cheering on their children as they race towards the imaginary tape stretched out across an improvised racetrack. I'm watching Wayne Dobbs, the tallest boy in year five romp home to win the hundred-metre sprint, I wonder how I managed to allow myself to get roped into this situation.

As giraffe-legs Dobbs waves to his father who's crowing with delight, my mind drifts back a few days.

***

Len had collected Saffron from school and after she'd changed out of her uniform she sat at the dining table tucking into a plate of beans on toast. "So, what did you do at school today?" Victor asked her as he leaned over with a kitchen towel and tucked it into her collar; just in time to catch an orange blob of sauce from her fork.

"We practiced for sports day next Wednesday."

"Well it's been a lovely day to be outside," I said, placing a beaker of juice in front of her. "Are you in any of the races?"

"I was going to be in the egg and spoon, but I'm not very good at that."

"I'm sure you are," I said, lowering myself into my chair.

"No, I'm not. I keep dropping the egg. And do you know what, Nan?"

"What?"

"It's not a proper egg, it's a pretend one."

"Never," said Victor.

"Yes, Miss Paxton said it's so we don't get yolk on our plimsolls."

"Makes sense," Len said as he lifted the lead from the coat hooks in the hall, sending the dog into a frenzy of whimpering and tail wagging. "Stand still you daft mutt." Len struggled with fastening the dog's collar "I'm taking the dog out for its business," he called from the hall with the dog straining at the lead. "Saffron, if you're not doing the egg and spoon, what are you doing?"

"Me and Jude Johnson have been practicing the three-legged race ... oh, and Fartuun."

"I beg your pardon," Len said, his head appearing around the door. "We'll have none of that language in this house, young lady." Saffron looked across at her grandad, her bean-stained mouth forming an O shape looking like one of Van Gogh's sunflowers. "Some people might allow babes to swear in their house, but I won't have it." Saffron's bottom lip began to quiver, and her chest heaved as she was pre-wail. "If we let it go unchecked, then where will it end? Today it might be farting but next week it could be the other F-word."

"Dad," Victor said, slipping his arm around his niece and pulling her close. "Saffron wasn't swearing. Fartuun is a Somali girl in her class. She's been practicing the race with her and Jude." Oblivious to the smear of tomato sauce on his shirt front I watched Victor hand his niece a tissue and a potential crying fit was avoided.

"O-rayt," Len said looking sheepish as he sidled out of the door. "I'm sorry little un… Better go or the dog not last 'till we get to the fields."

I took the tissue from Saffron, wiped her mouth and said, "Silly grandad, fancy him not knowing Fartuun is in your class."

"Nan?"

"Yes love?"

"Miss Paxton gave us all a note to bring home." Saffron retrieved the crumpled piece of paper from her coat pocket and smoothed it out over her knee before handing it to me.

"What is it?" asked Victor.

"It says the school are looking for some volunteers for sports day."

"To take part?"

"No, you dozy doorstep. It says they need some parents to act as marshals."

"Will you do it, Nan? Say you will." An excited Saffron clapped her hands with gusto. "Please Nan, it'll be fun."

"I'm not sure."

"Go on," said Victor. You might enjoy it."

"Please, Nan. Then you'll be at the front for when me and Fartuun do the three-legged race."

"I thought you were doing that with Jude Johnson?"

"I am. I'm in two races as there are too many of us in the class to fit on the track. I'm doing one with Jude and the other with Fartuun."

"I'll tell you what," I said rising from my seat. "I'll have a think about it."

***

So there you have it, that's how I came to be involved.

All of the marshals had been invited into the school midweek and the head teacher, Ms Thatcher had told us what was expected of us. Our duties include making sure parents stand at a safe distance from the participating children and keeping a keen eye out for anyone bringing in prohibited items, which include glass bottles, chewing gum and sports-enhancing supplements. I wanted to point out that the competition was between primary school children and not Olympic athletes but thought better of it.

The policy of the school governors is that the event will be non-competitive, with the children who fail to win referred to as supporting competitors. Ms Thatcher, however, being an authoritative force as strong as her namesake, very quickly made her feelings about this very clear. "I don't hold any truck with this non-competitive codswallop," she had said. "I believe that children need to know what it's like to attain greatness, and they cannot do that if they do not learn from failure." Mr Hussain attempted to interrupt her, but a steely glance soon had him back in line. "If we remove competition, then I ask you, who will strive to be the best?" No one responded, we all instinctively knew that she didn't require an answer. "The school can't afford to shell out for medals and trophies for individual events, but we can print off our certificates using the school's media suite. So, we need a parent with neat handwriting to fill them in. I'll leave you to decide amongst yourselves who will undertake that duty but do bear in mind that the school has quite a diverse ethnic mix and some surnames will have an assemblage of vowels and consonants you may not be familiar with." She looked at her watch and then continued, "I suggest we retire for coffee and after a break, I'll get a member of my staff to take you through health and safety and then we'll take your photographs for the I.D. badges." As she exited the staffroom we all remained silent until the door closed behind her, and then Mr Hussain said, "Bloody hell, she's harsh."

"I think she's magnificent," said Sue Hurley, one-half of the school's lesbian mothers. "I think we should have more women like her."

"I bet you do," sniped Elizabeth Nash.

"What are you insinuating?" said Sue.

"Make of it what you will."

"You're going the right way for a smack in the gob."

"Come along ladies," Mr Hussain said, stepping in. "Let's not fall out."

"Just make sure that she's not working anywhere near me on Wednesday," said Sue. "Otherwise she might be found behind the bike shed, bludgeoned by a rounders bat."

It was quickly decided that to protect her from harm, Elizabeth Nash should undertake the role of certificate writer and Sue should take up a position at the school gates to keep any undesirables out.

***

One of the downsides of having breast surgery is lymphoedema, which is the accumulation of fluid. In my case, it affects my legs and considering I knew I'd be spending the day standing up I cannot imagine how I had forgotten to wear my compression stockings.

Saffron is being dragged by Jude Johnson towards the finish line when the heaviness in my legs starts and I'm lucky enough to see them finish in third place when the discomfort becomes too much to bear. I notice that there is a spare chair beside Sue at the school gate and I'm walking up the drive when Sue's partner, Shirley appears. She's drinking from a bottle and as the two women embrace at the gate she puts the bottle down and I see that the label reads Lucozade. "Hello Shirley," I say sitting in the vacant chair, "how's things?"

"Very good, Mrs Bickerstaff. Thanks for asking."

"Shirley's entering the fathers' race," says Sue.

"Really?" I reply, trying not to raise my eyebrows, something I'm sure Doreen would have had great difficulty achieving. "I'll have to make sure I don't miss it."

"She's been training all week."

"Just a quick run around the block, twice a day, nothing too intense. Besides I don't really have a body designed for speed," says Shirley, her hands cupping her surgically enhanced breasts that the Montgolfier brothers would have envied.

"I've told her to strap them down," Sue says laughing.

"The size of these buggers, I'd need some marine rope and a couple of duvet covers." I join in the laughter and tell Sue I'll take over her watch. The two women stride over towards the playing field, where the crowd are applauding the start of the sack race.

After a half-hour of sitting down the discomfort in my legs is beginning to subside and I'm joined by Ms Thatcher. I spotted her making her way over and so I hid the Lucozade energy drink bottle in the waistband of my slacks. "It's been a successful day," she says. "Fartuun Ali has just won the five hundred metres, from the outset she had a substantial lead over the other runners."

"They're fast the Somali. My Len says it must be in the genes."

"It would appear so," she replies, a smile breaking through. "The fathers' race is about to start and it looks like it'll be an interesting one, Shirley Hurley has entered and she's in the lane next to Malcolm Nash."

"Please excuse me, this I must see," I say rising from the chair.

"You go ahead Mrs Bickerstaff, I'll put away the chairs and table. I don't think there'll be any more parents arriving now." I walk back towards the playing field and after looking behind me to check Ms Thatcher isn't watching, I lift the bottle out of my waistband and drop it into one of the waste bins on the edge of the playground.

The advantage of wearing a high-visibility jacket is that I can squeeze through the crowd to get a better view of the race. The fathers, including Shirley Hurley, are lined up, poised ready to sprint away when Ms Thatcher joins them ready to blow the whistle. I can see Elizabeth Nash deep in conversation with the head teacher, who is defiantly shaking her head.

The whistle sounds and the fathers are away. Very quickly, Shirley, arms across her chest to subdue her breasts is ahead of the pack, closely followed by Malcolm. It's safe to say it is – if you forgive the term, a two-man race. Malcolm passes Shirley who then catches him up and takes the lead again. "It's not right," Elizabeth Nash says, standing beside me. "Shouldn't be allowed. It's a fathers' race, not a bloody father and lesbian race."

When Shirley crosses the winning line first, the crowd erupts, Sue bursts into tears and Elizabeth stomps off to the certificate writing table. And I swear for fear of causing a Lucozade doping scandal, to keep the identity of the energy drinker a secret.

~ 35 ~

Monday, 5 July
This morning, I'm helping Mavis put up posters advertising the church's forthcoming summer fayre. In my opinion, the vicar's left it a bit late this year if he wants a good turnout, as it's scheduled for the end of next week. We'd just convinced Mr Tung to display one in the window of the Oriental Pearl takeaway and headed into the post office. It's my job to carry the posters while Vera is in charge of the box of drawing pins, which she now rattles loudly to catch the attention of Ken, the postmaster, who was sitting behind the counter, protected by its glass screen. "Can we put a poster on the noticeboard?" Vera calls.

"What's it for?" Ken asks morosely. He doesn't bother to look up and continues counting out ten-pound notes in front of the customer standing at his window.

"St Peter's summer fayre."

"Didn't know he was having one," says Ken, with a smile as weak as his joke.

"Very funny," says Vera and she begins unpinning an advert for a slimming club from the middle of the corkboard to reposition it next to a card advertising free pizza delivery. "Here look at this," she says, pointing to a garish sheet of A4, "What's the point of pirate classes?"

"What?" I say.

"It says that the community centre will be having pirates classes on Thursday nights."

"It's Pilates, you daft bat."

"What's that?"

"Exercise classes."

"Is it. I knew I should have put my readers in my coat pocket?"

"I think I might start charging folks to advertise on the board," Ken calls over as his customer tucks the ten-pound notes into her purse and leaves.

"Whatever for?"

"Because folks are always popping in, to pin cards and posters up. But no one ever comes back to remove them when they're out of date. No, that job's left to muggins here." The space in front of his window is now taken up by another customer.

As Ken takes his instruction, Vera leans into me and mutters, "Miserable sod."

Later that morning. We're sticking a poster in the window of Belly Busters café on Bridge Street and decide to stay and have a bite to eat. I'm blowing across the surface of my frothy coffee when my mobile starts to ring. "Your phone's ringing," Vera says, stating the obvious.

"It's Victor," I say, seeing his name on the screen.

"Is everything all right?" Vera asks as I end the call.

"Yes, he says Kirk is coming over tonight and he wants to see me and Len."

"Things seem to be going well with him and Victor."

"They do. Mind you Kirk's been away."

"Has he, somewhere nice?" Vera asks.

"Not on holiday, he's been working down in London this past week."

"I wouldn't have thought there'd have been much call for karaoke down there."

"Kirk's karaoke business isn't his day job; it's something he does on the side."

"So what does he do?"

"Something to do with underfloor heating," I tell her.

"I'm not sure I'd like that."

"Underfloor heating?"

"No, London." I take a sip of my drink and Vera says, "Maybe he's going to ask your Victor to get married and he wants Len's permission."

"What?" I splutter, spraying the air with a fine mist of frothy coffee.

"You never know," Vera says, sucking the froth off her coffee. "They can have a sort of wedding now … the gays." I look at her, about to tell her to stop being silly, but it's difficult to be mad at someone who has coffee froth on their lips making her look like a female Noel Edmonds, so I shake my head and cut my egg and cress baguette in half.

"Do you want half of my baguette, there's too much here for me."

"I've just had a doughnut."

"Suit yourself."

"Go on then," says Vera helping herself and taking a bite. "Those French folk must have good teeth."

"Why do you say that?"

"Stands to reason, you'd need good teeth if you're chomping on this crusty bread every day."

***

"Are you all right love?" Len says as he pushes his empty plate away. "You've hardly touched your cottage pie."

"I'm fine," I lie. "I had lunch with Vera in town and the portion was quite large."

"You don't want to go wasting money on lunch if you can't eat your tea of an evening, it's a false economy."

"I know love," I say collecting the plates from the table and walking into the kitchen, where the dog sits with an expectant expression. Truth is, just lately I've not had much of an appetite and as I scrape the remnants of my cottage pie into its bowl, I notice that the dog's put on a few extra pounds. "This is going to have to stop," I tell it. "Otherwise you'll be too fat."

"I'll get it," Len shouts after there's a knock at the front door. The dog lifts an ear but finds the extra meal more interesting than the visitor and stays in the kitchen.

"Is it Kirk?" I ask wiping my hands on a tea towel as I walk into the hallway.

"Give us chance woman," Len calls back, "I haven't opened the door yet… Yes, it's Kirk."

"Come in Kirk," I say as he pops his head around the door. "Do want a cuppa?"

"That'll be lovely Mrs B, thanks," he says and steps inside. There's a creak of floorboards and Victor appears at the top of the stairs.

"Come on love," says Len. "Let's put the kettle on, while the lads say hello."

In the middle room, we're all sitting and listening as Kirk tells us about his week working in London. "To be honest, it's too fast for me, I much prefer the slower pace of life up north."

"I haven't been to London for years," says Victor.

"We've never been, have we Len?"

"No, never had the opportunity."

"It's funny you should say that," says Kirk as he takes an envelope out of his pocket. "You know I told Victor I wanted to see you both tonight." Len and I nod our heads in agreement. "I've got another anniversary present for you."

"You needn't have—"

"I wanted to. Besides I won them in a work raffle." He hands the envelope to Len who says he hasn't got his reading glasses, so can I open it. I slide my finger under the seal and the flap opens. Inside are two vouchers. One for a two-night stay at the hotel where Kirk had been staying and the other for tickets to a West End show.

"You can't give us this lad," Len says. "It's far too much."

"Yes, I can, just accept it and enjoy the break."

"Thanks, it's very kind of you and a break will do the wife no end of good."

"You'll enjoy it, and Mum It'll be something new to add to your diary," says Victor.

"Yes," I reply, nodding and smiling like a bobble-headed dog on a car's parcel shelf.

At the end of the evening, after letting the dog out to cock its leg up the gate and locking the back door I climb the stairs to bed. Len is in the bathroom whistling tunelessly; his warning to me not to come in whilst he's in there. I slip out of my dress and remove my prosthetic and bra, placing them on the bedside cabinet. I know it doesn't make sense, but if there's a fire I don't want to be rescued with only one breast inside my nightie. I hear Len pull the cord, turning off the bathroom light and he pads into the bedroom in his stocking feet. I climb into bed as he undresses, folding his clothes and placing them on the chair beside the window.

"When you told me earlier that Kirk wanted to talk to us, I was dreading it in case he was coming over to ask for our permission to have one of those civil doodahs with our Victor."

"Would it be so bad?" I say, rubbing a little Vaseline onto my shoulder where the weight of the prosthetic has caused my bra strap to rub.

"Nah, can't say it would," says Len climbing in beside me. "But I'll tell you one thing."

"What's that love?"

"He can get hitched to our son if he likes, but if he thinks I'm going to sit through some fancy London show, where French peasants moan about how hard life is before they chuck themselves off the ramparts, well he's got another think coming."

"I guess it'll have to be Mama Mia then."

"Not bloody likely."

~ 34 ~

Saturday, 17 July
"She'd have had no trouble fitting in with the S.S." mutters Vera, as she bites into a jam doughnut. "I always call her the smiling assassin."

"Who?" I ask, confused.

"Her," she says, waving the doughnut about and flicking sugar in the direction of the television. "That weather girl, she's got a smile that could only be removed surgically. Look at her, grinning as she tells the people of West Yorkshire that they're in for a wet and miserable afternoon." I indicate that she has a blob of raspberry jam above her top lip that makes her look remarkably like Hitler, albeit with rollers in. After successfully removing it with the tip of her tongue she adds, "I hope it stays nice for the summer fayre this afternoon."

"What time do you have to be at Elkie's?"

"I told her I'd pop 'round at about eleven to pick up my Weight Watchers scales. Apparently, this year's cake is the biggest she's ever made."

"It's nice that she always makes the cake for the guess the weight of the cake competition," I say and collect the tea things. "What sort of a cake is it this year?"

"Carrot," Vera calls from the middle room, "with a cream cheese frosting. Are you on the tombola again this year?"

"No, the vicar thinks in my condition, I'll get tired quickly on such a busy stall." I walk back into the middle room and see Vera looking at her watch. "So, he's asked me to take a break this year."

"Hell, look at the time. I'd better get off if I'm going to catch the 22A to Elkie's house." I walk Vera to the front door and watch as she walks down the street and I start to feel sad that this year I've been asked to scale down my help with the church's festivities.

Saint Peter's church has had a summer fayre for as long as I can remember. As a girl, I'd come with my parents and we'd spend the afternoon guessing how many marbles a jar contained or trying to toss a bag of beans hard enough to dislodge a coconut. And how many waste bins made out of Party Seven beer tins, offcuts of wallpaper and upholstery trimmings were sold was beyond belief. Back in the 1970's it seemed like every home had a beer can waste bin. It's funny, when you look back to enjoyable days, you always remember the sunshine, but surely by the law of averages, there must have been rain at some point. A sodden fayre.

I began helping out after I got married and apart from 1986, when I had a particularly bad dose of cystitis, I've not missed a single year. I understood not being able to help out back then, No one would want to buy a raffle ticket from a sulky woman who had a knicker region similar to a volcanic caldera.

I told Len last night that now I'm minus one breast it could be more of a help than a hindrance when it comes to vigorously turning the tombola drum; there's less of me to get in the way of my winding elbow. Len said to look on the bright side, not having to count coppers into banking bags at the end of the day.

***

Thankfully the rain holds off and I walk to the church after lunch. I can already hear the sound of celebrations as I enter the churchyard. I walk past the vestry door into the car park at the rear, I can see children running after each other, eager to see everything in minutes. Over by the far fence, a bungee trampoline has been set up and the older children queue and fidget as they wait and watch others bounce up and down attached to a giant rubber band. In the corner, various stalls are positioned in an L shape: Everything from bric-a-brac to crafts. At one end of the stalls is local self-published author, Geraldine Malone, she's struggled with dyslexia all her life but has refused any help, which makes her books perfect for anyone whose native language contains lots of grouped consonants.

Elkie has a group of people inspecting her cake and paying their twenty pence to guess how many kilogrammes it weighs. How times change, I think. Now we're asked to guess the weight in metric, gone are the days of imperial weights and measures. I stand for a few minutes and wonder if I'll ever see this traditional English scene again. I shrug off the thought and wave to Reggie Boyle, selling his hanging baskets out of the back of his brother's hatchback and stroll over and blend in with the crowd.

Mavis and Doreen are sitting at a patio table on which stands a traditional sweetshop jar filled with boiled sweets. "You're looking better," Mavis says. "Last week you looked like death."

"Thank you," I say with a smile. "And hello to you."

"Thoughtless," Doreen says, her eyebrows almost meeting in the middle, underlining her frown. "Fancy a go, Beryl?"

"Go on, see if you can guess how many humbugs are in the jar." Mavis picks it up and rattles it like an over-enthusiastic charity collector.

"What have I told you." Doreen takes the jar from her friend and sets it down on the table. "If you keep rattling it, the sweets will break and how in the event of a dispute will we count them? I'm not sitting here piecing together broken humbugs."

"But we already know how many sweets are in the jar."

"Yes, minus the one you took out earlier."

"I popped a Pontefract cake inside in its place. Hello love," she says to a boy with a face full of freckles. "Have you come to have a guess?" Doreen shakes her head as Mavis hands the boy her clipboard. "Put your name in the first column and your guess in the second."

"Have you seen Vera?" I ask, watching the boy peer into the jar of confectionery while chewing the inside of his cheek in concentration.

"She was helping Elkie, the last time I saw her," says Mavis. "Come on love hurry up, there's other folks as want a go."

I say farewell and the boy hurriedly scribbles his details down. On my way over towards Elkie's stall I pass the refreshment stand, which is doing a brisk trade as usual. Margaret Watkins is handing out canned drinks while Julia, in between pouring what passes for tea into plastic cups takes the cash.

"Hello Beryl, how're you feeling?" Elkie drops a couple of coins into the cash box beside her huge cake.

"So what do you think of the cake?" Vera asks.

"It's magnificent," I say looking at the huge slab of frosted cake decorated with icing sugar carrots. "There's a good few slices in that."

"About fifty generous ones I think," Elkie says.

"Beryl," Vera says in a hushed voice, "you'll never guess who popped 'round to Elkie's this morning?" Before I have time to respond she continues; her eyes darting from left to right as she checks she isn't being overheard. "None other than…" she pauses for effect, "Doris Platt."

I didn't know you were friends with Doris," I say.

"She isn't," Vera says before Elkie can answer. She purses her lips and after looking over her shoulder. "We think she's cheated. Elkie had to nip out of the kitchen and when she came back my scales had been moved and Doris had some frosting on the cuff of her left sleeve."

"And…" Elkie says, dispensing with Vera's cloak and dagger approach to their suspicions "…she's gone and guessed the weight, spot on, she has."

"Can't you cut a sliver off, so she can't win?"

Elkie shakes her head as she hands her clipboard to a girl with her face painted with what looks like a giant butterfly. "I've no frosting left to cover it."

"You'll just have to tell the vicar."

"We can't prove it," says Elkie taking back the clipboard and the girl's payment.

"Don't worry, I have an idea," Vera says, tapping the side of her nose. "Why don't you have a go, Beryl?"

"What's the point, if Doris is going to win?"

"Never mind that I'll put in your stake and you can get off and enjoy yourself."

"Here," I say handing her a twenty-pence, "I'll pay for my go and you can put my guess on the sheet."

A few minutes later I'm waiting in line at the refreshment stall when someone taps me on the shoulder. At first, I don't recognise the woman smiling at me, and then suddenly I say, "Kate. Sorry, I was in a world of my own just then. You look different."

"It's this," she replies touching the wig. "I tried wearing a headscarf, but I couldn't cope with the sympathetic glances from strangers. I grew sick of seeing pity in their eyes."

"Whatever works for you is best," I say. "Do you fancy a drink?"

"A green tea would be nice. Well to be honest I'd prefer a Prosecco but I'll make do with the antioxidants in the green sludge."

"I'm not sure they're sophisticated enough for green tea. It's probably Typhoo and like it."

"I'll have what you're having then. Kate chooses a table and I purchase the drinks and we sit opposite each other with a view of children throwing wet sponges at adults fastened into makeshift stocks. "I'm glad I bumped into you, there's something I wanted to ask you."

"What's that?" I ask.

"I have a friend who works on the local paper and she's been doing a weekly piece on local heroes."

At that moment Vera saunters past. "Kate, this is my oldest friend Vera."

"Pleased to meet you," Vera says, "but she's wrong you know. Mavis's birthday is nearly three months earlier than mine."

Kate gives me that confused look that most people do when they meet Vera for the first time. "Pleased to meet you, Vera," she says, "I was just telling Beryl that I have a friend on the local paper who writes the weekly feature on local heroes."

"Didn't they run a story about a lad who found a missing lemon meringue in a wheelie bin?" Vera says as she bobs from foot to foot.

"Yes, that's right and inside the meringue was a lost engagement ring. Well, my friend, Pippa; she's the one that works at the paper asked me to nominate my hero, so I picked Beryl."

"Me?" I say, my tea going down the wrong way causing me to splutter, "Whatever for?"

"Because, without your friendship and support, I'd have gone stark staring mad. Say you'll talk to her and after if it's not for you, you don't have to go ahead."

"What a great idea," Vera says, "Nice to meet you Kate, but I must rush I'm dying for a pee."

"So?" Kate's eyes plead with me from across the table. Something is missing, they are dull, like pebbles that have dried in the sun and the shine has gone. How I want to pick up those pebbles and splash them with water to make them sparkle again.

"Okay, give her my phone number and tell her to give me a call."

"Thank you, Beryl." She reaches across the table and squeezes my hand, but the grip is frail and bird-like. I take her hand in mine and pat it. After our drinks, Kate tells me she's feeling tired and I walk her to the gates and watch as her husband, Gareth helps her into their car and drives away.

For the remainder of the afternoon, I walk from stall to stall. I deliberate over six crocheted egg cosies but decide against them, I know they will end up sitting in a drawer somewhere unused. As the day draws to a close the winners of the various raffles and competitions are announced. The boy with abundant freckles wins the jar of sweets and after the vicar tells everyone that the roof's restoration fund coffers have significantly swollen it comes to the guess the weight of the cake result. The crowd coo as Elkie's cake is wheeled out once again. "Ladies and gentlemen," the vicar says. "The winner of this year's, guess the cake's weight competition, with the closest weight of five kilogrammes and sixty-five grams is—"

The vicar's speech is cut short as Doris Platt calls out, "It can't be." The crowd turn to see her red-faced beside the empty refreshment stand.

"Do you have something you'd like to say Doris?" the vicar asks. I watch as she shakes her head and pushes her way through the crowd. "To resume," the vicar says pushing his spectacles back up onto the bridge of his nose, "the winner is Mrs Beryl Bickerstaff."

"Well done Beryl," Elkie shouts from the side of the stage.

"Yes, well done Mrs Bickerstaff," adds the vicar. "Will you need a hand to get this monster home?"

"Do you mind, Vicar," I say moving towards the stage, "if I donate it to the Friends of St. Peter's Hospice?"

"Not at all, I think that's a very generous gesture."

That evening we deliver the cake to the hospice and Mrs Logan the manager makes a small announcement before asking me to cut the first slice. I take the knife from her and I'm just about to cut into the frosting when Vera shouts, "Stop!"

"What's wrong?" Mrs Logan asks.

"Oh nothing is wrong," says Vera, "I just think it would be nice if Beryl cuts the first slice from this end of the cake so that all the people sitting over there can see." So I change my position and wonder what difference it makes to the people in the television room if they have my left profile rather than the right. I cut the first slice to applause and then hand the knife back to a young girl in a striped tabard.

"Let's sit over there," Vera says picking up the slice of cake, and we head towards some high-backed armchairs.

"What's going on, Vera?" she shushes me and after looking over her shoulder, she picks up the slice of cake and pushes a finger into its side and I watch as an AA battery plops into the palm of her hand. "What's that?"

"Extra weight," Vera says. "If you remember I'd loaned my Weight Watchers scales to Elkie, well because the cake was so big we had to weigh it in two halves and then stick it together."

"How—"

"Let me finish. Doris called at Elkie's house under some pretence and when she had the chance she weighed the two halves of cake."

"But how did the battery get inside?"

"Well, if you remember when you were with Kate, she'd said that her friend had written about the boy who found a ring in a lemon meringue pie."

"Yes, I remember."

"I thought about it and had what I can only call an excreta moment."

I wrinkle my nose. "Don't you mean eureka moment?"

"Yes, that's it. So I went to the toilet and what do you think I was doing in there?"

My nose remained wrinkled. "Do I have to answer that?"

"I remembered I had just bought some new batteries for the TV remote, so while I was in the toilet, I took the scales out of my bag and weighed one of them. When I got back to the stall I pushed it into the cake and hey presto it was fifteen grams heavier. When the weight was verified at the end of the day, your guess won."

"That's cheating."

"It's not really cheating … well yes it is … but I see it as a case of beating the cheat at her own game, and besides, look at all these happy people who wouldn't be enjoying a slice of cake without your kindness." I look around at the joyful faces, most covered in cream cheese frosting.

"Beryl, are you going to eat that?" I shake my head and with a laugh, Vera shoves the whole slice of cake into her open mouth.

~ 33 ~

Thursday, 22 July
I've been somewhat of a celebrity this week, albeit only in the local sense of the word, and if that wasn't enough I also entered the digital age, obtaining my own, bona-fide electrical mailbox.

It started on Monday morning, I was in the kitchen giving the net curtains a rinse through when the telephone started to ring, wiping my hands on my apron I walked into the middle room and picked up the receiver. "Hello, is that Beryl?" said a voice I didn't recognise. "I'm Kate's friend. Pippa from the local paper. I was wondering if we could meet for a chat."

"Oh, yes, she did mention it," I'd replied, still unsure if I wanted to be a part of the newspaper's local heroes feature. "When would be ideal?"

"I was hoping you'd be free on Thursday?" said Pippa.

"I'm not sure."

"Not sure about what, if you're free Thursday or the article?"

"Both."

"I understand," said Pippa. "Look, let's have a chat and I'll explain all about what the paper is looking for and if you're still not happy we can leave it there."

"Very well," I said, "you can't say fairer than that." We agreed to meet at an American coffee bar in the shopping centre just after midday and Pippa promised to bring along a couple of examples of her work for me to see. I replaced the receiver and went back to wringing out the net curtains.

***

Thursday arrives and I'm in the bedroom getting ready to meet Pippa, still in two minds about doing the interview, but I've promised to be there. I look at myself in the mirror. I look tired; worn like the dishcloth sitting in the sink tidy. "Come on Beryl, get yourself jiggered up," I tell my reflection. I run a brush through my hair and apply a smear of peach-coloured lipstick. I opt for a blue skirt and cream blouse before removing the lipstick that makes me look like I've just eaten an orange ice lolly and take one last look in the mirror. My reflection confirms I'm still tired looking, but this time a smarter shade of worn.

I meet Stella Murphy, who is at the bus stop with her granddaughter Tiffany. I ask how Sonia is finding married life. "Oh she's doing champion," she tells me. "She's just started one of those home education courses. She's studying architecture and its emotional effects on society."

"Really," I say, trying to sound interested but truly thinking it sounds like a waste of time. I'm of the considered opinion that if a building looks like a carbuncle, don't stress about it, just bulldoze it, "So does Sonia have to go to college?"

"No, she does it all from home. She sends her essays to her tutor by email, apparently a lot of it's done electronically nowadays."

"The bus is here, Nan," Tiffany says pointing.

Taking her seat, Stella says, "We're nipping into town to get Tiffany some new shoes."

"That's nice," I say and shiver inwardly. The thought of traipsing around town looking for shoes with a child doesn't bear thinking about. I already know how it will play out, an afternoon of tantrums, sulking and finally, bribery.

I smile at Tiffany, her neatly brushed hair is a golden mane, shining in the mid-morning sunshine and her cheeks glow healthily. Give her ten minutes and she'll have chocolate from ear to ear and hair so unkempt she could easily pass for something you'd find backwards inside a hedge. "I'm having new shoes," Tiffany pipes up.

"Yes darling, I know. What colour do you want?"

"She's having black," says Stella.

"Pink," says Tiffany.

"Black," reiterated Stella, raising her eyebrows in emphasis. Needless to say, the remainder of the journey is spent on idle chit-chat, observed by a petulant looking five-year-old.

The coffee shop is designed to look like how I'd imagine an American diner to look. You know the kind. Over-sized mugs and leather couches. I guess that the young woman sitting alone in the corner is Pippa.

"Hello, are you Pippa?" I ask. She stops tapping at the screen of her iPad and looks up.

"You must be Beryl? Lovely to meet you, sorry, I don't mean to be rude, but I've got to get this email finished and sent as soon as."

"I'll get us both a coffee," I say as she resumes her screen tapping. "What would you like?"

"Thanks, I'll have a super grande mocha-choco latte with vanilla and ask them for a receipt."

I stand at the counter looking at the board where it lists the selection of drinks on offer, they have vanilla flavour coffee, hazelnut flavour and amaretto – in fact, they seem to have every flavour apart from coffee-flavoured coffee. They have a choice of various sized mugs ranging from medium, which were twice the size of the mugs in my cupboards back home, to mega-grande the size of a mini skip.

"Can I take your order?" says a young lad with a floppy fringe and a blue plaster covering his eyebrow piercing. I think to myself, why do they bother? If anything it only draws more attention to the hole punched above his eyelid. But it isn't for me to comment so I give him my order and shuffle along the counter towards the till.

A bored-looking girl prods a few keys, looks at the screen and says, "Six pounds, twenty-five."

"Six pounds, twenty-five," I reply. "I only ordered two cups of coffee; I wasn't planning on paying off Greece's national debt."

The girl rolls her eyes and then starts speaking, "Your medium latte is two seventy-five and your—"

"One medium latte and a super-grande," says the lad who'd taken my order plonking a tray with two drinks in front of me. The girl drops my change and a receipt beside them and turns away.

Pippa is no longer engrossed in the email she was writing so I walk over and hand her what looks like a bucket of brown slurry.

"Thanks. I so need a mega caffeine boost. I was up late last night working on another feature for the paper."

"Two pounds seventy-five pence for a bloody milky coffee. I can get one of these in the bus station café for eighty pence and if the woman who serves you is in a good mood you get a free custard cream thrown in."

"How much do I owe you?" asks Pippa.

"Nothing"

"No, please. I can put it on expenses." She glances at the receipt and counts coins from her purse onto the table. "There. Now, as promised, I've brought along a couple of previous articles for you to look over." She hands me her iPad. "Have you used one of these before? They're new."

"Yes, my Victor's got one."

"Victor? Is that your husband."

"No, my son." I can see she thinks the name is archaic compared to the modern trend for rhyming names like Dwayne, Wain, Shane, etc. "I named him after Victor Fleming; he directed *Gone with the Wind*." I can see uncertainty cross her face so add, "And *The Wizard of Oz*."

"Good job it wasn't Victor Meldrew." Pippa's laugh sounds like a football rattle, not an attractive feature in a young woman. "Just run your finger across the screen to turn the page."

"Whatever will they think of next?" I say as the digital page turns, suddenly the iPad beeps and I look at Pippa, worried I've done something wrong.

"It's okay. It's just an email, I'll get it later."

I begin to read an article about how much dust the average pet dog carries in its coat, as she rises from the seat and says, "Excuse me; I need to make a call."

I watch her walk away and wonder how old she is. She seems to be winning the fight against the ageing process because I guess she has to be older than she appears at first glance. I place her in her mid-forties. I also bet she doesn't have any kids.

She's a thin-framed woman with no discernible shape, almost androgynous, the suit she's wearing adding to the deception. She has a luxurious mop of black hair, cut short into the nape of her neck, and sideways she bears a striking resemblance to the 1920's film actress, Louise Brooks. She is talking ten to the dozen into her phone cum camera cum media player cum dishwasher – well you never know what's around the corner, technology wise – when she must have sensed I was watching her. She glances across and feigns a yawn, which makes me smile. A few seconds later she's striding back to our table. Before she sits down she picks up her bucket of coffee and gulps a mouthful. I look at her long slender fingers, each one capped by an outrageously long and perfectly manicured red fingernail. How does she plump her cushions? I think, and I don't know how she'd cope if she had to insert a suppository.

"So, about the article," she says crossing her legs. "The idea is to let people know about everyday normal folk, who go out of their way to help others."

"I thought it was about local heroes, you know, people rescuing lost pets or helping to save pointless patches of wetland."

"It can be. Next week we have a feature about a labradoodle that contacted the emergency services when its owner got trapped in a portaloo. I don't particularly like the phrase,' hero' that's the editor's choice. He's young and inexperienced, but he'll get there eventually."

"Who, the editor or the labradoodle?"

"You're so funny," laughs Pippa, "I can see why Kate likes you." We chat for a while longer. Pippa explains that she'd already interviewed Kate, who talked about how I was instrumental in her facing up to her cancer and how much support I have given her. To be honest I felt a bit embarrassed. "I just try to be a friend," I say.

"I think Kate sees it as more than just friendship." Pippa gives me a brief outline of how the article will look. To coincide with a television campaign by a national cancer charity, the paper will do a two-page feature, Kate on one page and me on the other. "I'll email you the questions so you can answer them in your own time, and then we'll send out a photographer to get some snaps of you. You do have an email address don't you?"

"No. I don't know how they work."

"It's as easy as anything. I can set you one up now. What would you like the address to be?"

"Do you mean my postal address?"

"No, you choose what you want, for instance, you can have your name or something you like as your e-mail address."

"You mean like fudge? I quite like fudge."

"If that's your bag, so to speak. But I'd steer clear otherwise you'll be bothered by nutters who see fudge as a euphemism for something else." Whatever she was implying I didn't understand and just watch as she begins tapping at the screen again. "Here we go," she says looking at me through false eyelashes, "I've sorted out a web-based mail account and you can have Beryl dot Bickerstaff ninety-nine. Do you have access to a computer and the internet?" I nod. I don't feel she needs to know that I use Victor's laptop "Can I have sixty-six?"

"Sure, if sixty-six is an important number for you."

"It's the year I got married." She says nothing, just taps away at the screen then says, "All sorted, your address is beryl.bickerstaff66, all lowercase with numbers. I'll write it down for you." She scribbles down the details and tears a page from her notebook and hands it to me. "I'm sorry I have to dash, but I'll send you the questions later today, and if you need to know anything just fire off an email."

After she's left I sit for several minutes staring at the piece of paper. "Is everything okay?" I look up to see the floppy-haired boy standing beside me.

"Yes, everything's fine. I've just entered the twenty-first century."

"Okay," he replies picking up our empty mugs and with a confused look on his face he walks back to the counter.

***

When the paper arrives, I'm not keen on the photograph they've used which I think makes me look miserable and it's strange reading about myself. I'm glad I declined to answer the more personal questions. I had reasoned there was no call giving people around here any more ammunition than they need, but on the whole, it's a nice piece of writing.

Kate calls to ask me what I'd think and I tell her I'm pleased with it. Secretly I'm more concerned with how tired she sounds. I tell her I'll pop over one day next week and we can have a proper catch-up.

I've been stopped in the street a few times, by people telling me they've seen the paper. The other day Sonia Murphy said, "I saw you in the paper, you're a local celebrity, people will be asking for your autograph."

"I doubt it," I'd told her. "You'll be wrapping chips in it by next week."

~ 32 ~

Wednesday, 28 July
"Are you going to drink that pint or not?" I ask Len, as we sit in the theatre bar during the interval. "You've been staring at it for the past five minutes."

"Have I?"

"Yes. What do you think of the show so far?"

"Honestly?" he says, looking up, "it's a bit like this southern beer, could do with a decent head on it."

"Oh."

"I'm sorry love, I don't want to spoil your evening, but watching folks blurting out songs every five minutes doesn't do it for me."

"Thank goodness for that," I say, doing nothing to disguise the relief in my voice. "I've never been so bored; I can't believe I was actually jealous of my own backside when it went to sleep." Then came the call telling everyone the performance would resume in five minutes. I look at Len and he looks back; no words are needed and like children playing truant we skulk out of the theatre and laugh as we stroll along the pavement. "You do realise we'll have to lie and tell everyone we enjoyed the show."

"Don't make it too convincing," Len says, squeezing my hand, "just in case they buy us another ticket."

Underneath flashing lights that beckon people to buy tickets to watch shows, we stroll along hand in hand. We are so engrossed in each other that we could be anywhere. Len is amused by the speed of the other pedestrians who race across the pavements like Alice's white rabbit. I like the anonymity, here no one knows me, no one knows about my illness and no one knows part of me is missing. Here I'm just another woman walking along, although much too slowly. We stop and look into a bar filled with women in expensive-looking dresses and men in crumpled suits, probably straight from work. "Do you fancy a nightcap?" Len asks.

"No thanks, I find them a bit tight around the ears."

"Come here, you daft ha'peth," he says pulling me into him and kissing me. "I bloody love you, Mrs Bickerstaff." Caught out by this act of affection I just mutter something about going back to the hotel, to which he raises an eyebrow and winks.

"Not on your Nellie, Mr Bickerstaff."

***

We'd decided to come to London mid-week, assuming the weekend would be too busy. We'd taken the train down and arrived at the hotel mid-afternoon. We thought it was quite a grand place and very different to anywhere else we'd stayed; our experience of away from home hospitality being caravans and budget B&Bs. The bed was much bigger than the one we have at home, and on our first night we drifted apart under the sheets and because I couldn't feel Len close to me I woke up in a panic. The bathroom was the size of Victor's bedroom with a shower cubicle big enough for at least four people. Len joked that we should take home the complimentary toiletries, box them up and give them to Lisa for her birthday. "Save us a few quid," he said.

"Len Bickerstaff," I said laughing, "You can't come all the way to London and be a common thief and cheapskate. We'll get her something nice while we're here."

Kirk had told us not to worry about having anything out of the mini bar. We did look inside, but to be honest, Len's not a bottled lager man and when I saw the price of a tiny bottle of rosé, I closed the door quick sharpish. "Even though Kirk's paying I'll not waste his money on over-priced wine," I said. We did try the room service; something I've always wanted to do. I felt decadent as the young man wheeled the trays into the room and referred to me as Madam. I watched as he positioned the plates on the small table under the window and lifted the silver cloches. After he'd left the room we sat eating looking out over the city.

"So what do you think of London?" Len asked.

"It's all right, but I'm not sure I'd ever get used to the bus service."

"There's a lot to be said for familiarity."

We spent the next day before the show looking around. We didn't want to be tourists, so Big Ben and Buckingham Palace didn't feature in our plans. We did have a bash at the underground, but the map of multi-coloured spaghetti confused us and I wasn't taken with the smell of the braking trains. For lunch, we stopped at a small café and for the first time in his life, Len had a ciabatta sandwich, remarking, that when all was said and done it was just a posh cheese and tomato toastie.

Covent Garden was a pleasant surprise. We enjoyed watching three men in ballet tutus and wellington boots juggle with fish, the endless youths with guitars disguising busking for begging as they sang songs out of key did nothing for us and don't get me started on the living statues: what a pointless spectacle. We spotted a lovely silver bracelet in a small independent jeweller that was ideal for Lisa's birthday and Len treated me to an agate brooch.

Back at the hotel, we got ready for the theatre, Len wasn't happy putting on his suit, "Why can't I wear my comfortable trousers?"

"Because people dress up for the theatre," I told him.

"What's the point, they sit in the dark, so who will notice?"

"I will."

Despite the theatre being within walking distance, we took a black cab, another first for us. Len wasn't impressed; he said it was just a glorified mini cab with an expensive tariff but I liked it. There was lots of leg room and unlike the taxis I've taken back home it didn't have an air freshener hanging from the rear-view mirror giving off an overpowering smell of pine.

Once inside the theatre we didn't know the protocol so watched the couple ahead of us and copied what they did. Len followed the man who checked in the woman's jacket, so Len did the same with my cardigan and I followed the woman to the stall selling souvenir programmes. When I saw the price, I declined.

Len and I made our way back together in a pincer movement. He asked, "Didn't you want one of those booklets?"

"You're joking, twenty-five pounds for a programme, do you know how many loaves of bread that is?"

"Twenty-five if you get them from Poundland." Len smiled and squeezed my hand. "Come on let's find our seats."

Sitting on velvet seats while the orchestra tuned up, filling the auditorium with the sounds of strangulation. "Let's hope they play better when the show starts," said Len. Twenty-odd minutes later the curtains opened to reveal what looked like the inside of a pocket watch, singers filed on stage, and a man and women at either side of the stage started to sing, or as Len put it, they shouted across at each other.

I knew from the outset it wasn't going to be our thing. Musicals are okay in small doses; it took me a few instalments to get through a video of *West Side Story*. 'I Feel Pretty' loses its appeal when it's serenaded by a snoring husband.

***

I wake up the following morning with a headache like I've never had before, it is as if the inside of my head contains a jar of wasps, angrily buzzing and stinging the insides of my skull. I pad across to the bathroom and take a couple of paracetamol before turning on the shower and stepping under the spray. We only have an attachment that fits onto the bath taps back home so this is a luxury. I'd have liked to have had a shower fitted, but Len couldn't see the point when we had a perfectly good bathtub. The tablets begin to take effect and the wasps in my head fly away as the warm water flows over me. Stepping from the shower I grab an over-sized towel wrap it around my body and stand looking at myself in the steamy mirror; something I rarely do nowadays. I let the towel fall away and look at my scar, the horizontal reddish line underlining where my breast once was, emphasising its disappearance. For months after the surgery, I couldn't bring myself to look at it. I was scared of it. But now it no longer bothers me. It's remarkable how we adapt and accept, but I don't feel the urge to break out into song about it.

~ 31 ~

Wednesday, 4 August
We had a family gathering yesterday to celebrate Lisa's birthday, nothing too fancy just a few sandwiches and drinks. Lisa loved her bracelet and said she'd treasure it forever and it struck me as she showed it off to Mac, that this could be the last time I would see my first born celebrate her birthday.

When I'm no longer here, will there be a conspicuously empty space in the room, a vacant chair. At first, I imagine my name will be difficult to mention, but as the family gatherings keep coming around, I'm sure I'll become nothing more than a spectral guest.

After everyone had gone home, I closed the door to the front room leaving the plates and glasses unwashed. "I'll clean up later," I said. Len knew there was something wrong; you don't live with someone for forty-four years without understanding how they tick. "It's just a headache," I told him as he squeezed my hand. "I think I need a lie down."

"You get yourself upstairs, I'll see to the dishes."

I fell into bed and within minutes I was asleep. In fact so deeply that I didn't notice Len coming to bed or even getting up this morning. I opened my eyes and saw a cup of cold tea on my bedside table and a note telling me he'd gone out.

***

I get out of bed and traipse downstairs and after tipping the cold tea into the sink I make a fresh pot and slide a slice of bread under the grill. I'm feeling better today, no wasps in the jar. I fill the washing machine with our London clothes and go out into the backyard with a cloth to wipe the washing line. There's no point washing your clothes only to hang them out on a dirty line. I look over the wall and find I'm staring at my neighbour's washing line, which is full of pegs. The latch on the gate lifts and the dog rushes forward giving a half-hearted bark as Vera comes into the yard. "You were miles away then."

"I was wondering how her next door can hang out washing with dirty pegs, I don't think she's ever bothered to get herself a peg bag."

"Peg bags aside, how was London?"

"It had its moments," I tell her, snapping out of my daydream. "Fancy a cuppa?"

"Yes please, I'm gagging." We go inside and I'm arranging Malted Milk biscuits on a tea plate when she says, "Are you planning on going on holiday?"

"No. Why?" I say looking in from the kitchen to see Vera thumbing through a holiday brochure. "Where's that from?"

"It was on the chair."

"Must be Victor's," I say turning away as the kettle boils, "perhaps he's planning a holiday with Kirk."

"This looks nice," Vera says as I carry the tea tray into the middle room, "All-inclusive to Benalmadena."

"All-inclusive?"

"Yes. It says here that all your meals and drinks are included in the price of the holiday." I pour the tea and place a cup in front of my friend. "Only problem is," she says, "I don't have a passport."

"Me neither," I say. "If you could go anywhere, where would you go?"

"I don't really care, anywhere away from here would be nice, as long as they didn't serve foreign food."

"Well it wouldn't be foreign to them, would it."

"To whom?"

"Foreigners."

Vera stays for another hour and I tell her about the trip to London but keep quiet about leaving the theatre at the interval. She may be my best friend but sometimes she's prone to blurting things out and I'd hate Kirk to know. She tells me that Mavis and Doreen have fallen out over an aubergine-coloured handbag in the RSPCA charity shop. I tell her about the headaches I've been getting lately, and when she's leaving through the back gate I promise to speak to Dr Banerjee about them, during my check-up next week.

I'm just pegging out the last of the washing when the gate opens and Len steps into the yard. "Hello love," he says, "how are you feeling today?"

"Much better, thanks. Where have you been all morning?"

"Here and there," he says. "Shall I put the kettle on?"

"Not for me, I drank so much tea with Vera this morning I've got a bladder like an inflatable paddling pool," I say, as I smooth out a crumpled shirt sleeve that's flapping in the breeze. "You have one if you like."

"I'll wait 'till lunchtime, do you fancy something from the chippy?" I nod and turn my attention to a pair of Len's socks that are in danger of losing their peg.

***

"Her in the chip shop has had another tattoo," Len says as he divides the pies and chips onto two plates.

"What's she had this time?" I ask, pouring tea into his mug.

"She's had, 'love conquers all' written in Arabic on her neck."

"I didn't know she could speak Arabic."

"She can't, Shakeel from the takeaway translated it for her."

"She's taking a risk trusting Shakeel, he spells, discount with a K, for all she knows she might be walking around with an order for a large doner kebab printed on her neck."

After lunch, while I'm washing the dishes Len comes into the kitchen and says he has a surprise for me, "Well it'll have to wait until the plates are on the draining board."

"Leave the plates for a bit. I've got something for you." He holds out an envelope, so I wipe my hands on my apron and take it.

Inside is a sheet of letterheaded paper from the travel agent. "What's this?"

"Bloody read it, woman."

"It says you've booked a holiday."

"That's right," he says beaming, "it's a surprise for you, a week in a hotel at Lido di Jesolo."

"What, Where?"

"Italy. I've booked it through the Co-Op."

"But we can't afford a week in Italy."

"Yes, we can. Arthur's got to go into hospital for a new kneecap, so he's going to be off work for a few months and I'm taking over his shifts until he comes back. I've done the sums and the extra money means you can get your dream of seeing Venice."

"Passports. We haven't got passports."

"Don't fret love, Lisa's dealing with them. We'll nip into town later and get some photos taken at the booth in the bus station."

"Photos today. Oh no, my hair's a right mess."

"Looks all right to me."

The dishes have been put away before Len drives us into town; usually, we use our bus passes as he finds, (in his words) council parking facilities 'a bleeding rip-off,' but today he chooses to drive. As he feeds coins into the parking meter I spot Mavis. I don't mention the handbag debacle related to me earlier, but it doesn't take long before she broaches the subject. "I think Doreen's on the change," she says.

"What makes you think that?" I say presuming that at her age Doreen – like myself – would have passed through the menopause years ago.

"She's become right touchy," continues Mavis. "The other day we were looking at a purple handbag in the charity shop, and she got uppity over a remark I made."

"And what was that?"

"She was telling me that the woman who runs the adult art classes at the school thought she had interesting features and asked if she'd like to model for the class."

"That was nice of her."

"Well," Mavis says, "I pointed out that the art class had an advert in the paper last week and it said they were looking for life models." Mavis looks across the road and then lowers her voice. "You do know what life model means don't you ... nude ... naked ... undressed!"

"So did you tell Doreen she'd have to strip off?"

"Yes, and I told her she should pose with the handbag as the colour would go well with her varicose veins. Next thing I know she's raising her voice and storming out of the shop."

"I'm sure you'll make it up soon."

"Are you ready love?" Len says.

"Off somewhere nice?" Mavis asks.

"We're getting passport photos taken for our holiday."

"Ooh a holiday, where—"

"It was lovely to see you Mavis," I say cutting her off mid-sentence and linking Len we make our way to the bus station.

"Did you two have a nice chat?" he asks.

"It was ... interesting."

The photo booth is situated at the far end of the bus station, but the inside smells like a urinal and there's graffiti daubed on the interior walls. As we turn to walk away a young man wearing a Tesco uniform tells us the superstore has one. "It's down by the tills," he says. "You'll need five one-pound coins though as it only takes change."

"Five pounds for four piddling little photos," Len says as I fish coins out of my purse.

"Tell you what we'll do, you have two taken then nip out of the booth and I'll dart in and have my two done."

In Tesco, we stand reading the instructions on the machine when a lady in a tabard asks, "Is everything okay? Do you need change for the machine?"

"I think I'm okay for coins," I say. "We're getting our passport photos taken."

"Do you know how long it is between flashes?" Len asks her.

"Sorry, no. Why do you ask?"

"We've worked out that the missus will have the first two photos taken, then we'll change places and I'll have the last two."

"I'm afraid you won't be able to do that."

"Why not?"

"Because you have to send matching photos each for passports, the camera flashes once and you get four identical pictures."

"Oh." I put the coins back into the zippered side of my purse open the wallet side take out a ten-pound note and say, "I think I'll need change after all." The assistant takes the note and says she'll return with a leaflet detailing the rules regarding passport photos.

Looking at my photograph as we walk away from the booth. I say, "I look like a worn-out Judy Finnegan."

"You look all right to me," says Len, as he collides with a baby buggy. He apologises and receives a sarcastic riposte in return from the young mother who with her orange fake tan and scraped-back hair looks like a startled pumpkin. "Come on love," Len says taking the photograph from me as the mother wheels her baby away in the direction of the nappies and wet wipes. "I'll get us a nice bottle of Italian wine. We might as well get some practice in for our holiday." I nod and holding my hand he leads me to the wines and spirits aisle.

~ 30 ~

Monday, 9 August
"Bloody weddings," says Vera as we shuffle our way up the aisle of the bus looking for a seat. "I don't even like the girl."

"So why are you going?"

"Family. It's expected. Look at this." She hands me a gold-coloured card. "Wedding invitations, they're just problematic pieces of gilt card." I look at her confused. "They facilitate decisions you'd normally not want to clog up the inner workings of your mind. Things like hat or fascinator. Shoes, comfy or corn crushers. And then there's budget or bio-degradable confetti to think about."

"What's his name again, the chap she's marrying?"

"Maurice, he's a semi-professional footballer from Rochdale."

"I didn't know that."

"And she's changed you know. Forgotten that she was born and raised on a council estate in Fegg Hayes. Last week, she said, in her newly adopted telephone voice, 'When we're wed I'm looking forward to re-styling his new, three-bed detached in Bacup.'"

"And what did you say?"

"Me? I said people should never forget where they've come from. I mean, why she should feel the need to develop a new posh personality beggar's belief? Oh look, here's our stop." She presses the bell to alert the driver and after pointing out to a young mother that the position she's left her child's buggy in constitutes a trip hazard, we exit the bus.

Vera has dragged me into Newcastle. not the one in North-East England but the one in Staffordshire, it's posher than Tunstall with the nearby residents living behind hedges with gravel drives and more cars than they can use at once. "I've exhausted the shops in Burslem and Hanley," Vera says, "So thought I'd try the shops here. Doreen told me of an exclusive one, saying I should try it."

La Bella Figura isn't a shop I usually frequent, but as Vera gets changed behind the curtain I check the clipping from the newspaper is still inside my jacket pocket. Feeling it there I call out to her," Vera, I'm just nipping to the newsagent, I won't be a minute."

"Okay," she says from the changing room, "can you get me my slimming magazine while you're there?"

"Yes."

"And don't be too long I need your honest opinion on this outfit." The bell above the door rings as I step outside. Next to this shop selling ladies' couture is a take-away restaurant and between the two, a narrow alleyway. I duck inside and remove the clipping and reading the printed telephone number I take out my phone and dial. I conduct my conversation in a hushed manner and after gleaning the information I require I emerge from the alley and make my way to the newsagents.

"Morning," says the girl behind the counter.

"I'm looking for the health and fitness section," I tell her.

"Porn disguised as naturism or fat mag?"

"Weight loss."

"There's this one," she holds the publication aloft and red letters on the cover scream, 'Beverley's five-stone success story'. "Or there's this one that reckons you can drop a dress size in a fortnight."

"It's for my friend," I tell her. "It's the one where they count points." I notice she gives me a disbelieving look and she reaches up and takes down the magazine Vera wants from the stand. "My mum shifted fifteen stone of unsightly fat last year," she tells me as she scans the barcode.

"Did she? How?"

"She divorced it," she says followed by laughter that resembles a grunting warthog.

"Thanks," I say handing her the correct money. "If you don't mind me saying love, there's nothing more annoying than people who laugh at their own jokes."

"And if you don't mind me saying," she replies, "I hope your … *friend*, enjoys the magazine." I don't like how she's emphasised the word, 'friend' but I let it go and walk away.

Back at La Bella Figura, Vera's looking at herself in the mirror while making disapproving noises, "Do you think this shows off my back fat?" she asks turning away from the mirror.

"It's a bit tight," I tell her. "Don't they have the next size up?"

"I've already asked but Miss Snooty over there says this is the largest size the shop stocks." She nods towards the sales assistant, "Cheeky cow."

"I don't know why you're bothering shopping here; the prices are ridiculous and the service seems to be appalling."

"Is everything satisfactory?" the sales assistant says after sidling over like a cat with its eye on a sparrow.

"I'm not sure," Vera says, "I think I'll leave it for now, if you don't mind?" The sales assistant looks at me and I'm not sure if it's relief or contempt that crosses her face before she strides away to rearrange a hat display in the window.

We eventually find a perfectly acceptable mauve two-piece with elasticated panels in the front at Peacocks on Castle Street and decide it's time for a drink. Sitting in a nearby coffee shop – Vera's treat – she mumbles through a mouthful of currants and flaky pastry from her Eccles cake, "I think I tried on nearly every dress in that shop and they were all too tight."

"Must be the way they're cut," I tell her. "Anyway, how's the diet going?"

"It's not," she says as a currant escapes its pastry confines and lands on the table. "I've counted my points every day and still I don't lose any weight. I reckon it's water retention."

"More like pastry retention."

Vera laughs and spots the currant on the table, "I wonder how many points there are in a currant?" she says, as she pops it into her mouth. "They're only fruit after all, and fruit is point-free."

"Not when it's dried and covered with all-butter pastry it isn't."

"Shame, that." Vera stands up and brushes down her cardigan, the pastry flakes giving the impression it was suffering from a chronic attack of psoriasis. I pull on my summer jacket that used to fit me quite snugly but now feels loose around the shoulders.

"Vera, do you think I've lost weight?"

"A little," she replies, picking up the carrier bag containing her wedding outfit. "Haven't you noticed?"

"You don't do you when it's the same face staring back at you from the mirror each day."

"I guess not. You're lucky you didn't have to work at it." I see the realisation cross her face as soon as the words fall from her lips and she begins to stammer, "Oh Beryl love… I… I'm really sorry … I didn't mean…"

"I know you didn't mean anything by it."

"I can be an insensitive old cow sometimes."

"Yes you can," I say smiling, "and that's what I like about you. Come on, let's get off to the bus station." She makes another attempt at apologising but I brush it aside, slip my arm through hers and walk her towards the exit.

Passing La Bella Figura, my phone begins to ring. I rummage inside my handbag for it as Vera looks through the shop's window. "That lilac hat would go nice with my new outfit," she says as I push the green connect button. A few minutes later, as I end the call Vera says, "I wonder what that's like."

"You could always nip inside and try it on for size," I say as I drop the phone back inside my handbag.

"I'd look a bit stupid turning up to a wedding with that thing perched on the top of my head," she says. I look up and see that she's no longer looking at the hats but is outside the take-away staring at a mound of brown meat that's rotating on a vertical spit. "Have you ever tried one of these thingamajigs?"

"Doner kebab, no, but our Victor has one now and then when he's been on a night out; the smell lingers right through 'til the next morning."

"Shall we try one?"

"I… I'm not sure."

"Come on, let's live a little."

"Very well, but what about your diet?"

"Beggar the diet," she says, "I've got elasticated panels now."

~ 29 ~

Wednesday, 18 August
I had a terrible night's sleep last night. I feel like I've spent the night in one of Saffron's pop-up books. I'd slumber then suddenly, pop! I was wide awake. I'd drift off again and, pop! Eyes open. The persistent ache in my head didn't help. Of course, Len snored beside me, completely oblivious to my nocturnal throbbing and popping.

The laughter of the bin men outside as they wheel the waiting bins off the pavement onto the road with a bump urges me to rise. I look out at the three men in orange waistcoats and watch as they connect the grey bins to the lorry to be lifted hydraulically and relieved of their contents. "Morning, duck," one shouts, waving to me before calling out something to his two companions that results in ribald laughter. I let the net curtain fall back into place, pull the neck of my nightie closer and after pulling on my dressing gown I leave the bedroom.

I'm sliding the grill pan under the gas as Len enters the kitchen. "Why didn't you bloody wake me?" he says pouring himself some tea from the teapot, "If that bus isn't on time, I'll be late again."

"I didn't sleep well last night," I mutter, pulling the grill pan halfway out to check on the bacon.

"Slept like a log, I did," he says.

"That's nice." I slide the grill pan back into place.

"I wanted to go on the earlier bus today."

"Why didn't you set the alarm?" I say, removing the pan again and turning over the slices of bacon.

"Never need to, you usually get me up."

"Sadly I'm not a mind reader. I didn't know you wanted to get up earlier. You never said."

"Didn't I? Must've forgotten."

"Brown ale can have that effect."

"I won't have time for breakfast, I'll see if I can catch the Cobridge bus, might save me a few minutes."

"But the bacon's ready now." I look up and he's in the middle room, one leg up, foot on a chair fastening his shoelaces.

"Tell you what," he says, his foot back on the floor, "stick it between two slices of bread and I'll take it with me. I can have it at break time."

As the front door closes behind Len, I look at the two rashers of bacon intended for my breakfast and then without a word pick them up and give them to the dog.

I decide to take myself back off to bed and with a cuppa on the bedside next to my falsie I press the TV remote. I flick between the channels looking for something remotely interesting to watch. Breakfast news has finished and I tune into a show featuring a pair of lesbians from Warwick, who've adopted a lifestyle change. The two ladies have taken up animal husbandry and are trying to eke out an existence living the good life, so to speak. Sadly, it doesn't look that good to me, as they are constantly complaining about the cold and they only seem to own one decent cardigan between the two of them. The program concludes with a pair of Gloucester Old Spots copulating and a snapshot of some roasted belly pork. I change channels just in time for a programme about a couple from Bridgnorth embarking on a quest to find a holiday home in Billericay. "I'm not that bloody bored," I say aloud and put the TV into standby mode.

I pick up a magazine and flick through the pages of true-life stories with lurid headlines like, 'I Married my Sister's Killer' and 'My Allergy Led to a Prison Sentence'. Celebrity gossip doesn't keep my attention either. I scan an article about recycling with Kerry Katona – previous husbands no doubt. I attempt a few paragraphs of a feature about the mysterious appearance of a stray Friesian cow at a water treatment plant in Sandbach before I give up and try to sleep.

The telephone rings, waking me and I look blearily at the clock, I've been asleep for an hour. My knees crack as I get out of bed and being alone in the house I allow myself an audible groan as I straighten up. "Okay," I shout at the ringing piece of plastic downstairs. "I'm coming," then at a slightly lower volume I say, "If you're some berk telling me I can save money by changing my energy supplier, I'll…" I pick up the receiver and bark into it. "What?"

"Err… Hello."

"Yes!"

"This is Gareth… Kate's husband. Can I please speak to Beryl?"

Mortified by my attitude my voice softens, "Yes, this is Beryl."

"Kate has asked me to call you." I detect a tremor as he speaks. I can hear he's trying his best to keep his voice steady.

"How is she?"

"Not good. She's not been responding to the chemo." The tremor increases. "She was admitted to St. Peters' yesterday, It was very sudden."

Neither one of us spoke. The silence that raced between the two connected telephones booming. I didn't ask the questions, why or how, they become redundant when you already know the answer. I hear his voice catch in his throat and to save him from speaking first I ask him when it would be appropriate for me to visit. He says Kate's parents had already visited that morning and that they'd cut short a trip to Istanbul by a few days. "They still managed to get a nice tan though."

"That's lovely," I say.

He tells me that he's been there with Kate all night and is going home for a shower and that he has to call in work to let them know where to find some important files for a forthcoming meeting and also that he still needs to go to the post office to post a fishing rod he's sold on eBay. I let him ramble on. It's strange how at times of great sadness and upheaval we seem to talk about the most mundane of things. I assure him I'll visit Kate that afternoon and he whispers a thank you before the telephone goes silent again. I place the handset back and walk into the kitchen. The dog looks up from its basket, ever hopeful, and I gave it a half-smile and say, "Sorry, no more bacon."

***

The coldness of the brass plaque that reads, 'Donated by the Friends of St. Peters' Hospice' cuts through my summer jacket as I sit outside on a bench. I'm looking straight ahead at the flower bed opposite, but the summer bedding fails to lift the chill that I feel. I'm scared.

I stand up and smooth down my skirt and pick up the flowers I've brought with me. What if they don't allow flowers, I think? I haven't thought to bring anything else, just in case. My mind races, I can maybe walk to the newsagent to get a magazine or two, maybe something to drink, what about chocolates? "Stop it," I tell myself, "stop being silly." I walk towards the doors and with my arm outstretched I go to push them open, suddenly they slide apart with an automated swish and the receptionist looks up and I notice my hand is shaking. I quickly pull it back press it against my side and walk inside. With measured practice, the smiling receptionist says, "Can I help you?"

"I'm here to see Kate," I say.

"Kate?"

"Yes, Kate … sorry, Katherine Chelson." I watch as her nude-coloured nails tap at a few keys on her computer and with a pleasing expression she says, "She's in Bluebell. Turn right at the end of this corridor and it's fourth on the left." I thank her, and follow the directions, walking forward and turning right. The corridor is well-lit with strip lighting that discretely hums. The doors are yellow with silver-coloured metal kick guards fitted to the bottom and each one has a nameplate fixed at eye level. I read them as I walk along counting the doors on my left-hand side. Primrose. Snowdrop. Aconite.

It's bad enough that someone saw fit to name the doors to death's waiting room after spring flowers, but bloody aconite. I ask you. I'm still shaking my head as I reach, bluebell and pause. Once again I smooth down my skirt, check I have spare tissues in my pocket and knock before opening the door slowly.

Kate is lying in bed propped up by pillows. She looks small and fragile. I hope my face doesn't give away what my heart feels, but Kate has noticed and says, "I know, I look a horror don't I?"

Not at all," I say, knowing that if I can't convince myself then there is little chance of fooling Kate. "How've you been?" I start to say before realising how futile the question is, "Bloody pointless question. I'm sorry."

"That's okay, at least you didn't start with, 'bluebell, that's a nice name for a room isn't it.'"

"Really?"

"Yes, my mother-in-law. Bless her she didn't know what to say."

"Must be hard for her."

"I laughed when I first heard the room names," she says, "how ironic. Here we are at the end of our lives and the rooms are signified by new life. Spring for goodness sake and here I am in the winter of my time. There's something about illness and flowers, they always seem to go hand in hand," she laughs, nodding towards the cellophane-wrapped bunch in my hand.

"What would you rather I brought with me?" I was starting to relax.

"Gin."

"Maybe next time I can smuggle it in inside a water bottle." We both laugh, that awkward laughter that sounds hollow. I put the flowers down and bend forward to embrace her. I ease back, worried I might hurt her when I feel how thin she's become. "You've lost weight."

"Tell me about it. I've dropped two dress sizes and I'm not even going on holiday." I look at her puzzled, "Imagine how good I'd look in a bikini right now."

"You'd have to do something with your hair first," I say. "No one wants to see you with hair that a scarecrow would refuse, no matter how good the swimsuit looks."

"Thanks." She smiles and I watch an incipient tear threaten to spill over and shrug, unsure what I've done to merit her appreciation.

"So many people visit me with faces switched to neutral and all they can do is apologise for my being sick," she explains. "Thanks for being normal."

"I understand don't forget," I say taking a tissue out of my jacket pocket to hand it to her. "I guess I know more than most how you feel."

She nods before saying, "Shall I put your name down for daffodil or crocus?"

"Any of them, but not bloody aconite." We laugh again and she hands me a hairbrush, I slip the headband from her head and as I brush her hair which has now become thin and dull she tells me that just lately she's found herself having erotic dreams about George Clooney.

"Could be worse," I say, "it could have been George Osborne."

We chat about anything that isn't death or cancer related. I tell her about Elkie's latest hair colour and she tells me how she feels she's invested too much time lately watching catch-up television, in particular, *The Great British Bake Off*, I tell her about how earlier I'd been watching a pair of copulating pigs until I notice that she is beginning to fall asleep. "I'll see if I can get a vase for these," I say pointing to the flowers. "I'll only be a moment."

Outside the room, with my back against the door, I take a deep breath before walking back to the reception area and asking the girl behind the desk for a vase. "I'll send someone in with one," she says. "Bluebell isn't it?" I nod, the fact that she has remembered filling me with hope. Maybe it's not so bad here after all. I return to Kate who is now sleeping. I pick up my jacket and put the now crumpled tissue I'd given her into my pocket and start to leave. As I reach the door and grab the handle, Kate speaks. "Beryl?"

"Yes love?"

"Next time you come can you bring me some magazines rather than flowers?" I nod and she opens her eyes and winking says, "Preferably ones with pictures of George Clooney."

~ 28 ~

Wednesday, 25 August
I push open the door and gingerly step inside. My nose wrinkles at the smell, a sort of mixture of burnt onion and floor polish. I look at the signs pinned to an information board and see the directions to the room number I'd been given over the phone. The old Victorian doors to the classrooms have small square glass windows and over the years, layer upon layer of green paint has made the surface of the wood uneven. I stop and peer through one of the small squares of glass and see regimented rows of desks facing forward. "Can I help you?" A voice behind me says. I turned to see a man dressed in brown overalls holding a broom.

"I'm looking for room six," I tell him. "Am I right in thinking it's this way?" I point in the direction I'm facing.

"Yes. It's the one with the black paper covering the windows," he says, before shuffling off down the corridor.

I arrive at number six and pause a while to study some examples of art that have been tacked to a noticeboard next to the door. A picture of a suit of armour with a chicken sitting inside the helmet is called, Hen Knight, and another entitled, Chatterley Whitfield in March, a sombre-looking urban landscape is separated by a riot of acid-coloured flowers in acrylics. I take a deep breath and knock on the door, I wait and knock again, this time a little harder. The brass latch lifts and the old door opens inwards, dragging across the floor. "Needs a bit shaving off the bottom, does that," I say indicating to the point where the door has carved a semi-circular scuff in the parquet.

"Tell me about it." The woman who has opened the door says. "Beryl, is it?" I nod and she smiles flashing a gold filling. "I'm Miriam, do come inside, I'll only be a few minutes, I'm just preparing for this evening's class." I study her as she busies herself, laying out pencils and clipping paper to easels. She isn't how I'd expected her to be; although what I actually expected, I don't know. Maybe I'd anticipated a woman with wild red hair, dressed in a diaphanous blouse and a hippy-style skirt, instead, she's dressed in a suit with a shirt and tie and on her feet are a pair of men's brogues. She catches me staring and asks if everything is all right. I lower my gaze and mutter something about her suit being quite nice, and she starts to laugh. "I'm not a lesbian," she says, as she flaps open her jacket like a flasher outside a primary school. "I don't normally dress like this. These are my husband's clothes. He was supposed to be the life model for the class tonight but his sciatica is playing up."

"Oh…"

"I thought, if I dress in his clobber, the students can at least have a bash at aspects of the male form."

"A kettle in the corner boils and clicks, switching off automatically, "Would you like a drink?"

"Yes please," I say, "tea would be lovely."

"I've only got Yorkshire, I'm not one of those arty-farty types who's into fruit tea that smells like cat pee."

"Yorkshire will be fine."

"So you're interested in being a life model?" Miriam says as I accept the mug of tea and we sit down to chat. I explain my situation to her, telling her that I'm trying to fill my last days with new adventures, determined to live what life I have left to the fullest, to test myself.

When I stop talking she gives me that concerned yet detached look that strangers adopt when you tell them you have a terminal illness. "I'm a bit out of shape," I say, trying to lift the mood. "I'd look silly with this face and the body of a fashion model."

"The more mature the better," she says. "Most artists find a body that's been lived in much more interesting."

"You make me sound like an old sofa." I laugh and she quickly makes to apologise.

"Can I ask you, Beryl, how do you feel about nudity?"

"Well," I reply, putting my mug down. "When you get told you're likely to peg it in fifty-two weeks, your sensitivity changes and the importance of some things starts to diminish. I've been poked and stared at by so many doctors, surgeons and trainee doctors, that for me the most important thing about stripping off for an art class is, does it have central heating."

A knock sounds followed by the scrape of the door on the parquet and a young woman's head appears. "Can we come in, Miriam? It doesn't half stink in the corridor."

"Of course Gemma," Miriam says picking up my mug, it clunks against hers as she puts them down beside the art room sink.

Gemma flops into a chair, dropping her folder and shoulder bag at her feet as two more people came into the room, a gangly youth dressed in black and a man who looks like his shirt is losing the battle to contain his body. "Belly button, Brian," Gemma calls and he looks down and blushes, pushes his belly back inside his open shirt and forces the errant button through the buttonhole.

"What is that smell?" I ask.

"That's Jacquie Elphick. Well not Jacquie, per se, but the class, she runs, Flavours of Asia, in the kitchens two doors up."

"Yes, and it was murder three weeks ago when someone overdid the chilli in a prawn masala. We had to open all the windows. I'm Gemma by the way, are you joining the class?"

"Not really," I tell her.

"If you can join the others please, Gemma," Miriam says as she tilts her head, indicating for me to follow her. "Sorry about Gemma," she says. "She can be a bit full on." Several more people enter the room and the crackle of conversation begins to fill the air, Gemma's chatting to a girl who's just arrived and is showing her drawings in a sketch pad. Brian takes off his jacket and lowers himself into a chair and as he does his shirt button pops open again to reveal his hairy midriff.

A woman wearing sunglasses places her folder against a vacant easel, removes her jacket and slides it onto the back of a chair. "Hi Miriam," she says taking off her sunglasses, "What are we going to be doing in this session?"

"Hello, Camilla. I'll explain what's happening when everyone is here. Who are we waiting for?"

"Kelvin and Mary," Brian says as the door opens and a man with hair the colour of copper wire walks in, "Sorry I'm late, the bloody bus service gets worse."

"That's okay Kelvin. Did you see, Mary on your way in?"

"No, I think she said she couldn't come, as she's got tickets to see some play at the Regent."

"That's right, An Inspector Calls," says Camilla.

"We did that in sixth form didn't we, Noah?" Gemma calls across the room.

"Yes," the gangly youth replies without looking up.

"I didn't get it. Some girl kills herself after getting pregnant but is it really the girl they all think she is, and the inspector is he real or a ghost, and that Mrs Birling, what a bitch."

"Thank you, Gemma." Miriam claps her hands and strides over to the door and closes it before turning to face the group. "Good evening everyone, I know last week I promised you we'd have a life model for today's session."

"Looks like we'll be doing a still life again, more bowls of sodding fruit," came a voice from the assembled group of students.

"Thanks, Kelvin, if you can bear with me, please. Now I'm dressed like this for anyone who'd like to sketch me. I could pretend to be a man."

"Not with those bosoms." I hear muttered but can't identify the speaker.

"Miriam, I don't know about the others, but I'd like to have more practice drawing the human form," says Camilla.

A murmur of agreement follows and Noah stands up, "I could be today's model, Miriam, just as long as you don't mind me wearing my dad's underpants. Mine are all in the wash."

"Thank you, but that won't be necessary Noah."

"Oh Miriam, please, it'll be a laugh," says Gemma.

"Piss off," says Noah.

"Look guys, I'm sorry it's not worked out today and I promise next time I'll make sure I've got a backup plan. So, just for today, if you don't mind, can we work on this."

"See," the man with copper-coloured hair says, as Miriam produces a bowl of fruit from under her desk, "another bloody still life. I've got that many of these sketches on my walls that my flat looks like the fruit and veg section in Sainsbury's."

"It's really not on, Miriam," Camilla says.

"I'm sorry but—"

"I could do it," I find myself saying, cutting into Miriam's apology before I've even had a chance to think about it.

"I'm not sure," she says.

"Look, if I stand here thinking about it I'll never do it, so let's just get on with it."

"Can I have a quick word?" Miriam says taking me by the arm and leading me through a door into a room next door. "You don't have to do this," she says as the door between us and the class closes. "I appreciate you're trying to help."

"I came here to be a life model and that's what I'd like to do." I'm terrified yet unwavering in my decision, and after Miriam hands me a dressing gown she closes the door leaving me alone in the room. As I strip off I can hear her muffled voice as she explains to the class about my operation and the reason for my being here. I undress and trace my finger along my scar and after slipping into the dressing gown I turn the brass doorknob and enter the art room.

The silence in the room is palpable, expectant faces behind easels look into mine as if unsure of my intention to go ahead with the task. Miriam gestures towards a chair with a cerise curtain casually draped over it, beside the table with the bowl of fruit from earlier. "Shall I sit here?" I ask, and Miriam nods with just a hint of a smile. As I undo the dressing gown belt, my heart clangs noisily against my ribs and I'm certain everyone in the room could hear it, but in truth, the only sound is the sharpening of a pencil as Kelvin scatters shavings beneath his easel.

"Comfortable?" Miriam asks as I settle into the chair.

"Surprisingly so," I reply.

"Here," she says stepping forward and reaching for the bowl of fruit. "Let me just move this."

"No," cries Noah loudly. Then softening his voice, he says, "Please can you leave it there, I'd like to use it in my drawing. Is it possible I could just move it a little to the left?"

"Very well," says Miriam and Noah moves the fruit bowl and goes back to his seat and the room becomes inundated with the scratching of pencils on paper.

I'm starting to nod off when Miriam gives a forced cough and says, "Class, you have just ten minutes left." She turns to me and mouths the words, "Are you okay?" I nod and look at the clock, wondering where the two hours have gone.

With the class clearing away their art materials, Miriam refills the kettle and I pop next door to get dressed, "You did it, old girl," I tell myself, pulling on my cardigan, "but probably best not tell Len or the others about this."

Ten minutes later I'm finishing off my mug of tea when there is a weak knock at the art room door, Miriam walks over and opens it, there is a whispered exchange of voices before she turns to me and says, "It's Noah, and he'd like to give you something."

"Just give me a minute," he says as he steps into the room, in his hands he holds a simple wooden picture frame. He walks over to his easel and taking an aerosol he sprays the picture he had worked on earlier, filling the room with the aroma of pear drops. "That's to set the pastels," Miriam says as we watch him take out a pen and scribble something on the bottom of the paper. He blows across the picture and then places it inside the frame.

"Beryl, I'd like you to have this," he says and hands me the picture that is part pencil drawing and part coloured pastel. It portrays me sitting down showing my scar in detail, while my intact breast is hidden by the bowl of fruit in pastel shades. "I think you're very brave," Noah says, "I wish my mum had been as brave as you."

"Did your mum have breast cancer?" I ask and he just nods. "Thank you, Noah. It's beautiful." He smiles and says I hope you like the title, it's a play on words."

Miriam steps closer and we both look at the artwork's title written in his teenage hand. It reads, *Still Alive*.

~ 27 ~

Friday, 3 September
"I'm terrified," I say as I brush Kate's hair. "I once went on a Ferris wheel at Blackpool, I was so rigid with fear I kept my eyes shut from start to finish. I can't do that for the two and half hours it takes to get to Venice."

"There's nothing to it," Kate tells me. "It's safer than crossing the road they say."

"Who says?"

"Statistics." I clear the brush of hair that has collected between the bristles.

"Have I lost much more?"

"No, not today," I lie as I ball the hair and tuck it into my pocket.

"Are you flying from Manchester?"

"Yes, that'll be an experience too, I've never been to an airport." I pour some water into a tumbler and hand it to her, "Victor said, they're just oversized waiting rooms full of bored-looking people and screaming kids." Kate starts to laugh then chokes on the water. I pat her back, feeling her spine, prominent beneath her nightdress.

"That's about right," she says. "Once on our way back from the Algarve, Gareth and I had a three-hour delay at Faro airport. It started off okay but soon deteriorated into frustrated parents and bawling kids. I remember saying to Gareth at that point, that's it, no kids for us."

I watch her eyes move upward as she remembers, and I know it's a cliché, but it's as if a shadow has crossed her face, not in a Joan Crawford lit from below kind of way – Len had previously commented that Ms Crawford seemed to spend most of her film career with a shadow of some description obscuring her face.

"I didn't know you'd decided not to have children."

"It wasn't a definite thing, I think maybe Gareth and I would have eventually got around to it, but I'm glad now." I take the tumbler from her and place it on the bedside cabinet. "I'd hate to leave a child behind, at least that's one worry I don't have." Her face drops, "Oh shit, I'm so sorry Beryl. I didn't think."

"I know love, it's all right. It isn't as if mine are still babes in arms."

"Yes, but I should've…" Her voice trails off and her eyes fix on the picture of a springtime scene on the wall opposite her bed.

"More pain?" I ask and she nods, eyes still fixed ahead. "Shall I call someone?" She breathes in deeply and her chest rattles as she shakes her head. I sit beside her and stroke her hand as she rides out the pain. We've been here several times before and Kate has told me that she doesn't want a high morphine dose that will limit coherent communication with visitors. I've asked her about the pain and all she's said is, as long as she can feel it, at least it proves that she's still alive. Her chest rises and falls rapidly for several seconds and the only sound in the room is her panting, gradually she starts to breathe normally again and smiling she whispers, "It's passed."

As on previous visits, Kate takes a couple more sips of water and I wait until she has fallen asleep before I pick up my jacket and noiselessly leave the room.

***

My head aches as I sit on the bus, I don't know if it's sadness or the stress of worrying about the flight the following day or maybe it's just my tumour, feeling neglected. Rearing up to remind me it is still here. The headache starts to fade after I leave the bus and walk to Vera's house, the familiarity of row upon row of terraced houses feels like a comforting arm around me as I stride along the pavement that I've walked along so many times before. I press the bell and the sing-song trill of an electronic rendition of 'O Sole Mio' plays. The music stops playing and the door opens and Vera's head appears around it smiling, "Did you like it?"

"Like what?"

"The door chimes, I changed it from the usual tune in honour of your impending holiday."

"I didn't know you could do that," I say as I cross the threshold.

"It has twelve pre-programmed tunes," she tells me as she takes my coat and hangs it on a hook. "Most of them are tinny and horrid. Today's is listed as, 'It's Now or Never,' but it's close enough to the one cornetto song." She chuckles as I follow her through into the middle room where the table is already laid. "Before you go, I must let you hear the tuneless rendering of, 'A Whiter Shade of Pale,' and wait until you hear the version of 'Wig Wam Bam.' Is cheese and tomato okay?" I smile and she removes the foil covering off a plate of sandwiches and I make a mental note not to mention the musical door chime again for fear of being subjected to the remaining eleven tunes.

Vera pours cups of tea; unlike me, she uses a strainer and loose leaf. I tell her about my visit with Kate and remember I have the ball of broken hair in my cardigan pocket still. I'm tempted to touch it but know that to do so would only bring my mood down, so I reach for a sandwich and tell my friend about my concerns regarding the upcoming flight to Italy.

"Her across the road went on a city break to Barcelona last week, she said the flight was as easy as catching a train. Imagine that, a city break. You leave one set of congested roads, crowded shops and streets covered in dog mess for another one; continental and miles away."

Engrossed in my sandwich I mumble, "Imagine it. Continental dog shit."

After lunch, Vera disappears out of the back door as I wash the dishes and stack them in the modern X-shaped drainer that looks out of place in her outdated kitchen. "You shouldn't be doing that," she says as she comes back into the house clutching a small brown bottle.

"Where did you get this from?" I ask as I place a tea plate into one of the drainer slots.

"I got it out of one of those little catalogues they keep pushing through the door, it said in the advert that the air that circulates around the draining dishes makes it more hygienic."

"Was it expensive?"

"Not really when you consider that they deliver it the next week to your door. If you like I'll get the distributor, Kenneth to post one through your door."

"He'd never get a dish drainer through our letterbox," I say, drying my hands on a tea cloth.

"Not a dish drainer, you daft mare," laughs Vera as she follows me out of the kitchen, "I mean a catalogue."

"Don't trouble yourself," I say as I stand in the hall taking down my coat from its hook.

"Here, these will help," she says, handing me the small brown bottle she was holding earlier.

***

"I've come for your cases," Lisa calls as she lets herself in, "I hope you're all packed and ready?"

"They're in the front room love," Len calls just as the door opens and our daughter enters the room.

"Mac's had to park around the corner, there's no space in the street."

"Shall I take the cases to him?" Len asks.

"No, Mac can fetch them."

"Hello everyone," says Mac, poking his head around the door just in time to hear Lisa tell him our cases are in the front room.

"Try not to catch them on my skirting boards," Len calls after him as he disappears back into the hall. "I don't want to be touching them up again this year. Paint plays havoc with the wife's chest."

"Go give him a hand," I say.

"Mac can manage," Lisa says." I give Len one of my withering looks and he skulks out of the middle room and into the hall to help Mac take away our packed suitcases. "Now remember, you're allowed one cabin bag and a handbag on the plane. What's dad taking?"

"His case is packed already."

"I mean his extra bag?" Lisa says, "for his essentials during the flight. Newspaper, extra strong mints and stuff."

"I can't see your father sporting an extra bag as he boards the plane."

"I've got Mac a man bag."

"A man bag?"

"Yes," she says, "It's a square bag with a shoulder strap, designed specifically for men. Here I brought this one for Dad, it was only a couple of quid off the market."

"So basically," I say, taking the black faux leather bag from her and placing it onto the table beside the brown bottle Vera had given me, "it's a handbag, but for men?"

"Yeah, but…" Lisa says picking up the bottle. "You have remembered to put all your drugs into a see-through plastic bag and—"

"Relax. They're already packed with the letter from Dr Banerjee."

"So, what are these?"

"Vera gave them to me." Lisa's frown questions me. "I told her I was nervous about the flight and she gave me those."

"Lisa reads the label and then looks up. "Edna Norton. Who the hell is Edna bloody Norton and why have you got her tablets?"

"She's one of Vera's neighbours, she gave them to her a couple of years back when she was having panic attacks. Vera said they helped her no end."

"Mother." Once again Lisa's voice rises an octave. "You can't take someone else's pills."

"But…"

No buts about it. Especially not with everything you're taking already. Now stop being silly, I've told you already, you'll be fine."

"Everything okay?" Len says coming back into the room.

"Yes, Dad. Right, we're off. We'll pick you up at five-thirty. Come on Mac." Mac has barely entered the room as he turns around and begins to exit. "And Mum, don't forget the…" She indicates with a tilt of her head towards the man bag on the table and turns and leaves.

Waiting until the front door closes, picking up his now cold mug of tea, Len says, "What was that all about?"

"Nowt important," I say, holding up the bag. "By the way, Lisa got you a man bag for the holiday."

It's not a pretty sight watching an elderly man propel cold tea through his nostrils and collapse in a coughing fit.

~ 26 ~

Sunday, 5 September
The flight wasn't as bad as I'd thought it would be, in fact, Vera's neighbour was right, it wasn't dissimilar to travelling by train, but without the views. The seats were allocated and Len, Lisa and I had three together but poor Mac was two rows behind with Saffron, sporting one of her extra surly moods. I was rather disappointed when we disembarked, the rather grand sounding *Aeroporto di Treviso-Sant'Angelo* turned out to be a great draughty barn of a place with an obvious lack of seating and multiple litter bins that needed emptying more frequently.

So now we're waiting for the coach that will take us to the resort, while a good third of the people from the flight are gathered outside the terminal doors, sucking in nicotine after their enforced two hours and fifteen-minute deprivation. "How far away is the hotel?" I ask Mac who is struggling with a squirming Saffron in his arms.

"I want to go down," she squeals.

"No," Mac says, before turning to me, "It's about twenty kilometres."

"What's that in old money?"

"Put me down," yells Saffron, making another attempt to wriggle free. "I want to go down."

"I don't care," Mac replies, "You're not running around here, you'll get lost." He then takes out a bar of chocolate and unwraps it with one hand and gives it to Saffron before answering me. "It's just over twelve and a half miles."

"And who said men can't multi-task?" I say to Lisa as I nod in Mac's direction. "Lisa. Why did everyone clap when the plane landed?"

"They do it to thank the pilot for getting us here safe and sound."

"That's just stupid," I say rummaging for a tissue to hand to Saffron, whose fingers are now coated with chocolate that has melted at an accelerated rate in the Italian heat. "You don't get people giving the bus drivers back home a round of applause just because they managed to deliver you from the stop on the high street to the bus station without killing half of their passengers."

"The coach is here," Mac calls as people start to move towards the allocated bus stop several steps away from the meagre shade that the building is providing.

"We're not sitting by that man again are we Daddy?" I look up and she is pointing to a man with a bald head that's so shiny you could fix your lipstick in the reflection. "He smells," she adds.

"Saffron! Don't be so rude," says Lisa.

"She's right," Mac says, "he spent most of the flight breaking wind." With his arm held out he prevents us from moving onto the coach until the flatulent man has seated himself near the front and then Mac tells us all to move down the aisle and to deposit ourselves at the rear.

Once the final passenger is seated a young girl climbs aboard and closes the doors before taking a microphone and instructing us that her name is Veronica, she comes from Droylsden, and we'll be making our first stop in about forty minutes for everyone who is booked into the Hotel Primavera. As the coach trundles along I start to get a headache and by the time Veronica has pointed out a few points of interest through the window in her monotone Mancunian accent I am experiencing a full on, wasps-in-a-jar headache.

At the hotel Primavera several passengers leave the coach and Lisa asks if I'm feeling okay, I lie and say I'm just tired and close my eyes. The coach sets off again and I decide to rest my head against the window, hoping it'll be cool but it's hot. Len reaches up and twists a nozzle above my head and I'm bathed in a cooling breeze from the air-conditioning. "Our next stop is the Laguna Hotel, where there are two swimming pools and a really good shoe shop not far away." drones Veronica as the wasps fly from one temple to the other.

"Come on love, we're here," Len says stroking my arm.

"I must have nodded off."

"It's been a long day." Len taps Mac on his shoulder and the two of them leave the coach and walk to the rear with the driver to collect our suitcases. With Saffron yawning noisily in her arms, Lisa and I follow Veronica into the small hotel that, according to the information Len has been given, is family-run and typically Italian.

We are greeted by a short man, aged around sixty wearing faded denim with an open-necked shirt that displays a dense thicket of chest hair, he thrusts his hand out towards me and says enthusiastically, "*Buonasera*, you are the Mrs Beek-errrr-staff?"

"Bickerstaff," I say with no roll of the middle 'R'.

"You are welcome at the Hotel Giardino; they call me Antonio." As he shakes my hand I introduce Lisa and Saffron, whom he tickles under the chin calling her, *la bella nipote*. Len and Mac walk into the lobby with the suitcases and after Veronica leaves we are shown to our rooms which are basic but clean and comfortable.

As a family, we spend the remainder of the evening sitting in the hotel's tiny bar with a few slices of salami and some olives for company. We plan how we'll be spending our next few days. "I think," says Len, "we ought to have a relaxing day tomorrow and go to Venice the next day. What do you think?" Everyone agrees and a decision is made to spend the following day on the beach.

52 Weeks

***

I've slept for longer than I meant to but when I do wake the headache has gone. I almost feel like that new woman people are always bleating on about. Len and the others have already gone for breakfast so I follow them down to find them waiting for me in the lobby. The hotel breakfasts are a buffet affair with a choice of three fruit juices, cereals, yoghurts and pastries, there are also platters laden with cheese and cooked meats. I smile at the sight of Len and Mac looking on disconsolately as there isn't a sniff of a fried egg or a rasher of bacon in sight. I try a little salami, bread and cheese. Odd things for an English woman to eat for her breakfast but it puts me in an Italian frame of mind, and afterwards while everyone else goes back to their rooms to prepare for the day I stroll outside.

The morning is filled with new aromas; the smell of freshly brewed coffee floats on the air mixed with the perfume of flowers unknown to me. The village is small and seems to only have a handful of shops. I peer through a window and see fresh bread arranged on shelves, in another, packets of pasta sit alongside bottles of wine with price tags a third of those back home.

Len waves to me from across the road, "Do you need anything from the room love?" I shake my head and hold up my handbag to show him I have everything I need for the day.

It's nice to sit on a beach and do nothing. Mac plays with Saffron in the sea and Len promptly falls asleep as soon as we get there. Lisa is engrossed in the latest Katie Fforde and I just sit under the umbrella watching as the world passes me by, even the dull ache that has started in my temple can't distract me today.

At lunchtime, we do the tourist thing and eat pizza followed by gelato at a beachside café before we resume residence once again on the sand. "Walk with me in the sea, Daddy," Saffron says, pulling Mac to his feet.

"I want to sunbathe like Mummy," he complains.

"No," she says, "Mummy needs a rest. Come on, Daddy." She is pulling at her father's arm and I get up saying I'll join them for a stroll in the surf. Len and Lisa give me a questioning look and I smile, letting them know I'm fine.

"Come on sweetheart," I say taking Saffron's hand as Mac rises to his feet, following a look from Lisa that I'm not supposed to notice, a look that orders him to keep an eye on me.

The cool sea laps at our ankles as we stroll along the shoreline watching Saffron who runs ahead of us, occasionally stopping to pick up a shell or throw a pebble into the water. "It's nice here, isn't it," I say, "I'm glad you and Lisa came too."

"Yes, it's lovely. I'm glad of the break, to be honest. Work is pretty full on at the moment."

"That's a good thing isn't it?" As soon as I say this I notice Mac's expression change. "Is everything okay at work?"

"It's okay," he says, then looking down at his feet as he walks he starts to explain how he feels trapped in a job he hates and thinks he hasn't achieved anything of any worth.

"Don't be silly," I tell him. "You've got a good marriage, a lovely daughter, and a nice home. You achieved that."

"I know that," he says, "but I'd like more."

"Money?"

"No, not money, just… I don't know. Satisfaction I suppose. I know people think I'm stupid and that all I'm good for is manual labour but I feel like I'm wasting my chance to be something more." Saffron joins us to show us a shiny pebble she's found, "That's nice," Mac tells her and she drops it into his hand and runs off to look for more.

"So, what is it you'd like to do?" I ask as he takes his phone out of his shorts and starts to take photos of his daughter as she plays at the water's edge.

"Ignore me. As I said, I'll be okay after I've had a break."

***

The next day I woke early. I'm excited. I've read the tour guides so dress appropriately for our day in Venice. "Antonio has offered to take us to the water bus," Lisa says, as we have our breakfast.

"I hope he won't be going out of his way?" Len says tackling a hard bread roll and some salami.

"No, he said he has to drive past there this morning."

"Let's just hope we don't have to squeeze into one of those crazy-looking three-wheeled jobs they drive over here," Mac says, also struggling with a salami roll.

"You will all enjoy today?" Antonio asks as we set off in his people carrier.

"Mum's always wanted to see the big bridge," says Lisa.

"Ah, *Ponte di Rialto.*"

"That's the one," I say, mopping my brow with a handkerchief, I see Antonio look at me, his eyebrows knitted together as he observes me through the rear-view mirror. "*Fa caldo?*" I look confused and Mac volunteers to translate.

"I've got a phrasebook," he says, somewhat triumphantly.

"It is hot," Antonio translates as Mac flicks through the pages of his little book.

We arrive at the *Punta Sabbioni* ticket office and Antonio kindly goes to the kiosk and books our tickets, before giving us advice on where to visit and where not to eat. We board the waterbus and as Antonio waves us off we head for Venice. "*Vado a Venezia,*" I say to my confused-looking travelling companions.

As the waterbus nears our departure point the wasps inside the jar in my head are waking up again. I had hoped they'd have stayed silent today. When we disembark I wave them aside and wander over with a group of other tourists competing for the first photo of the Bridge of Sighs.

"It's smaller than I thought it would be," Mac says as he holds up his phone to take a photograph.

I can see Len looking at me, he looks worried. "Are you all right love," he asks as he opens the compact umbrella he's brought with him, "Here, take this and shade yourself." I don't want to be fussed over but have to admit the shade does give me some respite from the sun, however, it doesn't hinder the jar wasps that were now beginning to swarm. Of all days, why today? I begin to find it difficult to concentrate as we walk in the same direction as everyone else along the quayside.

St. Mark's Square with its pigeons and hordes of visitors is exactly as I had imagined. We stop and sit on some steps for a while and just absorb all that is around us. Saffron has fun running at pigeons that take flight all around her as Mac and Lisa stand watching her, their faces full of pride and love. I rub at my temples hoping to ease the pain just as Lisa's pocket camera is pointed in my direction. "Having fun?" she asks. I nod my head and turn away from her, hiding my face from the intrusive lens. I sneakily remove two painkillers from my purse and surreptitiously swallow them before we head off through the narrow streets towards the Grand Canal. The shaded streets give us a break from the sun and I am in awe of everything I see. Like a sponge I soak everything up; balconies swathed in geraniums, washing hanging lazily in the still air and the stall holders selling fruit and veg of every colour imaginable with locals going about their daily business.

"Not far now," Mac says, looking at the map, "just around this next corner." We emerge from a side street and with my back towards the Hotel Rialto with its pink-rendered walls I begin to feel like I'm standing inside one of those optical illusions where black and white squares seem to sway from side to side.

I open my eyes and five faces look down at me with concern, four of them I know but who is the moustachioed man in an apron? "You fainted," Lisa says as I'm helped into a chair.

"You went down as fast as a dog on a dropped chop," says Mac as the strange face disappears and reappears with a glass of water and hands it to me.

"Drink. Tired, you look," the man says, pronouncing tired as ty-red.

"How are you feeling love?" asks Len, the concern showing on his face.

"Like a right twerp."

"I should never have booked this damned holiday. I'll never forgive myself if—" he says, not completing the sentence.

"If what?" I say as the stranger returns with a tray containing four iced coffees and a bowl of ice cream for Saffron. "I'm not ready to peg it just yet, I just got hot and fainted."

"Just as long as that's all it is." The concern remaining in place on his face tells me he knows I'm holding something back from him.

From as far back as I can remember I've wanted to stand where I'd fallen. I've dreamed of the Italian sun dancing on the water as it was displaced by the Gondoliers and the scent of pelargoniums in the air as I drink in the sight of the Rialto Bridge. And now it is ruined. What was supposed to be special is tainted, time to chalk up another victory to cancer.

I watch as Saffron shovels the ice cream into her vanilla smothered mouth and realise the wasps are once again asleep. "Is *Signora* feeling better?" our moustachioed friend says as he collects the glasses. I nod my response as Mac offers him a twenty euro note that is politely brushed away, "*Gratis*," he says and places a beautifully wrapped chocolate in front of Saffron while looking at Lisa and saying, "It is okay, yes?"

She smiles and nods her head and before she can speak Mac flicks through his book and says loudly, "*Muchas gracias*."

"*Grazie*," the bar owner says and we all look at Mac.

"What?"

"*Muchas gracias*," Lisa says, then laughing. "*Muchas* bloody *gracias*, that's not Italian." She snatches the book from him and looks at the cover. "This is a Spanish phrase book, you daft cabbage."

"They didn't have an Italian one in the paper shop and the bloke behind the counter told me they were similar languages, so I thought there'd be some sort of crossover." Even Saffron looks at him questioning his logic, the only person not looking at Mac is Len, his eyes are fixed on me.

~ 25 ~

Monday, 13 September
Mac sounds his horn as he pulls away from the kerb and I wave as Len, with our suitcases at his feet inserts his key into the front door lock. "I'm ready for a proper cup of tea," he says elbowing the door open and pushing the small pile of mail lying behind it further up the hall then picks up the cases and steps inside.

"Put them in the kitchen by the washing machine," I say. "I might as well put a wash on when we've had a cuppa."

"I'll put the kettle on," he says disappearing into the middle room and I hang up my coat before scooping up the pile of envelopes and garish flyers advertising takeaway food and follow him.

Despite it being just after lunchtime the room is in darkness, I drop the mail onto my chair before opening the curtains to let the afternoon sunlight in. Turning away from the window I stand and look at my picture hanging above the dining table, still a bit wonky no matter how many times I straighten it. The Rialto Bridge is now just a holiday memory.

"Here you go," Len says carrying in two steaming mugs of tea, I take them from him and put them down on the side tables positioned beside both of our chairs and watch him as he removes his shoes without untying the laces. Normally I'd scold him for using his toe to heel it away from his foot but today I let it go. He plonks himself down into his chair and picking up his drink nods towards the mail. "Bills no doubt."

"And junk."

"Leave it until later, enjoy your tea for now."

"I'll just sort the junk from the mail and then it can wait until tomorrow." I pull flyers for the free removal of kitchen appliances and a special offer for organic veg boxes from the bona fide mail. "There's a handwritten letter here," I say turning the pale-yellow envelope over in my hands to see if there is any indication of the sender on the reverse. "Feels like a card. Wonder who it's from?"

"Well, you won't know if you don't open it." I slide my finger beneath the sealed flap to open the envelope and remove a card with a picture of flowers on the front. I take a sip of tea and open it. As I read the text I inhale sharply and the tea catches in my throat causing me to cough. I remove my glasses and wipe my mouth, but still the coughing continues.

"You okay, you've gone a funny colour?" Len says, then he springs to his feet gets behind me and starts banging on my back. "Come on, breathe you daft mare," he says, and another whack from his fist dislodges the trapped liquid and my lungs inflate. "There," he says walking back to his chair. "You went the same shade of red as Doulton's flambé ware then."

"Thanks," I reply feebly.

"It was no bother love. You're back to your usual pasty self now."

In the commotion, I've dropped the card, and as I bend to pick it up my temples buzz, a warning that my coughing fit will have no doubt triggered another headache. I look at the front of the card once again and this time I notice that the flowers are bluebells. Of course, they are, what else could they be? I shush my inner voice as I open it and look inside once more. The handwriting is wide and leans to the left with big loops and is obviously written by someone other than the person who has signed it at the bottom in a tight rigid text.

"So," Len says, "who's it from?"

"Gareth." I look at him and start to shake. He puts his cup down leans forward and takes my hand. "Kate has passed away."

"I'm sorry," he says and reaching over with his free hand he pulls a tissue from the box beside my cup of tea. "Here." I take the tissue but no tears come.

"She died the day that we went to see that damned bridge." I stand up and hand the card to Len before walking into the kitchen to begin sorting out the holiday washing.

***

"Have you had your pills this morning?" Lisa says as she bends me forward and tries to plump up my pillows. "I'll make you an appointment to see the doctor later."

"I'll be all right," I say, "I'm much better today."

"That's as may be, but you're staying in bed again today."

"I can't. There's washing needs hanging on the line, it's been in the washing machine two days now, it'll start to smell."

Lisa hands me the previous evening's local paper and after picking up my breakfast tray says, "Stop fretting. The washing's already done."

The news of Kate's passing has affected me more than I expected. It's so sudden and there is so much I wanted to tell her about my holiday; I know she'd love to hear about it and now she never will.

I had called Gareth the evening we returned and he told me that Kate had had a funeral plan in place, this means that they have managed to get an early date for her service and he'd very much like it if I could come. "Of course I'll come." Then he started weeping I listened and passed on a few platitudes before I hung up. The days since the holiday have been dreary.

I'm just finishing a news report about vandals painting giant phalluses on the walls of the library in Kidsgrove, when I hear Lisa's voice. I assume she's on the telephone, but as her voice is muted by the floor dividing my bedroom and the middle room below I can't make out what is being said. I begin to read a piece about a teenager from Berryhill who is due to travel to China to teach English as a second language when I hear Lisa coming up the stairs.

"It's all sorted," she says popping her head around the door frame, "Dr Banerjee can see you on Friday afternoon at—"

"No," I screech, "Not Friday."

"It's the only day he has free."

"But Friday is Kate's funeral."

"I'm sorry Mum, but you need to think about your health. We can always call in after and drop off some flowers if you like." I pull the covers back swing my feet out of the bed and slide them into my waiting slippers before I pull on my dressing gown. "Where are you going?" Lisa asks, shaking her head. I push past her and don't speak until I'm out on the landing and starting down the stairs.

"I have washing to hang out, and I need to call Dr Banerjee."

"Mum, see sense, please." I stop but don't turn around, I stare ahead and as calmly as I can I tell Lisa that I'm going to the funeral whether she likes it or not, and if she doesn't like it she can put her coat on and go home.

I'm pegging out Len's holiday shorts when I hear Lisa finishing off another telephone call. "Dr Banerjee says he can move your appointment to Friday morning."

"Thank you," I say watching as she takes her keys out of her coat pocket and after shaking out one of my blouses, I peg it onto the clothesline as I hear the front door close.

***

I wonder if the orange chairs outside Dr Banerjee's office have been put there to brighten up the waiting room, if so they're failing miserably. The room is as drab as a sparrow's underbelly and the buzzing from the overhead strip lights isn't helping with my headache. "Hello Beryl," Victoria says popping her head through the door, "I heard you were coming in today. Did you have a nice holiday?"

"Yes thanks, it was lovely, we went to—"

"Sorry, I'd love to hear about it but I'm not smelling so good at the moment." She points at a dark stain down her uniform. "One of the patients has just tipped the contents of his commode down my leg."

Dr Banerjee opens his door and gives me a half smile as he glances across at Victoria. "Should you be here?" he says.

"Yes, I have an appointment."

"He means me," Victoria says, rolling her eyes as her mouth forms an O and she giggles behind her hand to indicate she has been put in her place. I giggle too and Dr Banerjee looks from me to Victoria and back trying to decipher the reason for our mirth. "When you're ready Mrs Bickerstaff." I rise and begin to follow him into his office as Victoria blows me a kiss before disappearing behind the door again.

"So how have you been?"

"I've been better," I say answering his question. "I'm sorry Lisa called your secretary, I did try to tell her that the phone number was for emergencies only and any problems should be directed to my GP."

"Your daughter thought this was urgent. She said you've been having headaches."

"Yes, terrible ones lately," I tell him. I'm describing them as wasps trapped in a jar and say, "They're real humdingers."

"And have you had any blurred vision or forgetfulness?" I bite my tongue as I really want to lift the mood and say, I've forgotten, instead, I just nod, then add, "Nothing too serious, just losing my track while chatting or forgetting why I've gone into a room."

"And you've recently been on holiday I gather."

"Yes, we went to Italy, Venice actually."

"Your daughter told me you had an incident."

"My fault," I say trying to keep the anger I'm feeling out of my voice. How could she? I mean why tell him that, it has nothing to do with… I rein in my angry inner voice and make a mental note to have words with Lisa later. "I let the sun get the better of me."

"I did tell you at our last meeting that you need to take it easy, you're not a young woman anymore Mrs Bickerstaff, and your condition dictates your capabilities."

"Yes Sir…" he looks up at me through his eyebrows. "Sorry … Dr Banerjee."

"I'll write you a prescription for some stronger pain killers, you can collect them from the hospital pharmacy before you leave and if you have any more problems don't hesitate to contact your GP." He goes back to adding more notes to my file and I sit watching him for a while. After realising I'm still sitting in front of him, he looks up from his desk and says, "Is there anything else, Mrs Bickerstaff?"

"Just this." I reach inside my shopping bag withdraw a flat parcel wrapped in tissue paper and hand it to him. I watch as he unwraps the framed print. "It's the Rialto Bridge. I thought it might brighten up your office." I rise and as I'm leaving the room I hear, "Thank you Mrs…" he glances at the picture and then says, "Beryl."

***

"How did it go?" Len says as he lowers himself into his chair.

"The funeral or the hospital?"

"Both."

"The funeral was lovely. Kate had some lovely flowers. The church was full, so many people came to pay their respects and Gareth made a point of introducing me to his parents as one of Kate's best friends." Len looks up as I pause remembering the afternoon. He waits, never dropping his gaze as he watches the memories turn the corners of my lips up, then down, then up again as I smile. "They played one of Kate's favourite songs." Len's head tilts to the side. "The Spice Girls. 'Spice Up Your Life.'" His head rights itself. "I think it was to show how bubbly and fun-loving she was. A sort of celebration of her life. Gareth said she'd picked it herself."

"Perhaps she was saying don't waste a minute of your life, enjoy it every day?"

"Do you think so?"

"That's what I'd think if someone told me to spice up my life. And what did the hospital have to say?"

"The usual. Dr Banerjee's given me some stronger pills for the headaches. Enough about me, how was your day?"

"Same as usual, apart from Arthur popped in today."

"How's he doing?"

"In a wheelchair, but he's looking well. Says his new kneecap is smashing."

"That's nice. It's lamb chops for tea." I rise and go into the kitchen to start preparing our evening meal.

"Beryl love, where's the bridge picture gone?"

"I moved it," I reply, "I fancied a change."

~ 24 ~

Tuesday, 21 September
The primary school has an odd odour of Mr Sheen and gravy as we all trundle into the main hall and take a seat. Grown-ups are sitting on chairs designed for small children and the walls around us are covered in childish artwork and prints of paint-covered hands with a name written below in pencil. I'm staring at a splayed handprint in purple with a remarkably short middle finger. The name Rosie is written below it and I'm wondering if Rosie is the victim of a knife related middle finger accident or if she didn't cover her hand with paint effectively.

"They only had coffee," Lisa says lowering herself into one of the dwarfish chairs.

"Saffron seems happy here." I look up and see her with two other girls rifling through a box of what looks like old clothes. I take the cup of brown liquid I'm offered as the door opens and a short man, quite rotund with thin legs resembling a pickled onion on cocktail sticks walks in, followed by a much younger man with a feminine gait.

"Good evening everyone," the latter says, his voice as feminine as his walk. "Kenneth would like to say a few words before we get underway."

Thanks, Ashley." Kenneth says.

"I wonder if he knows our Victor," Lisa whispers.

"I don't think he knows every gay person in Stoke on Trent." I say, "It's not like they have special membership cards."

"Don't play with the costumes girls," Kenneth says, postponing Lisa's response. "Could the mothers stop their children messing with the company's property?"

"Sorry," three mothers say in unison, one of them being Lisa. The children are retrieved and Kenneth resumes his speech.

"Welcome everyone on behalf of P.P.P."

"Potteries Pantomime Players," Ashley interjects.

"Or as we affectionately call it, Three P's." Kenneth's voice has taken on an edge of irritation. "As some of you know, this year we will be staging Cinderella and need quite a large juvenile cast. However, I cannot guarantee that you all will be successful, at Three P's, we have exacting standards and only take the best singers and dancers for our shows." Lisa looks across at me, her eyes rolling like a fruit machine as Kenneth continues. "Well, you wouldn't enter a donkey in the Cheltenham Gold Cup, would you?" Ashley laughs on cue.

"It's only a bloody amateur pantomime," Lisa says to the woman sitting beside her and this time it's Ashley who shushes her.

"Before we start, I'd like to thank the school for allowing us to use their space this evening. So if the children could remove their outdoor shoes…" he checks his wristwatch "…we'll get underway in a few minutes." Kenneth picks up two folders from the table waddles over to a table at the end of the room and lowers himself into an adult-sized chair that has been reserved for his ample bottom.

I've just helped Saffron out of her shoes and frown at the hole in her sock as the door opens and in walks Elkie; she's now sporting a green streak through her fringe. Spotting us she waves and then walks over towards Kenneth and I see him pointing at his watch, his face beginning to redden. Ashley's nostrils flare and his lip curls as he looks at the CD that Elkie has handed to him.

"Okay my lovelies, if you can find a space we'll have a little warm up." I watch as the children assemble and following Elkie's instructions they twist, stretch, and spin to music. After she's happy that they are sufficiently warmed up she plays them a piece of music. "Okay boys and girls, I'm going to teach you all a little bit of a dance. It's called a gavotte and will be in the show during the palace ballroom scene."

Classical music plays from the CD player operated by Ashley and I watch as the children are gavotting – is that even a word? – which to me looks suspiciously like a lot of skipping from foot to foot with the occasional spin around. The CD player stops and Elkie and Kenneth give the children a round of applause. I notice Ashley is too busy writing in a notepad to join in and Kenneth informs us there'll be a five-minute break and during that time could the parents retrieve a numbered ticket from Ashley.

"Bloody forty-two." A woman in a cerise blouse says, holding the green raffle ticket under my nose. "I'll never get back in time for the second part of that new ITV police drama."

"Is it the one set in Barnsley?"

"Yes, that's the one, with the policewoman who's an ex-glamour model who's trying to hide her past from her partner, who's a hard-nosed businessman from Huddersfield, with a knitting addiction and an illegitimate daughter who breeds French bulldogs on the Isle of Skye."

"Is it any good?" Lisa asks leaning in.

"Oh yeah, dead true to life."

I turn away to hide my smile as Kenneth claps to indicate that the auditions are ready to recommence. A small girl with ticket number one gets up and walks over to the table where Kenneth is sitting. She hands him a silver disc and there's a brief exchange of words. I assume she's telling him her name, age and the song she's chosen to sing. We all watch as she walks to the cross on the floor made from electrical tape, Ashley puts her CD into the player and everywhere falls silent. Twenty seconds later an uninspiring round of applause fills the room and the small girl with tears streaming down her face tells Kenneth she's never forgotten the words before. Next up is Bentley-Brock, one of five, Broom brothers all with double-barrelled names and all beginning with the letter B. I remember telling Vera that it'll be a nightmare in later years to come if they're all still in the same house, who'll know which letter belongs to which brother if they all arrive addressed to a Mr B.B. Broom. His music begins and confidently he attacks the opening number from Miss Saigon, it's going very well until he's needed to sing a high note and his face goes the colour of cherry jam and he breaks wind loudly. Several more children sing and feeling my bottom and my brain going numb, I get up and leave the room, just before a dumpy girl in a short skirt that makes her look like a mini skip with a pelmet takes up her position.

"I'm outside pacing the corridor looking at pictures made from cut-up bits of fabric and broken spaghetti when I spot a copy of a free newspaper on a table. It's not one we get delivered so I pick it up and flick through until I spot an advert that catches my attention, it reads, background artistes wanted in Stoke on Trent, no experience necessary. I look around before tearing out the advert and stuffing it into my pocket. Next door I can hear our Saffron beginning to sing the Destiny's Child hit, 'Survivor', she's singing notes that possibly only cats can appreciate when all goes quiet and the door opens and Lisa ushers her daughter through into the reception area.

"How did it go?"
"What does he know?"
"Who?"
"Him."
"Kenneth?" I ask hoping to elicit more than a one-word response.

"He said Saffron was pitchy. It sounded okay to me. What did you think?"

"Sorry," I begin, diplomacy taking over, "I was in here. I needed a break so I missed it. I bet you were fabulous," I say to my granddaughter.

"Well, I think she was the best so far, and I'll tell you what, it doesn't matter if he begs, she's not doing his sodding show. Three P's can bloody well P off." I nod in agreement and Saffron just shrugs as her mother pulls her jacket around her shoulders before asking her, "What did you think darling?"

"It was all right but I don't want to be in the pantomime."

"Why ever not?" I ask, "It would be fun."

"Did you see that silly dance? I don't want to learn how to garrotte."

I guess you can't say fairer than that.

"So how was it?" Len asks as we arrive home. Lisa just sighs loudly, I shrug and Saffron tells him, "It was stupid dancing and a box of costumes that smelled of hamsters."

"I'm guessing we won't be needing to buy tickets to see the show then?"

"Thankfully, no," I say.

"I don't think my daughter is destined to be a diva."

I drop into my chair beside the fire and say, "I'm not so sure." Then notice she's not wearing the shoes she arrived in.

~ 23 ~

Wednesday, 29 September
"We're bloody well what?" Len asks as we lie in bed. "Has someone had your lid off and dumped a load of manure inside your head?"

"Come on, it'll be fun and we'll get paid."

"What do we know about the TV business?"

"Nothing, but the advert said no experience needed."

"What do we have to do?"

"Just mill around in the background, I guess." I see his forehead crease and I know he's thinking it over. He turns to me and says, "I guess this is another of those, living life to the full, first-time things for your diary that you need to get off your chest." I nod as his forehead furrows again. "Okay but don't say anything to anyone about this and if you start to feel ill we pack it in and come straight home." I smile as he rolls over to turn off the light, "So what time do we have to leave in the morning?"

"Around five."

"Bloody hell woman, you're certifiable."

***

We arrived at the semi-derelict potbank where filming was to take place and we were met by a girl in a yellow high-viz jacket. She checked our names off the list and pointed to a portacabin set up in the far corner of the yard. "Wardrobe's over there and behind it is the supporting artists waiting area." I thanked her, but it was ignored as she looked down at her list ready to repeat the tick off and point process with the next person in the queue. Len dragged himself behind me as we made our way to the portacabin, it's obvious he felt uncomfortable and I was beginning to think maybe I should have come on my own.

He hadn't been happy getting up so early and grumbled as he took the dog out for an earlier than usual lamp post leg-cocking session. I'd been grilling bacon when the backdoor opened and he returned shaking his head. "What's wrong?" I asked as I held up an egg for him to see while he unclipped the dog's lead.

"Bloody stupid dog," he replied as he shook his head indicating he didn't want the egg. "I was talking to Phillip from Parsonage Street who works nights, he was on his way home and this bloody stupid hound only went and peed up his leg."

"Well, he is rather tall, perhaps the dog thought he was a lamp post."

"And, you'll need a cardigan today as well as a coat, it's quite nippy out there," he said hanging the lead on the back of the kitchen door.

"Okay, you eat your bacon sandwich and I'll root one out."

"I'm not hungry, my stomach isn't used to being awake at this ungodly hour."

"Tell you what, I'll wrap it in foil and you can have it for your lunch."

***

We reach the wardrobe department just as a face we've seen many times before on TV emerges from the cabin, "I'm sorry," she says bumping into Len.

"That's all right love, no harm done." Suddenly my husband's lethargy dissolves and his eyes, not to mention his speech brighten as she flashes him a smile before she walks away. "That was…"

"Yes, I know who it was," I say.

"Is she the one as plays the ex-stripper?"

"Glamour model," I correct him.

"Is there a difference?"

"Background?" a woman says popping her head out of the cabin door. I nod and she steps outside. "I guess you'll be in the loading bay scene," she says to Len, "But you can't wear that cap, the checked pattern will play havoc with the cameras. Are you the woman in the shop or the dead librarian?" She's now looking at me.

"I'm not sure, I only answered the advert last week," I tell her as she nips back inside the cabin, re-emerging with a clipboard, "I think you'll be better suited to the woman in the shop, in fact…" she pauses and scans the pages clipped to the board "…you get a line."

"A line?"

"Yes, nothing too taxing, but it's supposed to be summer so you won't be able to wear that cardigan, in fact, step inside and Sylvia will sort you out with something suitable from the racks."

"Shall I wait here?" Len asks.

"Sorry, but no. You'll cause a bottleneck, there's a bus behind here and you can take a seat on board until you're called." I see a flash of concern cross Len's face and I give him one of my, practiced, I'll be all right smiles, that over the past weeks, I've become accomplished at. Sylvia turns out to be of a similar age to me and has a worn look about her that I assume comes from too many early mornings. She looks me up and down and says, "Size fourteen, I'm guessing."

"Sixteen," I reply but she shakes her head and points to a curtain that she wants me to go behind and undress. I'm behind the curtain in my bra and pants when a hand appears with a skirt and blouse on a coat hanger. "Give these a try love," Sylvia says. Taking them, I step into the floral skirt and fasten the button before trying on the fitted blouse. "How do they fit?"

"The skirt's a bit big, maybe I do need a fourteen after all."

"It is a fourteen," Sylvia says from her side of the curtain.

"I'm afraid I can't wear a fitted blouse like this." The curtain is pulled aside and Sylvia stands looking at me, the skirt is hanging off my hips and the left side of my chest looks deflated. "I'm sorry," I say, "I forgot to put my falsie on."

"I see," Sylvia says as she moves back to look for something else on the rail behind her. "I lost it to cancer. I'm sorry, it was so early this morning that I forgot to pick it up off the bedside. I've never forgotten it before." I'm waffling and I don't know why I feel the need to say this to a woman I've only just met. It baffles me, but the words just tumble out.

"No need to explain," Sylvia says hanging a new blouse on the hook fixed to the wall on my side of the curtain. "Here," she says taking my hand and pressing it against her bosom, "I'm wearing mine this morning." Beneath the fabric of her jersey I feel the familiarity of a prosthetic, Sylvia smiles and says, "I'd lend you mine love, but I'm a lot smaller than you so you'd still look a bit lopsided if we go with a fitted top. Now turn around and let me pin the back of that skirt for you, and when we're done here pop next door and ask for Karon."

So finally pinned into the skirt that makes me aware of the weight I've been steadily losing, yet choosing to ignore, and now wearing a loose-fitting summer blouse I go next door to meet Karon, a girl with large brown eyes and a kind smile. "You need to sign this form," she says after informing me that I'd get more than the daily fee of fifty-five pounds, "You're not needed until after lunch so you can relax on the S.A. bus."

"S.A.?"

"Supporting artists."

"Oh, I thought I was here to be an extra."

"We don't call background artists, extras anymore." She pulls a green sheet of paper from a folder and hands it to me. "You're in the shop scene and here's the line that you need to memorise." I take the sheet from her and as I'm leaving she adds, "You'll be called for a rehearsal just before the director goes for a take."

The bus behind the portacabin was an old beaten coach, the kind that has tables between facing seats. As I clamber aboard it's already three-quarters full, and at first, I can't spot Len until he stands up and gives me a wave. "You can't be sitting all day in that get-up," he says looking at the clothes I've been given. "You'll freeze to death. I'll go and have a word."

"No," I say, "I'll be all right, I can put my cardigan on top for now."

"What's that?" he indicates towards the green sheet of paper with a nod of his head.

"It's the line I've got to say. Oh and by the way, they'll pay me twelve pounds extra for saying it."

"Bloody good job, it'll cover the cost of the medicines you'll need after catching hypothermia. So what is it?"

"What's what?"

"You're line?" I look at the portion of script I'm holding in my hand and spot a section which reads:

INT. DAY

D.I. COOMBES STANDS BEHIND A CUSTOMER BEING SERVED AT THE COUNTER. A WOMAN PUSHES BETWEEN THE TWO CUSTOMERS AND SPEAKS TO MR BANASZEWSKI.
Józef, is this tuna ethically sourced?
CUT TO:

"It says I have to say, Józef, is this tuna ethically sourced?" Len looks at me confused "What kind of a bloody line is that?"

"I guess it's to add a touch of realism."

"If you ask me it's—" Before he has a chance to complete his sentence Karon climbs aboard and informs everyone in the loading bay scene that they are required on set. "Look after my cap," Len says before filing off the coach with the other men who are needed.

The coach empties, leaving just myself and four other people. Two young men are sitting at the back of the coach, one asleep and the other reading a book, they are dressed in white boiler suits, similar to those worn by forensic officers visiting a crime scene. A few seats down sits a plain-looking woman sucking a KitKat finger as she looks out of the window and behind her is another woman with a great mane of red hair, not naturally red but that odd cherry colour that comes out of a bottle. She smiles in my direction gets up and walks over towards me, "I'm not needed until just before lunch," she says sitting opposite, "I'm a featured artist you see. What scene are you in?" Before I can answer she's telling me, "I'm playing the librarian." I manage to squeeze out a couple of words to indicate that I'm happy for her when she thrusts a hand with a ring on every finger including the thumb towards me. "My name's Crimson, by the way, I'm a professional actress."

"I'm Beryl. Retired pottery worker and occasional babysitter." Crimson laughs loudly. A little too loudly, causing the sleeping man at the rear to wake with an expletive and the woman with the KitKat to tut loudly.

"That must be quite difficult?" I say indicating towards the KitKat sucking woman, Crimson looks puzzled. "Tutting whilst sucking a KitKat."

"It probably is."

"It'll be all right while the chocolate is covering it but once it's gone you're just left with wafer, must be like sucking sandpaper."

"What did you say?" KitKat woman asks.

"She said, she likes KitKats, Wendy," says Crimson. The woman looks about to speak again when Karon appears on the top step of the coach and calls my name. I ask to be excused and walk to the front of the coach.

"We just need a Polaroid for continuity," she says and I stand still as the camera flashes.

"Do you need me too Karon?"

"No, you're all right for now Barbara." I look back to where I was sitting and see Crimson's shoulders drop as Karon thanks me and steps down.

"Why did she call you Barbara?" I ask sitting back down.

"Crimson is my stage name," she says flicking a thick red curl over her shoulder, "Crimson O'Hare, it's a play on words a sort of homage to my favourite actress."

"Really?"

"Yes, can you guess who it is?"

"I'm not very good at guessing games."

"Here's another clue then, she lived on an American plantation known as, Tara."

"Sodding, Scarlet O'Hara." Wendy, having now devoured her KitKat shouts from across the aisle. Crimson tosses her an irritated look and turns back towards me, "How long have you worked in TV Beryl?"

"This is my first time, and to be honest I thought it would be much more exciting."

"There's lots of just sitting around waiting." Another raft of curls is tossed backwards with a flick of her head. "Still the catering's good on these Yorkshire TV shoots."

"Do we get fed?" I say thinking about Len's uneaten bacon sandwich in my handbag.

"We do. It's roast chicken or sausage hotpot today unless you want the vegan option."

"What's the vegan option?" I ask.

"Cardboard," Wendy calls out, followed by a grunt masquerading as laughter.

The morning passes with me listening to Crimson rattling on about her previous dramatic escapades, she tells me she'd once worked with David Jason, "Such a lovely man, but hates seeing himself on the screen." How she wasn't too keen on working alongside Patricia Routledge and that Jim Broadbent was an absolute blast, "He told so many jokes on set one day I nearly wet myself." As she launches into another tale with, "Oh, and I must tell you about the time I played a sex addict in a small-scale theatre tour." I'm wondering, if I strangle her with her own hair, will the judge show leniency because of my illness?

The men from the loading bay scene return and Crimson is called away by Karon. "Len, can I borrow you too," Karon adds after looking at her clipboard.

As my husband follows them across the yard, the coach fills with conversation and I listen as the people around me talk about the filming, what they have decided to have for lunch and which famous actors have been on the set that morning. Twenty minutes later Len returns and lunch is called.

We're enjoying our meal. I'm having the chicken with some vegetables and Len has the hotpot, to which he adds his bacon sandwich alongside a plate of chips. "This is a bonus," he says, "I didn't expect to get fed. Do you think they'll have some brown sauce?"

"I'll ask them."

"No, I'll go, you stay sitting down." I tell him I need to stretch my legs after a couple of hours of sitting opposite Crimson with her non-stop vocal abilities.

"Honest Len, she hardly stops to draw breath, I'm sure she has a pneumatic voice box."

During lunch, my husband tells me that this episode is about a bare-knuckle fighter who has travelled down from Barnsley to Stoke to take part in an illegal fight in a disused factory. He explains how all the men had to cheer as the two actors dressed in shorts, pretended to knock seven bells out of each other as they froze their nuts off in the old factory loading bay. Just before lunch is over, Karon approaches our table to tell me the crew is ready for me. "You'll be shooting the scene over the road in the mini market."

"It won't be too cold will it?" Len asks, "Only she's…" I give him a withering look and he stops speaking,

"She'll be fine, it'll be very warm in there under the lights. Don't worry, we'll look after her." I hand Len a tissue, he looks at me his eyes questioning. "You've got brown sauce on your chin," I say and get up and follow Karon.

In the shop, I'm introduced to Mike, the director and I'm told where to stand. Which way to look and how high to hold up the tin of tuna. Smiling, he tells me they'll go for a quick rehearsal. "Cripes, there's so much to remember," I say and his assistant leans in and tells me to stay calm and act natural, "You'll be fine, Mrs Bickerstaff."

"I hope so." Someone calls action and remembering my days with the local amateur dramatic society I project my line towards the camera, and almost instantly someone shouts, "Cut!"

"Beryl, can you bring the volume down please," the assistant asks.

"Sorry, I thought you had to project?"

"Not for TV, just speak at your normal volume."

My scene is completed in three takes, the first one I messed up getting the Polish shopkeeper's name wrong, the second is cut short due to an errant belch that no one owned up to and the third goes without a hitch. "See," the assistant director says as he helps me back on with my cardigan, "I told you it was easy. Once you've taken your costume back to wardrobe you can sign out and go home. It's been a pleasure meeting you."

"What about my husband, Len?"

"Karon will know if he's finished with. But as we've only got a couple of location shots to take, I guess they'll be releasing everyone pretty soon."

I thank them all for their time, the actress playing the ex-glamour model turned detective gives me a genuine smile and after changing back into my clothes I see the queue of people signing out, so go back to the coach to find Len. Climbing up the steps I spot him sitting opposite Crimson, a glazed expression covering his face as her mouth opens and closes, spewing forth her tales. "There you are," I say, "We can sign out now. Have you been all right?"

"He's been fine with me, I've kept him company, haven't I Les?"

"Len," he says standing up and putting his cap back on before looking her straight in the eye and saying, "By the way, Scarlet O'Hara isn't an actress, she's a bloody character in a book. Cheerio, Barbara."

Sitting side by side on the bus home he turns to me and asks if I've had a good time, I nod and tell him I have, but wouldn't want to do it every day as it was boring sitting around. "I think I'll leave the acting lark to the likes of Crimson O'Hare," I say.

"Acting," he laughs, "all she had to do was lie on the floor and pretend to be dead."

~ 22 ~

Friday, 8 October
Now don't get me wrong, I respect Doreen. She's been a good friend for years and despite her snobbish attitude I do love her dearly, but as she ages she becomes less tolerant and is in danger of turning into one of those grumpy old women. You know the kind that sit in the bus station sucking in air loudly as young people pass by. Those moaning matriarchs with an obvious loathing of the younger generation with their body modifications, Facebook and Harry Potter books.

To be frank, I'm not keen on those people who believe just because they've managed to survive sixty or more years that the world owes them something. That they are automatically entitled to respect. I can always remember my father saying to me, "Respect is earned not given away like cheap gifts." In fact I quite like young people, I like to hear their plans and the abandon they have, unaware of what lies ahead and where life will carry them. Don't get me wrong, I don't like all young people, particularly those on reality TV shows, who seem to be all cleavage and expletives with a hunger for rewards they don't have to work for.

The reason I bring this subject up is because yesterday while sitting in the bus station café with a frothy coffee, I watched as a young couple sharing a pair of headphones moved their heads in time with the music they listened to. "Just look at the state of him," Doreen said, her eyebrows as usual rising like chopsticks in an invisible hand, "Why would you want to do that to yourself?"

"In our day it was only sailors and prisoners that had tattoos," Mavis chipped in, her friendship with Doreen now back on track following the handbag in the charity shop incident.

"I quite like the colours," I said as I looked across at the woman behind the counter wondering if we'd be getting a complimentary custard cream today.

"There's only one thing worse than a man with tattoos." Doreen used a napkin to remove the sugar left behind from her jam doughnut – most people would just lick their lips.

"What's that?" Vera asked sucking the filling out her cream horn from the bitten-off end.

"Women with tattoos. It's common."

"Elkie's got one," Mavis said.

"Exactly, need I say more?" Doreen was on form this day.

"That's unfair," I managed to say before Mavis butted in telling us all it was of a sunflower positioned in the small of her back and known as a tramp stamp. Vera coughed and sprayed the table with half-chewed pastry, soliciting a thump between the shoulder blades from Mavis to prevent her choking, and demonstrating her annoyance Doreen closed her eyes slowly, "I've only just had this mackintosh dry cleaned she said as she wiped cream from the lapel.

"Do you think it hurts?" I asked.

"What," said Vera now recovered, "having your mac dry cleaned?"

"No, you daft dandelion. Getting a tattoo?"

"Why don't you ask him?" The young couple began singing off key, the way people wearing headphones do. "I couldn't possibly disturb them, they're busy."

"Probably listening to American rap music that objectifies women and glamourises crime."

"Doreen, you've not been the same since stumbling across MTV whilst searching for Gardeners' World," I said.

"Well if it's not that it'll be some crude and banal comedy no doubt." Doreen's eyebrows for once stayed still and looked like two horizontal strips of liquorice.

My chair scraped across the worn linoleum as I rose and walked over to where the two young people were sitting. "Excuse me," I said, rather meekly, and two eyes ringed with black kohl looked up at me through a fringe of orange crimped hair as the young man's female companion turned her attention my way.

"Yes?" she said.

"Can I ask you a quick question?"

"Sure."

"I was talking with my friends over there." They both turned to look across at our table, and Doreen looked away, feigning a new interest in her Mackintosh belt buckle and Vera gave them a wave. The young man raised his hand briefly and then looked back towards me. "We were … well actually it was me… I was wondering…"

"Yes," he asked.

"Does it hurt getting tattooed?"

"Not really, it can be a bit painful where the skin is close to the bone."

"Are you thinking of having one?" his friend asked, her accent indicating she wasn't local.

"Oh no," I said rather too loudly and quickly. Worried I may have sounded judgemental I added. "Not that there's anything wrong with them, I'm just a bit too old for one."

"You're never too old," the girl said. "But they say it hurts getting your bum cheeks done." I nodded, noting what she said as she proceeded to slide her jacket and the t-shirt beneath it off her shoulder. "I had this done a few months back." I looked at the image of a man with an elephant head sitting on a throne etched into her skin, the design took up the whole of her upper arm with the top of the shoulder decorated with colourful flowers that arched above the crowned head. "It's Ganesh," she said.

"It's beautiful," I told her truthfully.

"Thank you," she re-adjusted her clothing tucking the tattoo away from show before saying, "Josh, show her your new one." Her friend rolled up his sleeve to reveal a ring of ivy with small red hearts dotted among the leaves encircling his lower arm, they wound around before forming a heart shape at the wrist with the Roman numerals XV: IV: MMVII.

"It's my brother's date of birth," Josh said.

"You must love him very much?" I replied and Josh's face seemed to radiate happiness, behind his eyes something moved, maybe a memory.

"We took him to visit my parents in Cumbria, last weekend," the girl said.

"It was bitterly cold and rained most of the day," said Josh.

"But he loved it all the same, especially Brougham Castle. Show the lady Josh."

"Please," I said, "call me Beryl." Josh removed his mobile phone from a jacket pocket and tapped a button. Suddenly the screen was filled with a round face with almond-shaped eyes, a narrow forehead and a button nose. The smallish mouth of the boy with Down Syndrome spread into a smile and suddenly he was gone. The camera recaptured him laughing loudly running towards the ruined archway of a castle. Josh then came into view and the two of them mimed a sword fight with the younger boy winning as Josh was beaten into submission.

I felt my throat dry as the boy jumped onto his older brother and hugging his neck tightly, he kissed him. The video stopped and I thanked them for their time, Josh shook my hand and put away his phone and rising from their table I watched as the girl held open the door for her friend and the two of them melted into the crowd outside the café.

"Well?" Vera said as I rejoined my friends at the table. "Does it hurt?"

"Not as much as imagined." I took a sip of my now cold coffee and Mavis looked across at Doreen and then back to me before speaking. "So what was the video you were watching?"

"No doubt something unsuitable?" Doreen said.

"Shall we make tracks?" I said taking my jacket from where it hung over the back of my chair and walking towards the door.

That evening Mac and Lisa called over and I was telling them about Josh and the video when Lisa said that Mac had saved some good videos on his phone from our holiday." She nudged him, an indication for him to retrieve his phone from his jeans and show us all the footage.

We were watching a clip of Len trying his best to lick the ice cream that had dripped down his arm to his elbow, the background is an ochre-coloured palazzo and our laughter is the soundtrack. "These look professional, you should do this for a living," Len said and Mac shot me a sideways glance.

The videos were then replaced by a slideshow of images taken during our trip and as I went into the kitchen to fetch some glasses for the bottle of frizzante that Lisa had brought with her Mac followed me. "Need any help?"

"Can you carry these in for me and I'll grab some crackers and cheese," I said. "The photos are very good, as Len said, they're professional looking." He lifted the glasses and was about to leave the kitchen when I said, "Remember that chat we had on the beach."

"Yes."

"Is this what you meant by doing something else?" Mac nodded placed the glasses back down on the work surface and told me how he'd wished he'd been to college and trained to be a photographer. "Why don't you do it now?"

"Money," he said, "cameras are expensive and I need to work to support Lisa and pay the mortgage. I guess it'll always just be a dream."

"Doesn't have to be, love," I said and squeezed his arm. "Doesn't have to be."

Barry Lillie

~ 21 ~

Tuesday, 12 October
For most of this week I've been experiencing headaches so the last thing I need is an argument. "You've done what?" Lisa shouts her breath hitting my face.

"I've had a tattoo."

"Mother, you're sixty-four years old."

"So?"

"So! Is that all you can say? For crying out loud, you're not a bloody teenager."

"My age is irrelevant."

"What does Dad think about you defacing yourself?"

"He wasn't happy, but he understood."

"Understood… Hah! This is stupidity … reckless stupidity." She felt the need to do that inverted comma thing with her fingers. "Women of your age don't go getting tattoos."

"Obviously they do. I decided to have it done last week after talking to some young people in the bus station café."

"Come along Mother aren't you too old to be resorting to playground peer pressure," I say nothing in response, just look at her impassively, hoping that the pinging in my head and her outburst will both cease. "Come on then show me," she says, the volume lowering. I roll up my sleeve and show her the tiny Roman numerals inked onto the underside of my wrist, V: XI.

"What does it mean?" Lisa asks.

"5. 11."

"Five, eleven what's the… Oh I see. Come on I thought you were over all that?"

"It's not something you get over," I reply.

"But it was such a long time ago."

"The passing of time is irrelevant, besides it's hardly a date that passes inconspicuously. The fifth of November."

***

The latest bout of headaches is unremitting. Not the blinding ones that are debilitating, but a strange pinging sensation that's been repeating itself with a measured throb: a malignant metronome in my temple. I'm not allowing them to hold me back and four days ago, even though the incessant pendulum of pain made its presence felt I'd walked into SkinArt, a local body piercing and tattoo emporium. I'd had a conversation with Kal, who it seemed used his entire body as a canvas.

"There's only one part of me that's not inked," he'd told me, his eyes indicating to a lower portion of his six feet plus frame, "the soles of my feet." He'd laughed and I'd sat with the numerals drawn onto my skin and waited for the pain of the tattooist's needle to spread through my wrist. "Is that all right?" Kal asked and I nodded, the pinging in my head distracting me from the vibrations over my wrist. Fifteen minutes later with cling film on my wrist I was outside clutching a small card detailing the aftercare my blue/black marking required.

***

"So why now?" Lisa says, her face still blotchy with rage.

"Come on, give it a rest," Victor adds as he turns off the television.

"I was watching that," Kirk says.

"How could you with Lisa ranting on like a witch."

"Look, somebody has to say something."

"No they don't," Victor says, his head shaking as his sister stands defiantly with her hands on her hips. "It's none of our business if mum has a tattoo, and besides it's not as if it's indiscreet."

"So what do we do when she comes home with a bone through her nose, look away as if it's not there or say it looks good?"

I decide to stand at this point, and after smoothing down my apron I turn and say, "Anyone would think that you were the parent here and not me." I walk into the kitchen and the room falls silent. I busy myself with letting the dog out into the backyard, putting the kettle on and dropping two tea bags into the pot. As the kettle boils and switches itself off I tip some biscuits onto a plate and arrange mugs, a jug of milk and the sugar bowl onto a tray. I'm pouring boiling water over the bags when I hear Lisa say, "Have you told her yet?" I look out of the kitchen window, noticing that the dog has managed to escape from the yard again and picking up the tray I enter the middle room.

"Told me what?" I say as Kirk starts pouring everyone a drink. Victor takes a leaflet from his trouser pocket and hands it to me. I open the folded piece of paper and see an advert for photographs. A smiling family look out from the paper, an image promising that a studio posed photograph would bring familial harmony. "What's this for?"

"I thought it'd be nice if we had a family portrait," Victor says. "You could maybe hang it over there." He points to the space recently vacated by the Rialto Bridge. "It'll be a visual record of three generations."

"I don't want to be staring down from the wall when I've gone."

"Has it occurred to you that maybe we'd like to have something to remember you by?" Lisa says, her voice becoming edgy again.

"Why now?"

"Because I spotted the special offer and thought it'd be a good idea," Victor says, rising and putting his arm around my shoulder, "and Saffron will love it."

"You'll need to speak with your father."

"We already have," Lisa adds. "He's okay with it."

"Do you know something, Lisa?" I say. "Just lately, you and Doreen have quite a lot in common."

Glaring at Kirk who is stifling a laugh, she grabs her coat from the chair where she's left it and stomps out of the room. "Don't slam the…" Too late, the house shakes and we all burst out laughing.

"You do know she thinks you're losing it, don't you?" Victor says.

"So not only have I got a tumour to deal with, but Lisa now thinks I'm going senile."

"I told her you'd always been mad in my opinion," Kirk says laughing.

"Possibly, Kirk," I reply with a smile. "Possibly"

***

Garry, with two r's and Mary with just one, are downstairs setting up their equipment in the front room, Kirk and Victor have pushed the furniture back to make room and Garry has remarked that the space is intimate. Code I assume for small.

Len is struggling with a purple tie and I watch him grimace as he makes another attempt at tying it. I'm sitting looking at myself in the mirror, Gloria styled my hair the day before and I'm certain I can see the skin on my head moving where the pulse of the headache beats out its rhythm. I look into my eyes; rheumy pools of emptiness where my brightness once radiated. My mouth droops to one side slightly, maybe not evident to most people but clear to me. "Who are you?" I question silently, my thoughts passing between me and the reflection. "Who is this old woman that looks at me?" There is a knock at the door and Victor pops his head around to tell us that Lisa has arrived. I tell him that I hope she's come with a better attitude this time and he reminds me that she has phoned to apologise for her outburst earlier in the week. "Ignore me, I'm in a right cow of a mood."

"Buggery bollocks," Len says as he throws the tie onto the bed.

"Do you want me to do it for you Dad?" Victor asks stepping into the room.

"Why do I have to wear a bloody tie?"

"We all thought it would be nice if we were dressed smart for the photograph. Come here and I'll tie it for you." Victor fastens Len's tie and I look down at the blouse that Lisa has chosen for me, it's a pale violet to compliment Len's tie and Victor is wearing a lilac waistcoat. Lisa has told us that the image should have a uniformed theme, something she had been told by Garry with two r's when she'd booked the photo session.

"What's Saffron's dress like?"

"She looks great, it's a soft lilac-coloured satin."

"Is Mac in a complimentary shade?"

"He's in a purple shirt," Victor says as he pulls the bottom of his father's tie through, completing the knot.

Len looks in the mirror and then says, "I bet he looks like a walking blueberry." The woman in the mirror allows herself a tight smile and I catch it before Len goes on to say, "Once we're all assembled we'll look like a human paint chart. Forty shades of puce."

Once again the woman smiles back at me, a ripple spreads out, increasing circles in my eyes like a stone dropped in a pool, the waves making way for the light that seemed to be trapped beneath the irises. "Get changed," I tell her and leave her inside the mirror.

"If we're going to have this photo done, I'm certain I don't want it to be hanging on the wall looking like we're all wearing clothes that have been tainted by a misplaced purple sock in the wash." Just then Kirk pops his head around the door frame to say he's putting the kettle on and asks if anyone wants a drink.

"How come he's not wearing purple?" Len asks.

"Because I'm not in the photograph. It's family only."

"Well, as far as I'm concerned at this moment in time you're part of this family."

"But..."

"No point arguing with him," I say and he disappears downstairs to make the tea. When we emerge, Victor in a pair of black jeans and a red and blue checked shirt, Len in his best trousers and a white shirt with a green cardigan and I'm in a blue dress with a white floral motif on the cuffs and collar, the room falls silent. "You're in the wrong colour, Nan," Saffron says.

"It didn't suit me, love," I tell her and Kirk enters with a tray of drinks. "I just thought it would be nicer if we just looked like we normally do, we can still be smart but not organised like an art installation."

"Thank goodness for that," Mac says unbuttoning his purple shirt.

"Daddy you can't have your photo took with no shirt on."

"Taken," Lisa says correcting her daughter, before smiling and asking Victor if he has anything suitable that would fit Mac.

"Nothing with sequins though," jokes Mac as Victor goes back upstairs.

The sitting is relatively trouble free apart from when the dog gets under Mary's feet, tripping her up and causing her to land face first into Kirk's lap. "I think we have enough there," Garry says after we've smiled, grinned and gurned for twenty minutes or so. Everyone disperses to the middle room and Mary helps Garry pack his equipment away. I go to fix them both a cup of tea after he's hinted saying, "Thirsty work this photography lark."

Later, as we all sit around the TV watching a couple of magicians from Bletchley fail to crack the code that they hoped would get them into the final of a talent show, I ask Mac to give me a hand in the kitchen. "What do you need me to do?" he asks.

"Here," I hand him a business card. "It's off Garry, he says to give him a call and he'll let you help out on his next job."

"That's…"

"It'll be a bit of experience and he can answer any questions you might have."

"What about Lisa?"

"What about her, does she need to know?"

"I guess not," he says and kisses me on the cheek.

~ 20 ~

Thursday, 21 October
I'm around Vera's having a cup of tea, which happens from time to time. She may be my best friend, but to be honest I never really feel comfortable in her home. She has far too many antimacassars for my liking and every available space has a trinket of some sort languishing on it and life's too short for all that dusting. But one thing I like about Vera is her ability to say what she thinks. There's never been any skirting around the issue of my longevity and today is no different. After almost losing her top denture plate by opening a pack of bourbon creams using her teeth to tear open the packet, she says as she tips them onto a plate, "Have you decided what to do with your personal belongings when you've gone?"

The house and a few thousand pounds in the bank is practically all Len and I have to leave our children, and obviously, when I've gone it'll be up to my husband to make provision for when he's gone. With regards to personal items, there's my wedding ring and my new eternity ring, some other items of jewellery and a signed photograph of Joan Collins that Len found in an antique shop while on a work outing to Rhyl.

"Are you going to give Lisa your jewellery?" Vera asks as tea drips from her dunked biscuit onto the front of her dress.

"I don't think there's much she'll like," I say. "Most of what I have is costume or broken. Besides it won't be worth much."

"It might be," Vera says, devouring the last of the biscuit.

"I doubt it."

"Elkie was telling me she took all her odd gold earrings and broken chains and sold them to that bloke in the market."

"What bloke?"

"The one that buys old gold. She said it was just sitting doing nothing in her jewellery box and when she took it to be weighed he gave her sixty notes."

"Sixty pounds for some broken chains and odd earrings?"

"That's what Elkie told me."

"I'll give it some thought," I say and with Vera's attention once more focussed on a second biscuit, she begins telling me that an intermittent problem with her tumble dryer has returned.

"Honestly, Beryl the sheets would dryer faster in a cat's fart than that bloody heap of junk."

"Why don't you buy another then?" I ask her.

"Oh, I couldn't possibly do that. It belonged to my sister and she'd only had it nine months before she passed away.

"Maybe she's haunting it?" I joke.

"Don't," Vera says. "I've wondered that myself. You see her husband didn't want me to have it as he'd still got three payments left on it."

"Why would she haunt it?" I say shaking my head slowly at the realisation that we are sitting discussing a possibly possessed tumble dryer.

"Daniel O'Donnell," Vera says dipping another biscuit into her mug.

"What's Daniel O'Donnell got to do with a haunted tumble dryer?"

"Well, as you know my sister was a lover of Irish music and she was a fanatic Daniel O'Donnell fan. She'd play his CDs as she did the weekly wash."

"There's no accounting for taste."

"I told her husband that if he let me have the dryer I'd play her favourite CD while it was working, as a sort of tribute to my sister."

"Are you serious?"

"Yes. But, to be honest, I got sick of hearing him warbling 'Danny Boy' and 'One Day at a Time' in his lilting County Donegal brogue, so one day I put on one of my André Rieu CDs and that was the first time the machine faltered."

"I hardly think you can draw a comparison to playing André Rieu and the heating element failing in a tumble dryer."

"Ah!" she says rather too loudly, causing her cat to open one eye and look across at us malevolently. "I thought that, but the following week as I played Daniel O'Donnell, the heater worked perfectly well. In fact, it only seems to have problems when I play André Rieu."

"Can you blame it?"

"What's wrong with André Rieu? It's music for people of a certain age, like us."

"No, Vera love. No wonder your sister haunts the tumble dryer when you play it. André Rieu is not music for the elderly, it's music for the dead."

***

As the weather has turned drizzly, Kirk picks me up and gives me a lift home and as I look out of the window I realise that the high street is filled with signs that urge people to sell their gold, even the jewellers' seem to be cashing in – excuse the pun – on the new cash for gold culture. "It's a symptom of the modern condition," Kirk says. "It's a tragedy, mothers' selling their wedding rings just so they can feed their kids."

"I never realised there were so many of these shops."

"I reckon if you don't need them you don't notice how many there are. Why are you thinking of cashing in some of your treasures?" I shake my head and tell him the story Vera has told me about Elkie and her experience. I explain that like most women, I also have a small collection of broken pieces in my jewellery box that won't be worth bequeathing after I've passed away and maybe selling them will be the perfect solution. I tell him that I don't need the money as such and that maybe I can use it for something that will be more favourable as a bequest than a few broken chains and the odd earring.

"Whatever you decide I'm sure you'll make the right choice," Kirk says as he draws up outside the house.

With the engine cooling, he nods in agreement as I ask him, "Can we keep this between ourselves for now?"

The following morning I receive a call from Miriam at the night school, she contacted me to let me know that the picture that Noah had given to me is available to collect. "Thank you for letting him borrow it back," she says, "You'll be pleased to know that the selection committee have offered him a place."

"So, he's got into art college?" I say, happily.

"Yes, he's got a place on one of the top ten courses in the country."

"I am pleased, I must send him a card to say well done. Where is it he'll be going?"

"Goldsmiths, in London," she says. We conclude the call saying how proud we both are and I make arrangements to collect the picture later.

This other mention of gold reminds me of what Vera had said the day before and I empty the innards of my jewellery box onto the bed beside me and look down at the contents spread out across the duvet cover. "Not much there, Beryl," I tell myself. "You've never been in the same league as Liz Taylor." I pick up a tangle of old neck chains and a bracelet that is now battered and out of shape and put them to one side before picking up a brooch that I remember my mother wearing on special occasions. It has a leaf design, with white stones set into the now tarnished metal. I try to recall the last time I saw her wearing it, but as I attempt to picture her in my mind's eye it seems to ignite the buzzing in my temple, as if the memory threatens to bring on another headache. Ignoring this I still try to conjure up the image but nothing comes. I sit staring ahead, wondering if my illness has robbed me of the memory, or is it just that as time has passed it has faded away: Will I be an irretrievable memory one day? Forgotten or deliberately obstructed by a belligerent synapse.

I drop the brooch back inside the box, it is worthless in monetary terms but nonetheless important enough to keep. I find a broken earring, the faux pearl now missing from the gold post, and a couple of old sleepers that I remember I used to wear at work. There's a ring that is hallmarked, but I can't recall where it has come from. I sift through until I have a small pile of scrap gold and after tipping it into an envelope I put my jewellery box back onto the dressing table.

***

The man in the market smiles as I sit down, his large round face a perfect accompaniment to his cheery manner, and as he scratches at the metal and tests it with a chemical, I liken him to the pictures of the smiling moon often illustrated in children's nursery rhyme books. I watch as he weighs each item, jotting down numbers in a notepad beside him. He looks up and gives me a friendly wink then looking closely at the ring, "Is it worth much?" I ask.

He weighs it and then after writing in his notepad again he looks up at me. "This little pile here," he points to the broken chains, earrings and bracelet, "weighs 16 grams, that's £141.76."

"Really, for that little pile?" I say, assuming he's heard the question many times before.

"Yes, the price of gold is doing well today."

"And the ring?"

"Well, he says this is a different price altogether." I say nothing, waiting for him to continue. "This is 22 carat so commands a better price than nine carat, the scrap value of this ring alone is £85."

Who had I known that could have afforded a 22-carat ring?

Once again I search my memory but find nothing there to answer my question, I shake my head as I wander through my thoughts, but my brain is like a maze and at every turn I come to a dead end.

"Are you all right?" the man asks, his moon face now having a look of concern.

"Sorry," I say, "I was just trying to remember something."

"So, would you like to go ahead with the sale?"

"Yes," I tell him and hand over my passport so he can record the transaction. As he copies down my details I once again try to remember where the ring has come from, but it's like walking in the dark with no torch. In my temple, I can now feel the wasps starting to buzz, and pain shoots out coming to rest behind an eye. "Do you mind if I don't sell the ring?" I ask, the pain behind my eye tugging at my nerve endings, "I'll need to think about it."

"Sure," he says, then adds, "are you okay, you don't look well?"

"Just a headache." He drops the ring into a small plastic bag and hands it back to me and then after counting out the cash he gives me another smile before asking the man in the queue behind me if he needs any help.

It's nice seeing Miriam at the school when I collect my picture and the fact that Noah turns up gives me to opportunity to congratulate him in person and also give him the card which I have put inside a twenty-pound note. "Use it for some paints or whatever you'll need," I tell him.

"What will you do with the picture?" Noah asks,

"I have the perfect place for it," I tell him, "There's a space waiting for it in our middle room."

That night I'm telling Len about my day, and show him the building society passbook for the account I have opened in Saffron's name, he looks at me and asks, "You didn't sell your mother's wedding ring did you?"

"Don't be daft," I say, thinking of the ring in the little plastic bag that is now back inside the jewellery box on my dressing table. "As if I'd ever do that."

~ 19 ~

Friday, 29 October
"How much?" I say, my raised voice causing a few people to look my way, and I'm sure someone's tutted. "It should have been returned on time." The woman behind the desk says.

"But it's not worth that much."

"Fines are there for a reason. If everyone returned their library books when they felt like it, we'd be in a right mess."

"This isn't a case of returning it when I feel like it," I tell her. "I simply forgot that I had it."

"Yes obviously, twenty-three years ago."

I've been having a clear out this week. Sorting through the accumulated bric-a-brac that has been steadily increasing in the back bedroom that was built above the kitchen extension. Years of dropping off unloved and unwanted items has resulted in the clutter that I feel needs to be addressed before I die; otherwise it'll never get cleared up. The chest of drawers gave up its secrets easily. Most were filled with items of clothing that were either beyond repair or so old-fashioned that no one would choose to wear them again. I bagged up all that was clean and serviceable and dropped several bags off at the charity shop. At first I felt guilty taking what I thought was out of date but the girl in the shop appeared to be very pleased with my donations. "We're always looking for vintage clothing," she said, holding up a skirt I remember wearing in the late 1960s, before cooing over a pair of ridiculously wide flared trousers. "Don't you just love these retro flares."

Various kitchen devices that at the time promised to save time and simplify food preparation were gathering dust under a bed, their promises proving false. These were given to the man that drives up and down the streets looking for scrap metal, and books that had been read with pages folded over and creased covers were now packed into boxes, their words now silent had been delivered to the hospice along with several board games and a couple of jigsaw puzzles. Victor had painstakingly counted all the pieces to make sure they were all there. No one wanted the soft toys that seemed to have bred over time, "We can't shift them," said Mrs Hambleton who runs the Cats in Crisis shop and the vicar had shown me his garage which houses several large boxes stuffed with them, "We unpack them for every jumble sale and at the end of the day, they get packed away again." In the finish, Mac took them to the local incinerator for me. I had almost cleared the room, making space for the next generation of redundant items, when at the bottom of an old suitcase with a broken handle I found another book, this one was covered with a plastic film and had the details of the local library inside the cover. Inside the card pocket was my library ticket with the return date still clearly stamped upon it.

***

"Can I help?" A man says appearing behind the reception desk, the woman explains the situation to him and as he punches a few keys on the computer, she tries to out-stare me. "The book's no longer on our system," he says, looking up and causing his colleague to blink, meaning I win the eye-to-eye stand-off. "Thank you for returning it, I'll make sure it's re-catalogued."

"What about the fine?"

"There's no need to impose a fine, Sheila."

"But we have procedures. Rules." Sheila's eyelids lower as she says the word, rules.

"I think in this instance we can dispel with procedure."

"But Mr Burton…"

"Have you photocopied those internal memos yet?" he says, softly yet firmly and Sheila, turns on her heels and skulks off in the direction of the photocopier. "She's a stickler for rules," he says with a smile and his eyes take on a mischievous edge as he continues, "I bet board games are a laugh a minute in her house." We both participate in a moment of silent mirth before I explain that I'd found the book in an old suitcase, so must have taken it on holiday and as the case was damaged we had obviously not used it again and it had been forgotten. "Your library card's expired," he says. "Would you like to renew it?"

"No thanks," I say, and after thanking him for his assistance I go to join Vera who should be waiting outside Aristocrats, a new café that has opened in town. "It looks proper posh," she'd told me over the phone. "Has cotton napkins and olives in little dishes on the counter." She looks at her watch as I approach and I apologise for being late, telling her briefly about my run in with Sheila before we step inside. The tables are covered with white tablecloths and Enya is playing at a discrete volume.

"Just the two of you?" a woman with a smiley face badge that was at odds with her own, asks. Vera looks around as if expecting to find we've been joined by some other people before nodding. "Would you like a table in the window or one further back?"

"The window will be just fine." I snigger inwardly at Vera's affected way of speaking and we allow ourselves to be shown to our seats. "I hope someone we know walks past and sees us sitting here," Vera says, slipping out of her coat.

We take our seats and a young girl comes and places a trio of bowls down before handing us the menu. "Is this your first time at Aristocrats, ladies?" We both nod and she says she'll give us a few moments to look at the menus before coming back to take our order. We're sitting in silence scanning the list of sandwiches with names like the Dorset Delight and Avon Appetiser when Vera says, "They do five different types of coffee and twelve teas. I can't make my mind up. What's camomile like?"

"Looks like pee."

"What's green tea like?"

"Smells like pee."

"What about fennel?"

"Tastes like aniseed pee."

"I think I'll have a latte then, that's like frothy coffee isn't it, or is that a cappuccino?"

"Have we decided ladies?" our waitress asks, pencil poised over her pad. "We've no Dorset Delight today ladies, and the special of the day is a Wiltshire Wonder." We both order a cappuccino and I go for the Wiltshire Wonder while Vera opts for the Avon Appetiser.

Waiting for our drinks to arrive and without the menus to distract us, we turn our attention to the three bowls before us. At the bottom of one are four fat green olives, I'm about to comment on the portion not being very generous, when into it dips Vera's fingers. She retrieves one and holding it underneath her nose she sniffs. "What are you doing?" I ask.

"Smelling it, I've never had an olive before."

"Just eat it. People are staring."

"It smells like Germolene." I watch as she drops it into her mouth and almost instantly her face crumples and she half-chews it.

"Well, what did you think?" I ask, watching her swallow the olive.

"Bloody horrible."

"I quite like them," I say as I pick one from the bowl. "We ate lots of them in Italy."

Our drinks arrive and as we're waiting for our sandwiches, we inspect the remaining bowls. One has rice crackers inside it, some of which look like they'd been coated with brown dust. I gingerly extract one drop it into my mouth and instantly regret it. Fire sweeps across my tongue and my lips tingle.

"Nice?" Vera asks picking up three of the chilli-coated crackers and promptly dropping them into her mouth. Her eyes widen and she flushes before she spits them into her napkin and says, "Those are vile."

Our sandwiches are delivered to the table by smiley face badge and she asks if everything is all right and we politely nod our heads. "What are those?" Vera asks pointing to the bowl of contents that look like they should belong in a horticultural catalogue rather than on a dining table.

"Mixed seeds," she replies. "Pumpkin, sunflower, flax and linseed."

"Bird food," Vera says and we are left to eat our sandwiches that have arrived on oval plates with a handful of crisps and a small serving of salad leaves, some of which look like dandelion. "This salad's as bitter as an abandoned bride." My friend says, and so I push mine to one side and pick up a crisp.

"Bleeding hell, these crisps are hard," I say as my teeth do the best they can with what has been called, artisan chips on the menu.

"What's the Wiltshire Wonder like?"

"It's just ham and relish," I say.

"Must be Wiltshire ham."

"Ham's ham, regardless of its provenance, and the relish isn't wonderful either."

We were almost finished with our lunches when Vera spots Doreen and Mavis across the road. "They haven't noticed us," she says, as I see them stop and turn ready to cross the road.

"I think they're coming here," I say and with that Vera bangs on the window. The dining room falls silent and as Enya advises us that, we can sail, we can sail with the Orinoco flow, people are looking in our direction.

Just then Mavis spots us and waves. "Hah!" Vera exclaims, "They've seen us in here first."

"And is that important?"

"Of course it is, you know how Doreen goes on if she thinks she's discovered somewhere first." Smiley face badge comes over to ask if everything is all right for a second time, before walking away to greet Doreen and Mavis.

We pay the bill and after buttoning up our coats walk over to say hello to our friends. "Isn't it lovely here?" Doreen says.

"Yes it is, rather," Vera replies, affected voice again.

"Mavis treated me to lunch here last week. So today is my treat." I watch as Vera gives her a tight smile, "I wouldn't have thought this was your sort of place."

"The olives are nice," I say before Vera can respond with something colourful.

"Any idea what the Avon Appetiser is?" asks Mavis.

"Cheese and Branston," Vera says loudly; probably a little too loud. Our waitress looks across at smiley face badge and she shrugs as we leave.

"Cheese and pickle," Vera says once we're outside. "What's posh about bloody cheddar with Branston?"

"The price they charge," I say, and linking my arm inside hers we make our way towards the bus station.

"Did you borrow any books from the library?"

"No, why?"

"Because I've just read a good one you can borrow. It's the first in a set of three."

I stop and look at my friend and say, "Vera, I don't have enough life left, to invest in a trilogy."

"Oh yes," she says, "I'd forgotten for a minute."

~ 18 ~

Friday, 5 November
This morning Mac gave me a lift into town. Normally I'd have caught the bus but I needed to have a chat with him. "I was talking to a friend of mine, Miriam, last week," I tell him and he nods as he drives. I explain that she works at the night school and that she's asked around and found out that there is a new photography course starting up at the local college.

As he drops off outside the shopping centre, I give him an envelope.

"What's this?"

"It's got the details about the course and a little something to get you started." He opens the envelope and is shocked to see the money inside.

"I can't take this," he says.

"Cameras don't come cheap and besides it's just sitting in my account doing nothing."

"I'll pay you back," he says.

"There's no need. Now get yourself enrolled."

"Beryl," he says as I'm almost out of the car, "do you mind if we keep this just between the two of us?"

"If that's what you want," I say and I close the car door and walk away.

I buy a poppy from the man outside the market. "Ta duck," he says as I drop my pound coin through the slot in his tin.

"We shouldn't ever forget." I smile as I take the pin from him and walking away towards the flower seller, I fix the poppy to my lapel.

***

I never forget to buy a poppy and every year I drop my donation into the charity box. I remembered to buy sweets for the kids that will come trick or treating and I've remembered to buy the flowers that I'm carrying now. The flowers I buy at this time, every year.

Considering that recently I'd forgotten about my mother's wedding ring, I guess you could call this current spout of remembrance, ironic. To be truthful, I've noticed that with the headaches that now seem to be a daily occurrence, I've been forgetting things. Yesterday I remembered to send Doreen a birthday card, but as I addressed the envelope it took me a good few minutes to recall her postcode. Before that, I was talking to one of the neighbours and found that I couldn't remember her name and I'm thankful for my mobile phone and its electronic phone book, as telephone numbers also seem to do a disappearing act when they're required. I know it's not dementia, it's the tumour. Not content with killing me, the nasty little growth now chooses to rob me of my memory. I put something down and the next thing I can't remember where it is, memories from years ago seem to have dissolved and I've started to do that walking into rooms only to discover I don't know why.

I haven't mentioned it to Len, he has enough on his plate without having to think for me. Don't get me wrong, I don't for one minute think he hasn't noticed. He says nothing but I see the concern as it etches another permanent line upon his face.

Clutching the flowers to my chest I make my way away from the town centre. I walk past the tattoo parlour where I had my inking a few weeks back. I stop and fold back the hem of my glove and look at the little numerals, V: XI. Five, eleven. The fifth day of the eleventh month. A date that I cannot forget. An anniversary that I hope I never forget.

I walk through the Victorian pillars holding up the iron gates and stroll down the path that winds its way downhill. I have been here so many times that I no longer look at the gravestones that flank both sides. Concrete angels kneeling, guarding the bones beneath. Rows of marble and granite tablets with names and dates, standing in lines like hospital beds. I stop at the litter bin unwrap the paper around my floral tribute and drop it inside before taking a pair of scissors out of my bag and trimming the stems of the chrysanthemums. If ever a flower was perfectly designed for funereal tributes, it has to be the chrysanthemum. Beneath the tree that was little more than a sapling when we laid the small white stone is the reason for my remembrance. I brush away a couple of brittle leaves that lie upon it obscuring the writing. Simple black lettering that reads, 5th November 1968. Peacefully sleeping.

***

Forty-two years ago I felt a short stab, nothing significant just a twinge, I paid no attention until I felt the trickle, and then I knew something was wrong, suddenly inside me something happened, call it instinct, call it panic. I needed to get away, needed to see a doctor. Inside me, I felt that something was far from right.

I was shopping, looking at some flannelette sheets in Lewis's department store when the trickle occurred and in an instant, my mind resembled a bingo calling machine, questions bounced around like numbered balls: What was that? Have I wet myself? Is something wrong? Those balls bounced but no answer was forthcoming. My knickers felt wet and knowing I was leaking I panicked, knocking over a display of pillowcases in my haste to get out of the shop. As I lurched towards the entrance I knocked heavily into another shopper and receiving no apology she called out after me in anger: My haste removing my manners.

Once outside I was looking around for a public telephone box when a man asked me if I was all right. I remember asking him where the nearest phone was when the first pain came. It came from deep inside me, radiating out from my core until it reached my skin. "I need the hospital," I said as the second pain came, this one punched me hard, winding me and sending bile up into my throat and a blackness behind my eyes. When I opened my eyes, was it gunfire I could hear? Bangs, screeches and the screams of children. I turned my head and looked through the window, a multitude of colours exploded in the black sky. Tiny comets of red and green, their tails fading as they fell to earth. "Hello love," Len said. "You gave me a right scare."

"Where am I?"

"Hospital. You've had a funny turn."

"The baby ... is it all right?"

"You collapsed outside Lewis's."

"The baby?"

"You've been asleep for a few hours."

"I see," I whispered, his avoidance gave me my answer. My baby was gone. The life that had been growing within me; the first life I had ever carried was no longer there. "The doctor will explain everything when he gets here."

"There's no need, just take me home."

"We'll have to wait to see what the doctor says."

The doctor explained that I'd had a miscarriage, he waffled on and most of what he said went unheeded. I heard him say it wasn't my fault – a bloody stupid thing to say – of course it wasn't my fault. "These things happen from time to time," he said before shuffling off to tend to someone else.

"Mr Bickerstaff," the nurse said, "we'll be keeping your wife in overnight. It's just a precaution and nothing to worry about. Is there anything she needs?"

"I'm here, you can ask me," I said. She glanced across then turned back to Len. "Is she on any medication?"

"I've lost my sodding baby, not gone deaf."

This time the look I received was tempered with annoyance. "I'll leave you to talk with your wife."

She strode away and Len looked lost. I knew he'd find it hard to talk about, and truth be told I wasn't ready for talking. "I'll nip home and fetch you a nightie," he said. I nodded and turned over and lay there staring out of the window as fireworks lit up the night.

A week passed before we did talk about it. Len did his best to understand how I felt. Emotionally I was cold, I didn't cry; it was three weeks later when that particular landslide occurred. The hospital told me that I was fine and that they felt sure I'd still be able to carry a child to full term and that my insides were getting back to normal. If that was true, then why did I physically feel empty?

Painful days turned into painful weeks, those weeks into months, and although it was always at the back of my mind, I no longer thought about it every day. It took eight years before I felt ready to carry a life inside me again. It was my decision to try again, that prompted Len to buy the headstone. "There's no body there," I told him when he brought it home.

"I know. I spoke with the vicar and he said it's not uncommon for people to have little memorials. It'll be somewhere you can visit, even if it's only once a year."

***

I place the flowers down on the grass take a red ribbon out of my bag and tie the stems with a neat bow, "Sleep tight, little one," I say, before placing them on the small white stone beneath the tree. "I'll see you sooner rather than later."

~ 17 ~

Sunday, 7 November
Sundays are a relatively relaxed affair in our house. Len gets up first makes a pot of tea and brings me a cup up before taking the dog out for a walk. He usually returns to find me in the kitchen cooking breakfast and as his bacon crisps under the grill he'll make a start on the Sunday paper.

This Sunday is different, I've been tossing and turning all night and have woken up with a mouthful of ulcers – it's like being back on the chemo.

"You're just a bit run down," Len says. "You'll feel better after a lie-in." He lets me sleep for a further hour and wakes me with a gentle nudge and standing before me holds out a tray containing a cuppa and a soft-boiled egg and bread and butter. "When you've had this, I thought we could take a little walk."

"A walk?"

"Yes, it'll do you good to get some fresh air."

"Fresh air? It's like the inside of a meat store out there," I say as I watch him take a knife and neatly remove the top off the egg.

"Get this down you and I'll dig out your scarf." I dip the corner of a slice of bread into the yolk and watch as it rises and runs over the sides of the egg cup like a sun-coloured river.

Leaving the house we spot a few cars belonging to Sunday shoppers in the Lidl car park and huddled together in the bus shelter sharing a cigarette are three teenagers. I look across at Len as we walk towards town in silence, his breath steaming in the cold air. He's looking tired. Something is missing from his face. I don't mean he's suddenly lost an ear or misplaced his nose, but there's a glow, a spark that seems to have disappeared; it's something I can't quite put my finger on, like a shadow is muddying his eyes, preventing their light. "What?" he asks and I shrug.

"Just looking."

"Why? Have I got egg down me chin?"

"No," I laugh, "I was just thinking, you look tired. You'd tell me if you were unwell, wouldn't you?"

"There's nowt wrong with me woman, stop fretting." I want to tell him I'm not fretting; I'm just concerned he'll hide any ill health for fear of worrying me. But I know the subject is closed. He tilts his head in the direction of a café and asks if I want a cuppa. I remember Vera telling me they scored low in a recent Food Standards Agency inspection so I decline and we take a left down a side street we've not walked down for many years. "This brings back memories," Len says as we walk a path so familiar we could have done it blindfolded. "Can you remember when this road was full of men in white overalls?"

"And women in blue ones." We walk past the boarded-up front of a shop that in a previous life had sold loose tobacco to the workers that filed out of the factory gates.

"Can you remember the oatcake shop?"

"An original hole in the wall. Every morning Pearl..." I'm trying to recall her surname when Len reminds me.

"Pearl Leach. She used to come around the potbank for the oatcake orders. I used to have two bacon and egg with brown sauce."

"It's a wonder you didn't get fat." I smile thinking of the skinny youth he was back then, tucking into two breakfast oatcakes each day.

"Worked it off," he replies smiling back at me. "What did you have?"

"Bacon and cheese. But only one mind, and not every day."

"They don't make oatcakes like they used to." There was no need to respond. Things change, time moves on and no matter what, you can never shake that 'back then' notion that's ingrained within you. We reach the gates of the old potbank where we had spent most of our working lives, the shell of the building looks forlorn, its ruddy-coloured bricks unhappy in the mid-morning light. "It's a bloody shame," Len says looking at the barren building, blinded by vandal shattered windows and yawning where the doors had once stood. "I miss those days. Back then we were a community."

The cobbled yard that was once filled with activity stands vacant. Pockets of weeds have taken hold and a buddleia sprouts out from where the warehouse doors once were. Great open shutters where men would load ceramics onto lorries and where boys pushed barrows filled with recycled clay back down to the slip house. The top floor that once housed the lithographers and gilders is now home to pigeons and years of neglect and erosion have almost erased the name above the main entrance, its appearance echoing the poor decisions that were made that obliterated the industry from the city. I glance across at Len and the shadow lifts as he remembers and the light returns to his eyes. "You could hand your notice in on a Monday and walk into another job the following Tuesday. It was a grand time to be living in the Potteries." I nod in agreement. "I feel sorry for kids today, they'll never know how good life was."

"Was it really?"

"Oh yes. We might have been financially poor, but in reality, we were richer in so many other ways. We had real friends, not virtual acquaintances, we didn't have benefits paid into a bank account, we had a wage packet that made us feel worthy and we didn't need the internet, everything we needed to know was here in the people, the bricks and mortar and the industry." He leans forward and his forehead touches the metal of the gate. "It looked after us did the pottery industry, it gave us an identity and over the years those in charge became greedy, they squandered it and now we're lost." The light flickers and the shadow falls back over him again and he takes my hand and leads me away.

We return to the high street and I think about how when we were courting, we'd leave work and walk up the same street hand in hand. Now years later as we walk, we're still hand in hand but my illness has set us apart. "This is nice," I tell my husband as we reach the junction. "I can't remember the last time we walked hand in hand."

"How are you feeling now?"

"Much better. This walk was a good idea." I don't think he notices that I see him check no one is looking before he leans over and plants a kiss on my forehead. "We come from a time when marriage was worked at, not tossed away at the first sign of trouble."

We've been home for barely ten minutes when the front door flies open and a hurricane in the shape of an angry daughter arrives. The dog scarpers and hides in its basket as she stomps up the hallway. She's barely through the door and into the middle room when she says, "That's it!"

"That's what?" asks Len.

"Mac... It's over... Finished... End of..." She plops down into my chair and starts sobbing. I pull a tissue from the box and hand it to her as Len takes this as his cue to exit and put the kettle on.

"What's happened?" I ask her.

"He's having an affair. He's been going out in the evenings and when I ask him where he's been, he's secretive." Len pops his head around the door and asks if anyone wants a cuppa.

"Sod tea, do you have anything stronger?"

"I've some whisky in the sideboard."

"That'll do." The amber liquid calms her down and she's about to tell us what has happened when there is a knock at the front door. "If that's him, tell him to bugger off."

Len goes to the door and the dog pokes his nose into the room to see if it's safe to come back. Len re-enters the room followed by Mac and Lisa's volume control goes up to maximum again. "Get him out of here," she shrieks and the dog decides to leave for the second time.

"We need to talk," Mac says.

"I've got nothing to say to you ... you ... bastard." He just stands there. He doesn't try to defend himself; he just waits for the barrage of shouting and bad language to end.

"Are you finished now?" I ask Lisa, then turning to Mac, "Where's Saffron?"

"She's at my mother's."

"That's where you'll be going. Pack your things and go." Len pours four glasses of whisky and tells everyone to calm down and sit before he hands them out.

Silence shrouds the room as we all sip our drinks before Len says, "You need to discuss this quietly, there's no need to share your domestic situation with the neighbours. So lad, tell me, have you been having an affair?"

"No sir," Mac says.

"There you are, Lisa. Problem solved."

"Is it? No, it's bloody well not."

"Tell me, where did you get this notion from?" I ask.

"Here," she says opening her handbag, "proof." She throws several pieces of paper onto the floor and her father picks them up and turns them over in his hand.

"What do these prove?" Lisa snatches them back and holding one aloft she says, "Here. A hotel parking ticket for two Saturdays' ago when he told me he was working." She shuffles the other pieces of paper before choosing another and telling us all it is an invoice for a case and an umbrella, pointing out that they already have suitcases and umbrellas at home. And finally holding up another receipt she reads out that it was for three hundred and ninety-seven pounds.

"That's not pocket change," Len says.

"Too right, it's hardly pennies," Lisa is now getting her second wind and waves the receipt in the air and shouts. "What was this for?"

"A camera," Mac answers sheepishly and looks at me with a guilty look that tells me our collaboration is about to be discovered.

"A camera," Lisa says, "and where did you get the money from?"

"I gave it to him." Silence like an anvil suspended over a road by Wile E. Coyote in a Looney Tunes cartoon crashes to the floor and two pairs of eyes stare at me.

Mac just nods and Lisa quietly says, "You?"

Mac explains that he's been going to night classes to train to become a photographer and that he didn't mention it because he thought people would think he was too stupid to change his life.

"And the hotel parking?" Lisa asks.

"I'd been helping Garry. He did the family portrait; he's been paying me to get some experience."

"Mac told me on holiday," I say.

"Why didn't you tell me Mum?"

"Because it was Mac's secret, not mine. I had some money saved up and so I gave it to him to get him started."

"Well, we'll pay you back," Lisa says.

"I don't want you to pay me back, just sort this out and put a stop to this nonsense."

"Well?" Mac says. "Does that mean we're okay again?"

"Depends?"

"On what?" asks Len. I can tell his patience is being tested.

"The umbrella and case."

"It's a camera case and a pair of photography umbrella lights. I need them for Saturday."

"Saturday?" I ask.

"Yes, I've got my first professional booking."

~ 16 ~

Tuesday, 16 November
I put my bag on the floor as Vera leans over and deposits the mug of coffee and a cherry Bakewell in front of me, she's purchased one for herself and I watch as she picks it up and quickly nibbles the pastry from around the edge like a mouse on steroids before picking the glace cherry off the top and popping it into her mouth. "You're supposed to eat the whole thing together," I say.

"I know, but I've always eaten them this way. It's habit."

"It's lunacy," I mutter under my breath and stir a spoon of sugar into my drink as she peels the foil case away from the tart and takes a bite.

"What time do you have to be there?" she asks me, icing glued to her top denture.

"11:35."

"I didn't know you liked swimming."

"I don't," I say and cut my cake into two.

I explain to Vera what had happened when Lisa thought that Mac was having an affair and that it had all been resolved. Lisa had told him she didn't think it was silly if he wanted to look into changing his job to become a photographer and she'd support him. And Mac had said he wouldn't be doing anything rash just yet.

***

Following the stress of last Sunday's extra-marital misunderstanding, Len thought I should visit the doctor. So I was sitting in the surgery in front of some locum who was scanning my notes and occasionally looking up at me.

"So Beryl... I can call you Beryl, can't I?"

"Yes," I said.

"I'm Doctor Maczko."

Oh, I think to myself, so it's fine to be informal with my name but not yours.

"So you've been feeling a little under the weather lately?" I just nod, thinking, under the weather, is that how she sees living with a life limiting condition – oh dear my leg just been blown off by an IED but it's okay I can still hop – my thoughts are flippant today.

"Are you very active?"

"Not really," I said. "Some days I just want to stay in bed."

"That's not the way to be," she replied as she removed her glasses and turned to face me. "You'll feel much better if you're more active. I enjoy salsa dancing every Tuesday and I play badminton at the weekends, that keeps my energy levels up." I explained that my energy levels are at rock bottom and the occasional bout of mouth ulcers and strange bruising that seems to appear overnight doesn't make me want to take up salsa dancing. I tell her that some mornings my muscles feel like they've been replaced with plasticine."

"Swimming," she said as if the single word meant anything to me.

"Swimming?"

"Yes, it's good for all the muscle groups and helps with your cardio. Do you have a local swimming pool?"

"Following council cutbacks, I don't know where the nearest one is."

"I'll check for you." She put her glasses back on and turned towards her computer screen. I watched as she fingered the keyboard and then she said, "Here we are there are two pools. One is at Bodiezz."

"Is that the gym with two zeds in its name?"

"Aha, they're open to non-members at lunchtimes Tuesday and Thursday and the council facility is open weekdays from 10.00 am. I'll print out a timetable for you to pick up from the girl in reception on your way out."

I was a teenager the last time I went swimming. It was during a holiday somewhere in Wales with a school friend and the weather was so bad that her parents thought it would cheer us up to go to the local pool; it didn't.

I've had the odd paddle at the seaside since but I've never been keen on swimming in the sea, you never know what's floating around.

***

"Should you have eaten before you go swimming?" Vera says as we walk towards the changing rooms. "I'm sure I read somewhere you should wait at least an hour."

"I don't think one cherry Bakewell will put me in mortal danger."

The changing room is cold and unwelcoming. The air is heavy with chlorine and an abandoned towel lies in a corner looking forlorn. I share the space with a young mother with two small girls and Letitia, who is a full-bodied Jamaican woman who works as a lunchtime assistant at the primary school. We pass the time of day before I choose to change in a private cubicle; not because I'm prudish but because I feel the sight of a one-breasted woman might scare the children. Once changed into my swimming costume I double check the silicone prosthetic is secure before exiting the cubicle and stuffing my over-sized bag into the tiny locker. Vera, who has come to give me moral support, albeit from the viewing gallery offers to look after the locker key. The two girls, now changed into their swimming costumes squeal with delight and despite being told by their mother not to, they run. "Kids?" she mouths towards us as she follows them through the foot bath.

"Yeah kids," Vera says. "They're like farts. You can only stand your own."

I wade through the footbath that's as cold as a tyrant's heart and look up at Vera sitting in the raked seating, she waves and holds up a plastic cup and a bag of crisps to indicate that she's successfully operated the vending machine. I pad down towards the shallow end and stop at the ladder watching a couple of mothers bob their offspring up and down in the water as if they are dunking digestives in an oversized mug of tea. I glance up at Vera who has her head tilted backwards as she tips crisps from the packet into her mouth before I turn around and lower myself into the water. The water isn't as warm as I expect it to be and it makes me shiver as I immerse myself. Once away from the ladder, I stand up with the water level just above my ribcage. I spot Letitia as she emerges from the changing room and heads for the deep end and dives in. She surfaces and swims in my direction, the water makes her black skin shine and encased in a white swimming costume she looks like a killer whale as she cuts through the water. She stops just before me and stands up; her costume is now almost transparent and I avert my eyes as she falls backwards and backstrokes her way back to the deep end.

I swim a few widths, occasionally dodging the two fervent swimmers doing lengths, who are either training or in competition with each other. I make my way to the part of the pool where the floor starts to slope away and walk down until the water level is up to my chin. I'm actually enjoying being almost totally submerged in water; it doesn't feel cold any longer. I swivel myself around and lie on my back and with the minimal amount of movement I just drift. I close my eyes and I'm enjoying the moment when I hear Vera shout out my name. I open my eyes to see her pointing towards me, she's gesticulating wildly, making circular motions with her hands. Just then, Letitia, the human orca surfaces nearby and hands me my silicone prosthetic. "Thanks," I mutter, feeling my face flush with embarrassment as I stuff it back inside my costume.

"Na worry 'bout it, Beryl love" she says and with a twist, she's facing upwards and swimming away with her nipples visible to all and sundry.

***

Back home and sitting in the middle room with the electric fire on, Vera asks me how I feel.

"Bloody knackered," I reply. "I'm more tired now than I was before."

"Who knows with a bit more practice you'll be able to swim as fast as Letitia."

"She does travel through the water with speed."

"But someone should have a word with her."

"What about?" I ask.

"She really shouldn't wear a white swimming costume, her nipples were visible from the gallery, like two fat brown conkers in a handkerchief."

"Talking of body-related things," I say rising from my chair, "I've something to show you."

"If it's a boil on your arse I'm not interested," laughs Vera.

"Give over," I stand up and take a carrier bag off the table and hand it to her.

"What is it?"

"Just open it and take a look." I watch as she slides the picture out of the bag.

"Buggeration," she says, "is this you?"

"Yes, I posed for it back in August."

I'm telling her the story behind the picture and she nods in all the right places, but I can see that as I talk, she has a question on the tip of her tongue. "What?"

"Nothing," she says.

"Come along Vera, now's not the time to start being coy." She gulps her tea and instantly regrets it as it hasn't cooled sufficiently for a big mouthful.

"Were you naked?"

"Yes."

"Nude ... without clothes ... bare-arsed?"

"Yes," I reply. "I think you'll find the clue is in the picture." She looks at it again, turns it on its side, looks again and even peers closer, her nose is almost touching the glass.

"So did the people in the room see your…"

"My…" I'm enjoying watching her struggle.

"Your moo, did they see your moo?"

"I guess so, but they weren't specifically looking at it."

"Well Beryl Bickerstaff, you're a braver woman than me. You're … what's the word I'm looking for?"

"Brazen?"

"No. Conundrum. That's what you are, a conundrum." I ask her if she thinks I should show it to the family, and she says that the decision should be mine. I argue that apart from the scar there is no flesh on show that should be covered in polite social circles, and she agrees that it is tasteful and at least there is no moo on show.

Then she has an idea. "If you want a less liberal opinion you should show it to Mavis and Doreen. Just imagine Doreen's eyebrows. They'll look like amper-whatsits, the symbol for 'and' when she sees it."

~ 15 ~

Thursday, 25 November
Sometimes it doesn't pay to come into a conversation midway through.

Last Thursday as I collected the tray containing two frothy coffees and an herbal tea from the woman behind the counter of the bus station café I could see that Vera was already deep in conversation with Elkie. I sat down without interruption but almost choked on my first mouthful of coffee as Elkie said, "And as they buried him they had 'Rockin' around the Christmas Tree' playing."

"You all right?" Vera asked passing me a tissue.

"Yes. What the blazes are you talking about and who's been buried?"

"Lee."

"Who's Lee?"

"The school hamster," Vera said.

Elkie could see I was confused so explained that Lee the school hamster had passed away. "It happened while he was spending the weekend at Jade Smith's house," Vera added. Elkie went on to tell me that the staff decided that the school should hold a ceremony and they'd asked the head to choose a song to be played.

"Well," Elkie said, "'Rockin' around the Christmas Tree' was chosen with it being almost December, she thought it was an appropriate song."

"But why that song?"

"It's obvious isn't it," Vera chipped in, "it was sung by Brenda Lee and the hamster's name was Lee."

"I know it's a rather tenuous link," Elkie said before taking a sip of her herbal tea, which in my opinion smelled like damp compost.

"Tenuous, it's downright feeble."

"Have you thought about what song you'd like played at your funeral?" Vera asked with a moustache of milky froth clinging to her top lip.

"Depends," Elkie said.

"Depends on what?"

"Well, if I'm buried, then something like 'Going Underground' or 'Dig a Little Deeper' would work, and if I'm cremated I'd want something fitting like 'Hot Stuff' or 'Light my Fire'."

"What about 'Smoke gets in Your Eyes'?" laughed Vera. I couldn't help but add my suggestion to the already inappropriate suggestions, but the 'Theme from Chariots of Fire' didn't quite attract as much laughter as Vera's suggestion of the dance floor anthem 'Disco Inferno', followed by an off-key burst of 'burn baby burn'.

On the way home, sitting in the back of Elkie's car, I remarked that I'd not given much thought to my funeral and that their conversation had given me an idea, however, I wouldn't know where to start when it came to choosing songs. "Choose one of your favourites," Elkie said.

"That's just it, I don't think I have a favourite song."

"What song did you have for the first dance at your wedding?" asked Elkie.

"I don't think that'd be a good choice to have as I'm lowered into the ground," I said.

"Why what was it?"

"'I'm Alive' by the Hollies."

"Ha!" snorted Vera loudly, "I remember."

"Do you remember what was number one when you got married?"

"Something by the Beatles, a band I've never been partial to."

We tossed around ideas as Elkie drove, everything from the sublime to the ridiculous. We ruled out 'Chirpy Chirpy Cheep Cheep' because we felt the opening lyric of 'Where's your mama gone' to be inappropriate. Vera thought 'Stairway to Heaven' would be a good choice but a sidelong glance silenced her. Elkie offered up 'Love Is All Around' by Wet Wet Wet, to which my response was, No No No. I was starting to get bored with the game when Vera said choose a song that was number one on your birthday. These solicited more laughter for titles such as 'Grandad' and 'Tiger Feet', and we ruled out 'Bohemian Rhapsody' on its length and the risk of people singing along and attempting the falsetto 'Galileo'.

"What you need to do is borrow some CDs from the local library," Elkie said. "They might help." So with my mind made up to visit the library the next day and once again face Sheila with her policies and procedures I waved off Elkie and Vera as she called out of the passenger window, "How about Gracie Fields' 'Wish Me Luck as You Wave Me Goodbye'?"

"And how about, you bog off," I called back laughing.

***

Wednesday morning has arrived and I catch the bus to town and walk the short distance to the library. There's something about public buildings, they always seem to have that smell of old-fashioned floor polish even when they don't have wooden floors. I spot Mr Burton, the manager at the reception desk and ask for directions. He looks at me with that confused air of someone who knows they've met you before but can't recall where. "The music section is on the second floor," he says pointing towards the lifts, then I think, he's remembered me. "Do you have a valid membership?" I explain that I haven't and after filling in a form and showing him my bus pass he hands me a plastic card.

There are two other people in the music section, one is Sheila who is busily blu-tacking a poster to the wall that reads 'You are <u>only</u> allowed to borrow 5 CDs at one time!!' I suppress the urge to mention that I feel she shouldn't have underlined the word, 'only' and that the double exclamation mark is a tad over the top. The other person is a skinny lad with his underpants on show above low-slung jeans and black hair covering most of his face. Makes me wonder how he can see through that fringe.

Sheila walks back to her desk before saying to the boy. "Can I help you?"

"Do you have anything by Spear of Destiny," he asks, "or Theatre of Hate?"

"I'm not sure we'd have anything by bands that have the word 'hate' in their name," Sheila says. "Maybe you'd be better off trying the music shop in the precinct, they seem to sell lots of death metal or whatever they call it."

"Theatre of Hate isn't death metal, it's post-punk."

"Whatever it is I'm sure you won't find it in a respectable local lending library." She then turns to me and smiles. "Can I help you?"

"I'm just looking," I tell her and walk over to the stands where the CDs are listed in alphabetical order.

"Easy listening is in this section," she says pointing in the opposite direction.

"Maybe I'm not looking for anything easy," I reply as the young man looks up at me and smiles.

I start looking in the middle section and spot a few names I recognise, Spandau Ballet and Sting and there were some I don't know, the Stone Roses and Snoop Dogg, then I spot the infamous yellow and pink album cover by the Sex Pistols. I pick it up and notice that there is a piece of black tape over the swear word in the title.

"That'll be Sheila," the young man says. "I reckon she's the sort who'd Tippex the swear words out of books. So you into punk?"

"Not really, I just remember there was a great furore when this was released."

"It was groundbreaking in 1977 but sounds a bit tame now. Mind you, they were never really a proper band, more a manufactured piece of music industry merchandise, like most of the modern pop bands of today."

"You seem to know a lot for someone so young."

"I'm studying music at university; I'm doing my dissertation on dark genres and their influence on music history. So were you part of the punk scene?"

Sheila interrupts with a loud shush and I lower my voice as directed. "No, I was far too conventional back then. But we had a couple of punk rockers at the factory and they seemed to be having a great time with it all."

"Are you looking for anything in particular?"

"Not really, just something different." I pick up a CD with a red and black cover and holding it out say, "Is this what you're looking for?"

"Yes, thank you," he takes it from me, then he looks up and apologises, "sorry did you want this?"

"No love, you take it and make sure you point out to Sheila that if she did her job properly she'd have already known that the library has a copy of a Theatre of Hate album."

"I wouldn't dare," he laughs. "It'd be like poking a sleeping bear." This provoked another shush from Sheila's direction. "Here, give this a try," he says plucking a CD from the stand and handing it to me. "In my opinion, it's the best album to have emerged from the early London punk scene."

***

"Any chance of a cup of tea?" Lisa says as she walks in through the back door and Saffron runs into the middle room and launches herself at my legs. Lisa walks over to the CD player and lowers the volume. "Whatever is this you're listening to?"

"Siouxsie and the Banshees," I tell her.

"Whatever for. Don't you think you're a bit too old to be listening to punk rock?"

"I like to think of it more as post-punk," I say borrowing the young man's phrase.

"Whatever. Why don't you listen to something more age appropriate?"

The track changes and the jangling guitars of 'Mirage' start to play as Victor walks into the room. "I bloody love this song, turn it up." I turn the volume control up and Siouxsie Sioux's voice soon fills the room. "Going back to your youth, Mum?"

"Don't encourage her, Victor," Lisa says as she tries to stop Saffron from dancing around like a dervish.

"I've borrowed some CDs from the library." I point to the pile on the table and Victor picks it up.

"Bette Midler, Dead or Alive and Kasabian. Now that's an eclectic mix," he shouts over the music. Lisa leans over and switches off the player, asking why I've borrowed the CDs. I explain about the conversation I had with Elkie and Vera and the death of the school hamster.

"So you're telling us you've decided to choose the music for your funeral because of a dead hamster?"

"That's right."

"That's morbid," she says. "Anyway, it's the people left behind that usually choose."

"Well, this way I get to have the song that I like."

"I think it's a good idea," Victor says as he slips the Dead or Alive CD into the player and presses play.

"Well if you think you're having your coffin sitting in the church with 'You Spin Me Round (Like a Record)' playing, you can think again."

That evening I tell Len that I'm just listening to different songs to try to find one that I'd like to have played. "But surely you don't want some punk rock?"

"No," I tell him. I try to explain that I feel that marrying so young meant we had missed out on so much musically. I tell him about the young man in the library and how he seems to be passionate about his music, "It's a new experience, I'm not going to like all that I listen to, but take this…" I hold up the Siouxsie and the Banshees album. "It's full of energy and it has the vibrancy that I need to keep me going."

"Is this suitable?" he picks up the Bette Midler album and looks at the track listing. "What about 'Wind Beneath my Wings'?"

"My goodness, no. I listened to that earlier and it's a bloody dirge, a right moany droney song, although I did like, 'The Rose.' But songs like that are just too predictable for a funeral. I want something that no one else will have."

"Well…" Len says thinking out loud, "If left to me, I'd choose something that tells everyone exactly what you meant to me and how I felt about you."

"That's nice," I say getting up and walking into the kitchen and filling the kettle. "What song do you think you'd choose?" I call out to him as I drop two tea bags into the pot.

"'You're My World' by Cilla Black?"

"Len Bickerstaff," I say popping my head around the door, "I can appreciate the sentiment, but if you think I'm having my send off to a song from the scouse foghorn, then you can get up off your backside and make your own bloody cup of tea."

~ 14 ~

Saturday, 4 December
"Can you smell biscuits?" Vera says.

"That'll be the dog's feet," I tell her.

"What?"

"The dog's feet. Len commented last night that they smell like digestives."

Vera bends down lifts one of the dog's legs and sniffs at its paw. "He's right, they do smell like digestives."

"Come on you dozy dollop, we'll be late if we don't get a move on."

"How are you today Mrs Bickerstaff?" the vicar says as we arrive at the church hall to help out with the jumble sale.

"I'm as tired as Alice's dormouse," I reply. "I didn't sleep through last night." I omit telling him the wasps were buzzing in my head until I thought I'd go mental. "Len did his best sitting up with me but in the end, he had to sleep in the spare room as he's in work today."

"Well if you feel the sale will be too much for you I'm sure we can manage without you."

"Not at all Vicar, I'll be fine once I've had a cup of coffee." On cue, Vera arrives holding two mugs and the vicar slopes off to help set up the stall of stuffed toys that are being unpacked from their boxes for the umpteenth time. I watch as the woman helping him sniffs at a yellow rabbit before throwing it into a blue plastic box that I assume is for rejected toys. That's how I feel, I think to myself. I missed helping at the summer fayre and now the vicar has reaffirmed that they can cope without me. I wonder if there's a box for rejected old women. "You okay?" Vera asks. "You were miles away."

"I wish I was." She gives me a puzzled look. "Ignore me Vera, I'm just tired and miserable. So where are we?"

"I've looked on the list and you're on household. I'm on ladies' clothing."

What I like to term, the jumble rush starts at midday, the hardcore group of jumble groupies as usual were the first through the doors, the first port of call is always ladies' clothing and the elbowing and rummaging starts in earnest. Reggie Boyle looks across from where he's set up his stall of Christmas cacti and holly wreaths, he gives me a smile and a wave before I'm asked by a man who's forgotten his reading glasses how much a pedal bin costs.

"How much?" he says when I read him the price on the ticket, "It's got a dent in it." He haggles me down by fifty pence and I drop his coins into the sandwich box on the table.

"Are those storage jars new or used?" a woman wearing a Santa hat and scarf decorated with snowmen asks.

"I'm not sure," I reply and lift the boxed jars from the shelf behind me. At this point my vision blurs, I stumble and the box falls from my grip.

"Are you all right?" Reggie says coming to my aid.

"Yes thanks. I just went a little dizzy. Are they okay?" I ask pointing to the jars.

"One of them has broken," he says.

"Which one?" Santa hat asks.

"The one labelled, tea."

"Pity," she says, "if it had been the sugar one I'd have taken them."

Reggie fetches me a drink of water and I assure him after a sit down I'll be fighting fit again. The hall is now filled with people looking for a bargain and after a few minutes I'm inundated with customers. I've just sold a gravy boat with a souvenir of Ballybunnion written along its side when another wave of dizziness strikes and I stumble forward knocking a stainless steel coffee pot to the floor just as the vicar walks past.

"Mrs Bickerstaff is everything okay?"

"Yes Vicar, I'll be all right in a minute."

"I'll get someone to mind your stall, and you can have a rest over there." He points to the soft toy stall.

So the rabbit sniffing lady and I change places and I sit behind a mountain of stuffed animals as she sells the coffee pot to a severe looking lady in a spotted headscarf. The wasps in my head begin to buzz and I sit watching as people walk past without a second glance at the stuffed animals or the tired looking woman sitting behind them.

I must have fallen asleep as I'm being nudged awake by Vera who's standing over me with a paper bag and a plastic cup. "I've brought you a drink and a cheese bap. If you're tired why don't you go home and get some rest?"

"I don't want to go home," I snap and snatch the bag from her and place it down beside a purple elephant with a wonky trunk. "I'm…" I look up and the cup is on the table and Vera is walking away.

The afternoon drags on, only momentarily broken by a girl who comes over and fondles a couple of the animals. "Do you have any rabbits?" she asks. I look through the stock, sending assorted species of fabric animals tumbling to the floor but find nothing resembling a rabbit. I tell her I'm sorry but it doesn't look like we have any rabbits. Her chin drops and she walks away disconsolately.

The pain in my head shows no sign of diminishing and I'm about to concede defeat when Elizabeth Nash stops by the stall. "You look tired," she says as she starts to rummage through the items for sale. "How much for this?" she asks holding the wonky-trunked elephant aloft.

"Everything on the stall is fifty pence."

"I'll take it." She hands me a twenty-pound note.

"Don't you have anything smaller?"

"No."

"I'll need to get change." I saunter over to Vera apologise for earlier and ask if she could change the note.

"It's okay," she says. "I've skin like a rhino; it'll take more than a snappy old woman to upset me."

"Less of the old," I say with a smile and she counts change into my hand. I walk over hand Elizabeth her change and ask if she wants a carrier bag for the elephant.

"No. What I would like is the correct change."

"Sorry?"

"I gave you a twenty and you've only given me change for a tenner."

"Are you sure?"

"Are you calling me a liar?"

"Not at all I'm just—" I don't get a chance to finish my sentence before she launches into an attack, telling me that in her opinion if I don't have the mental faculties to effectively work on a stall then I should be sitting at home knitting or doing whatever it is old women do in their declining years. She then calls over the Vicar and as he walks towards us the wasps in my head go into a frenzy as Elizabeth continues her tirade I sit down put my hands over my ears, close my eyes and cry. The next thing I know Reggie Boyle is helping me to my feet and the vicar is standing between Elizabeth Nash and Sue Hurley, the three of whom are covered in what looked like white spots. "What's going on?"

"It happened so fast," Reggie says. "Sue Hurley was walking past and she overheard the Nash woman ranting and raving at you, and she grabbed the elephant from her and whacked her with it when the seams gave way and showered everyone with polystyrene balls."

"That was the funniest thing I've seen in ages," says Vera as she puts a tray with proper mugs and a teapot onto the table. "Look what I found in the kitchen." She holds up a packet of digestives.

"The dog's feet," I say and then remember something that has been playing on my mind all morning. I walk back to my stall and look underneath the table and there it is, the plastic box. I pull it out and reach inside to retrieve the yellow rabbit. I hold it to my nose and it has a musty but not unpleasant smell to it. My eyes search the hall and I spot the girl from earlier. I make my way over and tap her on the shoulder. "Hello," I say and hold out the rabbit to her. "Will this rabbit be all right?"

"Thank you, Mrs, but I don't have any money left."

"Don't worry about that, it's a gift from me."

"Are you sure?" I see her look up at a woman standing beside her, who just smiles, nods her head then looks at me and silently mouths a thank you.

"Just make sure when you get it home that your mum gives it a good wash."

"I will." I turn to walk away when she says, "Is it a boy or a girl rabbit?"

"As it's pale yellow I think she must be a girl."

"What's your name?"

"Mrs Bickerstaff."

"No," the girl says now holding her mother's hand, "not your big name the one your mummy picked for you."

"It's Beryl, why?"

"Because that's the name for my new rabbit." I cry again, just a little bit. But this time there are no wasps.

~ 13 ~

Monday, 6 December
I've been feeling out of sorts since the jumble sale. Len thinks I've overdone things but I feel days like this are becoming a regular and quite worrying occurrence. In fact with the exception of going to the toilet and having a wash, I've been under strict instructions from the family not to leave my sick bed. I've been lying here, drifting in and out of the safety of sleep that's punctured by the occasional barking dog, or drop of mail through the letterbox. My only companion is a fly that manages to escape Len's attempts to kill it only to reappear later to watch me from the opposite end of the room. I imagine it is waiting for me to slip away, or maybe it can see the decay that I feel is happening. Don't get me wrong, I'm not lying here swaddled in bed sheets and self-pity. I've not asked that question that many before and I'm sure many after me utter at some point. The 'why me?' enquiry that can never elicit a reasonable reply. I'm not saying that my time will never come, but as the pain and weakness starts to seep into my being, I'm finding it increasingly hard to remain positive.

I remember watching a television documentary about a scientist who had chosen to fly to Switzerland in a bid to die with dignity. We all have to make choices that suit our situation and I'm not saying it's wrong, but I'd never choose that option. Assisted death will always put your finality in the hands of another person, and it's the people you leave behind who will be left with unanswered questions about how things might have been.

Picking up the TV remote, I think about a quote from my school days, I don't recall which play we were studying, but I remembered that, Shakespeare said, 'Misery acquaints a man with strange bedfellows,' and once again, as with earlier in the year, mine is the television.

Before lunch, I endured the daily timetable of houses sold at auction with refurbishments that always go over budget. I skip a program about a man in Widnes who's been having a running disagreement for the past year with his neighbour over the positioning of his wheelie bins; programs like this are, in my opinion just televised anti-social behaviour. This leaves me the only other option. Alan Titchmarsh: Goodness me hasn't he done well for himself, if he's not handing out tips on how to get the best out of your brassicas, he's interviewing pop bands he's probably never heard of, and launching TV competitions to win a weekend in a country cottage.

How do people manage to sit around all day doing nothing? I'm so bored, I've started to list my favourite green vegetables in order of preference rather than catch up with the news – there's enough misery in my room and I don't feel the need to add to it. I look up as the door opens and Len brings me a tray with a bowl of soup and a slice of buttered bread for my lunch.

The afternoon schedule is – if you pardon the pun – peppered with food-related shows. I'm watching a woman making Vietnamese Bo' Kho which sounds exotic but is basically boiled beef and carrots with some chillies thrown in. This is followed by two Spanish chefs who show the TV viewing public how to make tapas; or as I've renamed it, fiddly bits of nothing. One of the chefs says that tapas is perfect finger food for sharing, while the other one devotes ten minutes to a recipe called, Patatas Bravas, which turns out to be griddled cubes of potato in a tomato sauce. Finger food? I'd like to see someone in a crowded bar juggle a glass of wine as they try to pick up a slippery potato cube. Another so-called celebrity chef attempts to show us what we can do with a handful of store cupboard essentials that include preserved lemons, sumac and gungo peas. What planet are these cooking fools on? My store cupboard has tinned ravioli, sage and onion stuffing mix and some out-of-date trifle sponges but no gungo peas.

Following this is a one-off special hosted by Paul O'Grady, where guests are wheeled in to promote their latest offering and beggar me who pops up again, none other than Alan Titchmarsh, this time to talk about his latest book; a gentle comedy about a banker who gives up the city life for rural Worcestershire and discovers a horde of Saxon artefacts on his allotment. "The dilemma is that the allotments are council-owned," says Mr Titchmarsh giving the plot away. "So the protagonist has to hide amulets among his onions to get them home."

More food later. This time in the guise of people cooking for strangers who then score them out of ten after secretly criticising their soft furnishings and choice of wallpaper. So I've decided no matter what there will be no more television today.

Len has gone out and I think about how detached from the world I am. It's odd as I've always been attached to someone else's life. I've never lived in a house that wasn't attached to another on both sides and yet as I sit here the world is going on around me, oblivious to what's happening here.

"The family across the road did a moonlight flit," Len told me last night as he sat up with me because my head felt like a puck being whacked across the ice. "You know the house that the builder rents out. They've left a right mess in the backyard."

I wasn't listening and felt dreadful for ignoring him; I hate this illness, it's robbing me of time with my husband, stealing from me those moments that we should be sharing. I had told him that I don't think I ever saw the tenants opposite, but now I'm wondering if they ever saw me. It's not important. However I'm thinking that they will never know I'm here languishing in bed, with a pain above my ear that's like someone is driving a screw into my skull, and a hacking cough that has rendered my stomach muscles painful, making each of my reedy rasps of breath an ordeal.

The pain isn't something I've prepared for, and unlike Kate, I find it difficult to handle. I remember sitting with her as she breathed her way through it and it gives me strength, because like my dear friend I am not going to spend my days in a drug-induced state of narcolepsy. Pain comes from different parts of my body like a game of pin the tail on the donkey and today my gums feel as if they've been shrinking and no longer fit my mouth properly. And bruises, they suddenly appear and then a day or so later they disappear only to resurface somewhere else. I know I've lost weight; I can see it in my face, the skin that was once filled out seems to have sagged, my cheeks have deflated and in their place is wrinkled skin that's sallow and unappealing and the dark rings around my eyes mean I resemble a death mask, not one of those vividly coloured Mexican ones but something left over from a Halloween party.

The dog barks from the kitchen which indicates that Vera has arrived, "Only me," she calls. "I know you haven't got the energy to shout down, so if you want a cuppa it's one bang for yes and two for no." I hear a little commotion downstairs and as I bang the walking stick beside my bed on the floor twice she shouts at the dog. She called in earlier and I asked if she had any used paperbacks she could lend me and she'd said she'd pop one around later, no doubt it'll be a historical romance. You see, Vera's a creature of habit. So much so, that you know if it's Thursday at 12:15, she'll be warming up a chicken and mushroom pie for lunch.

"Bloody stupid that dog is," she says as she comes into the room.

"What's it done now?"

"Only got its head stuck in the handles of my shopping bag and I tried to shake it off but knocked over your veg rack. But don't worry I picked it all up and put it back apart from an onion that rolled behind the cooker." She puts her shopping bag down on the bed beside me and starts to remove items that she's brought for me. A bottle of fizzy water is placed next to the unopened one she brought me yesterday and several oranges are added to the fruit bowl that's already overflowing on the dressing table. "Here it is," she says removing the paperback. "I thought you'd like this as part of it is set in Italy."

"What's it about?"

"It's about a man who has a restaurant. He goes on holiday to Italy with his wife and daughter, but the wife dies suddenly. It's a sort of evaluation of life for a father and daughter." Vera hands me the book and I look down at the cover a smile tugs at the corners of my mouth and already I'm feeling so much better as my oldest friend tells me, "It's by Alan Titchmarsh."

~ 12 ~

Tuesday, 14 December
Have you had those new council recycling bins?" Vera says, taking her coat off and placing her shopping bag on a dining chair.

"Yes," I say. "A man in a van delivered them yesterday." Just then the letterbox rattles indicating a delivery. Vera slips out of the middle room and into the hall, returning with a fist full of leaflets. "I'm fed up with all the crap you get shoved through your door." I take the brightly coloured mail from Vera and pull one out of the pack. "Look at this, it's a takeaway menu for a new fast-food outlet with the dubious name of Chubbies, which I assume is a warning of what the customers will become if they frequent the establishment too often. And look at this." I hold up a catalogue with a photograph of a commode on the cover with the name emblazoned above that reads, Home Help."

"What's it selling?"

"Mobility aids aimed at the bewildered and lonely. Everything from adult nappies to bedpans. Do you think they only target the elderly when they're shoving these through your front door? Is there a delivery person with a notebook that lists the approximate ages of everyone in each street?"

"Let me see it."

With Vera flicking through the catalogue I walk into the kitchen drop the leaflets in the new recycling box and pick up the tea things and the fruit pies I've laid out on a tray in readiness.

Vera takes a pie and sniffs at it. "Apple?"

"Yes," I say as the tea is poured. "What's in the bag?"

"An electric boot?"

"A what?"

"An electric foot warmer in the shape of one big boot that you put both feet into, Janice Bowman's mother has one. I've got it for Mavis' Christmas present." Vera takes a bite out of her pie and sounding remarkably like a sludge pump she begins sucking the filling out of the side. "It's nice this."

"Don't you think they're dangerous?"

"I don't think so, otherwise I don't think Asda would sell them."

"Not the apple pie, the bloody boot. Imagine if you forget you've got one on and the doorbell goes. Before you remember it, you're base over apex and cracking a rib on the coffee table."

"Wouldn't do for me with my memory problems."

"And what if you had a sudden attack of incontinence, you could be fried alive."

"Aren't you eating your pie?" and before I can answer, it's in Vera's hand, making its way up to her mouth, her lips pursed ready to suck.

"Who's Janice Bowman?" I say dropping a sweetener into my cup.

"You know. Doreen's friend. She bought the lock keeper's cottage on the canal by the bottle oven. Mavis always calls her Coronation Street."

"Coronation Street?"

"Yes, because her cellulite is so bad her thighs look like a cobbled street."

"Look at this," she says holding the catalogue open for me to see an advertisement for silicone toaster tongs. "It says they help you retrieve toast out of the toaster."

"Isn't the point of a toaster that it toasts bread, and then pops it up so you can take it out?"

"I wonder if there's ever been a serious toast, slash, finger-burning incident that prompted the manufacturer to make these."

"More than likely someone at the company brainstorming session said. 'Does anyone have any ideas for things that we can manufacture for the gullible to buy?'" It's my turn to flick through the catalogue. "Bloody hell look at this."

"What?"

"The price of mobility scooters. You can get a good second-hand car for the cost of some of these, and you can buy them on monthly instalments."

"Wouldn't do for someone like you who's going to peg it before the payment plan is complete, you'd never get the full benefit."

"Thanks, Vera, here." I hand the catalogue back.

"This looks fun. A leg shaving shelf."

"A what?" considering the rubbish advertised I'm baffled why I sound surprised."

"It's a plastic shelf that sticks to the wall and you rest your foot on it when you shave your legs."

"What's wrong with resting your foot on the edge of the bath?"

"I suppose they're for people with limited mobility or balance issues."

"If you have mobility issues you shouldn't be shaving your legs, you should be investing in a good walking stick."

"Let's get one for Doreen for the wet room she's planning on having." We are laughing when the letterbox rattles again, I go into the hall and collect the leaflets that are wedged in the door. "More junk?" Vera calls.

"Yes," I say telling her this time it's a flyer for storage units, a mobile hairdresser and a notice for a new pub that's opening.

Let's have a look," she says and I hand them to her before clearing the tea things.

"Beryl, listen to this," she says, calling to me. "Do you have too much stuff? Running out of space for your things? Is it getting you down? If so, why not hire a unit with, Tunstall Storage for as little as £19 a month?" I come back into the room and she holds up the flyer for me to see.

"I think I'll have some leaflets printed and drop them off after people have had this one delivered," I say.

"A leaflet for what?"

"Common sense. Mine will read. Do you have too much stuff? If so, save yourself £19 a month and have a bloody good clear out." I pick up one of the other flyers and read aloud, "There's a new pub opening called the Hearty Hog, says here it specialises in hog roasts. We had porchetta in Venice and I've often wondered if a hog roast is the same."

"Where's that?" asked Vera.

I turn the flyer over and then start to snigger as I see the address, "Next to the lock keeper's cottages by the canal. We should go one day, make an occasion of it.

Vera looks at her watch and says she must be off as she's meeting Mrs Khan who wants to have a look at a new shop that's opened on the high street.

"What kind of things do they sell?" I ask.

"I'm not sure, in the window they have a selection of crocheted tea cosies and dinosaur-shaped door stops."

"Can't see them staying open for long. They'd be better off selling what folk actually want, like ironing board covers and Hoover bags."

Vera's slipping her arms into her coat when she spots a card on the floor that must have fallen out of the mail and hands it to me. "What's it say?"

"It's asking if we want to sell the house for cash."

"What else would you sell it for, buttons and beans?"

"At this rate, I'll soon fill my new recycling box."

"Right, I'm off. No doubt when I've helped Mrs Khan and I get home I'll probably need a strong bloke to help me open my front door."

"Why, is it sticking?"

"No, but there's probably a mountain of junk mail behind it waiting for me."

~ 11 ~

Friday, 24 December
Vera and I have received invitations to join Doreen for mid-morning coffee and cake; or as Vera puts it, we've been summoned to see the new bathroom she's recently had fitted. "I'll be able to drop off her Christmas present," she tells me.

"What did you get her?"

"The leg shaving shelf out of the catalogue."

I snigger and pick up the carrier bag I've placed on my dining table.

We arrive at Doreen's and Mavis is already there and the three of us are ushered upstairs to view the new home improvement. "My nephew Carlton did all the tiling in just three days," Doreen says, "and he fitted the sound system." We stand looking into what had originally been a traditional bathroom but is now a vast expanse of tiles with a hole in the floor with Celine Dion's voice echoing around the walls.

"Where's the bath?" asks Mavis.

"You don't have a bath in a wet room," Doreen tells her.

"So it's basically a shower room?" says Mavis, "Like at the swimming baths.".

"No, it's a wet room," she reiterates. "There's no need for a shower cubicle as the far end of the room has a slight incline that directs the wastewater down towards the plughole."

"Isn't that a bit dangerous for someone of your age?" says Vera her size fives firmly placed in her mouth.

"What do you mean?" Doreen's eyebrows twitch and we all wait for their inevitable rising.

"Well, what if you slip on the wet floor and break a hip, no one will hear you with the water running and the 'theme from *Titanic*' playing. Right on cue, the eyebrows rise like Tower Bridge and meet in the middle, and without being asked, in silence, we file back downstairs.

The silence is disturbed by spoons against porcelain as we all stir our drinks until the moment passes and Mavis says, "I'm not sure I'd like a wet room, I like a good soak in a bath. In fact, it's one of the few pleasures I get."

"You need to get out more," Vera says before she's afforded a withering look from Doreen for picking up her slice of Dundee cake with her fingers, despite there being cake forks provided.

"I know but it's my guilty pleasure. I lie in the tub with a cup of hot chocolate."

"That's just a pleasure, Mavis," Doreen says.

"What do you mean?" I ask.

"Well, a soak in the bathtub with a drink is pleasurable, whereas the definition of a guilty pleasure is where someone enjoys something that other people would either find in bad taste or low brow."

"I don't understand?" Mavis says.

"It's like watching, *Birds of a Feather*?" says Vera. "You know you shouldn't, but you still do, just to see if you can spot where the writers have hidden the jokes."

"Exactly," replies Doreen giving herself a self-congratulatory smile.

"So, what's yours, Doreen?" I ask.

"Mine. Oh, I don't think I have any."

"Singing along to Celine Dion as she soaps herself in her new shower room," Vera chuckles, still sailing too close to the wind.

"Do you have a guilty pleasure, Vera?" Mavis asks.

"Oh too many."

Vera reaches across for another slice of cake and as she lifts it from the plate, Doreen hands her a napkin. "It will save getting crumbs on the carpet during transportation."

"I like to spend the day in my nightie and housecoat sometimes if I know I'm not going out," says Vera.

"Really," Doreen says, her remark a statement, not a question. "Don't you think that's a bit slovenly?"

"Not in the slightest, it's not as if I'm going outside. Okay, I might nip into the backyard to put something in the recycling. But I'm not like some of these mothers who drop their kids off at school still dressed in their pyjamas."

"I didn't know kids could go to school in pyjamas," says Mavis.

"Not the kids," Doreen says. "It's the mothers dressed in them as they walk to the school gates." We all sit watching Mavis until the realisation registers on her face.

"There's another I have that I don't think any of you know about." We all look at Vera, and I'm hoping it wouldn't be anything salacious; Doreen won't be able to cope if something scandalous is discussed in the vicinity of her Laura Ashley soft furnishings. "I have that painting of the crying boy."

"Do you?" I ask, "I've never seen it at your house."

"It's upstairs in the spare bedroom."

"Isn't it cursed?" Mavis says. "Don't houses burn down where it's hung on a wall?"

"Stuff and nonsense," Vera tells her. "I know folks don't like it, but I do and my house hasn't burned down in the forty odd years I've had it."

"It's an urban myth," Doreen picks up the empty coffee pot and starts to rise from her seat. "Besides, art is subjective."

Another confused look covers Mavis' face, "What's subjective?"

"It means individual, what one person likes another may not."

"Like a guilty pleasure?"

"Exactly Mavis. Now anyone for a second coffee?"

It is at this exact moment that Vera blurts out that I should show them my picture. I reach down beside my chair, pick up the carrier bag containing Noah's artwork, remove it and turn it to face its new audience. Silence envelopes the room and Doreen replaces the coffee pot noiselessly. Mavis' eyes are almost crossed, Doreen's eyebrows remain unmoved and Vera chuckles. "What do you think Mavis, is a naked Beryl subjective enough for you?"

We thank Doreen for her hospitality and leaving Mavis in a state of extreme perplexity we head off into town.

***

I hate Christmas shopping and tend to get mine bought and wrapped up before the end of November. That way all that's left is the grocery shopping. And I've never been one of those people who buys things for Christmas that I'd not buy at any other time of the year. There are no Medjool dates or bags of unshelled nuts on my table and not a sniff of a dried fig. I buy the bulk of my Christmas fare the week before and shop for perishables on the 24th. Which is why I'm in town now with Vera doing the last of our food shopping. Taking a breather, we decide to stop off for coffee in the bus station café as usual. I'm sitting looking out of the window while Vera goes up to the counter. Outside, the bus station is filled with people, some appear excited, others tired and mothers are scolding children like it's going out of fashion. Seasonal songs are playing, men are rushing around in their annual panic trying to decide what to buy for their wives and girlfriends and the pubs are filled with lunchtime drinkers. Friends celebrating their brief release from work.

"We've all been given a free slice of Christmas cake," Vera says as she puts the tray down on the table. "She…" Vera indicates towards the owner behind the counter "…is quite cheerful considering she lost her husband this morning."

"That's terrible. He was so young, should she be at work?"

"Oh, he's not dead, she just misplaced him in Superdrug. Says he'll turn up when he's hungry." I nod to indicate that I understand and stir a spoon of sugar into my drink. "What's left to do?"

"I've just got to pick up the turkey," I say. "I've ordered one from the local butcher that I'll collect after we've caught the bus back home."

We finish our drinks and cake, wish the owner a happy Christmas and go to catch the bus. There's a long queue and I enquire why there are so many people waiting and the woman in front tells me that two buses have arrived but they were so full of passengers they couldn't fit any more people on board. We stand as there's nowhere to sit, and to be honest if we went to sit at the benches nearby we'd lose our place in the queue. The cold is forcing its way through the soles of my shoes and I stamp my feet rapidly to try to warm them; I'm not the slightest bit worried that I might look like an over-enthusiastic flamenco dancer.

Three buses later and we're almost at the front of the queue when the fourth arrives. The doors open and two people get off. "I've only got room inside for four of you," the driver shouts.

There's a rumble of annoyance from the waiting public and I count that there are four people in front of us. "Looks like we'll have to wait for the next one," I tell Vera.

"We'll see. Excuse me, love," she says to the young man in front of us. "Do you mind if my friend goes before you? You see she's got a terminal illness and has to pick up a turkey before the butcher closes."

"That's a shame but I've got athlete's foot and need to get home and put some ointment on it before the itching drives me mad," he replies, before climbing aboard.

"And a merry Christmas to you too, you miserable bastard," Vera says as the bus doors close behind him.

Fifteen minutes later another bus arrives and we clamber aboard and squeeze between a woman holding a snivelling baby and a man eating a Cornish pasty. The journey seems to take forever, every stop is delayed as someone from the rear of the bus fights their way down the aisle of standing passengers in their endeavour to exit. Then the vacant seat will be immediately taken and those left on their feet shuffle back to create room at the front for the next person to come aboard.

"We'll be too late at this rate," I say as the man who's now finished his pasty brushes the crumbs off his coat onto Vera's shoulder.

Three more stops and we're finally free of the bus and after saying goodbye to Vera, I make my way to the butcher's shop. "Hello Mrs Bickerstaff," Eddie says as I enter the shop.

"I thought I'd never get here," I tell him. "The buses are a nightmare. I was worried you'd have closed up."

"I knew you'd get here so I stayed open a little longer. You can't have Christmas dinner without a turkey."

"You're not wrong Eddie."

"It's quite heavy and you've already got your arms full. Why don't I give you a lift home with it?" He pulls on his coat before going into the back of the shop to fetch the fresh, not frozen bird. "I've put you a dozen chipolatas in the bag too, they'll be lovely with some bacon for breakfast, and there's some scraps for the dog." As Eddie drives me home in his van I think to myself that this act of kindness makes up for all the pain I've suffered of late. These little moments redress the balance, making me feel more determined to continue on, despite knowing that this is likely to be my last Christmas.

~ 10 ~

Thursday, 30 December
I'm exhausted. As you get older you forget how manic the Christmas celebrations can be. Family visits, Saffron's noisy, battery-operated toys and the squeaky bone Vera bought the dog have taken their toll and for the past three nights, the pain has been unbearable. Len dosed me up with my medication but to little relief. I have tried my utmost to be as positive about my illness as I can be, but lately, I've been having periods where I'm angry with it. I've had moments where I've locked myself in the bathroom and cried as the wasps in a jar fly around my temple; their buzzing sending my teeth on edge. It feels like a swarm of wings beating against the inside of my skull making me feel sick. I've been sitting down looking at my face in the mirror and the pain seems to make my features distort. My eyes are blank screens, their emptiness belying the frenzy behind them. I've had a couple of occasions where the dizziness upsets my balance and I've lurched across the living room like a drunk at a party. There's been a continuous low-pitched whistling in my ear that's distracted me and kept me from sleeping. And finally, as if to add insult to injury, yesterday I was in so much pain I couldn't get to the bathroom in time and I wet myself.

"Are you sure you should be going out?" Len says as I pull on my coat and wait for Vera to arrive. "You look shattered."

"Thanks for pointing that out," I snap at him. My temper's frazzled and poor Len is getting the brunt of my irritability. He tells me it's understandable and I apologise, but I can see he's hurt. "I need to get out of the house, just for an hour or so."

The dog barks and Len remarks that Vera must be here, as he goes to let her in, I pick up the hairbrush and run it across my scalp once more.

"You look rough," Vera says as she enters the middle room. I don't rise to it; I just smile and tell her that Len has already pointed it out to me.

"Well, shall we get going?"

"In a minute or two," she says. "I've booked us a taxi."

"Whatever for?" I realise my voice has risen and rein myself in. "I am capable of walking."

"I know love," Vera says. "It's my arthritis, it's been playing me up the past couple of nights and means I can't walk far." I know she's lying for my benefit, but I can't mention it for fear of upsetting her.

This need for others to be put out to accommodate my illness makes me angry and it's an anger I cannot communicate. I'm unable to talk about this with my family and friends for to do so will make me sound ungrateful, which I'm not. But until you're in the position where people begin changing their lives to fit in with your sickness, you can't understand how debilitating it is and how powerless you feel.

A car horn sounds and Vera goes to the front door. "Call me if you feel unwell," Len says. I smile to indicate I've understood his request. "Enjoy your afternoon."

The taxi journey takes just ten minutes and we're outside the Hearty Hog, which has a great view of the canal and the old bottle oven. "What was this place called before?" I ask as Vera pays the driver, "I've forgotten."

"The Swinging Gate," the driver says before putting the car into gear and pulling off the car park.

"I think I preferred the old name," I say to the departing taxi.

"My," says Vera, "you're in a mood today aren't you."

We walk into the restaurant area and Mavis and Doreen are already waiting for us. Mavis tells us she had wanted to sit at a window so she could watch any narrow boats sailing past, but Doreen would have none of it.

"Well," Doreen says, "I don't want to sit with the lavatories in my eyeline."

"You could sit with your back to them," Vera says.

"But I'd still know they were there," replies Doreen.

Mavis rolls her eyes and beckons me to sit down next to her. "I've ordered a bottle of wine," she says. "Quite decadent for a lunchtime, don't you think."

"Expensive," says Doreen.

"I'd better not," I tell them, then add, "I didn't feel up to breakfast today."

"Of course," Mavis says and three heads shake in sympathetic unison. A good start to what we've called our, let's celebrate the New Year meal."

"So what's the food like?" Vera asks breaking the silence that follows. "I'm so hungry I could eat my fist."

"They specialise in hog roasts," Mavis says.

"Hence the name," Doreen points out. "But they do have other choices… Oh my goodness!" she suddenly says, her volume causing people at nearby tables to turn and look at us. "Just look at that." We all turn and look at a young mother holding her baby aloft and pressing her nose into its buttocks. "Mothers didn't pick up babies and smell their nappies in my day. Whatever or whoever teaches these young women such revolting practices?" Mavis shrugs and Vera chuckles and Doreen picks up her handbag and says, "I can't sit here now opposite that woman. We need to move."

After selecting another table that's to Doreen's liking, a young man with a confused look delivers the wine. "We've moved," Vera says and after ordering sparkling water for the both of us we sit and deliberate over the menu.

"The specials board is just around the corner," the young waiter says. "The salmon with fennel butter is excellent."

"I fancy hog roast," Vera says.

"I fancy the waiter," says Mavis, and we all watch as Doreen's eyebrows do their usual forehead gymnastics.

"Typical," Doreen says, "one sniff of wine and Mavis becomes a slattern."

"We order our lunch. Three of us choose the hog roast, the reason we have decided to visit in the first place and Doreen has the salmon, which she says is an excellent recommendation and can't wait to tell our young waiter. Vera and Mavis waste no time shovelling the hog and chips into their mouths, while I sip at my water and have a few forkfuls of meat, but mostly push my lunch around my plate.

"Is everything okay?" The waiter asks as he brings me another bottle of sparkling water.

"No, my head feels like it's about to explode, every forkful makes me want to vomit and to be honest I could cheerfully take this knife and end it all, here and now at this table," I say internally, but to the waiter I just smile and say, "Yes thanks, everything's fine."

"You're very quiet today," Mavis says with house recipe hog sauce running down her chin. Has she been having lessons from Vera? "Is everything okay?"

"Not really, I'm sick and tired of feeling like a wrung-out dishcloth," I say, and before I can take them back the words are out of my mouth. Cutlery stops moving, three faces look at me blankly and one chin drips hog sauce onto the blouse beneath it. "Ignore me, I'm just feeling sorry for myself today. Please don't let my moaning spoil your lunch."

"Nonsense," Doreen says, "If any of us has the right to moan it's you. Look at me I could turn moaning into an Olympic sport and you lot still put up with me." Mavis opens her mouth to say something but Doreen's raised hand stops her. "I know you must think me a stuffy old pedant at times and I'll be honest you do have to put up with a lot from me."

"That's because we're friends and that's what friends do," I tell her.

"I know that, but I guess what I'm trying to say is, that how you cope Beryl is an inspiration to us all. I can't cope with sitting opposite a toilet door, so how I would have survived in your situation I don't know."

"I'd have given up ages ago," Mavis says.

"No, you wouldn't," I say as incipient tears prick at my eyes.

Vera hands me a tissue, "Don't worry about us. If you're having an awful time of it, tell us."

"Yes we've all got broad shoulders," says Mavis.

"You certainly have," laughs Vera. "I've seen Russian shot putters with narrower frames." We all look at Mavis and laugh, not unkindly but because as friends we can.

After the laughter subsides and our plates are cleared, Doreen walks over to the bar to order coffee. "It can't be much fun feeling ill all the time," Mavis says, and I explain that I don't feel ill all of the time and although I never forgot the cancer is there, at times it has stopped having the front row seat in my thoughts. "Forgive me if I'm speaking out of turn, but is it difficult living with an end-of-life prognosis?"

"It's a bit like trying to eat spaghetti with a teaspoon."

"I don't understand?"

"It's not impossible, it just takes time."

Doreen arrives back at the table followed by the waiter who carries a tray with a pot of coffee and four glasses on it. "My treat," she says. "I think we could all do with a brandy." She looks at me and says, "No arguing, it'll do you good."

"Okay," I say, "but can we have a toast?"

"What shall we toast?" asks Vera.

"Friendship and how it's helped me to get through this year without ever having to say, why me."

~ 9 ~

Friday, 7 January
I have a secret. Yes, someone has trusted me with an important piece of information and I'm hoping that I don't forget it. Although forgetting a secret so that you can never blurt it out in company seems a perfect solution. Well, it would be if the secret didn't require me to be a participant in a covert operation.

Kirk has decided to ask Victor if he'll enter into a civil partnership with him. He spoke with Len and me a week ago and we both said we'd be happy and promised to keep it to ourselves.

Back when I was a girl I knew no same sex couples, in fact, you never heard much talk of them. Yes, there was the odd salacious rumour and accusation that spread through the factory quicker than a cold after the first Sunday of Advent. Of course, the fact that gay people would be persecuted and prosecuted deterred many from being open about themselves. Years ago if someone had said that one day two men could form a legal union together people would have laughed, but times change. I understand some people are opposed to it, Doreen for one, her point being that two men can't have children, which in my eyes is a redundant argument and frankly outdated.

There's a travelling fair set up on the site where the tile factory used to be and Kirk wants to propose to Victor on the rollercoaster. There's one small problem with his plan. Victor hates fairground rides, even as a child you'd be hard-pressed to get him on the swings at the park. "I don't think our Victor's ever been on a rollercoaster," I tell Kirk as we enjoy a lunchtime drink at the pub beside the canal.

"Well, we'll have to trick him then." A devilish grin spreads across his face as he rises from his seat and picks up our empty glasses, "Same again?"

"I'm not sure, I'm not used to drinking in the day."

"Let yourself go; it can be our naughty secret."

"I'm not sure I can carry the burden of any more secrets," I laugh and watch as he walks over to the bar.

I'm not sure how Victor feels about getting hitched, it's not something we've ever talked about. I'd be happy if he said yes. Kirk is a lovely man, who's slotted into our family really well and he's made my son very happy. Which is something I feared he'd never be when he first told us he was gay.

"I've ordered a basket of chips and a couple of sandwiches," Kirk says, returning to the table. "We may as well have lunch while we're here."

"Thanks," I say picking up my white wine spritzer, "a second one of these without food and I'd be squiffy."

We plotted and planned over lunch, coming up with and rejecting ideas of how we could get Victor onto a rollercoaster. "I've had a word with the man that runs it," Kirk says, dipping a fat chip into the dollop of mayonnaise on his plate. "I've slipped him twenty-five pounds and he's said if we come just before the fair opens tomorrow, he'll give us a private ride."

"I've got it," I say. "I know how we can get him there at least."

"How?"

"I can pretend it's a follow-up article that Pippa from the paper wants to do."

"Perfect," Kirk says, and we clink glasses to seal the deal, our lunchtime collusion now complete.

That evening after tea, the subterfuge begins. I tell Len and Victor that Pippa has called wanting to do a follow-up article on me."

"What for?" Len says, "What more can you say?"

Thinking on my feet I reply, "It's about moving on and enjoying life. Pippa says it might help other women in my situation." Len just shrugs as Victor says he thinks it's a good idea. "She's arranged for me to be photographed sitting on the rollercoaster at the fair."

"Whatever for?"

"Maybe to portray an image of fun," Victor tells his father.

"I think it's a daft idea," Len says, "but I'm starting to get used to them now."

"You wouldn't get me on one of them." Victor shivers as he speaks.

"So what time do we have to be there?"

"Five thirty before the gates open. You will come with me won't you?" Victor and Len both nod and I go into the kitchen to wash the dishes.

Saturday passes normally. Vera pops in for coffee and wolfs down half a packet of biscuits as she tells me her neighbour, Trevor popped 'round to take a look at her washing machine.

"Is he skilled in washing machine repairs?" I ask as she demolishes another chocolate Viennese finger.

"I'm not sure," she replies, the brown chocolaty corners of her lips giving her a look of Batman's enemy, the Joker. "I think he works in a chicken processing plant."

"I'm sorry I don't see your logic?"

"Well, he's used to having his hands inside small spaces."

"I think," I say, removing the plate of biscuits from within her reach, "having his hand up a chicken's bottom all day hardly qualifies him for washer repairs."

Vera rises from her seat stretches across and snatches another biscuit. "These are lovely," she says. "Were they on offer?"

"No," I reply and make a mental note to leave the till receipt out for future biscuit servings. "Will you be going to the fair tonight?"

"Oh no," Vera says. "I can't stand all the noise, not to mention the boys walking around with their hands down the front of their jogging bottoms. What is that all about? Are they afraid it'll drop off?"

"Maybe they're worried it might get stolen."

"Stolen," she says. "I wouldn't want it as a gift. A good Marian Keyes is the only bedroom entertainment I'll put up with nowadays.

***

A man in a striped shirt that's covered in engine oil and grease opens the gates to let us inside. He padlocks them behind us causing a handful of impatient teenagers to deliver a few choice words followed by that whining that they are apt to do when things don't go their way. Lisa asks Mac if he's brought his camera and he nods almost unbalancing Saffron who is perched on his shoulders, meanwhile, Len follows behind impassively. Music is playing on each amusement we pass; different songs and styles jostle as if in a contest and the pounding bass trembles in my chest. "Everyone's just making their final checks," the man says as we walk past what looks like the inside of Vera's washing machine as it spins around before tipping vertically.

"Have you done your last-minute checks?" asks Lisa.

"Yes love, did them this afternoon. Just needed a bit of grease and now my love missile is ready for action all night long."

"I beg your pardon, that's my wife you're talking to," Mac says, "and there's a child here."

The man looks confused for a few moments then smiles, "That's the name of my ride, the Love Missile," he nods his head towards the structure of twisted metal and there on the tracks sits a purple torpedo-shaped car with the name emblazed down its shaft in orange. "Bloody hell, you'd need a big pair of jogging bottoms to hold that one in," I mutter to myself.

"You all right Mum?" Lisa says.

"Yes. Why?"

"You were miles away and smiling like a loon."

"Just remembering something Vera said this morning."

"Right shall we get this over with before those teens start climbing over the gates?" the ride operator says and I climb aboard to begin the pretence. "When's the local paper coming?" Mac asks and Lisa shoots him a withering look that answers his question.

"Why don't you come and sit beside me Victor?" I say, but he just shakes his head and blows into his hands to warm them.

"Yes, go on," Kirk says.

"No chance. You won't get me on one of them."

"Come on," I say, "it'll do no harm to sit with me, I'd like that."

"Go on son, do it for your mum," Len says. "It'll make her happy."

"Very well, Dad, but just for one quick photo. Where's the newspaper's photographer?"

"They asked if Mac could take the photo and send it to them," Lisa says jumping in and then tossing a wink in my direction – I had to include her in the pretence to get them here.

Victor sighs and says, "Mac are you ready?" Mac lowers Saffron and takes his phone out of his jacket pocket and Victor clambers aboard and sits beside me.

"Just lower this so it isn't in the shot," the operator says as the safety bar comes into contact with our knees.

"Thanks, son, I appreciate it."

Mac begins taking photographs and the car shudders. "One more," Mac says and I'm about to change places with Kirk as planned when the car lurches then judders.

"Oh shit," Victor says as we began to travel along the rails. I turn and see Kirk talking to the ride operator who's shaking his head. Mac is still taking photos as Len and Lisa stand looking ashen.

"You okay?" I ask Victor who has his eyes closed as the car rises steeply before levelling off in readiness to plummet.

The car drops and the air rushes past me dislodging a few hair grips as we encounter a loop, sending us upside down and then the right way up. Almost horizontally we whizz past the others and Kirk shouts something, but I can't hear him. We climb again and I take drastic action, I ask Victor to open his eyes and as we slow before the drop I say, "Kirk wants to know if you'll marry him." Victor looks at me, his eyes questioning. "Well, will you?" My son's response is swallowed up in a scream as we fall and loop once more and as we pass the others I shout, "He said yes."

The gates open as the love missile slows with a hiss and the park is filled with the waiting crowds but I imagine that Victor and Kirk didn't see another person there.

~ 8 ~

Tuesday, 11 January 2011
A rare telephone call from my sister has me listening to her moan about how, in her opinion, the plastic bags at Marks and Spencer are not as good a quality as in previous years and if this is an indication of what this year has in store for us, then we may as well accept Armageddon. She's explaining that she'd been up town shopping and after accepting a lift from Sidney she put her shopping on the back seat of his ancient Austin Allegro and by the time they had arrived at her bungalow a parsnip had managed to work its way through the plastic, meaning when she picked up her shopping everything spilled out. "It was embarrassing, I had to get down on my hands and knees in front of the neighbours and rummage for a tin of stewing steak that had got lodged under the driver's seat."

Just then there was a bleep and salvation comes in the form of call waiting. I make my excuses and the new call connects.

"Mum, it's Dad," Lisa says with urgency. "He's been taken ill at work and they've called an ambulance."

"What's happened?"

"I'm not sure, I'll meet you at the hospital, Mac's on his way over to pick you up." Mac arrives and although he knows as much as I do, panic takes over and reason steps outside for a while. So as he drives I discharge a barrage of questions in his direction, all of which elicit the same, 'I don't know' response. He drops me outside the main entrance of the emergency department and a woman in a dressing gown who is lighting a cigarette calls out that we aren't allowed to drop off in an ambulance bay. "You mind your own sodding business," I say, "and should you be smoking whilst attached to an oxygen cylinder."

I find Lisa and she explains that Len had complained of chest pains at work and his supervisor had called the emergency services but as of yet, the hospital staff have not shed any light on his condition.

"Three bloody quid for parking," Mac says as he joins us. "So what's the news?"

"Lisa says the hospital hasn't told her anything."

"I'll go find out," he says striding over to the reception desk with the two of us trailing in his wake. Now to be fair, Mac isn't the sharpest knife in the cutlery drawer. Yes, he's a lovely man, a fantastic father and at times his wife's doormat, but this day he comes into his own. He approaches the receptionist who is much busier than it is fair to be. She looks up and the tiredness is evident in her eyes and we are ready for a generic but unhelpful response. However, Mac has her on board in an instant. "Hi, I understand that you're very busy, but could you please point me in the correct direction for enquiring as to the condition of my father-in-law who's recently arrived here." She looks down at her computer screen, and he continues with, "I don't know how you cope. I'm guessing, without you this place would grind to a halt."

"You can say that again," she says, obviously pleased that someone else acknowledges how important her role within the department is. "Some days I don't understand how this department functions without me. Name please?"

"Mac."

"Mac what?"

"Not your name, you daft ha'peth," Lisa says. "My father's name is Len Bickerstaff." The receptionist looks up and raises her eyebrows.

"Mr Bickerstaff is being attended to by Doctor Watson." She sees Lisa's mouth open in readiness and she adds, "You even think of making a Sherlock joke and I'll staple your hand to this X-ray folder." And as if to prove a point she holds the buff-coloured folder aloft. She places it back on the counter and smiles at Mac, telling him if he takes a seat she'll page the doctor to come over and have a chat with us. Mac thanks her for giving up her time to help, and she gives him a smile that I'm sure isn't handed out freely during her working day.

"You didn't have to flirt with the receptionist," Lisa says sitting down by the vending machine.

"I wasn't," says Mac.

"Well, she was flirting with you."

"Who cares who was flirting with who," I butt in. "If it gets us the answers we want I'll take her out on a date myself." Mac is standing behind a youth at the vending machine who can't decide between a Twix and a Bounty when Doctor Watson, who turns out to be a petite blond with a West Country accent arrives. She looks at her notes and tells us not to worry, claiming that Len is in good hands.

"Has he had a heart attack?" I ask.

"We're doing some tests at the moment, but it's unlikely. I'll know more in an hour or so." She excuses herself and we shrug collectively and go back to our seats.

Mac re-joins the vending queue that has now trebled due to the youth's indecision. "Come along son," a barefoot man in a tartan dressing gown says. "Make your mind up, coconut or caramel and biscuit."

I'm suddenly faced with the prospect that Len could be seriously ill. How will we cope? How will I cope if our roles are reversed and I become the main carer? Guilt starts to creep in and within minutes I've gone from wondering if the pressure of looking after me has made my husband ill to a full-blown self-accusation that this is all my fault. This in turn leads to other thoughts. Thoughts that I'd rather not admit to. We're all resigned to the fact that it will be me who dies first, but what now, what if Len dies? Will it be a godsend, will he be better off being free of watching me fade away? I'd be happy to spare him the heartache of having to see me pass away. Relieve him of the upheaval of change that my inevitable demise will bring. It sounds selfish but I don't want to be in that position. I'm not ready to be without him. We're like actors who've rehearsed our scenes over and over until we know them by heart, we've prepared mentally for our final scene so it has to be me that goes first and to change it now would mean it's been bloody pointless learning our lines and stage directions.

A plastic cup of brown liquid held out in front of me breaks my thought pattern and I'm, to coin a phrase, back in the room. Albeit a room full of the injured, ailing and worried. A young mother is frantic as she hands over her young son to a nurse and follows them into a curtained off cubicle. I'm sitting opposite an elderly gentleman who has fallen asleep and a wet patch is darkening the front of his trousers. The main doors open automatically and three teenagers carrying skateboards laugh as their friend hobbles over to the beleaguered receptionist.

I'm sipping the liquid that's masquerading as coffee when Doctor Watson arrives to tell us we can now see Len and we follow her as she escorts us through a pair of swing doors into another area with curtained off beds. Len who is wearing a blue gown and being propped up by three pillows looks relieved to see us. "You gave us a right scare," Lisa says as she hugs her dad then pulls back as he winces.

"It's okay," the doctor says. "He'll be a bit bruised for a week or so but there's no broken bones."

"What happened?" I ask.

"Nowt to fuss over," he says.

"His blood pressure's a little on the low side but there's nothing to worry about. We think he's overdone it recently." She turned to Len, "You're not as young as you once were, Mr Bickerstaff." Then back to me, "It was just a combination of fatigue and stress that caused him to faint."

"And the chest pains?"

"We suspect, heartburn."

"I missed breakfast," Len cuts in, "and I had one of those mega-man bacon baps they sell at the burger bar in the car park."

"So how come you've bruised your ribs."

"When I fainted, I fell into the snow shovel display. Sidney wasn't happy as he had to rearrange the buggers again as they'd all gone skewwhiff."

"It's all my fault isn't it?"

"What are you talking about woman?"

"The other week, if you hadn't spent your time worrying and sitting up with me, you wouldn't be so tired."

"And what was I supposed to do?"

"And If I hadn't felt so dreadful this morning, I'd have been able to cook you breakfast."

"Give over," Len says.

"I'm just saying…"

"No one's to blame," Mac says, putting his arm across my shoulders. "I know if it was Lisa I'd sit up with her every night until she felt better."

"Exactly," says Len. "It's in a husband's job description. Now if someone could ask that young nurse over there where she's put my trousers and socks, can we get out of here before someone I know sees me in this bloody blue frock."

~ 7 ~

Thursday, 20 January
The front door closes, a signal that everyone has left for the day. I dress and pick up the mug of cold brown liquid, that earlier had been hot tea. The plate of toast beside it is also untouched. This morning my stomach feels like a spin-dryer with a full load of bedsheets whirring inside it.

In the kitchen, as the plate and mug sink beneath the lemon fresh bubbles in my washing-up bowl, the dog wolfs down the toast. I look at the teapot sitting on the side. By now, I'd normally be having a second cup of tea, but as I'm also having one of those empty stomach heartburn moments, I give it a miss. I wander into the middle room wondering whether to suck an antacid tablet or not when I spot a small object lying on top of the fireplace. Upon closer inspection, it reveals itself to be a button. Not a loose button, but one trapped inside a small plastic packet with a press-together seal: The ones that come with new shirts. The button has a mother-of-pearl effect and I recognise it. It's the spare one from Victor's new shirt, the one he wore on New Year's Eve. I open the plastic bag and it slips out into my open hand. The surface is smooth and the brand name that's embossed around the edge feels rough against my fingertips. I drop the empty plastic bag into the front pocket of my apron and put the button on the table. I reach down beside my chair and retrieve the button box.

52 Weeks

The button box isn't a box, it's actually a round tin that at one time contained continental biscuits. For the past forty years, it's been sitting on the shelf beneath the round table that Len's aunt Maud gave us as a wedding present. In fact, in all that time I can only recollect opening it to retrieve and stitch on a button a handful of times. It's normally opened, like today for the sole purpose of depositing a button inside. I remember my mother having a button box, and her mother before her. Every female member of my extended family had one. I guess it stems from the make-do and mend era; something we've lost. Growing up clothes were handed down, patches applied and buttons re-attached. Back then it made sense, people worked hard for very little money and clothing came at a premium. Nowadays, with cheap imports and faddy fashions, the lifespan of clothing is short, almost akin to that of the mayfly.

I place the button beside the tin on the table and wander back into the kitchen. The dog looks at me, eager that there'll be some more toast going begging. "Sorry," I say, pushing it out of the way, "you'll have to wait now until teatime." I open the cupboard where I store, what I refer to as my dry goods. Standing on tiptoe I rummage around blind, my hand squeezing and feeling at the packages inside until I find what I'm looking for. I open the box of peppermint teabags that have languished at the rear of the cupboard for many months and hope that Vera's advice that they'll help with queasiness is accurate. The kettle clicks and I pour the boiling water over the buff-coloured teabag. A blast of mint fills the immediate area, the pungent medicinal aroma invading my senses. I toss the dog a dried pig's ear, and it retreats to its basket to chew the remainder of the morning away.

With the electric fire on two bars, I take to my chair, open the button box and drop the new button inside, where with a shake it disappears below the surface as if in quicksand. On top of this pit of buttons is a reel of blue-black cotton with three needles lazily stabbed into the threads, there's a piece of fabric attached, I can't remember where it came from and inserted into this is an upholstery needle; one of those curved ones that come in a set but never get used. Several knotted balls of thread, like rayon tumbleweed, sit upon the multi-coloured, multi-sized surface. I insert my hand into the buttons and move them around. I enjoy the rattling sound the action creates and look down as the contents race to the opposite side of the tin. I remove a small white button that catches my eye, from its shiny surface the smiling face of Piglet looks out. Almost as if I'm watching the opening credits of a film, my mind fades in from black.

"Oh please. You know I'd do you a swap if you wanted," said Celia Marston. I just shook my head and remained expressionless. "What about two Black Jacks and the liquorice from my Sherbet Fountain?"

"No. Not enough for Piglet."

"But I've already got Pooh and Eeyore." I shook my head again. "Beryl Pike, you really are too much."

"What else have you got?"

"Half a pack of Spangles."

"What flavour?"

"Blackcurrant."

"Urgh, they smell like cats wee."

"I thought you were my friend," whined Celia.

The memory fades back to black and I'm left smiling. I remember I was ten when Celia wanted to swap her sweets for my button. My uncle Bob had given me the button, saying it was one in a set of nine and if I collected them all they'd be worth a pretty penny in a few years. To be honest I didn't like Piglet, let alone the Winnie the Pooh books, I was just being awkward because three weeks earlier Celia had refused to share her copy of Bunty, saying I'd crease the pages.

I rummage a little deeper and pull out a small buff-coloured envelope. It's one of Len's old wage packets. On the front in faded green ink, I can make out his name and his clock number. Printed in neat script at the bottom, is his wage for the week, one hundred and forty-nine pounds and thirty pence. I remember, back then, with my wage and Len's overtime, we were one of the few couples in our street that were referred to as being well off. I open the envelope and two pieces of fabric slide out onto my palm. One is red and the other is green, they're Victor's swimming awards: red for the width of the pool and green for the length. I'm surprised to discover them inside the old wage packet. Once more my mind slips back in time.

"No Mum, you can't sew them onto my trunks."
"Why ever not?"
"Because you'll make holes with the needle."
"I'll need to otherwise I can't pull the cotton through."
"But you'll make holes."
"So?"
"If you make holes the water will come through and I'll sink."

You couldn't fault his logic. I begin to giggle at this snippet of my history and the dog, now bored with chewing the pig's ear walks into the room and gives me that look; the look that indicates it needs to go outside. I put down the button box rise from my chair and follow the dog into the kitchen. I notice the mug of peppermint tea, forgotten and cooling on the counter. "Silly me," I say to the dog, that is now sitting at the back door. "Fancy forgetting my tea, whatever next?"

Standing on the back step with a frigid January breeze nipping at my ankles, I sip at the tea as the dog wanders about, sniffing and looking for a spot suitable for a pee. Why, I think, does it always seem to have some urgency to urinate and once outside takes an age to finally open the floodgates?

After closing the back door and pouring the remains of the lukewarm tea down the sink, the dog settles in front of the fire and I fall back into my chair and once again pick up the button box. I delve into the sea of circular discs withdraw my hand and look down at the assortment in my cupped palm. A mock pearl button, a spare intended for the sleeves of my wedding dress prompts another smile, as does the tarnished brass button from my grandfather's uniform, a reminder of his national service and the only memento I have of the kind and gentle man.

I must have dozed off as I wake up and the fire is still on with the dog stretched out, its legs are moving as if it were running and the occasional whimper indicates that it's dreaming. I'm feeling peckish now, so scoop up the buttons that have escaped into my aproned lap and drop them back inside the tin. The dog wakes and follows me into the kitchen. Thankfully my earlier nausea has passed as I prepare some lunch. I remember that there are a couple of slices of ham in the fridge so retrieve them and the butter before removing the bread from inside the bread bin. The dog sits motionless, looking up at me with eager expectation. "Bugger..." I tell the hound "...the butter's too hard to spread." I light the grill and stand the block of butter on top to soften as I slice a salad tomato. I tear the fat off the ham and toss it to the dog. It snaps at it mid-air, catching it, the fat hanging on either side of its bottom jaw like a thin white worm before it disappears into its cavernous mouth.

Back in my chair in front of the fire I begin to eat my sandwich. I enjoy the sweetness of the honey-glazed ham when something catches my eye. I put my plate to one side and reach into the tin of buttons. I look down at the small circle of plastic in my hand. Its sunny yellow colour is bright against the paleness of my skin. I touch it gently with my index finger, pushing it around the palm of my hand. I'm remembering this button when the front door opens, "Hiya Mum, just thought I'd pop over, and spend some time with you before I go to pick up Saffron from school," says Lisa as she enters the middle room. "What is that bloody awful smell?" Suddenly she dashes into the kitchen and I hear something clatter into the sink and the tap being turned on. "Bloody hell," she says coming back into the room, "are you trying to burn the place down?"

"What's wrong?"

"You left the grill on and there was a packet of butter on top. The paper was on fire and there was butter burning in the grill pan."

"Oh dear, I must have forgotten to turn it off."

"You need to be more careful."

"I'm sorry, I was distracted… Look." I open my hand to reveal the yellow button. "Do you remember this?"

"What?" Lisa asks, sharply.

"This is one of the buttons from the dress you wore on your first day at school."

"Mother, we need to talk about this, it's important."

"So is this."

"No, it's not, it's a sodding button."

I look at her. I can see her concern and I understand, "I'm sorry."

"It's okay," she says, her arms falling around my shoulders. I'm pulled in and breathe in her perfume as she bends over my chair and holds me. After she has straightened up, she's looking down at me, her face wearing the mask of anxiety that I've seen so many others wear this past few months. "It's just a button out of your button box."

"I shake my head, "It's more than that." Lisa steps back and sits in Len's chair. "On the morning of your first day at school, you were dressed in a yellow blouse and brown corduroy pinafore dress. You looked beautiful, your hair was held back by a yellow headband, but something looked wrong."

"What?"

"The dress had ugly brown buttons on the shoulder straps. I remember taking them off and as you stood on the dining table I sewed on these yellow ones. If you look closely, you can still see the remains of an eye at the top right." Lisa takes the button from me and studies the surface of it. "The picture's worn away over the years, but it used to be an image of a smiling sun. I told you it was there to keep you happy at school."

"And did it?"

"Well, Miss Winterbourne did say that you were the only child who didn't cry on the first day." Lisa smiles and for a brief moment the mask falls away and she looks relaxed. "So you can see," I say, pointing to the biscuit tin on the table, "this isn't just a button box, it's a museum of memories."

~ 6 ~

Friday, 28 January
This morning was bright and sunny. There was a frost earlier and the street glittered as I waved Len on his way to work, but now the skies are leaden and threatening rain. I bring the dog in from the backyard and pour water over the teabags in the pot. "Sixty-five years," I say carrying the tray into the middle room. "This week, I'll have been on the planet for sixty-five years."

"So will you be doing something special?" Vera asks.

"The family asked me how we'd mark the occasion. I told them, quietly and without fuss."

"And what was the reaction?"

"There was some complaining. Victor even mentioned having a surprise party. I told him, in my condition surprises could finish me off and knowing there was a party looming would take away the element of surprise.

"Len keeps asking me what I want for my birthday, but truth be told, there's nothing I want."

"I wish I'd known," Vera says, "I could have saved myself the ten-pound that I spent in Debenhams on your gift last week." Dunking a ginger biscuit into her tea she continues, "I saw Elkie while I was there, she's had one of those new-fangled phones. I saw her taking a selfie by the bedsheets."

"I saw two girls on the bus taking them yesterday, all the way from Burslem College to Hanley, they must have taken hundreds."

"Have you ever taken one?"

"No," I tell her. "Besides why do they always hold the camera up above themselves when they do it?"

"I think it's more flattering, like when you photograph someone in a wheelchair." I look at her confused and she continues, "People in wheelchairs are always looking up so they benefit from never being photographed with a double chin."

"Vera!"

"Oh stop it, you know it's true," she says. "Here shall we have a go?" She withdraws her phone out of her handbag and holds it above her head and smiles as the sound of the shutter clicks. She looks at the screen and laughs, reminding me of the girls on the bus. "Come on, your turn," she hands the phone to me. "Just press the button."

"I can't," I say. "I look a right mess."

"I know," she laughs. "Your hair's messier than Katie Price's personal life. Now take the bloody picture." The shutter clicks and I hand the phone to my friend who starts to laugh again.

"Show me."

"Oops. I've accidentally deleted it," she says and continues sniggering as she drops the phone back inside her handbag. I don't know why, but I don't believe her.

***

I open my birthday cards over breakfast, there are tasteful ones from Mavis and Doreen with pictures of cats and vases of flowers on the front, there is an assortment of comedy ones from family and Elkie and a dubious one with a picture of a naked man on the front from Julia Watkins. Len's card has the words, For My Wife, in large gold letters on the front and he kisses me on the cheek as I read the verse inside.

The sound of a key in the front door distracts us and Victor calls to let us know it's him and Kirk. "Happy birthday mum," he says as he enters the room.

"That's a bit racy," Kirk says picking up Julia's card. "Let me guess, is this off Vera."

"No, I've not had one off Vera," I say as Victor hands me an envelope.

"Maybe she'll give it to you later at the meal."

I catch Kirk frowning at him. "What meal?"

"Nothing special, just an afternoon meal out with the family and some friends," says Len lowering his eyes from mine.

"I told you I didn't want a fuss."

"It's not a fuss mum, just a meal out," Victor says.

"How can I go out looking like this?"

"Like what?" Len asks.

"Like this!"

"You look fine to me."

"Typical." I huff and stomp off to take a look at myself in the hall mirror. I comment that I look a horror when Victor tells me that he called Gloria earlier in the week and she said she could fit me in for a shampoo and set and that my appointment is in twenty minutes.

"Twenty minutes, how can I go in twenty minutes, I'll never have enough time to get sorted."

"Why what do you need to do before you go?"

"She has to wash her hair," laughs Kirk.

"Exactly," I tell them. "Now get out of my way and Len go and plug me the hair dryer in upstairs."

***

"You ought to let them spoil you," Gloria says as she teases at a curl that refuses to be tamed.

"I don't want all this fuss."

"It's not a fuss, it's because they love you and want to spend what time is left with you." I'm always grateful for Gloria's no-dressing-it-up style of conversation; no skirting the issue, just telling it how it is.

"Back in the day my mother would have spit in her hand and dampened that bloody curl into submission," I say looking back at her through the mirror.

"I find customers aren't keen on being spat on," Gloria says as she looks triumphant as the unruly element is now in its place. "There you go Beryl, this is on the house, a birthday treat." I try to argue but she has none of it and after a final defiant spray of lacquer she kisses me on the cheek.

Kirk has been waiting patiently for me while the others said they'd go on ahead and meet us at the restaurant and he's offered to give me a lift there, it also gave him a chance to tell me something he's been keeping to himself. "There's been a wedding cancellation at Ford Hall in February. I know it's only been three weeks since I proposed to Victor, but do you think it's too early to set the date?"

"I'm not the person you should be asking," I say.

"Without sounding maudlin, I'd like you to be there and—"

"I understand…" I pat his knee "…and I appreciate your thoughtfulness." We pull up outside the public house that now serves carvery meals and he turns to me and says, "I'll speak with Victor later."

"Perfume," I say suddenly. "I've got no scent on,"

"Hang about…" he starts rummaging in the glove box "…will this help?"

"Lynx antiperspirant?"

"Not that… This." He holds up a bottle of men's cologne and after nodding, I lift my chin and he gives my neck a liberal dousing.

When we enter the dining area I see that a section has been roped off and my family and friends are waiting for me. I thank everyone for coming and Vera comes over to give me a card and a gift. Mavis is sitting next to Doreen and Elkie has changed her hair colour for the party. Saffron is squirming in Mac's arms trying to wriggle free to no doubt run around the room. I'm surprised to see my sister sitting next to Sidney, who has given her a lift in his Austin Allegro cum gas boiler. I'm more surprised, but pleasantly so, to see Gareth. I want to go over and ask how he's been coping since Kate's passing, but I'm steered over to a vacant seat by Lisa and instructed to sit down. With Len at my side, I look around the room that is filled with the people who mean the most to me and I feel a tremble in my gut that threatens to rise into a full-blown bout of sobbing. So taking a deep breath I say to the assembled guests, "So, how long do I have to wait before one of you buys me a drink." There's a trickle of laughter and Mac heads off to the bar.

"What's that perfume you're wearing?" Len says.

"It's Kirk's aftershave."

"Oh," he says, then after thinking about it says, "do you mind if I don't kiss you while you're wearing blokes' scent." I shake my head thinking, you might think you're a new liberal-minded man, Len Bickerstaff but sometimes, just sometimes, you revert to type.

At the end of the meal, Vera announces to everyone that they have to gather around and with much chair shuffling and pushing I'm surrounded and Vera puts a cardboard box in front of me. "What's this?" I ask.

"Open it and you'll find out," she says. I open the box and inside is a cake, decorated with something that almost makes me swear aloud. It is decorated with a dreadful photograph of me, and not one I have seen previously. And before I can close the lid, Vera takes the cake from the box and introduces everyone to my one and only selfie.

~ 5 ~

Thursday, 3 February

There's a knocking at the front door. Well to be honest it's more like hammering than knocking. I call out that I'm coming as I wipe my hands on a tea towel, but still it continues. "All right," I shout as I close the middle door and make my way down the hall. The knocking carries on and as I open the door, there stands a burly man, his fist that had previously been making contact with my door still raised.

"Look," he says his eyes indicating down.

I look down and see a small dog; when I say dog it is more like a cross between a poodle and a lamb.

"She could be pregnant."

"Congratulations," I say, "but what's that got to do with me?"

"It's your dog's fault."

"Excuse me?"

"It keeps jumping over our wall and having a go at Cybil."

"Cybil?"

"My dog, Cybil. She's a pedigree, not like that mutt of yours."

My hackles start to rise, not only has this man seen fit to bang his fists on my front door but now he's starting to insult my family – well, the dog. "Now look here," I say rising to my full height, "you can't just come around here accusing our dog of having relations with your poodle."

"Poodle," he says his face going puce. "Poodle! For your information, Cybil is not a poodle. She's a Bedlington terrier."

"I don't care what she is love, you need to calm down. You can't just go around banging on people's doors and accusing them of possibly impregnating your dog."

"I was due to show her but now I can't. If she's pregnant, she's ruined." This man who must be at least six feet five and possibly the same across the shoulders stands opposite me and he's about to cry. "I had high hopes of a rosette at the Cheshire Terrier Society," he blubbers. "The show's in Congleton next week." His shoulders lift, hold their position, then drop and the shaking starts as tears roll down his face.

"Let's see if we can't sort this out." I pull a yellow duster from my apron pocket and hand it to him. He apologises and dries his eyes before blowing his nose on it and offering it back to me. "That's okay love, you keep it. I've got a drawer full in the kitchen."

"I'm Russ by the way," he says stuffing it into his jacket pocket.

"Let's see if we can sort this out peacefully." Now I'm not usually in the habit of inviting strange men into my home, but I guess if he dares to take to the streets with a dog that walks like a ballerina en pointe and cries in front of an ageing woman then he must be a gentle soul. He takes a seat and Cybil settles at his feet and I go into the kitchen to put the kettle on and turf the dog into the backyard as a safety measure.

"You must think I'm a right wet blanket," he calls.

"Not at all," I lie, opening a packet of Rich Tea fingers before walking back into the middle room. He takes one and gives half to Cybil, who nibbles at it like an anorexic under surveillance. "How are we going to sort this mess out?"

"I'm not sure, the vet said if she does fall pregnant there's a pill he can give her to terminate it, but I'm not sure I can put her through that."

"She's a dog, love, I don't think she'll be bothered one way or another."

"I can't afford the vet fees."

"I'll have a word with my husband and maybe we can help with the cost. Leave me your address and we'll pop over when he gets home and we can talk about it." He finishes his tea and before he leaves, promises to wash the duster.

**

"You said what?" Len says.

"I just said we might be able to help."

"And who's to say his dog hasn't been seen to by all the other dogs in the neighbourhood?"

"He seemed certain it was ours."

"Right, well let's go and see shall we? You go on ahead and I'll take the dog to do its business and meet you there." Len puts the dog on its lead and leaves through the back gate and I grab my coat from the hall and set off to the address that Russ has given me. I round the corner onto the high street and suddenly find myself standing still with my breath visible in the February air. I can't remember which direction I need to go in. I look down at the written address in a vain hope it will jog my memory. I've lived here all my life and I thought I knew all the streets. It's frustrating and frightening, knowing that my memory is failing. I look up at the street sign fixed to the house on the corner and nothing registers. I look around for a landmark familiar to me, but nothing helps.

At that moment a woman carrying a string bag filled with cauliflowers walks past and thankfully she gives me directions. Sadly, this is of no comfort to me, it only highlights the problem. What if next time it happens no one can help me? What if I'm away from home and end up wandering around aimlessly? What if… "Stop it, you silly woman," I think. I mentally tell myself to get a grip. I refuse to be burdened with 'what ifs'. "For goodness' sake, it's just a mixture of age and brain cancer." After giving myself a dressing down I turn into the side street where Russ lives.

I knock on the door and wait for a minute before knocking again. I hear him call from inside that he's coming and the door opens and he's standing there red-faced and obviously annoyed. "He's at it again," he says. "In my backyard right now."

"Who?" I ask.

"Your dog, he's got in again."

Just then Len turns the corner and I point to him. "Here's my husband now, and that on the end of the lead is our dog."

"But…"

"No buts Russ."

"I was certain…"

"You were certain? Let me tell you about certainty. You can guarantee that one day what you're certain about will abandon you. What you know will cease to be known and you'll be alone and bewildered." My outburst stuns him and he stands looking at me open-mouthed. "You can live all your life in one place and think you know it like the back of your proverbial. Then one day, through no fault of your own, an invader can start to eat away at you until unexpectedly something you're certain of, something you've been aware of since always is gone. So, Russ, may I suggest that in future before you throw accusations around, you make sure you have the facts straight." He says nothing and I bid him goodnight and walk over to my husband put my arm in his and together we walk home.

***

"What's on next?" I ask as the credits roll, signalling the end of the TV program we've been watching.

"That program where there's lots of girls trying to get a date with some daft bloke."

"Turn it off," I tell him. "That Paddy McGuiness is about as funny as nettle rash." Len gets up and turns off the television and asks, "Do you fancy a nip of that brandy left over from Christmas?" I nod and as he leaves me sitting alone in the middle room I think about my altercation earlier. I realise that my outburst wasn't about the dog, it wasn't even about Russ. It was about me. It was something that I needed to do. Call it cathartic, call it what you will, but now I realise, because I've been feeling so ill lately, I've started to let the cancer win. My hidden invader is gaining, winning every daily battle, and I'm just rolling over and allowing it to defeat me. I needed something to kick-start me, to reinvigorate me. I needed to get my positive attitude back again. I needed to lose my temper today, to reset so to speak.

I hear something fall through our letter box and Len enters the room carrying a jiffy bag and the brandy bottle, "This just came through the door." Len pours the drinks and I tear open the package and inside is a freshly laundered and ironed yellow duster and a note that simply reads, "Sorry."

~ 4 ~

Friday, 11 February
This morning is a rush, Len has gone to work and I must have fallen back asleep and when I wake I look at the clock, it reads 11:45.

I'm panicking as I have a hospital appointment and I always like to be there in good time. I dress quickly and without so much as a mouthful of tea, I grab my coat and leave for the bus stop. The journey to the hospital requires two buses and I arrive at the bus station as my second bus is pulling away. So with 25 minutes to wait for the next one, I pop into the café.

"Hello love," the lady behind the counter says as I unbutton my coat and order a tea. "In a hurry this morning?"

"Sorry?"

"You've got your cardigan buttoned up wrong."

I look and the buttons and holes don't correspond. I smile, nod, and take my drink. I shuffle over to a table by the window where I can see the stand where my bus will arrive. Bloody typical, I'm halfway through my mug of tea when a bus arrives early and I get up and leave the café and dash across the concourse and climb aboard. "This goes to the hospital?" I ask the driver who then asks me for the fare. I look down and realise I haven't got my handbag. I apologise to the passenger standing behind me and I'm about to leave the bus when the woman from the café leans in through the open door and hands me my coat and bag. "Here love, you left these in your rush." I feel embarrassment colour my cheeks and as a man in the queue huffs loudly. I thank her and show the driver my bus pass.

I take a seat and look out of the window and the bus pulls away. I focus on the houses that slide past in a blur when the ache in my temple starts to build and I search inside my bag for some painkillers. Finding none, I close my eyes and try to block out the pulsating thump.

"Did you want the hospital?" a teenager asks shaking me awake.

"Yes," I say, my head feeling like someone had filled it with treacle.

"I thought so," the girl says, "We passed it two stops back." She presses the bell to alert the driver and she calls down the bus, "Excuse me this lady's missed her stop."

"I'll pull in here," the driver calls back, "but you'll have to be quick love. I'm not supposed to unless it's an official stop." The girl helps me down the aisle and the man from earlier huffs again as we walk past, she supports my arm as I leave the bus, and after thanking her she steps back and the doors close behind her.

For a few seconds, I try to get my bearings and decide I know which direction to take and I set off. After several minutes I know I'm lost as I don't recognise where I am. A passing dog walker informs me that I'm on the right road, but this one leads to the rear of the hospital. "You'll need to walk into town from here and then catch another bus," he says. I thank him and set off in the direction he has pointed in.

The walk into town is pretty straightforward or rather would be if I wasn't feeling drained, but eventually I make it under the subway and back up again into the shopping area. Another passer-by gives me directions to the correct bus shelter and exhausted I drop onto the hard plastic rectangle posing as a seat and wait.

I can feel myself falling asleep as a bus arrives and I ask the driver to confirm that I will arrive at my intended destination, and he kindly tells me he'll give me a shout when we get there. I thank him and sit down. Looking at my watch I'm angry with myself for being late, and for the whole journey I sit stony-faced looking out of the window.

The hospital waiting room is filled with people sitting on plastic chairs when I enter, breathless and with another attack gearing up in my temple. I present myself at the reception desk and hastily tell the girl behind that I'm sorry for being late, then without any encouragement I begin to blurt out the trials that have so far plagued me, until without warning I'm standing sobbing in front of a room full of strangers. I don't know who assists me but I'm helped to a chair and within minutes the door opens and I see Victoria walking towards me. "Whatever is the matter, Mrs Bickerstaff?"

"I'm sorry for being late."

"You're not late," she says. "You're early." She helps me up and walks with me to a side room where after handing me a tissue she explains that my appointment isn't until the following week.

"But look," I say showing her my appointment card, "it says Friday and 11."

"Beryl, that's the appointment time, it's for 11:00 am next Friday." I look down at the card and realise she's right. I mumble something about being a stupid woman and make my excuses to leave. "No you don't," she says. "I'll ask if Dr Banerjee can see you today." I'm about to protest but with a deep intake of breath her enormous chest swells out and I know not to argue with her.

"Dr Banerjee says he'll see you in ten minutes. Let me get you a drink and is there someone you'd like me to call?"

Dr Banerjee is sitting behind his desk which appears to still have the piles of paperwork that were on it at my last visit. He asks me how things are going and I tell him about the memory loss and bouts of confusion. "Is it your long or short-term memory?"

"It's a bit of both," I tell him and he then goes on to explain that medicine still doesn't fully understand how the memory works. "Science now thinks that there's no one single place in the brain where memories are stored. So it's difficult to predict with tumours the extent of the memory loss you can expect." He asks me about the pain and he now refers to them as my wasps in a jar. This simple thing cheers me; knowing he's taken notice during our previous consultations is a comfort. I explain how the pain lasts for longer but isn't more painful than previously. He sees this as a positive but I see it as a pain in the arse.

Victoria pops her head around the door to tell me Victor is here to pick me up and after Dr Banerjee explains that my extended sleeping patterns could be my body's way of dealing with pain relief. He then says he thinks it might be a good idea to reinstate the laser therapy. I decline his offer and he prescribes me some stronger painkillers but reiterates that the proposal is still there.

I thank him and he tells me there's no need to come to see him the following week, but to make sure if things become difficult to contact my GP. I stand up to leave and he adds, "You're doing remarkably well Mrs Bickerstaff, considering you're such a long way into your initial prognosis. Whatever you're doing, keep it up. But promise me that you'll take things easy."

"I didn't tell Victor about earlier," Victoria says as she walks with me back to the waiting room. "I just called and said I thought it'd be nice for you to have a lift home rather than get two buses."

"Is everything okay, Mum?"

"Yes son, everything's fine." I smile at him.

Victor slips his arm through mine and as the electronic doors open noiselessly, I hear Victoria say, "See you soon Mrs B."

~ 3 ~

Friday, 18 February
Reminiscent of the A.A. Milne poem, I'm halfway down the stairs when there's a knock at the front door. "I'll get it," I call and make my way along the hallway and open the door.

"Victor Bickerstaff?" a man with a red nose that resembles a rosebud asks.

"If I am I shouldn't be wearing this housecoat and slippers."

"Sorry I don't get paid to experience humour," he says, "I've five more deliveries to make before I can have a toilet break." I sign his delivery pad and I'm ready to receive the box from him when he says, "Keep them somewhere cool until they're ready to be worn. Let me suggest outside in a safe place and keep the lid shut to prevent pigeons pecking at the leaves."

I take the box as he walks away. I say a questionable, "Thank you," and close the door with my heel.

Fifteen minutes ago I was sitting up in bed finishing a poached egg. Victor has always made the perfect poached egg, mine are like bullets, whereas his are deliciously runny. After today he'll be gone, and there'll be no one here to poach one again. It's funny how something as mundane as a poached egg can bring on an unscheduled emotional response. Today is the day Victor and Kirk tie the knot and I promised myself I wouldn't cry but my eyes start to leak and with the box in both hands, I'm unable to wipe them. Len steps into the hallway and says, "Who was that?"

"Flower delivery."

"Are you okay, love?" he takes the box from me and using a handkerchief I wipe my eyes. "Not another headache?"

"No," I tell him, just feeling a bit emotional.

"Well take it easy, you don't want to overdo it today of all days." I follow Len into the middle room and he places the box on the dining table.

The kitchen door opens and Vera appears, "Morning. I've let myself in."

"You always do," I hear Len mutter under his breath.

"Can I hang this somewhere?" she's holding up a hanger with some clothing protected by an Asda carrier bag. "What've you got there?"

"Flowers for—"

"Have the flowers arrived?" Victor says entering the room.

"Yes they're here," Vera says. We all look on as Victor lifts the lid to reveal buttonholes and corsages made up of greenery, blue sea holly and yellow wallflowers that give off their subtle perfume."

"There are three ladies' corsages," Vera says. "Who're they for?"

"One's for Mum, another for Lisa and of course there's one for you Vera." I've never seen her lost for words and I can tell by the sniffle that she's touched by Victor's thoughtfulness.

"That'll go lovely with my outfit." Vera removes the carrier bag off her hanger to reveal a two-piece woollen suit in powder blue. "What do you think?"

"Very nice," says Victor.

"It's lovely," I say.

"I'll put the kettle on and take the dog out," says Len. He's never been much good at what he calls women's talk – knickers, menopause, net curtains. He picks up the dog's lead and exits through the kitchen.

"Where did you get it from?" asks Victor.

"La Bella Figura, in Newcastle," Vera replies, her chest puffed up like an amorous pigeon.

"I thought you didn't like that shop?" I say.

"Oh, it's not the shop I dislike, it's the owner I can't stomach."

"But last time you said nothing fitted you."

"Well, this time I tried on everything in the shop that was my size or near enough. I was determined to get something to fit just to prove that woman wrong."

"And it looks like you did," Victor says.

"Yes, by the time I'd finished she was breathless. I left her looking like an airbed with a slow puncture... Oh Victor, I need to give you these." She roots through her bag and hands him two envelopes. "They're cards." It was obvious that she'd looked at them. "One is from Mrs Khan, I know it says, congratulations on passing your driving test, but she said it was all the newsagents had this morning."

"Who's the other from?" I ask.

Victor opens it and with a puzzled look says, "Thelma?"

"Thelma?"

"Thelma Roper," Vera says. "The woman with skin like a schoolboy's satchel. Owns the tanning salon."

"Oh, that Thelma," Victor says shaking his head and shrugging.

When Len returns we all have a cuppa before retiring upstairs to get dressed. Len puts on his machine washable suit with a new shirt and tie and I slide into a lilac dress that I found in the Matalan January sale. I'm determined that I won't have a headache; there's no place in today's schedule for a visit from the wasps in a jar. I pick up my handbag and check, double and triple check I have my painkillers before making my way downstairs. "The car's here," Vera says, and one by one we file out with Len bringing up the rear after shutting the dog in the kitchen.

***

Ford Hall, a restored mansion house and now a hotel on the outskirts of the city has done a superb job of decorating the venue and upon arrival, we are directed to the Moorcroft Suite where people are gathering for the ceremony. "Bloody hell," Len says as we enter the room, "what side do we sit on, groom or … groom?"

"I don't think it much matters," I tell him as we take our places at the front. "To think, today our Victor's moving on."

"Don't think of it as losing a son but of gaining a … err … another son." I'm about to answer him when a small, stooped woman wearing an enormous maroon hat with an exaggerated golden feather enters. We watch her take a front seat adjacent to us just as the music fades up and the ceremony begins.

Everything goes according to plan and I'm glad that Mac has set up a video camera to capture the event for us to watch again later. The boys' pledges are quite emotional and at one point I don't realise I'm crying until Vera hands me a pocket pack of tissues; the act of which reminds me of the day I met Kate: She would have loved being here.

After the – yes, I'm calling it the wedding breakfast, we all take ourselves back into the suite to enjoy coffee as the hotel staff prepares the dining room for the evening reception. Vera's nibbling on a shortbread biscuit when Mavis and Doreen arrive. "I know we're a bit early," says Mavis. "Gives us a chance to hear how it went before the disco drowns us out."

"Where do I put the present?" Doreen asks. "Just a little something from the both of us." We all follow her eyes down to the gaily coloured package she's holding.

"I'll take it through and put it on the gifts table," Vera says taking the box from her. A waiter delivers two fresh cups to our table and Vera returns. "I've put it on the table next to the gift from Sue and Shirley Hurley."

Doreen suddenly clutches her throat. "Oh my goodness. The tag." Her eyes widen horror and her eyebrows flatten.

"What tag?" I say.

"On the present. It has both our names on it … oh my … people will think we're …"

"A couple?" questions Lisa.

"Lesbians," Vera says, coughing back her amusement as her joke falls as flat as a hedgehog on an A-road.

We stay for some of the evening reception until Len decides the music is too loud and we should make our way home and leave the drinking and dancing to the young ones. Victor and Kirk thank us for coming and as they see us into a taxi Kirk leans into me and whispers, "Thank you."

We're back home in our middle room when Len pours two brandies and we sit in silence and sip. The day is replaying in my mind when he says, "Who was the strange woman with the hat the size of Jodrell Bank's satellite dish?"

"That was Kirk's mother."

"I thought his family didn't approve of his –"

"They don't. I think it's hard for his parents to come to terms with."

"Some folks are like that," says Len. "Doesn't make them bad people though." I nod in agreement. "But how did she know about the ceremony?"

"I called her."

"I didn't know you had her number."

"I don't. I looked in Kirk's phone while he was out of the room a week ago and wrote it down."

"Does he know?"

"I think so, he thanked me earlier."

"You're lucky, it could have backfired."

"I know but it was a risk I was prepared to take."

"It was a good day all in all, wasn't it?"

I nod and think to myself, it *was* perfect and I've not had a headache all day.

~ 2 ~

Wednesday, 23 February
If the specialists are correct I'm already mid-way through my penultimate week; obviously, I'm being flippant. When they gave me the twelve-month end-of-life prognosis I'm sure they didn't mean that's all you have Beryl, and exactly one year from this date you'll peg it. Surely there's a bit of leeway on either side. If so I've beaten the worst odds and in a week I guess I'll be on borrowed time. That said a prognosis is just a forecast, there's no exact science that can give the actual length of time left, just an average based on experience.

It's been an eventful year, I started out with lots of ideas for things I'd like to do, new places to visit and new experiences to have, but now I'm too ill to be throwing myself into new things. If I'm honest the last thing I need now is any added stress and a change of routine, so I think it's best just to let life continue unhindered.

It's funny using the word, life when I'm thinking back on the year that was predicted to be my last. But it's been an enriching year, a year where I think I have achieved my aim to live more. I learned to drive, albeit in a car park, I did some TV extra work, I went to Venice and London and of course, I rubbed oil into a stripper's torso. There are a few things I didn't get around to doing, I wanted to have a go at making pasta and paddling a canoe: Obviously not at the same time.

There have been some highs and lows, meeting and losing Kate fall into both of those categories, Victor and Kirk getting together was a nice surprise and seeing Mac finally achieve his goal and being a part of that has made this past year special.

I have nothing major planned for this week, I'm going to just get on with it, and keep to my usual routine which means before lunchtime today it'll be tea and biscuits with Vera and a dose of her acerbic wit. We'll maybe walk into town and have a quick look around the market and then I'll be back home in time to make Len his tea as he takes the dog out and after I'll wash up before we settle down to an evening in front of the television. Some may say it's a mundane existence and I am aware that there's not much excitement in my everyday timetable, but as the back door opens and Vera calls out that she's here, I smile because it's that ordinariness that reminds me that the cancer hasn't yet beaten me.

"I just don't get it," Vera says as I place the tray down on the table. She's back from a visit to see her niece in Bacup. "Why would you put cushions on the bed only to take them off every night?"

"I guess it dresses the room."

"But who for? You get up, arrange the cushions on the bed and then leave the room. The only person who's going to benefit from the display is an overly nosey window cleaner."

Vera's telling me that Maurice has a hamstring injury that's meant he's been unable to play football for the past three months when the house shakes as if the street is collapsing. "Bloody hell, what was that?" The dog starts barking in the kitchen and outside, burglar alarms start to sound. "Let's go and see." I put my cup down and walk into the hall and before I open the front door I can hear a commotion in the street.

"What is it?" Vera says peering around me as we stand on the step.

"Half of number six seems to be missing. There's rubble everywhere."

"Do you think it was a terrorist attack, a bomb maybe?"

"I'm not sure, but I doubt it was a terrorist attack. What would a fanatical faction gain from targeting a rented house in Tunstall?"

"Looks like a gas explosion," a man walking past says. "These bloody dodgy landlords never do the proper checks," and he walks on chuntering to himself.

"He sounds like a cheerful soul," Vera says as a siren sounds and a police car and ambulance arrive. The onlookers are asked to move back and a policewoman who looks like she's barely out of high school takes up a position outside next door.

Another police officer gingerly picks his way over the rubble to get into the house when a car pulls up with the occupant from number six. There's lots of animated conversation and head shaking between the girl who lives at the property and the police officer. "Poor thing," I say to Vera, "she can't stay in a house with half of its front missing."

"Do you know if she has family nearby?"

"I don't, she only moved in a couple of weeks ago. The previous tenants did a moonlight flit."

Quickly the onlookers lose interest and start to disperse as a gas van arrives and workers cordon off the street. I turn to the girl who is now standing next to the policewoman next door and ask if she'd like a cup of tea. "I'm not sure," she says and the policewoman nods her head.

"There's nothing you can do for now, and if they need you the police will know where you are." She smiles and tells me her name is Natalie and Vera pops inside to put the kettle on. A fresh pot of tea is made and Vera takes two mugs outside for the police officers while I pour three cups for us. "That's not a local accent," I say to Natalie as I hand her a cup.

"I'm from Cardiff originally," she tells me as I offer her a biscuit. Vera joins us and before long we're deep in conversation. We discover that Natalie has relocated here as she's been transferred through her job.

"What is that you do?" asks Vera.

"It's boring, I work at a bank."

"Behind the counter?"

"No I work in the back, I'm not customer facing."

"Like a secretary?" Vera asks.

"Not as such, I investigate allegations of corporate money laundering and fraud. That's why I'm always moving around the country. Before I came here I was in Edinburgh for eight months."

"That must be exciting?"

"Not really. It's all numbers and spreadsheets." Looking above the dining table, Natalie says, "That's an interesting picture."

"Yes," says Vera. "The artist didn't paint her moo, thankfully." I toss her a look that tells her to button it and Natalie reaches for another biscuit when there's a knock at the door and the policewoman tells us the landlord is on his way to secure the front of the premises and they think she ought to remove any personal belongings before it's made safe.

"I suppose I should look for somewhere else to move to?"

"You can stay here tonight if it helps," I tell her, and it's Vera's turn to throw me a disapproving look.

"Thank you, Beryl, that'll help as I have an important meeting tomorrow, and won't have time to find a new place until the day after."

As Natalie goes with the police to collect some of her things, Vera scolds me, telling me I don't need the upheaval of inviting a stranger into my home saying, "You know nothing about her."

"Why, do you think she could be a serial killer?"

"Looking at her hips," Vera says. "She's more likely a cereal killer."

"What are you like," I laugh and there's a knock letting us know Natalie has returned.

"It's just a normal day in the Bickerstaff household," Vera says.

"Of course, now open the bloody front door."

Vera says goodbye after telling us she's off to buy a cushion to place on her bed to enrich the life of her window cleaner. Natalie looks at me confused and I just shake my head. I take her up to the room that until recently was Victor's and after she's settled in, she apologises saying she needs to get back to work. "That's okay love, I'll just catch up on some afternoon TV so I'll be here when you get back."

With my trip into town with Vera now postponed I settle down in my chair and pick up the TV remote. The afternoon schedules are awash with soaps; catch-up slots of the evening shows for the unemployed and night workers. In fact, there's enough soap to see Widow Twanky through the current economic depression. There's Mancunian soap, antipodean soap, 'by eck as like' Yorkshire soap, and if you want proof that there's always someone worse off than yourself, there's cockney sparrow soap. I'm not a follower of this East End drama, I don't have the time to invest in someone else's misery also I'm worried I'll become caught up in a scandal where one character has swapped twins at birth and I'll die before I know who the culprit is.

I continue to flick through the channels and the option that's left is cookery programs. I don't feel like spending half an hour watching either, sweary, lispy or droney, tell me they have fifty illuminating ideas for root vegetables. So, with one final attempt to find something to keep me entertained, I'm now trawling the higher numbered channels, where presenters wearing an excessive amount of hairspray, equal to an entire nation's airborne emissions, try to sell me gemstone rings and pressure washers. As I'm not in the market for a deluxe, make your own celebratory jigsaw puzzle kit complete with safety scissors I turn off. How people can be holed up all day watching this collective drivel is beyond comprehension. I'd be bored senseless, I can tell you, Anne Frank and her family go up in my estimation.

~ 1 ~

Tuesday, 1 March
Here we are. The final week has arrived and I'm doing my best not to think about popping my clogs in a few days. (I jest, obviously, this hasn't been a NASA countdown.) I've decided to get organised for Len's benefit. In four more days, I will have survived fifty-two weeks and now is the time to put a plan in place for his life without me. I start by looking through the pantry section of our kitchen cupboards to check what tinned goods we have that will help my husband to subsist without me. I make a list of things that he'll be able to add to a pan to make himself a meal. He'll only eat beans if they come with sausages in the can so I add four tins to my list. Next is a root through the freezer; out goes a bag of something brown that I've stored from an earlier dinner but have forgotten its origin. At the back of one drawer is a frozen bunch of coriander; something we thought we'd try so long ago that it's probably been there for over a year. Len said it tasted like soap and so it's consigned to the bin along with the insides from one of Saffron's Hallowe'en pumpkins.

It's a Tuesday so the buses are relatively quiet. I show my pass to the driver, take a seat and look out of the window as the streets that I've known for so long glide past. Familiar sights that are comforting despite the dereliction, empty shops where the past hangs on memory hangers and the indoor market where I've worn out enough shoe leather over the years to create a whole new cow.

The supermarket doors open with a silent swish, it's one of those hyper-types that sells everything from mackerel to microwaves and socks to soda bread. I find supermarkets have changed, now they're places where friendly people lose their patience, where severe foot tapping is obligatory and teeth sucking is the norm. Everyone seems to be in a rush and if there's a lack of product on the shelves, normally sane people take it as a personal affront. I steer my trolley to the tinned section and stock up on beans, tomatoes, green beans and those tins of peeled new potatoes; all of these are simple things that Len will find easy as he explores cooking for himself. I'm just reaching the end of the aisle when Marcia Hamill appears, a shopping basket balanced on a pushchair but no child. "Hello Beryl," she says as she spots me. "I've not seen you at Slimming World for a while."

"I've stopped going," I reply.

"Must say though, look at you, you look good, how much weight have you lost?"

"I… I'm not sure."

"Whatever you're doing it's working for you. What plan have you been following?"

"I've just cut down on calories," I say. She's about to speak again when a disembodied voice calls her name over the public address system asking her to collect her granddaughter from the fish counter.

"Not again," she says exhaling loudly. "Bloody kids. We got a six-month ban from Tesco last week after Rioja ate a handful of grapes, half a parsnip and a red onion; she was sick on the kumquats."

"Best get over there," I say and she waves as she rushes away.

Knowing I'd be buying so many tins I ordered a taxi home and sitting on the back seat in a moment of nostalgic need I instruct the driver to take me past the old Doulton pot bank where I used to work; it's earmarked for houses but thankfully I won't be around to see this.

I've just poured water over tea bags and I'm stocking up the freezer when Vera opens the back door. "I swear you can smell a pot of tea two streets away," I say as she steps inside.

"It's my superpower," she chuckles. "I've brought cakes." I place the last ready meal in the freezer drawer as Vera takes down the tea tray, loads it and carries it into the middle room. "Did you get everything you went for?" she asks as I join her.

"I think so. I got some of those frozen dinners that Len can just pop into the oven and have a meat and two veg tea."

"You know I'll keep an eye on him."

"Thank you." Vera opens the bakery box to reveal four angel cake slices and I pass her a plate. I watch as she separates the coloured sponges and starts to eat the yellow layer first.

"You're supposed to eat every layer at the same time," I say.

"I'd never fit it all in my mouth," she replies.

"Not all at once you daft dollop, I mean bite through all of the layers."

"Ooh, I'm not sure about that, I like to save the icing until last."

I know I'll have no conscious comprehension when I've passed on, but I will miss Vera's idiosyncratic way of eating cake. I shake myself out of morbid thoughts and tell her that I ran into Marcia and the request that came over the P.A. system.

"Bloody liability that child is. Last summer her mother, Verity had to take her to A&E as she'd sniffed a flower and sucked a bee up her nose."

"Did it sting her?"

"Who knows? Mind you, between you, me and the dog I think Rioja is a stupid name for a child."

"Yes, Marcia told me a while back that Verity thought Chardonnay was becoming too common, so chose a different wine for her daughter's name."

"Honestly, that woman is as thick as Oxford marmalade. What will she do if she has another baby, call it pinot grigio or move onto spirits and name it Bacardi."

"Heaven forbid she had twins."

Vera laughs, "Imagine their first day at school. What are your names? Rum and Coke." We spend a few hours enjoying trivial conversation before we pull on our coats and walk into town.

Two years ago Alexandra Retail Park opened and that's where we head. Vera says she wants a new sink tidy, "What's wrong with your old one?" I ask her.

"It's untidy."

My mind boggles and I shake my head.

We're having a mooch around Matalan and spot a sale rail, "Let's see if we can grab a bargain," I say disturbing Vera as she rifles through a display of discounted gloves.

"Oh, I like these," she says holding up a pair in beige suedette with a fake fur trim.

"What size are they?"

"One is a four and the other's a nine," she says trying one on.

"But they're two different sizes. They're not a proper pair."

"That's why they're reduced to one pound twenty."

"But, who has one small hand and another the size of a shovel?"

"Bugger," she says trying on the other glove. "They're both left-handed." She throws them down into the display basket. "Shame, I'd have had those if they were a proper pair."

"But they weren't."

"I know. Two left hands." I shake my head and walk over to a rail where last season's leftovers are marked up for sale. "This is a nice summer dress," Vera says holding up a floral affair. "It'd look nice on you."

"I'm not spending good money on a summer dress for it to sit in my wardrobe unused until Lisa donates it to the charity shop.

"Why wouldn't it be used?"

"Because the chances are, I'll be gone before summer."

"Oh yes, I forgot. Shame I'd have liked it myself, but now it'll just remind me of you."

"Why would it remind you of me?"

"Because you've got one hanging in your wardrobe unworn." I shake my head again; lately being with Vera involves so much head shaking I'm beginning to wear my neck out.

Normality returns in the men's underwear section where I choose three vest and pants sets and a pack of socks. "Are those for Len?"

"Well, I've not taken to wearing Y-fronts."

"Nothing to pop out of the front pocket."

"Exactly Vera."

"What about this thong?"

"Can't see Len getting used to one of those."

"Not for Len, for you."

"Why?"

"Eradicates VPL."

"VPL?"

"Yes, it says it here," she shows me a label attached to the handkerchief masquerading as knickers.

"Visible panty line," I say. "At my age I couldn't care less if my knickers make it look like I have double yellow lines painted across my backside."

"You're tetchy today, Beryl Bickerstaff."

"I'm sorry," I say, "there's so much I want to get done before…"

"Before what?"

"Nothing. Ignore me I'm being a grouch."

"You're probably tired," Vera pats my hand.

"Yes, that'll be what it is. Now let's pay for Len's pants and get off home."

I'm putting Len's new underwear inside his drawer when I see the envelope that he's kept there for years. I take it out and lift the flap; I know what is inside, it's not a secret. I tip the contents out and dried petals land on the duvet cover before I remove the faded paper. Len the old romantic has kept these petals from my bridal bouquet along with a copy of our marriage certificate. My mind slides back to our anniversary party in June and I turn the eternity ring on my finger. The first tear eases itself out and balances on my bottom eyelid before it drops and signals others to follow. I'm alone, and despite having been strong-willed for the past year, I allow myself a moment to cry and feel sorry for myself: So much for my never having a 'why me' moment. But truth be told, I'm not crying for myself, I'm crying for those I shall leave behind. I pick up one of the now almost transparent petals and bring it up to my nose, there's no perfume, it's lost its scent and this makes me realise that in passing, it will be me that ultimately loses. I will lose the constant in my life, I'll lose Len. I'll miss all my family: Stands to reason, but today is all about Len. I worry about the long nights that he'll endure alone in this bed. The mornings when he wakes and for a brief moment has forgotten he's on his own. Those celebratory dates that he'll no longer want to celebrate. Those minutes that will feel like hours when he'll be enveloped in silence. The empty moments when he'll stand in the kitchen, a solitary saucepan on the heat with the dog looking up at him.

~ Extra Time ~

Sunday, 6 March
Len pulls the curtain aside and looks out of the bedroom window, "There's been a ground frost," he says and I ask him to open the curtains. The frail daylight enters the room and I ask if he'll open the window for me. "It's cold outside. Are you sure?" I nod and afterwards Len leaves the room and heads downstairs to make a pot of tea, leaving me lying in bed. A blast of cold air rushes into the room and I shiver although the feeling is pleasurable. I look at the vase of blue irises and daffodils that Natalie gave me, a herald of new life, of hope. At first, Len was surprised to see we had a house guest, but after two nights with us her landlord found her another property.

I hear a car door slam and an engine firing. Heels clatter across the pavement and the sound of a conversation, muted and undecipherable floats into my bedroom.

I have finally decided upon the song I want to play at my funeral. It's not an old favourite, in fact it's a relatively new song called, 'The Performance of My Life.' I discovered it after borrowing a Shirley Bassey CD from the library. I chose it because of the opening lyrics, they seem to conjure up how life has been this past year. And what a year it has been.

I wondered if by getting this far I'd feel like I was on borrowed time, but to be honest I feel no different today than I did yesterday and the day before that. I can, however, honestly say that I feel more alive and much more positive than I did on this day, a year ago.

So I'll think of this as extra time in the battle between myself and the cancer. Thus far the scores are the same, so this extra period will be played on in this game called life until there is a clear winner.

Beneath my window someone is whistling, the world below continues and I'm still a part of it.

Isn't life grand?

~ Acknowledgements ~

"You've written a book – wow! But it must be a lonely pursuit, locked in a room with just a keyboard for company."

If only that were true. It takes a lot of people to create a book and this one is no exception, so there are a few people to thank.

Beryl as a character was conceived back in 2008 and thinking back, I have to thank Rachel Brookes who endured listening to the early attempts to give my creation both a life and some funny lines. (Even if she did throw paper clips at my head.)

This book grew out of an idea my mother had.

When diagnosed she removed the darkness from her illness and just enjoyed her life rather than be defined by the cancer, so I have to say, thanks Mum and I miss you every day.

Throughout the writing process, there have been many people involved and I'd like to take the opportunity to thank as many as I can remember, Peter Coleborn. Mick Walters. Bev Adams, Jem Shaw. Malcolm Havard. Nic Hale and some others I have forgotten no doubt. Thank you all for listening to the drafts of Beryl's story as it evolved.

52 Weeks languished unpublished on a hard drive until 2023 so a massive thank you goes to my 'beta babes' Jan Edwards and Misha Herwin who reminded me about it, asked me to dust it off and give it (another) final edit and replace a couple of chapters. As the best beta readers in the business, Jan and Misha always put me right when I think I know better.

On a final note, this novel is set in Stoke on Trent because that's the town of my birth. It's where people are welcoming and whatever your (or their) gender they call you duck. It is where the decimated pottery industry was once populated by forthright men and strong-willed women in a real sense of community. Most of the references here are true, however, the bus number is fictitious, as is St. Peter's church and hospice and the Ford Hall wedding venue.

The 1934 film, Boots! Boots! starring George Formby and produced by Blakeley's Productions, Ltd. (later Mancunian Films) did have its premier in Burslem, Stoke on Trent rather than London.

"To live is the rarest thing in the world. Most people exist, that is all." — Oscar Wilde

If you have enjoyed this book, please go to Goodreads or Amazon and leave a review, just a star rating is enough. If you loved it tell your friends and family and feel free to share it with anyone who needs to smile when they feel life is heavy.

Barry Lillie

~ Coming in 2024 ~

Saving Springbrook (Kim and Eddie Book One)
Under Italian Stars
Kim and Eddie (Book Two)

For news about new releases and free content
sign up for Barry's Book Club here:
www.barrylillie.com

Flatfield F

Printed in Great Britain
by Amazon